Doin' Jimmy

Doin' Jimmy

W. Allen Werneken

Writers Club Press
San Jose New York Lincoln Shanghai

Doin' Jimmy

Writers Club Press
an imprint of iUniverse.com, Inc.

For information address:
iUniverse.com, Inc.
5220 S 16th, Ste. 200
Lincoln, NE 68512
www.iuniverse.com

ISBN: 0-595-09675-1

Printed in the United States of America

For Jimmy O'Dea who admonished me for complaining, and showed me by example that it's never too late to change your life. To my family, Nancy, Sarah, Steve, and Tom, for allowing the change to occur.

Acknowledgements

Thanks to Joe O'Brien for his legal expertise and Dr. Michael Preston for his medical expertise; to Vickie Dyckes for the cover layout, to Larry Boothby for his photography; and especially to Bruce Unwin who graciously insisted on painting the original art that adorns the cover of this book and now my mantel.

Thanks also to my agents, Mike Vidor and Anne Sheldon of the Hardy Agency, to William Symons at the Bluebird for his support when he needed it himself; to Tony Ciafardini, Dr. Margaret Mary McGovern, and, of course to 'Uncle Bubba', Steve Combs.

I

It was July in Detroit. It was hot. And the night was over. Bobby pushed the door, and with the uncertain choreography of drunkenness, stepped outside into the darkness, toward Cass Avenue and the Corridor. He felt the small, warm wind as it made it's way around the parking structures and the tired brick apartment buildings. There was always somethin' blowin' at you, he thought. Struggling to stay balanced, drunk, he swayed nearer the curb as he made his way to the corner, closer to the alley where he would sleep off the liquor.

Heat didn't bother him. But to an old southern redneck, cold was awful. He remembered many nights of shelters and wood scraps and trash burning in oil drums and the relentless Northern winter. He grinned at the thought of describing it to anyone in Monroe, Arkansas. Heck, those idiots had never even seen snow. The memory sent a chill through him, and gave cause for a sip from the pint he kept in his pants. Always keep the whiskey warm. First rule.

A car passed slowly behind him as he turned the corner and went east on Parsons. It was rich boys from the suburbs, he was sure. This was the time of the morning when they would cruise the ghetto looking for hookers and drugs, when the bright lights went on and the bars closed. If this was a lucky night, they might find some girls from the university stumbling back to their apartments after a night out. He liked the school. It kept the neighborhood safe and offered what little public protection he felt he was due.

He slowed as he approached the alley, turned in a few feet and stopped. Bobby Merimac Wilson pulled out the bottle once more. He drank all but the little bit he would keep for morning then shoved it back into his pants. Reaching behind the down spout, he found the plastic garbage bag containing his possessions and yanked it forward. Fluffing it as though it were a fine feather pillow, he arranged it in the corner, where the brick building met cement. Then, in one slow weaving motion, after aiming his numb body at the spot, he turned his back to the wall and like some giant drunken lizard, slid down slowly, so he wouldn't break the precious container nor the sensitive surrounding anatomy.

He sat for a moment before his eyes went heavy against the hypnotic noise of city streets. Before long, he passed out.

To Bobby, life was simple and it was hard. It had been almost forty years since he had left that guaranteed poverty of his future in the South in exchange for something more hopeful in the big factories of the industrial North. For a time, during the war, there was work. Then there was the drinking and the end of his job and the hard landing here at the bottom of life.

Though they were difficult to see through the overgrowth, his face bore the scars of urban combat. Those who had come to know him called him 'Devil Bob', not so much for his demeanor, but because they had never known how any human could survive what he had, and live to be sixty-two, without having entered into some unholy tryst. Often, being somewhat superstitious, they would actually bring him offerings of scraps of food and more importantly, liquor.

The car approached again, slowly, and stopped. Two men jumped from the rear doors and approached Devil Bob rapidly in silence. One of them grabbed Bob's arm and pulled him to his feet.

Startled, barely awake, he tried to defend himself. "Hey," he shouted in his groggy southern drawl, "What da heyll is this?" but they were on him. He felt the tight grasp of the first man's left hand closing on his bicep, followed almost instantly by the searing thunder of the right, the knuckles ripping his fleshy cheek. He fell back against the second man and felt the sting of the cold liquid as it dripped into the bleeding wound from the saturated rag that was slammed to his nostrils. He began to lose consciousness, but he fought hard nonetheless. It was not the first time some Yankee tried to get the best of this old Arkansas boy. He kicked hard at the night, his feet flailing airborne, but missing any significant target. "Hey! Hey!" he screamed as loud as possible, but only a muffled hum escaped the ether-soaked cloth. The whiskey bottle dislodged and shattered on the pavement as he was dragged from the alley to the waiting car. The stars faded in the bright light from its door as the backs of his worn shoes disintegrated. His heels ripped open on the sidewalk, creating bloody pools under the clear glass fragments.

In the car, the two hit him again and again, but he felt nothing. They ripped his clothes from his body and the beating continued, smashing a rib, breaking his teeth. As Bobby lay across the back seat, face up and barely conscious, one of his assailants covered his filthy nakedness with a clean white cotton sheet, while the other opened the trunk, removed a two gallon gas can, and returned to the alley. He added the clothes that Bobby had been wearing to the pile near the drainpipe and doused it with gasoline. He backed away to avoid the explosion, tossed a lighted match at the heap, and ran, setting on fire everything in the world that was Devil Bob's.

The alley erupted in flame and Bob, lying semi-conscious across the back seat could see the bright reflection in the limousine's rear window glass above him, growing dim as the long black car pulled slowly away, quiet and noticed by no one.

When Bobby wasn't there the next day waiting, at noon, when the bar opened, the bartender became suspicious. Devil Bob was always there to help him put the place in order. He would mop the restrooms and wipe down the tables and in return, accept food and a refill of the warm, but empty pint. Then afterwards, drunk, he would recede into a dark corner booth where he would sleep; where he should be now.

The bartender walked out the back door and down toward Parsons, into the hot bright sun that baked the dirty alley. He immediately saw the huge area of newly deposited black residue; carbon climbing ten feet up the wall or more. Squinting, he noticed a shred of bright red material lying on the pavement and bent to pick it up. It was the burned corner of a small confederate flag and he recognized it as one that Bob used as a handkerchief. Eight feet nearer the street he knelt again to examine the charred bottle cap still clinging to a shred of blackened glass. He knew then, he would not see Bobby again, but he also knew that things like this happened on the Corridor and there was little he could do about it. For a moment, he thought of reporting the disappearance to the police, but reconsidered, knowing that nothing would be done. He pushed the ashes and the broken glass aside with his foot and returned inside.

In the weeks that followed, there was much speculation around the Cass Corridor as to Bob's demise, though none included his incalculable suffering nor the actual horror of his death.

There were some who suggested, over beer and cynical laughter, that what happened could have been some sort of supernatural occurrence, and that sometime during the warm morning of July

14, 1975, whatever deal Bobby Merimac Wilson had made with the darker side had finally expired...

...and Devil Bob had simply combusted, spontaneously, and evaporated into Hell.

2

Resting his bike against the granite foundation, the messenger, hurrying, ignored alternate steps as he ascended from Fort St. to the entrance of the MacNamera Building, through the revolving doors and to the metal detector.

The uniformed guard rose for the inspection, "To see?"

"Keenan," he answered, "205, with a package."

The guard took the large manila envelope and laid it on the long table next to the arch of the weapon-sensing equipment. A second uniform motioned the courier ahead through the unit, stopping him a few feet on the other side. Behind him employees from the many agencies above produced government ID and scurried past him. At the completion of the scrutiny, he asked directions.

"Take the first elevator on the left; the local, up to two, or if you're really in a hurry, up those steps, second floor, end of the hall on the left."

He was on the first step before the sentence ended. The long hall at the top was crowded. It was just after lunch. It was difficult to see the room numbers, their gold leaf faded and blending with marble walls. 201-202 Justice Department, Drug Enforcement Division; 203. Bureau of Alcohol Tobacco, and Firearms; 204 and, finally next to last door, 205. And on the crinkled, opaque window pane, badly worn and hardly decipherable, was written, Charles F. Keenan, Special Prosecutor, U.S. Attorney.

He turned the knob to enter the small outer office. In the far corner the brass floor lamp provided a sixty watt incandescent glow. There was no furniture except the secretary's desk to his left, piled high with communication and dust. From the large oak door directly ahead there emerged the only actual daylight to dare entry, followed by the tempered voice of the people, "Yeahooisit?" it asked.

The messenger had no idea what it said. "Package? for Keenan?"

"Tha'd be me," chewing the last of his sandwich, "Keenan," the suspendered emanation identified itself as it entered, reaching forward to take the envelope with one hand, while wiping a small bit of mayonnaise from the corner of his mouth with the other.

"Right here, sir, line 26," the courier indicating where he should sign. "Thank you," and he was gone.

As this big man returned to his office, so did the silence. He tossed the newly received information down on the far corner of his desk and continued with more important issues; his newspaper and his lunch.

Charley Keenan was one of those guys that everybody liked instantly. It had always been that way. With his natural talent for conversation and humor he had made his way from steamy adolescent roots in Tifton, Georgia to the U.S. Navy where he expected to see the world but saw mostly Norfolk, Virginia. After his tour of duty, he settled in Richmond where he spent six years in the service of that city's police force while he worked nights and weekends studying law. It was then that he met Anita Fennery, from Michigan, and the University of Virginia in Charlottesville. With the interminable energy of a young man and a sense of duty to his heart, Charley drove there every Friday and back every Sunday night from the spring of 1968 until 1969 when she graduated.

No one was more excited than Anita when he passed the bar and became an attorney the following year. Nor was anyone more dedicated to his profession or his beautiful bride than Charley Keenan.

His first job as an officer of the court was as an assistant to the federal prosecutor for district nine in Columbus, Ohio, a move that appealed to Anita since she would be closer to home and could visit regularly. Two years later he was offered an opportunity to work in Washington, in a position which others in his office openly coveted, and, as was the curse of his affable nature, it was his if he wanted it. He was regarded by all to be on what was classically considered to be, the fast track. When he declined the promotion, his peers were astonished. But he saw how happy Anita was and he just couldn't bring himself to ask her to make the change. Instead he requested that he be assigned to the Detroit office as soon as a position there was available. It took two more years.

Anita was thrilled when he told her of the move. She started packing before he had issued the final words of explanation. He never mentioned Washington, or the consequences of his refusal. He was content to make her happy, and happy himself with the relative obscurity of his life.

So accepting was he of what he presumed would be his perpetually placid condition, he had actually laughed in disbelief, years before when one of the FBI guys from upstairs showed up at his office.

"Looks like you got the big one this time, Charley," he had said, adding to Charley's suspicions. "If it isn't one stupid asshole it's another. I don't know why we don't just let' em kill each other. Shit, when you can't find guys like this, I figure that's good news." He laid a folder on Charley's desk, "Go ahead, check it out."

"You guys don't have anathin better ta do?" Charley smiled, certain he was being had. "Y'all gotta mess with the big dumb southern boy, don't cha?"

"Open it," the agent insisted, now more serious.

Charley looked at the folder. It had the usual red-ink stamped lettering, "Confidential-FBI" and a sign-out log below it. As was required, he scribbled his initials on the next available line, right under the agent's. At the bottom was an additional stamp that was not usual. It simply said "HOT," with a single line attached to it that contained initials he did not recognize.

He broke the tab allowing the thick folder to be opened. Stapled to the left, inside, facing the mound of various documents, was a black and white photo of a course looking, middle-aged man. Charley lifted it to see the back. There, handwritten in black marker, was, "J.R.H."

"You got it now, Charley." He seemed relieved, "Briefing at eight-thirty tomorrow up on four. And I gotta tell ya, the media's all over this one, so get ready. They think this guy is some kinda hero. As far as I'm concerned, we can just wait for him to wash up somewhere down in Toledo, but we're gettin' pressure, so we gotta get movin' on this." He was halfway across the room when he stopped, unable to resist final comment. "Hey, this could be the big break you've been waiting for."

Even though it was almost twenty years earlier, Keenan remembered the agent's sadistic chuckle. He remembered pouring through the file until late that evening and every evening for days and weeks that followed. The weeks since had turned to faded years. But the recollection of when it began, remained vivid. It was August 5th, 1975; the day he was unexpectedly dislodged from his comfortable bureaucratic cocoon and made to fly reluctantly into the public eye; when he was appointed the first and still Special Federal Prosecutor in Charge.

Of the investigation.

Into the disappearance of James Riddle Hoffa.

3

During the long course of the investigation, Keenan had received thousands of envelopes; most from psychos claiming to have committed the crime, or from amateur detectives who were certain they knew where Hoffa's body could be found, or worse, from people who thought they had recently seen Hoffa in person. The arrival of another one was not unusual, and, as was a matter of procedure, he would again contact the FBI.

After an hour or so, Inspector Frank Doran arrived and now sat in Charley's office, feet up on the desk, casually chewing at the illegal remains of an unlit De Christo Capo cigar and listening as Keenan reviewed the evidence.

The letterhead was plain and authoritative, "Law offices of Ferrand, Mascio, Stein, & Swain. Tenth floor. Buhl Building. Detroit, Michigan." and along the left margin next to the salutation, a long list of associates.

The letter began, "At the posthumous instruction of my client, Mr. Dominic V. Baglia, deceased and so pronounced on the fourteenth day of June, 1995 and in accordance with his wishes as specified in his last will and testament and on behalf of the estate of the aforementioned I convey to you the enclosed." Then continued with the obligatory disclaimer, "I neither personally, nor as a representative of this firm, make any representation as to the veracity of the enclosed nor do I/we claim any knowledge as to the nature of it's contents." It was not signed.

The enclosure to which it referred was a simple white business envelope. Handwritten in pencil, smudged and barely legible across the aged, wrinkled paper was the name, "Keenan." The envelope had practically disintegrated as he opened it. Inside, written in the incoherent printed stroke of the illiterate Baglia, was one yellow sheet of lined legal paper containing the criminal's final message to the prosecutor and the world.

"Read it again, Charley," requested the soft spoken, white-haired man. "I want to make sure I get this straight. We checked out Baglia. I think it's bullshit, but go ahead read it again anyway."

Doran was a career agent who had moved up through the ranks to head the Detroit office of the FBI. He was from the east side of the city, a local boy who grew up on streets lined with elm and maple trees where he played baseball and rode his bike. It had once been an area of large, brick two family flats, now replaced with empty fields and buildings, and no more than camouflage for the drug trade inside. He was the best success of six siblings. He had worked hard, it was generally thought, and had earned everything he now had. Years of intense competition for domestic conversation had resulted in his quiet demeanor. "Go ahead." It was almost a whisper.

Charley read, *"So I'm dead if yer redin dis. Da fukin Teninos cant kil me ani mor thin that. I took care of that Hoffa prick tho an I can prov it. So I hop the hole bunch of em dies to. An for the Domatis go to hell. Baglias not gonna shut up ani mor so you can all die to. wat ar you gonna do. Keenan hers wer the prick is. go up 75 an taka left to kalkaska go all the way thru Travers an keep goin to 22. then thers this rod to leland but you dont go to that town you go left wer it ends an thers a little fukin dirt ther you go in an thers thes littl house an ther on this lak i dont know but the 1 aint*

*it its 2 down with a boat an shit an in betwen the boat plac an the
hous is him. prbly fukinrotin in the same plastic bag I picked up at
that lot.*" The note went on with bigger capital letters, "*YOU
GUYS AR SO FUKIN STUPID BUT YOU THINK IM LYIN SO
HERS A LITTL PRESENT. I WISH I WOOUDA KNOCKED IT
OUT A HIS FACE WHEN HE WAS ALIVE.*"

"May I see it?" Doran asked, and Keenan passed it over. "I
thought I'd seen everything. We're supposed to believe it's one of
Hoffa's?" He rolled a decayed molar in his fingers. "I'll send it to
the lab." He wrapped it up carefully in a scrap of yellow paper.
"Let me have the whole thing. I'll send it all in. Who knows if this
is even from Baglia. Use your phone?"

"Sure." Charley replaced the tooth into the original envelope
and handed it to Frank who spoke into the receiver, "This is
Doran. See if you can round up Garnetti and Karen and meet me
in the conference room in ten minutes. I'm down in Keenan's
office. I'll fill ya in when we get there." He spoke rhetorically to
Charley, "Doesn't this just figure? I'm gonna end up spending the
last three months in the bureau diggin' holes up north lookin' for
Hoffa. Jesus, doesn't this thing ever end?" Doran rose. "You
ready?" He threw the butt in the waste basket. "Lets go."

It was almost ceremonial; the two men walking down the busy
hall. Even the younger employees knew, though it didn't happen
frequently, what it meant. Intermixed with the "Hey Franks" and
"Hi Charleys" was the inevitable, "Find him again?" and this
time, from some far corner, a horrible Flip Wilson impression
while they waited at the elevator, "Charley gonna find Jimmy
Hoffa." And laughter as the doors opened.

When they got to the conference room, the two agents were already seated. "Agents Morse and Garnetti, I believe you know Prosecutor Keenan."

With introductions completed, Doran placed the items on the conference table and began, "Here's what we've got and I'll let Charley tell you how we got it...Charley."

"Yesterday, by courier, I received an envelope from the law offices of Ferrand, Mascio, Stein, & Swain. In it was that business envelope and note presumably from a guy named Dominic Baglia, that Frank's showing you, and this letter from his lawyers. It claims that the message was to be delivered to me when he died. So I can only assume that he did."

"Here's the note," Doran added, "And look at this; it's supposedly one of Hoffa's teeth. It was wrapped up inside." Careful not to touch, the agents leaned in for closer examination. Frank continued, "Baglia says that after picking up the body at what he refers to as a "Lot" and I don't know what that means, he took it up north somewhere near Traverse City and buried it. Karen, you go up there, right?"

"Uh huh."

"Could you get a map, please?" Frank quietly ordered and she left the room. "Bob, I want you to mark this with an evidence number, get it in the log, and send it to the lab. Also, see if you can get a profile on this Baglia guy."

Karen returned quickly with several maps and unfolded them on the table. "This is the general area."

Garnetti rose, "From the description in the note, I'd say he was talking about somewhere in here."

"Leelanau County." Karen said, and went on to indicate specific towns. "This is Sutton's Bay, Northport; and over here on Lake Michigan, that's Leland."

"He said you 'don't go that way but left.' Could that mean here?" Karen nodded in agreement.

"And what's that? Duck Lake? That would be at the end of the road going toward Leland?"

"I wonder why he was so specific." Frank now swiveling around to the window and standing. "I mean it's as if he were told exactly where to put the body. What's Baglia say there, Bob?"

Garnetti read aloud the broken language, "...'the 1 aint it its 2 down with a boat an shit an in betwen the boat plac an the hous is him'."

Frank continued, "Why such a clear recollection? And why now?" Without giving time to answer he turned to the prosecutor. "Charley, I'll be so fuckin' happy not to have to do this anymore." Then, his voice raised slightly. He ordered, "Bob, you and Karen stay on it, get the names of the property owners and get search warrants, but please try to do it quietly. The last thing we need is for the TV guys to think we're on to something."

"Especially when we're not," Charley added.

After the two agents left, Keenan began, "I remember this guy Baglia, he was nothing. I doubt if he even knew anything about Hoffa."

"Why do we get the note now? What possible difference would it have made had he clued us 'stupid guys' in twenty years ago? He was already in prison."

"Maybe he's trying to get to heaven," Charley offered, but he could tell Frank wasn't paying attention. "It doesn't say he had a thing at all to do with the murder or whatever; maybe he was just supposed to dump the body. It doesn't make any sense. If he'd already gotten away with it, why is it so important for us to find the body now? I mean it's not like someone can get any more dead than dead. At least not where I come from." Charley chuckled.

Doran's quiet voice was much more serious. "Why now?"

There was too much silence. Charley stood to leave. "Maybe Baglia was pissed off at you and he's just tryin' to make your last two months more memorable." He slipped into his drawl for effect, "Maybe it's what you all Yankees call a practical joke. I'll talk to you later." And he left.

"Yeah," Doran responded without turning or breaking his reflective surveillance of the downtown landscape. Silent through the huge glass, it had no answer. "Why now?" He really wanted to know.

And in no more than a breath too small to reach the pane, he asked again, "Why?"

4

"...Shelby? Can you get that?" There was no response. "Shelby?" John Russel called as he hurriedly wrapped himself in a bath towel and rushed toward the ringing phone. He heard the sound of the hair dryer and his wife's thinly recorded voice on the answering machine downstairs in the kitchen.

"You've reached the Russels. We can't answer the phone right now, but please leave a message and we'll call you back." And the beep. And another familiar voice. "John, this is Bob Kellett. I know this is gonna seem kinda strange, an' I hate to bother you. I know you're busy, but I got this call fr..." John picked up the phone.

"Bob, this is John Russel. What can I do for you?" He pushed his hair back, drops of water falling onto his shoulders and into the deep carpeting.

"Were you calling me?" Shelby entered the hall, hobbling while she attempted to get the second, black, high-heeled shoe to remain on her foot. "Who is it?" She surrounded his wet torso with her arms, her short dress absorbing some of the dampness that remained on his back.

"Go ahead Bob. Yes. Uh huh," she whispered in his free ear, "We've got to get going, we're gonna be late," she scolded, knowing this conversation had created a considerable opportunity. She slid her hand under the edge of the towel, touching him just slightly as he waved furiously and silently for

16

her to stop. "And they what? You've got to be kidding. Hold on a second." He covered the receiver.

"Stop it. I thought we had to go," John whispered back.

By now she had taken a full grip and began to move her hand slowly over him. He continued into the phone but found it somewhat difficult to concentrate.

"Well I suppose we have to let them do whatever they want, but they better damn well be careful. I know, Bob and I appreciate it. Thanks for calling. I'll tell her. Thanks."

The clean smell of Shelby was overpowering. Her black velvet dress was soft against him. She, now approaching forty, was the same incredible woman that he had married fourteen years earlier. The towel dropped to the floor and he looked at her, still astonished that her physical beauty and sensuality had not faded. "That was the Sheriff." It took a moment for her to realize what he had said. She stopped. "Sheriff Kellet?" John nodded, hiding his disappointment that the act would not continue. "What did he want?"

John reached down and replaced the towel strategically to cover himself, "I gotta get dressed."

Shelby followed him into their bedroom growing more curious, "Well?"

"The FBI has a warrant, a search warrant, for the cottage. And...well...several other places, too, but mainly, this is only what Bob says, they want to search *our* place."

"The cottage? For what? What are they looking for?"

"It's too ridiculous to even discuss."

"Go ahead. Give it a try."

"First of all, remember how they are up there. There are a lot of rumors about this and that, but none of 'em ever turn out to be anything." He paused, "They're looking for a body."

"On our property? C'mon."

"Actually, they're looking for Jimmy Hoffa."

"All right, fine. If you don't want to tell me what's going on, fine." She was pouting into the mirror while she finished her makeup.

John couldn't help the nervous giggle, "That's what Bob just told me, Shel. That's all I know."

"Fine."

John Russel pulled up the sharply creased slacks, tucking in the shirt, adjusting the tie. He brushed his dark, wavy hair until the sides met perfectly behind his head. He grabbed the navy suit coat from the end of the bed. "Shel, we'll talk about it in the car." He leaned to give her a tiny kiss on the back of her neck. "Now c'mon, we've gotta get over to Henry's."

Shelby smiled, "I hate Henry's engagement parties."

"Now, Shel, you know it wouldn't be so bad if he didn't have 'em so often."

It was true. John had attended at least three. It was good for business. Most of his clients would be there.

He had never cared much about such things, and after many years of dodging them, he had theoretically matured sufficiently to appreciate the necessity of such social events; largely as a result of Shelby's constant tutoring. He owed much of his social success to her. He was sure, that without Shelby, he never would have known anything about handling money, let alone advising others on how to handle theirs. But that's what he did.

He was always amazed that he was paid so handsomely for what seemed so obvious. But he just kept meeting people who insisted that he work for them.

He knew Uncle Henry had something to do with it. Since his father died, Uncle Henry had something to do with everything in John's life. Some of his best investment tips came from Henry Swain; and some of his best clients, too.

John remembered a conversation in 1981, just days before Great Lakes Overland Freight went chapter eleven, when Henry had advised him to short the stock, as much of it as he could get. Coincidentally, John also received calls from three new investors on the same day, who insisted he do the same for them.

It was ridiculous. In the thirteen days that followed, Great Lakes not only declared bankruptcy, but four members of the board of directors were indicted for fraud or embezzlement, and two of them were purported to have ties to the Domati crime family. The president, who was not charged, committed suicide by shooting himself in the back of the head, a curiously gymnastic accomplishment, John thought, for a man under duress. Most of the employees were let go and, in what seemed a heartbeat, Harborside Trucking ended up with all the trucks and equipment and what little else was left of the company.

When it was all over, in less than a month, between commissions and his own profits, John had made over seven hundred thousand dollars. So, John figured, if Henry Swain wanted him to be at one of his parties every day of the week, that would be fine.

In the car, Shelby's curiosity resurfaced, "Why would they think Jimmy Hoffa's buried at the cottage?"

"The Sheriff said they got a tip. They needed some help locating the properties and ours was one of 'em."

Shelby pulled down the visor mirror to complete her lipstick, "After twenty years somebody says 'Oh, by the way, Hoffa's over at the Russel's house'; sounds more like a joke."

"I wouldn't worry about it. I just hope they don't wreck the place in the process. I spent half the summer planting those front beds. Jesus, look at this."

Parked halfway down Windmill Pointe Drive on both sides of the wide green boulevard were limousines and their respective drivers. John refused to park at the end of such a long line of vehicles, preferring instead to proceed directly up the main driveway. He passed the brick kneewall of the large front courtyard and circled the fountain counterclockwise past the marble columns of the main entrance then out again to the side drive and to the right and the well hidden garage behind. He made an abrupt and immediate U-turn toward the back yard, and with a tiny squeal of rubber, positioned his car in such a fashion as to block two of the five garage doors which housed the most necessary vehicles.

"There," he said, proud of his vehicular dexterity.

He and Shelby walked back around to the front. As they approached, John nodded dutifully to the tuxedoed man holding the huge oak door, and stopped, allowing Shelby to enter first.

Inside, the floor of the front entrance hall stepped up twice into an ocean of blue slate from Europe. The walls rose fourteen feet in natural stone. It was like walking into a hotel lobby. There were hundreds of people crossing the monstrous oriental rug from the rooms on one side of the common area to those on the other. Various seating arrangements had been placed strategically within the room, but everybody was standing. Every corner of the large hall, on every square foot of wall, everywhere that John looked, was adorned works of art; most ugly, all expensive. It would be impossible, even with one's best effort to replicate the bizarre effect that had obviously been created by Swain's excessive wealth rather than any knowledge or love of art.

"Look at this place." John was almost embarrassed for Swain. "It's unbelievable."

Shelby was quick to agree, "It looks like a cross between the art institute and the Marquis D'Sade's favorite whorehouse. The sooner we're outta here the better."

Ahead, flanked by two complete suits of medieval armor, were six beveled glass doors. They claimed the full height allowed and married the ceiling to the sky and the sky to Lake St. Clair beyond. Out on the perfect lawn, a huge yellow and white striped tent had been erected, replete with musicians, white tablecloths and a large buffet.

They moved into the yard, each step sinking deeply into the bent grass lawn, leaving footprints behind. "I must say this is the first time I've gone to a reception before the wedding," Shelby noted.

"Henry's marriages usually haven't lasted that long. This poor girl probably wanted to make sure she got one."

"He's such a letch. I can't stand being anywhere near him."

"We won't stay long."

They walked out past the guests at the tables. If there was one good thing about Swain's events, it was the odd assortment of attendees that showed up. Henry's dubious and checkered background had produced this eclectic array once again. John couldn't help noticing that each table had a distinctly unique character. From some came the empty-headed chatter of social climbing one-upsmanship; the Junior Leaguers. From others, foul mouthed street talk; his clients. At one of these was perhaps Swain's most notorious, Benito Tenino. Dark, with the same curly hair and piercing eyes of his father, he was the old man's youngest son and had, at one time, worked with both Henry and John Russel Sr. loading vegetable trucks. Eventually, after his brother and old man Tenino were murdered, he inherited the operation. It was widely speculated that his interests ranged well beyond the legal, but, with Uncle Henry's help, he had thus far avoided conviction.

As they made their way through the crowd, there were the usual greetings and questions and small talk. As far as John was concerned, it was all pretty silly, but he had learned to go along. It was desirable, Shelby had instructed, to be *seen*. It was not necessary to actually converse.

Shelby was well versed in such etiquette. She had been blessed or cursed, depending on one's point of view, to have been born of the womb of the social elite, which was more a matter of lineage than of wealth. John had not. His father worked hard. He was a doctor, a researcher, and they lived well. John's childhood was good by any estimation, but lacked both the bloodline and the secretive, messy soap operas exclusive to those of privilege. He was normal.

The day they met, John was moonlighting as a bartender at a reception at the Country Club, long before becoming a member himself. She was twenty, a senior in college, and absolutely overwhelming. He was twenty-four. He remembered her date laughing when John, so completely stricken by the depth of Shelby's hazel eyes, could not recall what drink she'd ordered.

Later that year, just before Christmas, Dr. Russel and his wife, John's mother and father, suffered an automobile accident and died. They were on the way home from a party. The brakes failed. Unable to control the car, they slid over the embankment and into the lake, crashing through the thick ice to the bottom, where they drowned.

John was mentally paralyzed by the loss, until, as though by some miracle, he once again met Shelby. This time at Uncle Henry's, where his status was substantially elevated from servant to family member, and they could gaze at one another from an equal plane, without fear of criticism. Their love was as immediate as their friendship. And together that day they walked the same lawn that was now under them, and left behind the first of many inseparable footprints.

"John?"

"Oh, sorry Shel. I was just..."

"Isn't that Henry?"

In the far corner of the vast striped canvas tent there was a man waving. As he moved closer, John heard his strong voice growing louder, "Johnny! Johnny how are you?"

Even Shelby had to admit that the old guy was dashing. His deep tan and white hair belied his seventy plus years.

"Uncle Henry, congratulations."

"Thank you, Johnny, thank you. She's a good one, this one." Turning to Shelby, taking both of her hands in his, he softened, "How are you, beautiful Shelby, will he never leave your side?" Henry leaned in for the obligatory social half kiss.

She backed away, but smiled, "Not as long as you're on the other, Henry. Congratulations."

"Wait'll you meet Carla, she's unbelievable." John noticed a very tall woman approaching, a flute of bubbling wine in each hand. She was no more than thirty-five. Her skin was as white as he had seen and her long, straight, auburn hair moved hypnotically back and forth with each step. She was by any measurement, outstanding.

Henry Swain was an uncle in title rather than in blood. He had become so forever after a pre-adolescent summer of cigarettes and joyrides long before John even was. John's father and Henry Swain, after being caught stealing an Oldsmobile from a local car lot, were banished to separate schools; Mr. Russel to Weylan Military Academy in St. Louis, Mr. Swain to Oakbrook in Bloomfield, Michigan. Institutions from which each would be expelled after less than one full school year, returning afterward to public education where their friendship grew stronger and they became inseparable virtual siblings until John's father's death in 1976. Perhaps as a result of such direct experience, Henry Swain had developed an interest in the law. He had begun his career as a public defender, but soon afterward took a position with the Wayne County Prosecutor's Office. He had a reputation as a formidable trial attorney, particularly with regard to organized crime. Then, after nearly twenty years, he abruptly quit to join Ferrand, Mascio, and Stein, as a partner in one of the city's largest firms.

Since then, Henry Swain had shot like a meteor from public servant to social dandy, in the process becoming quite wealthy. But persistent rumor remained that his flamboyant lifestyle and his procession of ex-wives did frequently outpace his earnings. Still, considering this mansion by the lake and the unbelievable beauty of this latest woman who had pledged herself to him, it was difficult to believe that he was not of substantial financial resources.

"Carla, I would like you to meet John and Shelby Russel; Johnny, Shelby I give you my betrothed." As he spoke Swain put one of his long arms around each of the women, pulling them close in to himself.

John should have been prepared for just about anything given Swain's historical propensity for importing his wives from such exotic places as Venice, California and Las Vegas, but this one gushed with a syrup so strong that his teeth hurt from the first utterance.

"She's from Nashville. She's a singer, aren't you sweetheart?"

"Well Henry, don't y'all just say the sweetest of things. Isn't he somethin'?" The singer kissed Uncle Henry's cheek as he reached down simultaneously patting both Carla's and Shelby's backsides.

"Why don't you girls get to know one another. I want to have a word with Johnny." Swain dislodged himself from the group and motioned for John to join him. The two walked slowly toward the water. "That Carla's something isn't she?" Swain began, and turning to make sure they were out of earshot. "...doesn't have a brain. It's amazing she knows when to breathe. But when she does," he continued with a laugh, "it's a sight to behold." Swain lowered his voice. "John, I heard about the warrant. I just wanted you to know that if I can do anything, I mean legally, I certainly will."

"Jesus, lunacy travels fast. How the hell did you find out about that, Henry?"

"I've been around a long time. It pays to know what's going on."

"But they only called me an hour ago. I guess they're going to dig around the cottage. I'm sure it won't be anything, but if I get arrested I'll call you."

"Well, in that case, I hope I never hear from you. C'mon, let's get a drink."

When they returned, the group had grown. The singer had drawn her first northern social audience, comprised primarily of errant husbands, now apparent recent converts to the country music genre. "She's like a damn magnetic hood ornament," Swain boasted.

Shelby, who was holding her own on the periphery, was shooting the look as she politely nodded in half-hearted agreement with the various ignored spousal assemblage. John signaled toward the house. Shelby made her escape. When they connected, she started, "That's about as engaging as I want to get. Let's get the hell out of here. What did he want?"

"He knew about the cottage."

"How?"

"I don't know, Shel, maybe lawyers put their ears to some imaginary steel rail on the information railroad. Maybe they can hear cases rattling toward their bank accounts. I don't know."

"I'm serious. Don't you think it's strange he would know? How long does it take to get a search warrant?"

"This is really gettin' to you, isn't it?"

Shelby found the situation intriguing. The two walked through the monstrous hall without speaking; John making necessary good-byes and she merely nodding acknowledgment while she tossed the various wild scenarios around.

In the car on the way home, she suggested that maybe it would make sense to go north to find out what was going on and John responded, "I was planning on driving up tomorrow, but there's no reason for us both to go. I just want to see how badly they dug up the place and make sure they put everything back."

"Aw c'mon John," She had slipped into a baby's dialect and he knew this was going to be tough. "I just wanna see what the big ol' policemen are doin' with their backhoe," Shelby paused and moved her left hand between John's legs, "...first hand." She squeezed him gently, sliding closer and whispering, "Please, Junior?"

"Shel, why? I'll call you when I get there. You take care of things here and I'll be back the next day. Okay?"

Shelby was pouting again and refused to speak for the remainder of the ride home.

5

The trip to Leelanau County was long, at least four and a half hours, but Shelby's company did make it more enjoyable. John had realized that it would have been impossible to deny her the satisfaction of her curiosity, and had acquiesced to her wishes. He watched her sleep now and marveled, as he often did, at her being. Shortly after they met, she graduated from Stephens College. It was a great collision between the street and the Tau Beta. John's complete ignorance of such things, rendered him a charming social challenge, one which Shelby gleefully accepted, having been left no choice by her immediate and uncontrollable passion for him. She had once told him that if indeed a woman makes the man, she would make him a god, and he had grown to believe that. She alone, he thought, may actually possess the angelic ability to perform such a miraculous transformation.

Many years before, Dr. John Albert Russel had named this only child after himself, but Shelby was the only person to have ever called him 'Junior'. And not then until he was almost thirty. He was sorry that she had never met his parents, but grateful that she was there, as an angel, soon after their death. Shelby had become his family. She was like a sponge that absorbed his history as though it were her own. She had never seen him on the playground, or in braces, or riding his bike, but knew through his stories, every detail; what color it was; how he felt invigorated, riding alone, dodging the piles of freshly raked, golden elm leaves that rained from the arches above his street. She knew. And she had absorbed much of his earlier life, too, before his family was able to move to such a stately neighborhood.

The Russel's had lived near downtown Detroit. John's father had worked at the Eastern Market, where the farmers brought the fresh daily cargo of poultry and produce. He arrived each morning at three-thirty at Tenino's loading dock. He would work until seven-thirty loading vegetables into wooden cases and onto the endless army of trucks to be taken to the restaurants and markets of the city. He would return home by eight and take John to school, then continue to the university and to his own heavy load of classes requisite to obtain a medical degree. This was his routine for over five years, requiring the extra income to raise his son and keep his wife supplied with the wherewithal to run his modest household.

Then, as if suddenly hatched from a long dormant egg, life began. The memories of the tiny apartment where the Russels had lived cracked into jagged pieces and John emerged from his shell, the son of a doctor; Dr. J. A. Russel, Sr. of Grosse Pointe.

Things for John were newer. His friends were different. At school there were mohair sweaters and suntanned second graders. The rough language of Tenino's was gone, replaced with a delicate substitute which seemed to have no definite national or regional origin. It was through this new life that John would ascend toward adulthood. It was the life of a doctor's son.

John glanced at Shelby, she still dozing as they drove north toward Grayling on I-75. He had traveled this course many times as a boy after his family had bought the cottage. It was a place his father had loved, the direct opposite of the doctor's stark research laboratory.

For at least two weeks every summer, and the week between Christmas and New Year's, they would forget about every other aspect of their collective lives and concentrate on the act of simply being and being together. These times provided a kind of natural syrup which sweetened their relationship and stuck them to one another.

After John's parents' Chevrolet went off the road into Lake St. Clair, this was what was left; the glue that joined the ice over them and reflected the Christmas lights from the Lakeshore mansions back up into the December darkness.

For someone to violate this connection, to intrude into John's past was unconscionable. For the FBI to suspect, however briefly, that his family could somehow be implicated in the Hoffa disappearance, even by physical accident, angered him.

"How we doing?"

"Almost to Traverse."

Shelby stretched her neck slowly to relieve the stiffness. "Good." She turned toward the window and drifted off again.

It was a little past one when John pulled to a stop at the intersection of M-204 and M-22. He jogged to the left and then made an immediate right into the gravel-covered dirt road. He passed the row of green plastic cylinders which accepted the Traverse City newspapers, and the rustic, carved wooden sign at the end of Bill Holloway's driveway. 'Holly's Retreat' it read, proudly announcing his neighbor's secret location. On the next mailbox, the number four. John turned into the gravel two-track and, winding through the tall pines, caught the first hint of Duck Lake and the cottage.

"Wake up, Shel, we're here."

She slowly opened her eyes. "What's that, John?"

About fifty feet from the house toward the water and the boathouse was an area marked by slender, three foot tall wooden stakes. Draped between them was bright yellow plastic tape.

"I don't know." John was seething. Leading to the cordoned-off section were several deep gullies, each marked with the unmistakable interwoven angular impressions left behind by the tires of some form of heavy equipment. They stretched like dark brown zippers in the mud through what had been a perfectly manicured lawn just days earlier. What remained was a flat green trampled triangle, pointing like a huge arrow to the site of the investigation.

"Jesus Christ! Look at this! Godammit!" He slammed the car into park before it had even rolled to a stop. Pushing open his door and exiting in a single movement, he walked to the spot to get a closer look. Shelby got out and hurried to catch him. She placed her arm around him and tried to comfort his obvious anguish, but in his building rage he was oblivious to her touch. The two stopped at the elevated yellow line, staring, amazed at the result of this federal violation. John ripped the tape and stepped forward to the edge of the hole. "Jesus Christ!" he said, looking down, "Do you believe this? It's gotta be ten feet deep." It was not an exaggeration. Cut through the earth and mature roots was one large, nearly square excavation, about twelve feet on a side. "Goddammit!"

Shelby, still standing at the original line, broke the tension. "They must think this Hoffa guy was pretty big." Even as angry as he had become, he could not help laughing. "Let's see what else they did."

Initially the cottage looked pretty much as usual. The wide wooden steps were as solid as ever, resting on the stone foundation. At the top they opened to a screened porch that ran the width of the front of the brown wooden structure. Each window was framed in forest green and almost as high as the total height of the room itself. To the right, as they entered, John and Shelby could see Duck Lake and the forest beyond as a perfect inverted reflection in it's still surface. To the left, through the deep northern woods, Lake Michigan, almost half a mile away, yet the sound of the great lake's waves pounding down on the sand could be heard clearly.

John opened the screen door and crossed to open the more substantial door to the house. It was never locked. He turned the knob and nudged the big door open. Before it traveled halfway, the well-oiled hinges refused to propel it further. Abruptly, with timing of almost slapstick precision, John collided with the wooden adversary. "Ow! What's wrong with this?" He muscled in far enough to facilitate passage. "What happened in here? Jesus fucking Christ! I thought Kellet was gonna keep his eye on this place. I'm calling the bastard right now. This is bullshit." John stepped over piles of books dislodged from the empty bookcases that enclosed two walls of the main room. He carefully moved past chairs, upside-down, their bottom linings torn and fabric cushions sliced into foam rubber shards by dozens of parallel cuts. The kitchen cabinets were open and the contents distributed on the floor. The wall phone, normally attached next to the refrigerator was buried under a stainless mountain of flatware and utensils. Shelby stood frozen in statuesque disbelief at the door. John picked up the receiver and dialed. The calm woman's voice answered and John let her have it. "You're God damn right this is an emergency. Russel. John Russel….no nobody's been injured, *yet*," and then raising his voice again after a pause, "But if the bastards who fucked up my house have got the balls to show up here again, then I'd send a fucking ambulance or two if I were you! Oh. Someone is. Isn't that nice. Well I hope it's Sheriff Kellett because as far as I'm concerned this whole deal is his fault. No, I will not stay on the line," He slammed the handset down onto the carriage, sending plastic shrapnel flying.

"Social call?" Shelby bent to pick up a book. Realizing he didn't appreciate the humor, she went on, "I'm sorry, John. I can't believe it. What were they looking for in here?"

"They weren't supposed to be in here at all. That's what Kellett said; 'Oh, it'll just be a minor thing, no reason to give it a second thought.' Well, I'm damn glad I did, this is out of hand."

They were just beginning to pick up the rubble when they heard the sirens drawing closer. The lights flashed in the dark woods, coming closer down the driveway. One county car then a second, finally a third each spinning to a perpendicular stop in the dappled light of the front yard. Doors open. Two men in the first two cars, kneeling, guns drawn, sheltered by the sheet metal. Another siren, and then a fifth. Twin ambulances skidded to a halt. From the third patrol car emerged the tall figure of Bob Kellett. Slowly he approached the cottage. "John?" he inquired, "You all right?"

"All right?" John yelled back, "Have you seen this place?" He stormed through the porch door, not noticing the pair of pistols aimed directly at his head. He continued, "I've never seen anything like this. You promised me this was nothing. Now I get up here and it looks like somebody's gettin' ready to pour the foundation for a new high-rise on my front lawn. I'd say *that* was something, wouldn't you Sheriff?"

"Put 'em away boys, it's Mr. Russel. You guys can take off, I'll take care of this," Sheriff Kellett instructed, "Calm down, John."

John went on, "Wait'll you see what they did inside? C'mon I'll show you. Then tell me if you'd calm down."

Shelby stepped back from her vigil by the door. The two men ascended the steps and silently entered.

John, being first, crossed the main room and visually referred to various heaps of belongings, his gestures not dissimilar to those of a model on a game show pointing out the prizes to be won. With a slight flourish of wrist, he elevated both hands drawing the sheriff's attention to the two broken side windows. Stepping briskly over the inverted love seat, he landed dead center in the room, pointing down to the pile of his father's ledgers, journals, and various books. With a simultaneous choreographed circular motion of his forefingers, he directed the sheriff's sight beyond the broken lamp, which he kicked aside, to the scattered photographs below. This absurd, sporadic dance through the turmoil punctuated the rape of his father's memory. When he stopped, he lifted his arms part way up on either side of his body, and, with a slight shrug of shoulder, physically demanded an answer.

"Jesus, John, I don't know what to tell ya. This is horrible." He bent down and picked up a book. After a brief look, he handed it silently to Shelby who managed a slight smile. She walked dutifully to the bookcase and placed it back onto a shelf.

"Bob, I think somebody owes me an explanation, don't you?"

The sheriff examined the scene. He was careful not to step on anything as he walked to the front window. "That's where I was, outside, while they were digging. I never saw any of 'em come in here. They only had a warrant for the outside. As far as I know, John, no one from the FBI or anywhere else was in this house; nobody from the county went anywhere near the place." He looked directly at John, "After they found the body, they left. I was on the way out here to tell you."

"The body?" Shelby wasn't sure she had heard correctly.

"Yes, ma'am. About ten this mornin'. They loaded it up in some special kinda van and took it over to Northport. That's where they are now. Said they didn't want to disturb the evidence. They're waitin' for some hotshots to get in to evaluate the situation. But they found it. Right out there." He gestured to the excavation.

"They don't think it's…"

"Hoffa? Of course not, Shel." John reassured her, "But it is pretty strange to find someone buried…"

The sheriff interrupted, "They do."

6

The hours after Bob Kellet left were almost imaginary. Shelby and John having run out of expressions of disbelief of the situation, could not help landing on the obvious.

"I don't believe it," John spoke as they were picking up items from the floor, returning them, to the best of their recollection, to the proper places. "I just don't believe it. Shel, do you realize what all this means? What sort of implications this has? I mean, they've been lookin' for this guy for twenty years."

"What's this?" Shelby held up a black notebook, legal size, with burgundy triangles on the corners.

"It's one of Dad's journals. There are dozens of 'em. Look over here." Under a cover of paperback books was a mound of similar journals. John, already seated in the rubble, picked one up. "See?"

"He used them for his work?"

"You know how he was, he wrote everything down. If he did anything, it's in these."

"Look at this John." She'd opened one of the records and brought it over to him. "Every entry is dated, with times, and I guess he wrote down the results of each procedure. That must be what this is." John inspected the page. From top to bottom each line of the narrow-lined ledger was numbered at the extreme left and then followed by a series of what appeared to be chemical formulas or mathematical equations and finally at the right, in a column headed 'confirmation', a check mark or nothing, depending, John assumed, on the results of that particular test.

"It's not voodoo. I've been lookin' at these all my life. The guy was a research scientist, this is the kinda shit he did. I don't know, Shel, it's just…stuff he wrote down."

"Well, I don't know who was in here today, but I do know they wanted something, something that's here…in this cottage. You think it was the FBI guys; what if it wasn't?"

"Who else would it be?"

"I don't know…anybody."

"Shel," he didn't know how to present this, "Are you saying that somehow my family is involved in this? I think you've got an overactive imagination."

She was edgy. "Well, I didn't imagine that hole in the yard, or the broken windows, or this fuckin' mess. Something is going on. Right here. And you and me *are* your family, and we're in it, whatever it is and I'd like to know what it is, thank you."

"Shelby, listen, what these people thought they found or whatever, it has nothing to do with us. Sheriff Kellet was probably too busy kissin' up to the FBI agents to even notice whether someone came in here or not. I'll tell you Shel, this whole thing is bullshit. Now, let's just take it easy and get some rest, and tomorrow we'll be able to figure out what's goin' on. Okay?"

"I'm sorry." She was all hugs. "I'm gonna get ready for bed, you coming?"

"I'll be in in a second."

It was interesting, John thought, to see the notations of his father. He scanned the handwritten book with pride. To be able to rise from nothing was a worthy accomplishment.

After completing school, the elder Russel had chosen to continue medical research, to teach, and to write. He had never left the sanctity of academia for the world at large, nor had he ever felt compelled to actually treat a patient. It was as though he thought, that after orchestrating his own arrival on the doorstep of his adoptive mother university, to leave her would be treason. So he stayed. His laboratory grew with his recognition, as did his staff. From a solitary, one man room, his domain expanded to an entire floor in the basement of the medical center. His work with genetics was renowned among his peers. John remembered visiting once when he was young. He remembered the cages with the monkeys and the rats and the birds. And asking his father if he was a veterinarian. This thought made him chuckle silently. He rose from the area he'd cleared in the center of the living room floor, and walked to the bookcase to return the journal, but stopped, instead taking it with him to the bedroom.

Shelby was asleep when he got into bed, but stirred slightly. "Goodnight Junior," she whispered. John leaned and kissed her gently. "I'll call Henry in the morning." With that she smiled and fell back into sleep.

John propped himself against the pillows to review his father's ledger. Page after page was filled with medical drawings and notes about various procedures. There were references to Subject A, specimen VII/24B, and long lists of chemical formulas. A date was placed ahead of each section, which then went on to fill whatever space it required. It wasn't long before the penciled scroll dissolved into a blur. The northern air, with more than it's share of oxygen, worked as a sedative. John turned out his lamp and was asleep before the last wave of incandescent light had vanished from the room.

Then the flashes. Lightning. There should be thunder. They were so bright, he could see them with his eyelids closed, but heard no sound of rain. Gradually awakening, he looked toward the window. This lightning had direction. It was man-made. It was close. He saw figures outside, in the yard; people moving around out by the big hole, taking pictures.

Leaping to action, John grabbed something to throw at the mob, the nearest thing on the night stand, and ran from the room. "Junior? John?" Shelby was dazed, "What are you doing?" He was already gone. Spinning, tripping in the dark. The wild burglar dance played against the walls in random silhouettes, his contorted shadow strobing in momentary bursts from the trespasser's flashbulbs. Out through the door, to the porch, screaming, "Hey. Hey! Get the hell outta here!" But instead the flashes became more frequent and closer. "Get the fuck outta here!" John yelled as loud as he could. He heard the sounds of vehicle's engines starting. The photographers stopped, all but one. He came closer, within fifteen feet. And aimed the final burst. Wham. John was completely blinded by tungsten. He missed the first step, falling wildly out of control, his would-be weapon flying through the air above him, "Ahhhhhhhhhhhhhhhh." The press, frightened by this odd behavior, scurried into the night. He landed on his knees in the cold dirt.

"Nice act." Shelby tried to suppress the convulsing laughter that shook her body. "But I think it would be much less dangerous if you practiced your acrobatics in the daytime." She had been standing on the porch, and had witnessed the entire event.

"There's no way I'm going back to sleep now," John was up, "I'm gonna make some coffee." He brushed the black soil from his body.

"I'm scared, John."

He took her hand as they reentered the cabin. "So am I, Shel."

Shelby righted a wooden chair and sat at the huge antique farm table while John made the brew. The heap remained, and in the area at her feet was an empty box and scattered photographs. She picked it up along with several of the shots and started putting them away. "You know, John, there has to be a reason for this.

Even if this body, whoever it is, isn't Hoffa, there is still something here that somebody wants badly enough to break in."

John sat with her at the table. "I think we should finish cleaning this place up; when it's light, I'll board up those windows. We should get back and talk to Henry as soon as possible, hopefully this afternoon. He's a lawyer, he should be able to tell us what recourse we have. I still think this mess is a result of the search. What's that?"

Shelby was looking at an old black and white photograph. "It's your dad."

"Let me see." She passed it to him. The emulsion, once smooth and shiny, was an aged mosaic of hairline cracks. "Look at how young he is."

"Who are these other guys?"

"That's when he was working at Eastern Market, at Tenino's. I don't know, but this guy looks like Uncle Henry, I know he used to work there, too. The others, I don't recognize."

"I think we should take it with us, and the rest of these, too. If something happened we could never replace them."

"Sure." John put two cups of steaming, black coffee on the table. He noticed a faint glow on the lake. "The sun's coming up. I've got some plywood in the boathouse and some tools. I'm gonna start on the windows."

While he was outside, Shelby finished with the box of pictures. She began leafing through the ledgers, putting them in chronological order on a shelf. They were dated beginning in 1961 and continued through the doctor's death in 1976. She too looked at the drawings of organs, the descriptions of procedures, and the long lists of chemical equations and none of it made any sense.

John was outside driving nails into the pine, each blow echoing from the trees that surrounded the peaceful lake when Shelby called, "John! John, c'mere!" He dropped his hammer and ran inside. "What Shel? What's goin' on?"

Shelby sat transfixed with her discovery. She handed the book to John, pages open to the spot. "See? See what I mean? Look at that." On the left, the date July 23, 1975, on the right July 28, 1975. "They're missing. You can see where someone tore them out; the pages in between. Where are they?"

"Shel. Calm down."

"Why those pages?"

"I don't know."

"Right before them, there are notes about new procedures and something called 'HLA', and then he wrote all these symbols. I looked back at the rest of the book and it's pretty much the same as all the others, but then look ahead at the pages after the ones that were torn out. You see anything different?"

"Not really. What do you mean?"

"Look. See all the chemistry stuff in the front?"

John nodded.

"Then look back here. It's the same kind of stuff, except this new notation shows up."

"Lemme see." Shelby pointed out the notation.

"And," she said, opening two more books, each of a later date, laying them on the table, "It keeps repeating. Here." She passed the journal to John, "And here," she passed another, "And in all of them...until he died."

"My God." John could not deny the truth of what she had discovered. He scanned each page with disbelief. "We'd better take these, too. Why don't you pack 'em up and we'll get outta here. It'll just take me a couple more minutes to finish boarding this place up, by then I can call Henry. Jesus, this is weird."

Shelby agreed, "You're not kiddin'." She looked again at the pages. She tried to imagine what had been written on the ones that were no longer there and what John's father had to do with any of this. She examined the coarse, torn pages. And the dates. "Hey, John?" but the hammering had resumed.

Shelby didn't really want an answer. "Junior?" She asked anyway, more quietly and to herself.

"When did Hoffa disappear?"

7

Leelanau Memorial Hospital, where the remains had been taken, sat horizontally along the ridge of a small hill overlooking the wind kissed water of Grand Traverse Bay. It served the medical needs of the northern part of the county and the seven hundred or so residents of Northport. With it's single story architecture of beige brick, and large, evenly spaced windows, it could have easily been mistaken for an elementary school.

Behind the building, a road entered from one side, widened into a parking lot, and then, as it went down the slope, once again became a road. Usually quiet, and a frequent shortcut for those who knew the town, it was now blocked. Two black Fords nosed in across the entrance, two more at the exit. They were positioned in such a way as to make it necessary to zig-zag to gain access to the area. Posted at each were two plainclothes agents who checked every vehicle entering and leaving and kept the ever-swelling gang of reporters at bay. At the rear of the lot, newly painted in bright yellow, was a huge "X", twenty-five feet across.

It was upon this target that the thunderous sound of the helicopter descended through the tranquil August air. From the rear of the building a small group of men appeared, walking quickly toward the landing area. From the aircraft, emerged two others who joined the group halfway across the lot. "Welcome, doctor. We've got you set up right in here." They continued into the building.

The emergency room doors slid open. "Norman," came the quiet voice from inside, greeting the doctor and his assistant, "Glad you're here." The voice discarded the cigar butt into a container generally reserved for medical waste.

"Hi, Frank...finally found him, eh?" The doctors removed their sport coats and replaced them with light blue uniforms. "Where is he?"

Frank Doran directed them to a second small room, instructing his agents as he walked. "This is Dr. Hoffman, from Bethesda. Please give him whatever he wants."

Hoffman introduced the second doctor who would assist and all proceeded into the adjacent room.

Inside, it was cold, the air chilled by two large units which had been set up in the main room. Twelve inch flexible ducts carried the steady flow of cooled air to the work area. In the center on a stainless steel table was the large black vinyl bag that had been removed from the hole in John Russel's front lawn. Bright white lights on tall metal stands stood in the two far corners, raised almost to the ceiling, their halogen reflections ricocheting around the green and yellow ceramic tile.

"This is what we found; didn't want to open it up 'til you got here," Frank explained.

"Well," the doctor responded, "Let's take a look." His assistant wheeled a stainless steel cart containing dozens of surgical instruments, various drills and saws, and hand tools closer to the table. From one of several cases, he removed a small video camera. From another, a collapsed tripod. After he had completed the setup, he nodded to Dr. Hoffman, indicating the equipment was ready.

Doctor Hoffman began with a utility knife, slicing the opaque plastic bag as if it were a package of bacon, his careful insertion just far enough under the surface to be effective yet not disturb whatever human meat may linger beneath. He cut a small rectangle which included the zipper pull and, with tongs, placed it into the plastic bag his assistant was holding. "Give it a number please and start an evidence table." Through the hole he had created, the doctor could see the first hint of bone. He again used the utility knife, this time to cut the bag completely, lengthwise, parallel to the rusted zipper track. Reaching into the slit with both hands, he slowly separated the sides and, like a giant black baked potato, he peeled back the skin until it was completely opened.

Frank, curious, leaned in. He was always amazed that after a time there was no odor, the flesh and interior organs having long ago eroded. What remained wasn't even a body. He could see that the largest bones were still connected with thin yellowish threads of tawny tissue, but many of the others had dislodged and found their way to the corners of the bag, explaining the almost musical percussion the discovery had made as it was transferred to the table.

The two pathologists worked silently, methodically measuring. Only an occasional medical fact was spoken, and then, only for the benefit of the video recording. "We appear to have a male. Caucasian. Age sixty to seventy. Evidence of prior traumas...number one, simple fracture of the right fibula; looks like an old injury." He turned to Frank. "We're gonna need a big table in here to reassemble and inventory the skeleton."

Doran left the room momentarily and returned with two of his men who carried a long wooden table with folding legs. "Set it up over there next to the operating table," he ordered, "Have you got the Hoffa records? And the films?" Doran asked.

"Right here." The agent raised a manila file.

"Good, we'll need 'em."

Frank took the folder and handed it to Hoffman's assistant who immediately removed a dozen or so X-rays. He switched on the wall-mounted light box and clipped each so they could be seen clearly by the doctor.

Reaching back into the potato, Dr. Hoffman exorcised the first scrap of preserved calcium. "Fifth ungual phalanx," he announced, and placed the tiniest bone from the small toe down on the new table. With a micrometer the assistant measured and announced for the record, "1.03 centimeters." From a nearby crease, Hoffman removed what he suspected was the adjoining bone, "...second phalanx, four or five..." and placed it in a position adjacent to the first. With some adjustment he was satisfied that the two did indeed fit together. Smiling, he began to reassemble the anatomy of the mysteriously deceased.

Frank Doran watched as bone after bone was put into the puzzle. He lit a new cigar and watched as the exhaled smoke circled in the wash of the air conditioning. Each piece measured and compared to the film. The occasional nod between the doctors. The last thing he had ever expected to find was this body. The timing still troubled him.

"Frank?" It was Agent Garnetti, "Can you spare a second?"

"Sure." Doran joined him in the emergency room which now resembled a command center.

"I got the prelim from the lab. It looks like Baglia's prints are all over the note and as near as anybody can tell, it's his writing, too, but that's not for sure."

"Where's Karen?"

"She went to get the sheriff."

"Good. What about the tooth?"

"They took some pictures, but Hoffman needed it here. I guess it's up to him to figure out if it's a match." Garnetti opened the manila folder. "Background; Dominic V. Baglia, arrived Detroit

'53 from New York; born San Salima, Italy, 1927; worked the docks, trucks, usual stuff; connected with the Domati family; odd stuff; enforcement. We checked him out early in the investigation. Nothing stuck. He was twenty-five to life at Milan."

"Charge?"

"Murdered a college kid in seventy-nine, a boy. Apparently it was a sex thing. Anyway, he is dead; last week, pneumonia; AIDS."

"All right. Let me know when the sheriff gets here." Doran walked down the hall toward the small empty waiting room, stopping at the pay phone. He raised the receiver and punched in the numbers. With a practiced oral dexterity he moved the lit butt from one side of his mouth to the other, waiting for an answer.

"Keenan," came back through the wire followed by a final swallowing and the ever upward inflection of the south, "How may I be of service?"

"It's Frank."

"Well, well...did we find our little teamster in the woods?"

"It could be."

"You're kiddin'." The significance had not yet been fully absorbed. "Well, isn't that somethin'? Who you lookin' at?"

"Hard to say. We're checking the guy who owns the property; Russel? Ever heard of him?"

"No."

"He lives down there; has a cottage here; in Leland on Duck Lake. I'll make sure you get the details. You're probably gonna want to talk to him. But I wanted to warn you, you should get a haircut, I think we're about to get popular again."

"Does that mean I gotta watch you every night on the news? 'Cause that's enough to make me swear off television forever," he chuckled.

"I'll get back to you later, Charley."

Frank walked back to the main area. Karen Morse was talking to a tall, broad shouldered man in a light khaki uniform. The room was alive with technicians and wires and phones. The public relations people were preparing a response to the gathered press which would certainly involve his on-camera presence. He had chewed the illegal tobacco into a slippery pulp and, not finding a more appropriate means of disposal, placed the remains in a convenient bedpan. When he entered Hoffman's room he was surprised at the progress. Both legs were assembled and in position on the second table. The doctor was holding the pelvis bone up to the light, adjusting the proximity to match the corresponding view on the film. It was with an odd grin that he acknowledged Frank's return; and with a slight raising of brow that he arranged this large calcium piece to complete the apex of the lower part of his growing puzzle of death.

"Well?" Frank asked.

Hoffman removed his surgical gloves. "It's early, but so far I'd say it's a match. I'll know more when I get to the head, which really shouldn't be too long. A lot of the rib cage is pretty much in location, some of it intact; so it could be an hour or so; but that'll really help us determine who we got here, Frank."

"Lemme know." Doran left them to their work. He motioned to Karen Morse, who approached from the other side of the emergency room.

"Yeah, Frank."

"Who's that?"

"Kellet. County sheriff."

"I want to talk to him. Have we got a room somewhere?"

"We've cleared the whole hospital, you can go anywhere you want."

"That won't make anybody wonder, will it Morse? C'mon bring him in here."

Karen returned with Bob Kellet to the semi-private room Frank had chosen.

"Shut the door, please," he ordered, "Have a seat, Sheriff." He gestured to one of the beds, himself sitting on the other. Karen Morse stood by the door. Doran reached into the inside pocket of his sport coat and removed another Cuban export. He carefully unwrapped it and, with a small tool designed for such purpose, sliced off the tip.

"You can't smoke in here." The sheriff was definite, but Frank ignored him completely and instead, with a push of a button, raised the head of his bed, put his feet up, and with quiet deliberation began to do just that.

"Given his present condition, I don't think this guy is gonna mind a little secondhand smoke. Do you, Sheriff...?"

"Kellet."

A huge blue-white cloud rose in the stream of northern light, illuminating dust in the air. Without eye contact, Frank started calmly, slowly. "What do you know, Sheriff Kellet, about the people who own the place where we found the body?"

"The Russels? I've known 'em since I was a kid around here."

"You're from here?"

"Yeah."

"Go on."

"Well, John's dad was a doctor, hell of a guy, and they used to come up here for vacations and stuff, you know. Half the county does the same thing."

"But we found a body in his half." Doran's voice increased in amplitude briefly, "Any trouble that you know of? Did they have lots of different people coming and going from the place? Any known criminals livin' there Sheriff Kellett? Agent Morse here says that lake, what is it?"

"Duck Lake, sir," she answered.

"...is a former haven of illegal activity. In fact, apparently Al Capone himself used to hide there to avoid prosecution. So, Sheriff..." Frank took a hit of the cigar and swung his legs back onto the floor. He leaned intently and too close into the face of the officer and spoke quietly, almost whispering, "I want to know what the fuck the deal is with these Russels and how the fuck Hoffa ended up as fertilizer for their front lawn. So if you know anything that might have led to that result, I think it might be wise to tell me." The additional oxygen from his tirade had stoked the cigar to magnificent combustion. The exhaust filled the room. Frank spoke again. "Don't you, Sheriff Kellet?"

Bob Kellet was a large physical man. He had grown up in the rural county the third generation of Finnish carpenters. His father could build almost anything, and in fact, at one time, not only were most of the buildings in the area of his hand, so was most of the furniture inside them; the county providing nearly an endless supply of birch, cherry, and white pine. The elder Kellet had encouraged his son to also pursue such tasks, but Bob found it too boring and sought more adventure than Leelanau could ever provide. He became a marine in 1970 and remained in the service for eight years; long enough to know that there was no point in reasoning with assholes like Frank Doran. Instead he stood up and towering over his surroundings, slowly removed the burning tobacco from Doran's lips and put it, lit, into the inspector's front pocket. "You can't smoke in here." He turned and with a wink to Karen, opened the door and left. He heard swearing behind him and the warning, "You better keep this to yourself, cowboy, I mean it. Keep a lid on tight." But the comments were soon overtaken by the noise of the others in the main area and finally disappeared totally when the electric doors parted and Kellet was accosted by a barrage of inquiry, a chorus from the press on both sides of the lot.

"Hey, Sheriff, Sheriff!"

"What's going on in there?"

"Did they find him? Is it Hoffa?"

Bob Kellet returned to his car which he had parked near the southern entrance and, without a word, got in. Slowly he worked his way through the security vehicles and out to the public side. When he was clear of the crowd on the other side, he stopped. He got out of his car and stood silently until he was noticed by the reporters. Sensing some importance in this action they now were completely silent. Bob Kellet stood with the erect presence of a military officer, and into the dozens of tape recorders, cameras, and microphones, he simply said, "Yes."

They rushed forward, suspicions now confirmed, seeking more information, but none would be had from the grinning sheriff as he descended the hill and vanished.

Inside, the ossified mosaic continued to take shape. All but the head now lay on the table. Like a modern Hamlet, Doctor Hoffman lifted it to the bright lights to take a closer look, pondering what tragic events may have led to the man's demise.

After it was compared and measured, he put what was left of the skull in position and stepped back to admire his work. "Let me have the tooth." The assistant opened the numbered plastic baggy and passed it's contents to the doctor. Hoffman held the off-color molar to the light and then against the film itself. He put it on the table next the to skull and reviewed dental sketches that were laid out on the cart. His comparisons complete, he turned back to his specimen and, with gentle precision, he placed the tooth into what he now knew would be it's socket. The rough edges of the tooth interlocked with the jaw exactly as anticipated, and left no doubt that it had come from that bone.

"Ask Frank to come in, please."

Hoffman stood alone in the room with his man. He pondered the complexity of the anatomy, the way it all fit together, one bone into the next. He was amazed at how he could read a life just from the bones that remained; how he could see the pain of the past and the physical torment to which this man had been party.

He could tell this man's leg had once been broken; that his jaw had also been injured, and two of his ribs.

"Okay Norm, what do you think?" Frank Doran and the assistant had returned.

"This is one union president who has seen better days."

"So it's him?"

"We still have to do the DNA, but as far as a prelim goes, I'd say yes. I am bothered by something, though. I can't find any record of amputation."

"What are you talking about?'

"See here." Hoffman pointed to a spot on the table near the left hand. "The first, second, and third phalanges appear to have been amputated at the fifth metacarpal. Right there." The doctor indicated the spot.

"He's missing his baby finger?"

"That's right. But there's no mention of it anywhere in his history."

"And the tooth?"

"It's his."

"When do we get the DNA?"

"That'll take awhile, at least a few days. I've gotta take him back to D.C. We've got all the control samples there." Hoffman removed his surgical clothing. He stretched, stiff from the long hours of work. "Congratulations, Frank."

Doran was lost in his own thoughts, "Yeah."

"Hey, it's better than a gold watch."

The comment pulled him back, "I'm sorry, I was wondering about the finger. Thanks."

Hoffman's assistant wrapped the entire table containing the bones with one continuous sheet of plastic from a large roll. Once they were completely covered, he used a hair dryer to shrink the covering until it was tight enough to hold the puzzle in place. With the help of Frank's men the whole package was placed in a new black body bag. The assistant disassembled the electronic equipment and returned everything to the proper cases. The group moved swiftly through the main room and out through the sliding doors.

"See ya later, Frank," Hoffman called back, his words obliterated by the engine noise and voices of reporters. "I'll let ya know."

The agents loaded the bag onto the helicopter. With a wave, the doctors followed.

The commotion made it easy for Frank Doran to slip back into the rear hallway. Checking to make sure no one was watching, he dialed the pay phone again. He was certain he was alone in the back corridor, but still spoke more quietly than usual. "Yeah, I did." Hoffman confirmed the initial ID. "Waiting for the DNA. It better fuckin' match, that's all I gotta say. Who? Yeah, I talked to him. No. He's a hick. He doesn't know shit about anything. I didn't even let him in the room. He's got no idea about the missing finger. No. I'm sure." While he listened to the other person, Frank removed the dead cigar from his mouth and dropped it to the floor, but immediately realized his mistake and bent down to retrieve it. That done, he moved his shoe back and forth to disburse any trace of ashes, then put the brown flat butt in his pocket instead. The inspector was focused on his conversation. He never saw the light beige of the man's uniform, though it was not ten feet away, concealed behind a slightly open door. He was careful. He never suspected that anyone but the man on the phone could hear a word he was saying. He was wrong. Everything he had spoken had been absorbed by the acute military senses of Sheriff Bob Kellett.

"Hey, you wanted us to find him," Doran whispered, "And this time we sure as hell did." He was upset. His voice now more intense than ever, "I know that. I will."

And then, "...but at least now we know what we're looking for."

And so did the hick.

8

It was difficult to negotiate the large, brass, revolving door of the Buhl Building, considering the boxed cargo of old photographs and Dr. Russel's journals, but they had, and, exhausted from the ride home and the inability to sleep, John and Shelby ascended to the tenth floor in an antique Otis elevator and a bleary-headed haze.

The doors opened into the lofty silence of the law lobby. Ahead, a beautiful young woman stood to greet them, "You must be the Russels." She walked from behind the green marble receptionist's desk and hurried forward to help with the boxes. "Mr. Swain called and asked me to have you wait if you would. He's in court this morning, but he said he'd only be a few minutes late. Can I get you something?" John was afraid to answer this one, given the stunning figure which had presented itself before him, but Shelby didn't hesitate.

"I'll have a coffee. Black, please. John?"

"Uh, yeah, that's fine." He watched as the woman departed.

"You can breath now."

"Sorry, Shel. I'm just astounded at the women Uncle Henry has around here."

"I told you. He's a letch."

The receptionist returned with the coffee, "Why don't you wait in here?" She motioned to an adjacent conference room. The phone on her desk was ringing. "Excuse me."

The boxes were dragged into the large room, once the library of the original partners, but changed soon after Henry Swain began his reign and ordered it converted into a personal monument to himself. The rich patina of century old oak exuded an inherited silent wisdom; a strength of knowledge, absorbed by osmosis, from what must have been many hours of secret conversation between counsel and client. A huge mahogany table dominated the central space and bookcases comprised three walls from floor to ceiling. The fourth, with its tall windows, provided a view of Canada and what appeared, from this height, to be miniature ore-carrying freighters on the river below. On the marble wall between them was an oil painting of a Parisian cityscape, a Monet. On the polished stone floor beneath it, there was a cowboy and stallion, an original sculpture by Remington. The shelves were filled with plaques which had been bestowed upon the litigator by colleges and charitable foundations. There were photographs of Uncle Henry standing posed with Walter Mondale and Joe DiMaggio. There was one with Larry Fine, the Stooge, pretending to poke out Uncle Henry's eyes with his fingers while the astute attorney defended himself, his hand dividing the fingers of the mock assailant, and flat as if saluting sideways from his nose.

John noticed an old toy truck on one of the shelves and leaned in for closer inspection. It was a perfect replica. He lifted it to test its metallic weight and was surprised by its mass.

"You like that, Johnny? It was a gift from your father just before he died." Swain had returned.

"Uncle Henry, how are you?"

"As well as can be expected, I guess. And lovely Shelby?" He crossed the room reaching to lightly shake her hand.

"Fine, Henry. Thanks."

He turned to John, "Your dad gave me that; said we should never forget where we came from, no matter how we ended up."

Swain picked up the toy from the shelf, "Said it reminded him of Eastern Market, loading the produce. It wasn't long after, he was gone. Oh," remembering his audience, "Sorry, Johnny."

He put the model back, wiping a bit of dust that had lodged in the axle between the chrome wheels, and then, with the long practiced air of his profession, completely changed the subject.

"So, what the hell have we got here? Sort of a skeleton in the closet, I'd say, eh, Johnny?" He smiled his paternal smile that John had seen so many times as a child. "Here, put those boxes up on the table. Let's take a look."

From the first one, John removed one of the journals and opened it to a page near the back. He pointed to the formula. "We found these up in Leland and I didn't think much about 'em, then Shelby discovered this. You can see it's a formula of some sort..."

"That's not unusual."

"...But here's the thing," Shelby interrupted from across the table, remaining skillfully beyond range, "...that particular one doesn't show up at all..." she turned back the pages to the spot where some were missing, "...until after here. And then, it's everywhere. It means something."

"What happened to these?" Henry examined the book closely noticing the torn edges.

"Don't know, but it was whoever broke into the cottage, I'm sure of that," Shelby insisted.

"But why tear the place to shreds, Shel? They must have wanted something more than a couple of pages of medical notes."

"What else have you got?"

"A bunch of old pictures. We don't know how they might fit into this, but the way things have been going, I didn't want to leave them there either. There are several of you and dad."

"Look at this." Swain held a small photo of John's parents standing arm in arm at the beach on Duck Lake. "That must have been after they first bought the place." Another caught his attention. "I remember this one."

It was the same one Shelby had noticed before. Her curiosity had resurfaced. "That's you, right?"

Swain nodded.

"And there's Dr. Russel. But who are these other guys?"

The details in the faces had faded, cracked and become anonymous to all but those captured in the initial exposure. "These are Tenino's son's; Michael and Benny, next to John and me; and there's the cop. He was always around. And back there, Johnny, you're not gonna like this, that's old man Tenino...and..." He paused just an instant. John Russel locked onto the face he would never have suspected to be in a photograph with his father. He had already silently guessed who it was, this tough looking young man, somewhat older than his father, embraced forever by the happy Italian. He was the only one in the picture who did not smile, "That's Jimmy Hoffa."

"My God." Shelby could not resist and moved around next to the two men. "That's Hoffa? He knew him?"

Swain seized the opportunity to touch her, his arm meandering slowly down her back as he spoke.

"You have to understand, Shelby, things were different then. It was a smaller town. When you wanted to work, you went to where you could get it, and, you couldn't choose who was working next to you. You got your paycheck and went home. That's how it was."

"So it's possible that dad *was* involved with him?"

"No more than any of us, Johnny. He was around. Tenino was having problems with some of the delivery guys. Hoffa said he could fix it. Apparently he did. Right after that, Tenino set up his own company."

"What 'problems'?"

"Hoffa had convinced some of the drivers that they should get more money. He started strikes. Tenino's business was hurt pretty bad. He had food sitting there rotting. No one would move it. After he met with Hoffa, he started Harborside."

"There must have been other truckers."

"For a while, there were, 'til Hoffa squeezed 'em out. His guys'd strike the other companies until they went under, then Tenino bought their trucks and hired their drivers. He paid the higher wages that Hoffa demanded and Harborside never had any trouble. The two of them were pretty close."

"How could Tenino stay in business like that? How could he pay more?"

"Well, Johnny, this is just speculation, but we all figured Tenino became kind of a 'partner' with Hoffa and Hoffa used the relationship to prove how well the thing worked and get other truckers to join him. Besides, eventually Tenino owned all the trucks, so he must have saved some money there. I really don't know."

"How was my father involved?"

"None of us were really 'involved', but we were smart enough to know not to mess around with the situation."

"Get a check and go home." Shelby, loose from his grasp, moved to the window.

"It's the way it was, Shelby," Swain said conclusively. "They backed the trucks in, we put the vegetables on. That's it."

Swain noticed the time. "We'd better get going, the prosecutor's got a few questions. Just leave this stuff here for now. If he wants to see it, he can ask."

Shelby was reluctant, "Maybe we should take it home, so we can..."

"It'll be fine Shel." John reassured her.

Henry Swain was already out in the main lobby area with John closely behind. Neither man saw Shelby put the photo in her purse.

Swain spoke to the girl at the desk, "Christine, will you please have the car ready in the lower level? Thank you. We don't want to be accosted, do we Johnny?"

"What are you talking about?"

"You're big news now. What'd that Warhol guy say? Something about fifteen minutes? This must be yours." While Christine spoke on the phone, Swain winked at her and reached around her leg into the shelf just under the top of the marble desk, drawing back, with a slight brush of hemline, a tabloid. "See for yourself."

John Russel stopped, frozen. It was as though he had instantly reached the absolute end of a long emotional rope and the elastic that was connecting him to this bizarre event would stretch no more.

"Junior?" Shelby sensed his shock, "What's wrong?"

It was all he could do to release the paper into his wife's curious hand. The life-giving liquid that usually circulated through the capillaries in his face ceased to move. Weak and pale, he drifted to the marble bench adjacent to Uncle Henry's private elevator and sat down, the headline burning in his mind. Shelby's abdominal muscles, toned and beautiful, began to vibrate with humorous delight at the stolen image on the page. The gorgeous Christine was blushing and giggled the chirp of a schoolgirl. Finally, Henry Swain, unable to restrain himself, began to roll. His years had not diminished the volume of his gregarious laughter, and it was amplified by the stone and marble. It reverberated like a Hollywood soundtrack, an echo from the prince of darkness, laughing from the eternal flames below; who must certainly, John thought, also be a lawyer.

He could hardy speak, "Jesus!"

Shelby squinted at the front page, her eyes managing just barely to remain open against the heaving, convulsive waves. There, in the photograph, on the front page, diving toward the camera, oversized boxer shorts flapping wildly like fins at his sides, was her husband, three feet from any solid object, mouth wide open, screaming. His eyes burned through the image with the red reflection of a mis-timed flashbulb. High above his head, six feet or more, the blur of a white princess phone, grabbed hastily in the night, receiver rotating around it as a satellite and, with slow shutter, creating a ringed Saturnesque halo above John Russel's left ear. The dwelling behind could not clearly be seen in the darkness of the night, but minute reflections of distant tree limbs and buildings were eerily illuminated by a second lucky flash, triggered by coincidence during the height of the rainless storm. A third, brighter bulb outlined perfectly, in sharp focus, a huge rectangular hole in the ground, into which it appeared the weightless man was about to jump. Now, seated in this lobby, indefensible against the uproarious and treacherous onslaught, he certainly wished he had.

Above this photograph, in letters as big as Shelby's thumb was the last humiliating nail in the flying man's coffin, "PHONE FLINGING MADMAN GUARDS HOFFA GRAVE!"

The stainless steel doors opened to the quiet bell and Swain, now more composed, entered and held the door for Shelby and his recent client. Still in shock, John stood, shuffling into the elevator, making what he could of a polite smile in the direction of the lovely Christine. The misfortunate combination of apparel and physique made it impossible to disguise the tiny jiggle of her breast while she struggled to return to serious disposition. John was horrified that, after years of elevator doors closing in his face, these seemed somehow blocked by the immensity of his humiliation and would not close at all.

"Good bye, Mr. Russel." Christine vibrated through the finally diminishing opening.

"Jesus," John whispered, "Good bye."

9

It was nearly impossible to move through the crowd of reporters on the steps of the MacNamera Building. From the moment Swain's long black car had arrived, they were surrounded. John pushed first, never losing his grip on Shelby's hand, while Swain, perhaps a bit too closely, brought up the rear. His voice raised above the questions. "Nothing to say at this time," he yelled, "Nothing to say." He pushed forward, up the stairs.

"Mr. Russel. Mr. Russel. Can you tell us how it happened?" one of the press yelled.

"Were you in it together? With your dad?" Another shot.

"How long was he in the mob, Mr. Russel?"

The volley of questions kept coming. Photographers, television cameramen, reporters and various other non-descript pundits poured from the building, like water from the revolving door in the center of the entrance. The big brass paddle wheel issued an endless stream of interrogation, rubbing against the Russels and counsel. Inside, a second wave.

"Have you been charged?"

"Did you help bury him?"

"How long did you know he was there?"

They moved as swiftly as they could toward the metal detectors. The guard moved forward to provide some much needed blocking. The interrogators surged ahead, hoping to break through. They were nothing more than a blurry gang of animated shouting faces. It was impossible to identify anyone.

It was perfect camouflage for the dark-haired man in the far corner, studying carefully, memorizing John's features; watching.

He stared until he could no longer see the Russels, even a few minutes more, after they disappeared up the marble stairs. Then he left.

Swain and his clients were comforted by the relative silence of the secured interior. Once upstairs, Henry spoke.

"John listen. These people have no evidence of anything. The best thing you can do is keep quiet. We wouldn't want you saying something that would give them the wrong idea. I know Keenan. He's a good guy. The FBI people...who knows. We'll just take it as it comes."

John and Shelby were stunned by the scene out front. They could not believe this was happening. Neither one had ever been inside the walls of this building except to get passports. Two days ago everything was as it should be. Now this. What were those reporters talking about? Did they actually believe we had something to do with this?

Shelby sensed that Swain knew much more about this than he was letting on and she didn't like it one bit. Perhaps he had no problem confronting the justice system, but it was far from anything she had ever expected to experience and she was frightened.

"What are they gonna ask us, Henry?"

"Oh, Shelby dear, don't you worry, Uncle Henry'll take care of it. You just relax."

Right. She was ready to wet her pants. "I've gotta make a stop."

The two men waited in the hall while Shelby was in the ladies room. Before she returned, she splashed cold water on her face, patted it dry, and carefully reapplied her makeup. She noticed in her purse, the picture from Eastern Market and stopped for a moment to look at it. They were all together. John's father, Swain, Hoffa, Tenino. Except for Swain, all dead. And there were those others who looked on in the background. There were Tenino's sons. She had a minor urge, instantly suppressed, to give this photo back to Swain.

They reached the federal prosecutor's office and were greeted from within by Keenan's disarming southern manner.

"Is that you, Henry?" the jovial advocate entered his small lobby. "Why, it certainly is. And these must be the Russels." He shook all hands, "How are you? C'mon in." He gestured to the inner office.

The curtains, now pulled wide, allowed the light into every corner of the room. His desk, though still dominant, had been joined by a small conference table on the other side of the large room. Keenan motioned for them to sit while he reached across his desk and with one artful move retrieved his blue blazer from the back of his chair while discarding the remains of an empty White Castle wrapper into a nearby wastebasket.

"Inspector Doran, I think you might know him, Henry, in fact, I'm pretty sure you do; anyway, he'll be joinin' us all pretty soon. He's got some questions I know he wants to ask; shouldn't take too long and we'll have you on your way. Now, can I get you folks anything? Coffee?" Charley was not accustomed to visitors and actually looked forward to the interrogation with pleasant anticipation. He had obviously spent much time earlier straightening the office. The light bulbs in every lamp were shining. The piles of books and mail had disappeared. There was no dust anywhere, and, with the notable exception of the tiny square hamburger's thin paper sleeve, not a trace of the numerous meals and snacks which had undoubtedly been consumed already this morning.

"Now," Charley took his place at the end of the table, "We'll try to make this as painless as possible." He turned to John. "First of all, I want to let you all know that we don't suspect you in the least. Why, Mr. Russel, you were no more than a boy when all this started."

"I was twenty-four."

"Just when was that?"

"Well, you know, when he was..."

"I'm sorry Mr. Russel, who we talkin' about?"

Swain jumped in, "I think my client is referring to the summer of 1975. Weren't you, John?"

"Yes."

Uncle Henry continued, "...and that was your age at the time when Mr. Hoffa disappeared?"

"That's right."

"Ya know, Henry," Charley opened an official looking folder, "I have that information right here. I shoulda thought of that. Of, course, Mr Russel you were...yes, here it is, twenty-four." Keenan looked up, directly into John's eyes and with a smile as big as Virginia said deliberately, "Just as you said."

John heard the door to the outer office open and voices; the first, a woman, then the quiet tones of the man, enter. Keenan stood to greet the new arrivals. Shelby nervously hoped it was a pizza delivery, but the aroma was more of Caribbean tobacco. Charley attempted, but lost his chance at first speech. The quiet, smoky voice spoke first.

"Counselor. Charley. Let's get started." Doran would not look at either of the Russels. Agent Morse was more courteous.

"Hello, I'm Special Agent Morse," she began, nodding to both Shelby and John.

Uncle Henry, well aware of this potential romantic opportunity, was up, hand extended to the agent, "Good afternoon, Ms. Morse. It is indeed my pleasure."

Not yet it's not, Shelby thought, hoping that maybe this once he could drag his filthy legal mind out of his shorts and pay attention to the proceedings at hand.

"Henry." Her raised eyebrows conveyed the unmistakable message, "Please sit down." Like a puppy caught in the trash, he did.

Doran did not sit with the others, preferring instead to pace slowly from the center of one window to the center of the other, blowing minuscule puffs of blue through the rays of sunlight.

"Mr. Swain, with your permission, I will address your clients directly." Without hesitation, he went on. "It seems, Mr. Russel, that we have a slight dilemma. You see, we've got a guy who, for the last twenty years, the best of the entire law enforcement community has been actively searching for, who now has turned up as if by magic under your front lawn." His attempt at eloquent dialogue was amusing. John began to respond, but Doran was too fast. "Now, hang on, before you say anything, let me just ask you, can you see why we're just a little bit curious about how he got there?"

"Are you making accusations, Inspector?" Swain was back.

"No. I just wanted these people to know where I'm comin' from on this, Henry." He chewed down on his cigar, cranking up the intensity. "We have the preliminary autopsy report, don't we Karen?" agent Morse nodded her agreement. "Let's start there."

She opened the manila folder and referred to her notes. "The deceased is a Caucasian male, approximately sixty to sixty-five years of age; cause of death appears to be blunt force trauma to the head, although, due to the deterioration of the body, there's some question about that. There was evidence of other trauma too, but it does not appear to have been fatal." She turned the page. "The preliminary DNA is in and it confirms a match between the deceased and Hoffa. The body was intact except for…"

"That's enough, Agent Morse, thank you," Doran interrupted.

Keenan tried unsuccessfully to lighten things up, "Looks like we got our man," he chuckled.

Doran continued with his questions, still pacing. He asked how long John had owned the property, how often he went there; had he ever been burglarized. He asked about weapons, and income, and social contacts, and a thousand other personal things. John, for the first time since they found the body was beginning to worry.

Shelby studied Doran carefully, trying to disguise her stare by shifting her gaze to the windows each time he looked at her.

"Now Mr. Russel," he slowed for effect, and bowed his voice to a level just above silence, "I'm gonna have to ask you some pretty personal questions. I hope you don't mind."

The words hung with his smoke in the stagnant office. It was not as if he hadn't been prying distressingly far up John's behind already, Uncle Henry was too busy making eyes at Agent Morse to chime in, and Shelby for some reason had begun to poke John in the calf with the pointed toe of her shoe. "No, go right ahead," he said.

"Let's talk about the relationship between your father and Antonio Tenino. What do you know about that?"

"He worked for him. When he was going to school. You know, to pay for tuition."

"Uh, huh," Doran sputtered, "And what sort of things, what kind of work did he do for him?"

"I don't know. He loaded trucks at Eastern Market."

"How much money do you suppose he was paid for this 'truck loading' do ya think? A hundred bucks a week? A hundred and fifty?"

"I don't know. Yeah, I guess that's about right. I don't know." John was impatient, "My dad wasn't in the habit of discussing his personal finances with his children." Shel gave him a swift one. "Uh."

Doran walked to the table, now sensing, John supposed, that his prey was about to crack. "Then you would be surprised if I told you that every single bill for his education was paid by Tenino...every...one!"

"That's bullshit." John snapped. Shelby was bruising his leg badly by now.

"You think so, Mr. Russel? Show him, Charley."

Keenan launched into his easy southern manner, "Well, I believe what the inspector is referring to, are these." He passed sheets of copied canceled checks and receipts across the table. The sound of shuffling papers, like some sort of legal alarm clock, jogged Swain from his comatose romantic fantasy. "Lemme see those," he exclaimed, affixing reading glasses to the bridge of his nose. "Uh, huh," as he looked them over. "So what?" Swain's beeper sounded. He pulled it from his pocket, looked at the number display and put it back.

"Soooo, Henry," the prosecutor began, "It just doesn't seem possible to make two or three hundred thousand dollars loading vegetables into trucks. At least not in my neighborhood, and...if it were the case, I sure as hell wouldn't be working as a civil servant knowin' I could be gettin' rich slingin' ripe watermelons into semi-trucks. So naturally, I'm a little curious, you understand."

"Then there's the prints," Doran added. Swain was riveted. "Agent Morse."

"The forensics lab found two sets of identifiable fingerprints on the vinyl bag that the body was in. The first belonged to Dominic Baglia. The others were Dr. Russel's."

"Oh, for Christ's sake!" John was indignant. He slapped the table with his open hand. "That's ridiculous. My father was no more near that body than I was. You guys are nuts." Swain gently squeezed his arm, a reminder that it was not good to antagonize these men.

"Go ahead, Karen," Doran commanded quietly, without moving his eyes from John.

"And one other smeared set that we have not been able to identify yet."

Doran turned his back to the table and walked to the window. "Maybe those belong to your client here, Henry."

Swain squeezed John's arm again, this time to let him know that he would speak on his behalf. "Doran, you know as well as I do that none of this means a thing. Now what do you want?" His beeper went off again, but he quickly reached in his pocket and turned it off.

"Just a couple more questions, that's all."

"Well get to it, 'cause as near as I can tell this is a waste of all of our time." He wanted to get back to his office as quickly as he could.

"Mr. Russel, was your father a particularly secretive man?"

"Not really."

Did he often use that cottage for meetings, maybe with business associates, that kinda thing?"

"No."

"Did he talk much about what he was working on?"

"Not to me."

"All right." He relit what was left of the butt. "Did your father ever have occasion to have met Mr. Hoffa?"

"Well actually, I didn't think so...until this morning." Shelby was kicking him with both feet, making it almost impossible not to react. He shot her a look. What the hell do you want? Stop kicking me.

Keenan joined the conversation, "My heavens, this morning? And you had no idea 'till then. Huh. And what, if you don't mind me prying, caused you to discover that fact at that time, Mr. Russel?"

"Well, we found some stuff at the cottage, some pictures and books, and we brought them back down here and we were looking through them and wondered who was in this picture we found..." Shelby was coughing and snorting and mildly convulsing at this point.

"Can I get you water, dear?" Charley asked. "Hang on a second, Frank." Keenan jumped into action, hurrying across the office to a small refrigerator. He opened the door, and after digging through leftovers from various fast food places, found a bottle of mineral water. He opened it and poured some into a small paper cup for Shelby. She drank slowly, glaring intensely at her conversational husband.

Doran would not be so easily stopped. "And these photographs, where are they at this time?"

"They're at Uncle...I mean, Mr. Swain's office."

"Charley, if you would, please." On Doran's cue, Keenan produced an official looking document from the inside pocket of his jacket. "What the prosecutor has there is a warrant to search that office. It is a copy of the one that Agent Garnetti has at this very moment presented at those premises. Look it over, Mr. Swain. I think you'll find it's okay."

Frank Doran drew a long satisfying drag from the cigar and relaxed like a satisfied house cat, warmed by the afternoon sun on his back, as he relaxed on the windowsill. He surveyed the damage he had caused to his victims. He had spent years perfecting his technique and if Swain or the Russels cracked, they would not have been the first. "Mr. Russel, is it possible that you may have removed something else from that cottage?"

"Besides the journals and pictures? No. I don't remember anything else."

"I'm curious, Mr. Russel, did your father collect things or keep things locked up? Did he have a safe? Was he..."

Henry was on his feet. He confronted the inspector face to face at the window. He raised his voice, "Just what the hell is this, Doran? What are you looking for?"

"Settle down, Henry," Keenan pleaded, "Take it easy."

Everybody at the table jumped up, but Shelby managed to catch John's sleeve. She leaned to his ear and whispered, "Don't say any more. I've got to show you something." They stood in silence as Swain continued.

"You got a lot a balls, searching my office, you bastard."

"Why, Mr. Swain?" he gloated, "Whatdaya got up there, anyway?" Doran threw his cigar butt into the wastebasket and moved his face into Henry's so close that the pungent stale tobacco odor surrounded him. "If you're trying to hide something, Henry, we're gonna find it."

Swain spun away and instructed, "That's enough, we're getting out of here. C'mon John, Shelby, let's go." He moved toward the door.

"Henry, wait." Charley tried, but it was no use. Doran would not relent. Keenan had never seen the inspector act this way. It was personal. He spoke in anger, with his voice uncharacteristically loud, calling after the trio as they made their exit.

"You still work for one of the Tenino boys, don't you Swain? Don't you?" They were well down the hall. Doran returned to his usual manner and spoke softly to Charlie. "I think they oughta consider getting a different lawyer."

On the way down the stairs, John asked the steaming attorney, "What the hell is going on? What was all that about, Uncle Henry? It sounded like he was after *you*."

Henry was too mad to answer. He huffed, "I'll call the driver to bring the car around, and I gotta call the office. You guys wait here."

He walked to a bank of pay phones near the elevators, calling back, "And don't say anything to anybody. I'll be right back."

Shelby and John waited at the base of the huge staircase. When she was certain no one was watching, Shelby spoke quietly, "Junior, look at this." She opened her purse just enough for John to see the picture.

"What are you doing with that, Shel?"

"Never mind, c'mere." She maneuvered him into a marble corner and pulled the photo out. "I know who this is." She pointed to the policeman who watched from the background as the group next to the truck posed for the picture. "This cop here, standing with that other man in the back. Here, take a look." She shielded it with her body from any wandering eyes that may be passing behind them in the hallway. "Do you recognize him?"

"Shel, I don't really feel like this now."

"C'mon." She pointed.

"I don't know. It's some cop."

"Yes. It is. Not just some cop, look at his eyes."

Oh my God. It was true. He had seen this man. About five minutes ago.

"It's Frank Doran. Isn't it?" She asked.

And he knew immediately that it was. Younger, and not with the others. Hoffa, Russel, Uncle Henry, Tenino and Tenino's two sons prominent in the foreground. Doran, in the dated uniform of the Detroit Police Department watching with another man as the others posed. "It sure as hell is."

The Russels jolted at the sound of Swain's voice behind them, "He'll be around with the car in a second." They hoped he hadn't overheard what they said. Shelby crammed the picture back into her purse and smiled innocently at Henry to distract him.

He didn't even notice. "I'll drop you off at your car. I have to go up and see what's going on. We can talk later. Ready?" They nodded. "Let's go."

They passed the metal detectors and the surge of unwanted attention resumed. Questions flew past them, indistinguishable in the anxious haze of recent inexplicable revelation. They rushed out, this time through the revolving door which acted as a lever, hurling photographers backward into the lobby as they rotated out toward the street, through the commotion on the sidewalk, and finally to the waiting car.

Inside, Swain offered drinks. He wasted no time creating one for himself.

John accepted. "Scotch please. Shel?"

"I'm fine."

They drove in relief and silence. The asylum of Swain's limousine was not lost on John. He could see how the very famous or very rich could come to depend on such conveyance as a daily necessity rather than an occasional luxury. This long, dark Lincoln with its soft leather, was like a rolling cocoon, providing protection for those who sought to avoid public scrutiny. He understood fully now, why it was the preferred mode of transportation of both the notable and the notorious; of idiot ingenue and suspected felon alike.

He drifted into his relaxed subconscious. It was the trial. Uncle Henry stood looking somewhat younger and more polished than ever, standing before the packed courtroom. He spoke to the jury, his final argument commanding attention with his grand voice, low and clear, and pointed at John Russel.

"Does this look like the face of a mobster; a kidnapper and a murderer?"

The thousands of interested onlookers turned simultaneously to stare as one at the accused. There, in his pressed blue suit, he was:

John Jr., a boy, only about ten. Standing next to him, in his white lab coat was his father.

"Yes!", the crowd shouted, "Yes! That's him!" and then they began the chant, "Yes. Yes. Yes. Yes."

"Junior? John?" It was Shelby's soft voice that alerted him. They pulled to a stop in the underground lot of the Buhl Building where they had parked. "We're here."

Henry Swain was already out and on his way to the private elevator by the time John was fully awake. The nap was good and much needed, given the stress of the day. Sensing her husband's fatigue, Shelby volunteered to drive. They exited the security level of the lot, reserved for tenants, and soon headed east, down Jefferson and home.

John noticed a few stray reporters hanging around by the parking lot, but they did not pursue. He assumed there was no need, since, no doubt, a swarm of their associates would already be camped at his house, ready to suck from them whatever information they could when they arrived.

Shelby was good at the wheel and moved expertly through the rush hour traffic. She was adept at advantageous lane changes, providing those cut off justification for obscene signals; communication from which she was prohibited by dignity from acknowledging in any way.

John leaned back, relaxed in the comfortable seat, and was nearly asleep again when he caught a brief motion; dark sheet metal in the side mirror. A car, several back, which seemed to replicate her moves. "There's someone following us," he said, not at all surprised.

Shelby looked in the rearview and slightly increased her speed, changing into the left lane as she did. Instantly, the car following did the same. She performed several other maneuvers before slowing again to a comfortable pace in the middle lane. She was pretty sure who it was. "Probably one of those news guys. They're unbelievable."

"Can you see him?" John saw her looking back at the car in the mirror.

"Yeah. He's wearing a big sign around his neck that says, 'I'm an asshole' just like all of 'em at the Federal Building." She laughed briefly. "Hell with 'em."

No longer concerned with the car behind them, she turned to John. "This is bad, John. This whole thing is bad. And we've gotta find out what's going on. This deal with Henry and your father...and now Doran, it's frightening. Did you know about the money from Tenino?"

"No." The fact disturbed him.

"...and Doran goin' after Henry, my God. That's pretty scary. Don't tell me those two don't know each other."

"Shel, I'm telling you, Dad didn't do anything. I know it. He wasn't like that."

"He knew him."

"It could have been a loan, I mean, we don't know. I'll bet he paid it all back. I bet there are canceled checks. We'll just have to look."

"And remember when that woman agent was reading the autopsy stuff?"

"Morse?"

"Yeah. Doran cut her off. She was gonna say more, and he cut her off. So they've got more information that we don't even know about. I'm glad I took the picture, 'cause by now they've got everything we brought to Henry's office, too."

"Damn. They've got all the journals. And I think you're right, there's something in those. You know how Dad was, Shel. If he were somehow involved in this thing, he would do anything he could to protect himself...and to protect me, too."

"Like what?"

"Like maybe...I don't know...leave a clue, in case..." for the first time it occurred to him that perhaps his father's death was not accidental, "...in case something happened to him."

There was silence. Something had happened to Dr. Russel. On the way home from dinner, he had mysteriously driven off the road into Lake St. Clair, crashing through the ice to the bottom where both he and his wife had drowned.

Shelby turned up the residential street. Moments later the car following did the same. It was several blocks to the Russel house, each separated by an intersection with a stop sign. Every time they stopped, the car behind stopped five hundred yards or so behind them. It was a silly procession in this deadly peaceful neighborhood. It was not the best way to go unobserved.

When they got to the corner just before home, they noticed a second dark car parked in the 'No Parking' area just past the intersection. Inside, two men sat doing nothing. The license plate bore the 'X' markings of an official vehicle. The word 'Government' across the bottom confirmed ownership.

"Oh look, Junior, visitors from the FBI. Great." Shelby smiled and waved at the men as she accelerated past the surveillance. The man who had followed them from Swain's office turned quickly to the left and disappeared from view. "Looks like we lost our friend."

"Somehow, I don't think we're going to be lonely." John pointed to the dozen or so reporters who had gathered on the sidewalk in front of the house.

Shelby pushed the button to activate the automatic garage door. This alerted the group to the arrival of their prey and they moved as one, descending on the Russel's car as it inched up the drive, pyrhannas nibbling at the succulent iron pig. They screamed questions at the closed windows, but their voices were attenuated as, once inside, Shelby again pushed the button, lowering the motorized door, separating the mob from the Russels and the sanctity of the garage.

John sighed, relieved that he was finally home.

Shelby switched off the ignition. She slid over next to her husband, taking his head into the bend of her arm. She hugged him gently and whispered, "I wrote down the equations from the journals."

"You're an angel, Shel."

IO

The FBI warrant specifically requested materials relating to the Russels. It had further requested any files or information on Benito Tenino, hoping, of course that these would somehow implicate him, not only in the current conspiracy, but perhaps provide evidence of other illegal activities. The big bonus from Doran's point of view was that if anything was found that could even remotely implicate Swain himself, all protection under attorney-client privilege would be suspended and he could expose the whole Tenino operation.

Henry Swain was well aware of this. He had spent the remainder of his afternoon seeking a restraining order to stop the search. By the time such an order was granted, the agents had already seized the journals and the photos. They had also pilfered just about everything from the file room and from Henry's private office. The other lawyers' offices had been searched, but most of the files were left behind.

During the commotion, Christine had remained at her desk as Swain had instructed. They had been over the procedure many times. If there was a search, she should immediately page Swain, inputting his private office number. If he did not respond, she was to wait five minutes and try again. No response the second time was confirmation. She was then to begin to dispose of all of her files. For this purpose there had been constructed within the massive reception desk, a drawer which, when opened, allowed documents to slide underneath its bottom and into a wide slot at the back of the drawer opening. From there, they traveled down the smooth stone and fell through the floor, in between the girders, coming to rest within the wall in the dentist's office directly below on the ninth floor.

Swain felt that leaving these files virtually in plain view was the best way to hide them. He had marked each with innocuous titles like 'vacation schedules' and 'current benefits' so that even if they were discovered, there would most likely be no immediate interest in them. He reasoned, correctly in this instance, that the search party would be so intent on reaching his inner sanctum, they would walk right by the front desk.

So, for over three hours during the FBI search, with agents everywhere, Christine had systematically and clandestinely emptied the entire incriminating contents of her desk into the secret chamber.

Swain was satisfied that the FBI had found nothing. He was exhausted and looking forward to the evening ahead. His car pulled up his side drive and he saw the reflection of the nearly full moon rising over the still lake behind the mansion. There would be enough light on this clear warm night to cork one of his many fine wines and sit on his rear verandah admiring Carla. Maybe even sex on the lawn. Such moments were his reason for life, his addiction.

The symptoms appeared early, during his first marriage, when he was only twenty. He had become infatuated with his wife's sixteen year old sister to the point of obsession. He tried every way imaginable to seduce the young girl, but she would not break. He concocted incredibly imaginative scenarios; passion-laden fantasies where they would somehow end up together, but she had no interest in him. Her resistance drove him to such acute frustration that he ultimately and suddenly divorced, without explanation to his wife, just to be away from her sister.

Even after as many years as he had lived, there were less than a dozen nights in his life that he had been alone, and five of those were spent at the hospital after bypass surgery.

It was the process of falling in love, rather than the ongoing situation of being in love that followed, that was the drug. The adrenaline, the anticipation of the first sensual moment, was what fueled his passion. Every aspect of his being was touched by this obsession. Even the Oldsmobile he and John's father had stolen as teenagers was, to him, only the means to impress a Junior High School fascination. To Henry, the successful conquest was where the romance must necessarily end, where the next must begin. Henry Swain loved women. More than once, this had caused trouble.

The limousine dropped him at the side entrance and went on into the night. Soon, Carla was there.

"Hi, sweetheart," gushed the slow southern syrup. "Did y'all have a good day, Henry?"

"It's certainly getting a whole lot better in a hurry, honey." He met her at the door and together they walked through the kitchen service area. "Why don't you get relaxed and meet me outside. I'm gonna see what kinda wine we've got."

"Henry?"

He stopped, sensing some urgency in her voice. "What is it, Carla? Everything okay?"

"There are some men here to see you. They're in the library."

"What?" Swain could not believe that Carla would be so stupid. "Why the hell did you let 'em in? Are they cops?"

"No." Carla started to whimper.

Swain realized that his harshness was too much for her. He embraced her lightly, "Oh, honey, it's all right. I'll get rid of 'em. You just go on upstairs. I'll handle it."

He walked deliberately. He was mad. Those pricks had crossed the line. He marched through the great hall and into the paneled room where the men waited. "What the fuck's goin' on?" he asked, before he even knew who was in the room. "What the hell do you want?" When he looked up, he stopped dead. "Oh my God."

Standing across from him was an old, frail man, supported on each arm by men much younger. The man's suit was expensively tailored and fit perfectly, which was remarkable considering his diminutive and bent stature. After a long silence, one of the bodyguards spoke. The other walked over to Swain, searched him for weapons, then returned to the small man's side.

"Mr. Swain." There was a horribly long pause like those that occurred when a judge enters a crowded courtroom, or when they open the envelope at an awards show. "Mr. Domati wishes a moment of your time."

Henry was stunned. "Of course, I…Here, would you like to sit down?" He gestured nervously to a large chair. "Can I get you a drink? A glass of wine?"

Although Henry was addressing Domati, the younger man answered again. "Mr Domati does not drink."

Henry was already at the bar, pouring a brown liquid from a crystal decanter into a large glass. He gulped the first half inch or so from the top. This was not a good situation. Vincenzo Domati was one of the most powerful men in organized crime. He knew how deadly he was. This was the man who most agreed, was primarily responsible for Hoffa's murder; who now controlled the underworld of Detroit directly, and the International Brotherhood of Teamsters indirectly through an untraceable web of well-placed underlings. He was eighty-six. He had grown weak over the years, but his strength, what was to be feared most, was not physical. And knowing this, when he spoke to Swain, it was eerie, like death itself.

His words were slow and deliberate, "Henry, I'm very disappointed with the way this Hoffa thing is turning out." He both coughed and cleared his throat as he talked. "It was never supposed to get to this point. So I ask, after twenty years, do I need this shit? Do I?"

Henry recognized a rhetorical question and, wisely, did not answer. Domati continued.

"I've known you a long time, Henry, since you were a boy, since the trucks. And I know you don't like me much. But I know, too, what you and Tenino, and that doctor friend of yours did. Why try to get me on it? Did you really think I'm that stupid, huh? Why do you think Baglia dumped the body where he did?" He began coughing uncontrollably until he brought up some phlegm. Everyone in the room waited for him to spit it out into his handkerchief and for him to finish what he was saying. "It doesn't matter. I just know everything is fine, then I get a call and everything is not fine. That's what I know."

"Listen, Mr. Domati," Swain was a little more forceful. "I don't know what you're talking about."

Domati interrupted again. "No. You listen to me." Domati stood more erect. He sputtered. He was mad. "I've spent most of my life in this country. I've raised six children here. I started just like you, with nothing. Since it turned out Hoffa was missing, I've probably turned six or seven hundred million. With absolutely no problem. Now, do you really think I'm gonna let my family go down because of some piss ass lawyer? I don't think so. So, why don't you just give me what I want?"

"I don't know what it is. Mr. Domati...please."

"You are a stupid man." The old man was enraged, "What the hell were you thinking? Why did you send that shit from that queer Baglia?" Domati surveyed the teak paneled room, lifting his arms to present his surroundings. "What more do you want, Swain? Isn't this enough for you? If you woulda left everything alone, this would be different."

"I never sent anything from Baglia," Swain protested. "Look," Swain was candid, trying to be as diplomatic as he could. "I have no idea what you're looking for, Mr. Domati. I don't know how I can help. Yes, I represent one of the Teninos, and Dr. Russel's son, but that's as far as it goes. I don't have anything to do with this." Domati shuffled forward. His breath was on Swain now and it stunk. He leaned in and whispered with his disgusting internal air, so close that only Henry could hear him.

"Before I killed that fat ass Tenino, I cut his balls off and while his blood was dripping down like a woman, I held them up in front of his face while his son watched. So he would know who not to fuck with. If you think that little prick Benny's gonna do one fuckin' thing to help you, you're wrong. I want this to go away." He stepped back.

"Mr. Domati..." Henry pleaded, but he could tell from the glare in the eyes of the old man's protectors that Domati was finished talking.

Then a bit of hope. It was Carla, sucking every eye toward her as she entered. She was wearing a short, deep blue, sequined cocktail dress, low cut in the back. Far too formal for the evening that Henry had been planning.

"I'm sorry to interrupt, but I was wondering if there was any little thing that I could get for you gentlemen? A snack, perhaps? Y'all have to be pretty hungry, aren't you?" Her accent had never been so welcome.

"It's okay, honey, our business is finished," Henry replied, hoping her intrusion would end the interrogation. "They were just leaving."

With help, the old man slowly moved toward the door where Carla stood. When he got there, he turned back to the frightened attorney, but Swain couldn't take his eyes off Carla. He barely heard Domati's orders to his men.

"Go out and tell him he can come in and clean up now. We're finished in here." He motioned for the two men with him to leave the room. When they were gone, his tone became almost friendly.

"You know something, Henry?" He wanted Swain's full attention. He looked at Carla, "Sometimes balls are not such a good thing to have," and at Swain, tanned and still in good shape, then shaking his head back and forth, with some disappointment, he said to Carla, "Kill him." And he shuffled away.

It was like the whole house falling down on Swain.

"Carla? What are you doing?" He watched, horrified as she walked slowly to a small mahogany glove table, opened the drawer and retrieved a chrome pistol from where it had been hidden. Swain dropped the drink, the glass shattering on the slate floor. "What's that? What the hell is that?" He was becoming more terrified as the reality of this horrible conspiracy became clear. She was part of this right from the beginning when they first met. For all of his street savvy, he had been fooled. And now this gorgeous woman stood in his mansion and held one of his own revolvers tightly in her delicate hand, pointing it directly at him.

In a midwestern voice as clear as a Chicago night, Carla issued commands.

"Stay there, Henry."

This was almost laughable since he was nearly catatonic; faint with disbelief and betrayal.

"Oh my God, Carla. No." His voice was low. He began to weep. "No." He knew he would never have her again.

"You're disgusting," she said, and raised the pistol, firing two shots directly into his chest. The blood was instantaneous. It exploded from the opening in his back and splattered across the room, a thin dotted line angled downward, over the desk lamp and drapes, up to the corner of the ceiling as the immensity of Henry Swain collapsed on the slab, dead before he hit.

Immediately, a dark red puddle began forming around the upper part of Henry's body, flowing from his chest. It soon became a lake. Careful not to step in the liquid, Carla moved next to him to put one final bullet in his head, but before she could, a soft voice interrupted from the doorway.

"This is nice." The sarcastic voice was confident. A puff of Cuban smoke preceded it. Carla instinctively spun to the sound, ready to shoot again, but she recognized the man. "That's a good way to get shot, Frank."

"Relax. Give me that," he said.

He casually took the loaded weapon and, holding the barrel, wiped away Carla's fingerprints with his sleeve. "Tear this joint up a little bit," he said. "Make it look like you two were fighting."

She instantly obeyed, pulling books from shelves, breaking Chinese pottery on the floor.

"Rip your dress a little. So it looks like he attacked you. And throw a couple more glasses on the floor." Carla wondered what difference it would make.

"I thought this one was a break-in."

Doran ignored her. "Did you find anything?"

"Everything that looked important is in here." She lifted a large leather briefcase from beside the door and placed it on the table. "There are a lot of contracts, real estate closing statements; I don't know if that'll help. Oh, but I also got the will he did for the doctor; Russel. It's in there, too. The rest of the stuff from his desk is in boxes in the garage."

"What about the safe?"

"Money."

"Where's that?"

"In the boxes in the garage."

"Good. Anything else?"

"I've been watching him from the beginning. Nothing." She ripped the seam at the top of her dress. "I've searched this place every day since I moved in. If he had anything important here, I would have found it."

"Anything to do with the Russels, I want it."

"It's all out there, Frank."

"Good."

"Thanks."

Swain's body lay on its side. Careful not to touch it with his hands, Doran used the points of his elbows to roll it to its back. While Carla was busy destroying the room, he put the gun in Swain's right hand, wiped his own prints from it, and, wrapping Swain's index finger around the trigger, raised the dead man's hand to take aim at the arresting beauty before him.

"Hey Carla?"

When she turned around, he shot her. Once. Through her forehead. He stared into her eyes and wondered if they still saw him as she was hurled backward into the bookcase from the force of the bullet. She slid downward to the floor. There was very little blood.

Frank pulled her closer to Henry's body; close enough to use Swain's left hand's fingernails to gouge flesh from Carla's face. With her heart no longer pumping, there was not enough pressure to push the blood to fill the deep gashes. So Doran reached his arm around her to a position where, by compressing her chest between his hands, he could manually pump it out from the organ through her veins to the wounds. He pushed hard several times, careful not to break her ribs. Finally, it began to flow, first from the hole in the back of her skull and then into the cuts. That done, he maneuvered her hand to Henry's head and, using her thumb and first two fingers like pliers, ripped out a portion of Swain's white hair. He then returned her body to the bookcase, placing it again in a seated position to duplicate where she had fallen originally, carefully aligning her head with the trail of tissue which remained behind on the shelves. He stepped back and surveyed the scene for authenticity. Satisfied with his work, he paused for a moment.

It was a shame, Doran thought, for the world to lose such a woman. He knelt down close to Carla's incredible body and ripped her clothing further, so he could clearly see her breasts. He lifted her dress, pulled her panties down, and marveled at her perfect anatomy. He reached out and touched the red liquid that was now nestled in the marks on her face, transferring the smallest bit to the tip of his finger, and, after a moment of hesitation, he looked at her again, lifted the drop to his lips, and sucked her cool blood into his mouth.

He could wait no longer. He removed a small wrapped package from his jacket pocket. Inside, were two wafer-thin strips of magnesium ribbon, each about two inches long. Doran inserted one end of each into the top and bottom plugs of a nearby electrical outlet. After stoking his cigar until it glowed bright red, he used the parts of the ribbon that protruded, and carefully sliced through the wrapper about one inch from the lighted ash, so it was suspended between the two plugs, like a handle across the plate. He reached back into his pocket and produced a small aerosol container of hair spray. Again, he moved Carla; this time slightly downward, so her hair would reach the receptacle. Grabbing several strands, he wrapped the ends around the magnesium strips near the cigar and glued them in place with the spray. He used the rest of the contents of the small canister to coat her face and neck, assuring complete combustion and eradication of forensic detail.

Doran collected the briefcase from the table and left. It would be about seven or eight minutes before the cigar butt burned down far enough to ignite the magnesium. Enough time to load the boxes into his car and drive away unnoticed.

I I

When John and Shelby returned home, their answering machine was full. Most of the messages were from reporters, but there was also one from Bob Kellett. John was curious about its vagueness. The sheriff had been oddly nonspecific and obviously did not wish to leave any important information on the tape. Or maybe, Kellet also suspected that the line was tapped. Either way it wasn't good.

When he returned the call, the conversation became even more oblique.

"Hello."

"Sheriff Kellet?"

"It is."

"Hi Bob, this is John Russel returning your call."

"Where are you? Are you home?"

"Yeah."

"Oh." There was silence.

"What?"

"Nothin'. Hang on." John could here the sheriff talking to a woman in the background mixed with the usual household noises. "I've got John Russel on the line. Was there something else?" The sheriff was back. "Rebecca just wanted to know if you were gonna be back up here, she's put up some fruit or somethin'. Anyway, do you have any plans to be up this way?"

"I guess. Bob, what's going on?"

"Oh geez, they're radioin' me from the office. I gotta go. Listen, gimme a call if you're up this way. We can get together then, okay?"

"Sure, Bob, fine." John heard him hang up the phone and then a series of strange clicks. He hung up.

John relayed his fear that their phone was tapped by writing Shelby notes during dinner. If they got to the phone, he reasoned, maybe the whole house was wired. This covert activity only excited her further. She wrote back, 'ISN'T THIS WILD?!!!!' but John was not amused. His whole life; his whole perception of his father was under siege. The notes continued.

"I HAVE TO TALK TO HENRY. I WAS GOING TO CALL, BUT I'M GOING OVER THERE INSTEAD," he wrote.

"THE REPORTERS WILL SEE YOU."

"I'M GOING TO WALK. I THINK I CAN SNEAK OUT THE BACK."

Whoever was listening, if anyone was, must have assumed that the Russels had ravenous appetites, since they barely spoke during the meal. Eventually, John pushed his chair back and standing, loudly announced, "That was great, Shel. I'm a little tired." He spoke directly into a house plant for effect. "I'm gonna go upstairs, watch TV and crash."

Shelby joined the rouse. "Okay, John. I'll just finish cleaning up around here and then I will be up." It sounded like a high school play, but Doran's men didn't look smart enough to know the difference. Maybe they didn't go to high school. John grinned and gave his wife a wink. He wrote another note.

"DON'T LET ANYBODY IN. I'LL BE BACK IN A COUPLE OF HOURS. LOCK EVERYTHING. I'VE GOT KEYS. I LOVE YOU."

Shelby wrote back "I LOVE YOU, TOO."

Before she knew it, he was gone.

Next to the kitchen, in one end of the family room, was the Russel's small office. Shelby set up shop there. She took the picture out of her purse and laid it on the desk next to the computer. She studied it while she waited for the machine to start.

First the canned voice, "You've got mail." With a few clicks of the mouse, she retrieved the message. It was from Bob Kellet.

It read, 'can't talk on the phone.. may have something. need to talk. you should come up now. ASAP reply by e-mail only. you see my address at the top of this window. use that.'

She typed her response, 'Why? What do you have? What's going on?' and clicked to send it to Kellet, hoping he was still online. Her next step was to access the database at Wayne State University and, more specifically, the medical center, where Dr. Russel had worked. She hoped that she would be able to make some sense of the notations Dr. Russel had made in his journals. It was worth a try. Before long, she was deeply into the archive.

John, meanwhile, had managed, with only minor scratches from the rose bushes, to elude the press by exiting through the back door of the garage and then silently darting across his backyard and climbing several of his neighbor's cyclone fences, popping out occasionally to cross streets, then ducking in again to secluded yards. He was three blocks from home when he reemerged onto the sidewalk, undetected.

Swain's mansion was no more than a mile away and John had walked it many times. His step was brisk, fueled by adrenaline from fear, and anger that Uncle Henry was involved and that he had dragged John's father into it as well. He should have told him. Why maintain some ridiculous charade? John had to admit, at least to himself, that it was no surprise that Henry was involved with the Mafia, but, John assumed, as a lawyer and nothing more, certainly not as an accomplice. He decided he would confront Swain with all of this when he got there.

His concern was growing for his own and Shelby's safety. He didn't like the fact that his phone was tapped and that his house was most probably bugged. He was grateful for this short, quiet walk, since it gave him an opportunity to sort things out.

Nobody could possibly think the Russels had anything at all to do with Hoffa's disappearance, no matter where they found his body. Still, it was big news and implications would be drawn. John considered approaching the issue head on, maybe with a press conference. He wanted to ask Henry about it.

He crossed East Jefferson Avenue and headed toward the lake. Of the things that had happened, one of the more disturbing was Doran's verbal attack on Swain. It was obvious that he was looking for some particular piece of evidence, but why did he seem so certain that Swain had it. Doran, John recalled, had seemed intent on getting to Henry. The interview was an excuse.

After his father's death, John had gone through most of the possessions and papers, but never got around to the cottage. It had been his intention to do so, but he never did. So if there was something that tied his dad to the Tenino family or the disappearance, it would be up there. Others knew that, too. After all, the place was ransacked. Doran and the FBI did it. John was sure about that. They had to. Lying pricks. Those missing pages in the journal. They've got those, too. Swain knew all about it and tonight, so would he.

John turned onto Windmill Pointe Drive. In the distance he heard a siren. The sound was distinctive and he recognized it as a fire engine. It was coming closer.

The faint smell of burning wood touched his nostrils. Ahead he could see the low stone wall that marked the entrance to the attorney's estate. Speeding down the road behind him came the roar of the engine and the obnoxious repetitive monotone of the horn; then another and another. Ladder trucks and pumpers rumbled past him, shaking the sidewalk as they did. Their lights flashed from the windows of the immense homes as lights began to come on inside. The sound was deafening.

The smell of smoke was definite, though John saw no fire. He was only moderately curious until he noticed the trucks turning into Henry Swain's driveway. Then he began to jog, slowly at first, then gradually picking up his pace to a full run.

He could see the intense yellow white glow on the oak trees behind the house. Airborne cinders rose like stars, shooting up to the August sky. He was running to the open front door leaping over hoses, past firemen furiously dragging them to the hydrants. John ignored the commands to stop and bolted through the opening into the great hall. The air inside was clear except for the top three feet nearest the ceiling where black smoke was beginning to accumulate, forming a sinister darkness over the eclectic gallery. He walked quickly ahead, screaming for Swain.

"Uncle Henry! Uncle Henry!" John hurdled at top speed to the second floor, still calling out for his uncle. He checked the bedrooms but found no one. Maybe they weren't home. He continued his search, back to the first floor. In the few minutes he had been upstairs, the smoke cloud had descended. It was just above his head. He would have to leave the house soon, before all the oxygen was gone. Room after room. Where was he? "Uncle Henry! Where the hell are you? Are you here?" John belted from his lungs. But his eyes burned from the smoke and his throat hurt.

Finally he got to the library. He was too late. Fifteen minutes earlier, the magnesium ribbon had ignited and instantly exploded in a chemical flash, dissolving the electrical plugs, so that it looked like that was where the blaze had started. The hair spray burned like napalm melting Carla's flesh in seconds. Her clothes had caught next, spreading the flames to the rug and the bookshelves. The teak wood and books provided fuel as the fire grew. Across the floor for a split second there was an almost transparent blue flame from the scotch crawling toward Swain. The slate floor heated like the burner on a stove, and the blood boiled and turned grayish white as it cooked. Seconds later flesh burned again. The windows on the French doors imploded, unable to hold back the air from the outside that the fire demanded and the room exploded in a white hot fireball.

John felt strong arms grabbing him from behind.

"C'mon. You gotta get outta here." The fireman threw him toward the door as he donned his oxygen mask and opened the valve, spraying hundreds of gallons of water at the flames. John had to duck down to breathe as he made his way out to the front yard. From deep within the house he heard one fireman yell to another in the darkness, "Looks like we got two in here." and he knew exactly what he was talking about.

Stunned, John breathed in the fresh air and watched as the flames worked their way through the house, eating the carved oak and the oil paintings. Every few minutes a beam the size of a tree would crash to the floor in flames. Soon, it was too dangerous to be inside and the best the firefighters could do was shoot constant streams of water from the tops of the ladders through ever expanding holes in the slate roof.

It was too hot to stand in the courtyard and John walked sadly away, down the drive to the edge of the street. He turned and watched the grand old home collapse, nothing more than embers.

"John! John!" A woman was running toward him. "John, are you all right?" It was Christine.

"I'm fine." He realized he was covered in soot. "Really, I'm fine."

"The alarm company called. What about Henry? Is he all right?" She could tell from John's expression what had happened and she broke down, leaning forward to embrace him. "Oh no", she whispered, "Oh no."

She cried silently. "Carla?"

"I think she was with him."

"Good," she said, then straightened, wiping away the tears. "Would you like to get some coffee or something?"

John was quick to answer, "Let's get a drink." They walked down the street past the fire equipment and official cars to where Christine was parked.

"Would you mind?" She handed the keys to John.

"Not at all." He closed the passenger door behind her and walked around to the driver's side. Just as he was about to get in, he heard Doran's quiet voice behind him.

"Like I said, Russel," he paused, "...you're gonna need a new lawyer."

Christine watched from inside, but couldn't hear what he was saying. She watched as John reeled back and, swinging with full force, delivered a blow that sent the cigar flying out of the inspector's mouth and the older man backward to the ground. John slammed the door and drove away.

"Prick." It was all he could say.

He waved to the guard at the club's gatehouse and proceeded slowly up the long drive. On either side large sprinklers sprayed the fairways and greens of the golf courses. He pulled up under the stone overhang at the main entrance and stopped. Both doors were immediately opened by valet attendants.

"Good evening Mr. Russel;...Ma'am." Neither seemed to notice his appearance or care who he was with. It was one of the great privileges of this affluent, old money community; anonymity.

They walked to the club room. John nodded 'hellos' to some of his fellow members who were seated at the small tables and proceeded to the bar, pausing to allow Christine to be seated first.

They were greeted by the bartender, "Good evening Mr. Russel; Miss. What can I get for you?"

"Hi, Jimmy, I'll have a scotch, large, up. Christine?"

"Same."

The dark-skinned gentleman was off, his starched white jacket crinkling as he reached up to take the glasses from the overhead rack. John loved the country club, because even with all of its pretensions, it did provide refuge when it was most needed. He could walk in here, as he had this evening, smelling like charcoal, with a tall blonde in her twenties and snuggle up to the same bar that Henry Ford had frequented, and no one would say a thing: partial discretionary invisibility. The drinks arrived. He leaned to Christine, gently holding her hand.

"Jesus, this is awful." He was trying to catch his emotional breath. She nodded.

"We'll have another." The first shot had gone down too easily for both of them.

"He was afraid something might happen to him. He knew it." she said.

"What do you mean?"

"Ever since they found the body, he knew."

"You mean you think he was killed?"

"Yeah." she said confidently, "I know it." Christine downed the second drink.

"By whom? Who would do that to Henry?" He lowered his voice to a whisper, looking around to see if anyone was listening. "Who do you think did it?" John motioned for another round, but Christine signaled no.

"I'll have water." she said. "Henry was into a lot of things, John. Some of them are better left alone. But I've been with him a long time and there was a really good side to him. He paid for my whole education; everything, right through law school."

"You're a lawyer?"

"I'm Henry's lawyer. It's something we worked out a long time ago. He thought it was best if no one knew, so I could handle some of his dealings under privilege. He was very pragmatic. He knew he wouldn't live forever and he said after he was gone, I could hang my shingle in the lobby. He made all the provisions in his will to make me a full partner."

"How did you end up with Henry?" John figured this girl was too young even for Swain.

After a long silence she said almost under her breath, "He's my dad." The quiet tears came again, dripping down on the bar. "I thought you knew." John took her into his arms and held her tightly. "Maybe I will have another one, John, if you don't mind."

He caught Jimmy's attention and ordered for both of them. "I don't know what to say, Chris."

"I told you, Henry was into a lot of things." This broke the tension. They laughed. But she continued, more seriously. "I think you could be in trouble, too, John. These people aren't screwing around. I think they killed Henry. I think that bitch Carla had something to do with it too. I checked her out. She was from Indiana for chrissake. But he didn't care." She was loosening with the liquor.

"Why would I be in trouble? I've got more cops watching me than the president. Who's gonna do anything to me?"

"I'm serious, John, there's evidence that they want. Henry used to joke about it. He said as long as Hoffa stayed missing, there was no way they knew what it was. I never knew what he was talking about. When the body turned up, though, he talked to me about it. And about your father."

"And?"

She moved closer. "Apparently, and he never told me what, they had physical proof that they thought would protect them;

Henry and your dad, from something they had done. Together. With the Teninos."

"What? What are you talking about? My dad was a doctor."

"I don't know. After they found the body, he told me they'd find out and come after him, but there wasn't anything he could do. He said your dad hid it, years ago, that's all he knew. And, he said, if something did happen, to tell you he was sorry. That it was because of him your parents were killed. He said you should search through everything of your dad's until you find it. And then he said I should beg you, for your own safety, to give them what they want.

I know this is confusing, John, but he said he couldn't tell me any more, that it would be bad for everyone."

"Who is 'them'?"

After having dropped all the other bombs, she whispered this one. "Vincenzo Domati. His family."

"My God, Christine." He was getting drunk. His mind could not absorb any more horrible information and it shut down. "I loved Uncle Henry, you know." He fell silent.

After many more drinks, the situation became somewhat foggy.

The last thing he remembered was holding onto red velvet curtains for balance. He had no recollection of the car, or leaving the club, or the ride. Then he was here, at home, jarred into consciousness by another flash from a photographer's camera as Christine dragged him from the passenger side of her car to the porch. Fortunately, she was strong enough to hold him up while he fumbled to insert his key into the locked door.

Shelby, hearing the commotion outside, assumed it was John returning. She was anxious to tell him what she had discovered and hurried to let him in. What she encountered when she opened the door caused her to stare with disbelief. The couple standing there looked like they had crawled from the wreckage of a recent automobile accident. She did have to admit, though, that the man did resemble her spouse, and his ingenue companion, Swain's receptionist, were an unlikely team, she thought.

The woman's long blonde hair flew in every direction. Her makeup was badly smeared. The man's face looked bruised, black with soot, interrupted with drops of perspiration and clear lines from tears. He stood, shirt tail out, rumpled, weaving ever so slightly back and forth, supported solely by Christine, who embraced him from behind.

Shelby knew she would receive an acceptable explanation from John eventually, so she decided to play the situation for what it was worth.

"You must be here for the Accident Victim's Anonymous meeting." She started in on him. "Well, my friends, you've come to the right place. In fact you're the first to arrive. But that's no problem, come on in and trip over a few tables." She motioned toward the living room. "Can I get you something? Maybe a handful of Advil and a couple of gallons of coffee?" Her antics were met with chilling silence.

John took a deep breath and said, as clearly and definitely as he could, "Henry's dead, Shel."

12

With the morning after Swain's death came more reporters, dozens of them; so many now that two local officers had been assigned, at John's expense, to control the crowd. The discovery of Hoffa's body was front page everywhere and the lead on the national news. Hundreds of incoming calls made it impossible to use the phone. Every so often one would actually get through to the Russel's machine and the voices as they were recorded, echoed from the kitchen. So and so from NBC, the National Enquirer, and representatives from the talk television shows, from Oprah and Geraldo. The phone had become useless to the point that John's usually friendly neighbors, no longer able to complain about the commotion by voice, had resorted to nasty notes slipped through the mail slot in the front door and rude gestures as they drove by.

John was happy to be driving, to have escaped from home, to have time to think and talk to Shelby. Even with the torrential summer thunderstorms which had for hours rained down on them, so heavily that at times they could barely see the road, this was better than the scene they had left behind. Of course the press would find them again, and it wouldn't take much to figure out where they were going, but after the horror of the evening and the way he felt this morning, as hungover as he had ever been, John figured this was probably as good as it could get.

After punching Doran, John was sure he'd be arrested. In fact, the more he thought about it, he wondered why he hadn't been arrested on the spot.

The fire at Henry's mansion played over and over, clearly in his mind. He tried to put it together. From what Christine had told him, he assumed that it was not an accident. He was in shock. He wanted to know more, to pick her brain, but the situation at the house made it impossible. Besides, it wasn't the time. Swain's daughter. He couldn't believe it. He didn't even know her last name.

"I've got to get something to eat." John put his signal on and turned toward the exit and the fast food places. He hadn't eaten breakfast.

For three hours, as they drove, Shelby had been reviewing the information she downloaded from the Wayne State University Medical School database, trying to unravel some of the equations, to find more of Dr. Russel's records; something Doran hadn't found.

It was raining harder now, until they pulled into the drive-through and the car was sheltered by the overhead canopy. They were the only customers and were able to quickly pull around the building and up to the window.

Through the curtain of water, passing on the road, John recognized a car. "Look, Shel. Isn't that...?"

Shelby looked up from the printout and spotted the black Ford; the only vehicle on the highway whose headlights weren't on. "It's Doran's guys." she said.

"Jesus." He wasn't as much surprised as reminded that the FBI inspector could not be trusted. Who knows what his motives were. "Jesus."

Back on the freeway, John devoured the greasy food while nervously scanning his mirrors, looking for the car that he was certain was still following, but all he could see was water.

Sheriff Kellet had been emphatic. He wanted them to get there as soon as they could. He said he had something, but wouldn't say what. The puzzle just kept getting more complicated.

Through a series of mercifully silent notes slid back and forth on the kitchen counter, Shelby learned from Christine how potentially dangerous a situation this was. As long as they were suspected of having some sort of evidence, even if they didn't have it or know what it was, they were in trouble. John wished he did have whatever it was they were looking for. He swore he'd hand it over to the first person who asked just to get his life back to normal. At least this morning.

Eventually the women decided that Christine, as the Russel's attorney, should approach special prosecutor Keenan with their suspicions about Doran. John was dead set against this idea, complaining that there was no way to know who they could trust, or even if Keenan himself was not involved. But the women worked on him and somehow convinced him that they needed an ally inside the system. Christine knew the prosecutor and Swain had told her more than once, that Charlie Keenan was honest. Besides, Shelby had a good feeling about the guy…intuitively. This last thought had John's already delicate stomach spinning. We're gonna invite ourselves to the electric chair because you *think* you can trust a guy who probably has backyard barbecues with Frank Doran? But, no matter how big he wrote, or how forcefully he shoved them in front of the women, his notes were overruled.

Chris was on her way to see Keenan.

The information that Shelby brought with her was a result of hours spent the night before, searching, but she hadn't discovered anything in the computer data that was surprising. There were bibliographies of published papers, lecture schedules, and phone directories. There were spreadsheets for various research projects indicating costs for laboratory animals and equipment, and thousands of pages of blood donors. She had located files which contained information from the seventies and specific references to Dr. Russel's work. There were many references to the medical research library and to particular volumes: 'DECOMPOSITION/RAT/DNA #6-12882/vol 17343' but nothing having to do with Russel's repeating formula from his journals. She had tried to input the formula and search through the database, but the response always came back, 'NO MATCHING ITEMS FOUND'. It was a frustrating reality that most of what she was looking for was too old to have been inputted into the database.

But, when Christine told her about the possibility of evidence that the doctor and Swain may have hidden, she became even more determined to discover what it was, if it existed at all. She printed out several of the files containing references to the time period between April and August 1975. She searched again. This time, out of exasperation, she even typed 'EVIDENCE' and 'HOFFA' and even 'MURDER' but, of course, the message was the same.

Before they left to drive to Leelanau, Shelby had gathered all of the pages the computer had printed so she could study them on the way. Now they were spread across the entire front seat, draped over the back, and cascading from the pile on her lap to the floor. "I can't find anything in here." She sounded defeated, "We're no closer to knowing something now than we were three days ago."

"But we're far more popular."

"Lets go over it again," Shelby continued, ignoring his remark. "The journals are just a bunch of technical crap, and as far as I'm concerned there's no rhyme or reason to them at all. Then, all of a sudden, in July, he starts to repeat the same formula. He puts it on every page of every one until he...well, from then on. Where he puts it on the page doesn't seem to have any relationship to the rest of the stuff on the page, and actually, on a lot of 'em, if I remember correctly, it's written in the margins. It's obviously a message."

"Maybe he was just doodling in the margins."

"How can you say that after what Chris told you?"

"I wouldn't put it past Uncle Henry to be involved in something, he had some questionable clients; remember those guys at the engagement thing? But, he could have told her anything. It doesn't mean that's how it happened, that's all I'm saying, Shel."

"Well, what if it is true? Then he would certainly want to create some way of letting somebody know, wouldn't he?"

"Like...?"

"Like the equations. Junior, listen. I know it's hard for you, but we have to try to look at what's happened...objectively, if we can. So help me out with this. Please?"

John knew she was serious. "All right, Shel, go ahead. Let's go over it again."

She dug through the stack of papers again, finally coming to a handwritten scrap. "Okay, here it is." The small piece of lined paper was filled with hastily scribbled letters and numbers, reproduced as accurately as possible from her memory of the journals. "'H does not equal 2H' she read. 'H=2H-x and x=Pt+(3NO3+H2SO3)' and then under that it says, '2H=1-71575/15877.' And then there was this little one at the bottom of each page, 'CHS4++'."

"Sounds like dad's usual stuff. H, that's Hydrogen. I remember that from high school. And N and O, those are Nitrogen and Oxygen; and some of those other notations are compounds."

"Okay, so why would a scientist write something as simple as H doesn't equal H2? I mean, that's obvious. Of course something doesn't equal twice itself. Right?" Shelby stated rhetorically.

"And...?" John took the bait so she could make the point.

"Unless H doesn't mean Hydrogen. It means something else. Maybe it's an initial."

They had gotten this far before. "Maybe it stands for Hoffa, or help..."

"...or for Henry."

"...or hangover." John smiled.

"And maybe this 'Pt.' stands for pain in the ass, which you are." Shelby opened her eyes wide as she chastised him.

"No, I think 'Pt.' is platinum." He grinned back.

"Let's say it's Hoffa." Shelby was thinking aloud, "Hoffa doesn't equal double Hoffa. Hoffa is Hoffa too. Is means the same as equals, right?" She didn't wait for his answer. "Okay, so let's try Henry. Henry is not Hoffa."

"It takes two Henrys to get one Hoffa."

"C'mon, Junior, I mean it. Quit screwing around." She sat up. "Wait a minute. This last one, 'CHS4++'. Could that be 'see...Henry Swain for 'and the plusses are 'more'; See Henry Swain for more. That's it. That's it, John!" She was obviously excited. She was a detective now and worse, she may actually be on to something.

"Jesus, Shel, that could be."

"But these other numbers, what are they all about? They look like something, something I saw. Where, though?" She began rifling through the computer pages.

John scanned the rearview again. He noticed several sets of distant headlights through the downpour, but none close enough to be recognized. It was becoming more difficult to deny that somehow his father was involved in Hoffa's disappearance and the thought made him sick. It meant Christine's warning should be taken seriously, that if they found evidence that could implicate the Domatis, they would indeed be in danger. He already knew that they would kill if they had to, and he assumed that was what happened to Henry Swain.

"I thought so," Shelby held up a printout, "Look. See these numbers? These are the reference numbers of the medical records in the archives of Wayne's medical library. See '7-100773, 4-62682', and so on. And you know what they are? They're dates, all of them dates of experiments! And after the slash, those are journal numbers! Lookit!" She was throwing papers over her shoulders and into the back seat, flying everywhere until she found the scrap. Then she stopped and quietly turned to John. "And that is what this is. She read, '1-71575 slash 15877'. It's a date; July fifteenth, nineteen seventy-five; and the reference number of the written record in the library. And the '1', I don't know what that means, but I'll bet you anything that your father will tell us more if we can get that book."

"My god, Shel, you could be right. Jesus."

The rain fell harder than ever now. He reached across the seat to touch her hand. They didn't talk for almost an hour.

They were almost there, in Leelanau and just turning onto Duck Lake Road. The rain had eased a little and, as dusk approached, the sun had begun to dip under the flat, gray clouds. Spears of bright yellow, sifted through branches and flashes reflected from the wet leaves as they were tossed by the lake breeze. The birds still sing after a rain. Even if your life is in total turmoil. And there is nothing more secluded or more peaceful than a lake.

Then, loud enough to rock the car, "BOOM!" an explosion in the woods. John slammed on the brakes and the car skidded on the damp gravel, stopping abruptly about an inch from the carved 'HOLLY"S RETREAT' sign. "Get down, Shel! Get down!" John ordered, his ears still ringing from the blast. He knew all too well that it was the sound of a shotgun. "BOOM!" It rang again from the woods on Shelby's side, severing a maple branch above them, which came crashing down on the car. "Stay there!" John yelled and opened his door, pushing through the leafy barrier. He ducked down along the driver's side, and using the vehicle for shelter, called out as loud as he could in the direction of the shots, "Hey! Stop it! What the fuck are you shooting at?"

There was a long quiet pause.

"Is that you, John Russel?" An older voice responded from deep in the woods. And then yelled, "Answer me or I'll blow the shit right outta ya!" "BOOM!" The report echoed over the lake and again from the hills. The treetops rattled as birds escaped the attack.

John suddenly realized it was his neighbor. "Jesus Holloway, stop it! Of course it's me. Who the fuck did you think it was?"

There was longer silence and then footsteps came crunching toward him from the direction of Holloway's cabin. Then the glimpse of Bill Holloway's constant blue bib overalls followed by the man himself.

He stood up from the car. "It's okay Shel. It's just Mr. Holloway." She sat up in the car, her heart slamming inside. She put her head back on the headrest and waited to catch her breath.

"Jesus Bill, what are you doing? You could kill somebody."

"Ahh, baloney. It's just rock salt. This place has been like a three ring circus ever since they found your body there. I'm just tryin' to maintain a small amount of God-given peace and quiet. Sorry. Hope I didn't scare ya too bad."

"We're all right."

"It's jes those damnable reporters and guys with cameras...I'm gonna teach 'em to come stompin' around here. Besides, I knew your father and he wouldn't like what they're doin' to ya one bit, not one bit, ya know."

"I don't care if you shoot em all." John laughed. He dragged the branch off the hood. "Listen, we're gonna be around for a couple of days, Bill, but you can bet we'll let you know when we leave."

"I'll make sure they leave you alone." Holloway patted the twelve guage. "As long as I got this, we'll have some privacy. Those CNN guys'll be too busy pickin' Morton's outta their ass to bother us."

The two laughed at the prospect and waved. "See ya later, Bill." John returned to the car.

Shelby was chuckling. Some of these guys had been around here forever and they never appreciated intrusions. "Looks like we've got our own militia."

"I hope he shoots the photographers first."

13

"Good morning, Ferrand, Mascio, Stein, & Swain." The voice was different; no longer Christine's. For a moment, Shelby didn't know what to say.

"Yes, I'm calling for...Christine...and I don't really know her last name. I'm sorry."

"Ms. Ferrand. And whom shall I say is calling?"

"Shelby Russel."

"I'll connect you."

"Hey, Junior," she said in a course whisper, covering the mouthpiece. "Christine Ferrand?..."

"Ferrand?" John said realizing that Shelby was on hold. "Isn't that one of the original partners? I bet there's a story there somewhere."

Christine picked it up. "Hi. Chris?"

As Shelby began her conversation, he turned his attention back to the papers that were spread out on the table. He'd scrutinized every word since dawn, convinced that Shelby was right and that his father had left oblique messages hidden in his journals.

John was happy to be at the cottage and away, at least temporarily, from the onslaught of the press.

He'd opened all the windows after they arrived and now full of the nights air, the place was fresh. He could tell it was going to be hot. When he got up, the thermometer already read seventy-three degrees. The water was almost mirror-still, except for the odd swirl of a water snake or the occasional circular waves after a fish jumped.

Last night was the first time in two days that he had really slept, and John felt the benefits. He was relaxed. The coffee smelled perfect. The bacon was just beginning to crackle in the pan. Things were damn near normal.

He surveyed Shelby's figure, as she stood, leaning on the counter in her white, short robe and marveled at how she radiated immediately after waking up, long before the makeup. He no longer had any interest in the computer printouts. He was instead, as he had been from the start, totally captivated by his wife's being. He watched her thin lips as she talked. Quietly, he crossed the room.

"...and we'll be at the sheriff's office later. Right. I wish I could tell you more, but the phone...well, you know...sure. That's what we'll do. And, thanks again, this is really important...okay Chris, thanks." She hung up.

John's arms wrapped around her from behind and locked his hands together. He kissed her gently behind her ear. "I love you, Shel." She turned around in his arms, reaching behind her as she did to push his hands low on her bottom. She kissed him lightly. "I love you, too." She kissed him firmly. She reached into the fly of his pajamas and guided him out into the air. She kissed him again while she held him tightly, then turned around, removed the robe and reached back to find him again, this time taking him inside her. "You know Junior, this has to be the best place in the world to make love." Shelby knew that he could see past her to the shimmering sunlight on the lake and feel the air, and smell the pines, and that no one could hear them at all, even if she screamed, and she loved him and how it felt, and she heard him behind her, and she knew he was happy. And nothing could take away this perfect moment.

"John? Are you about out?" She called into the bathroom where he was showering.

"C'mon in," he yelled back.

She stuck her head into the steamy room. "I told Chris we'd call her later. We'd better get going. Kellet called. He's waiting."

Outside in the bushes near the kitchen window, a dark pair of eyes watched intently, while struggling to hear their conversation. The large man ducked as Shelby returned to the room. After a few minutes, when he was sure that she had gone to the back bedroom, he made his break; running, careful where he stepped, back into the dark woods.

Just as John opened the bathroom door, a shotgun blast tore through the quiet morning, echoing as it had before across Duck Lake. Then another blast and the sound of a car speeding away, retreating to M-22. He gave his wet hair several rubs with the towel and said almost to himself, "I love that guy."

On the way out, past Holly's place, John nudged the horn, a signal to Holloway to let them pass, and no shots were fired. They headed into Leland to meet the sheriff. Behind them the black car followed. Occasionally, John caught a brief look at it in the rearview as it emerged from a bend in the two lane blacktop. He no longer mentioned these sightings to Shelby, since they occurred so frequently.

When they arrived, the black car parked on River Street, about a half a block from the county offices. From the lot in front, John could clearly see it and the silhouette of the driver inside. It was difficult to be discreet in a town this size and the stripped down Ford looked ridiculous. As they walked to the door, John added to the absurdity, waving broadly toward the car and the man who watched.

"John, come in. Shelby, dear, how are you? C'mon back here in my office." Bob Kellett, always the gentleman, led them past the front counter and a common area where several deputies were working, to his office in the rear corner of the building. "Coffee?"

"No thanks, Bob, we're fine." John answered.

"Have a seat."

The office was twentieth century northern sheriff. The outside walls, originally exposed brick, had been covered, presumably by a predecessor judging by the wear, in smooth finished knotty pine. Kellet had decorated it with certificates from various law enforcement academies and photographs and fish. One of the biggest and ugliest was poised to strike and prominently displayed on the wall behind him right over his head. "Nice," John said, pointing at it.

"Big Leo. Caught him after three years. Right up here in the river. Beautiful, isn't he?"

John nodded. Shelby smiled, but wondered how you tell.

The sheriff got to the business. "Thanks for coming. I think we've got something that could be important." He walked behind the Russels and shut the door and, returning, half leaned, half sat on the front edge of his desk, so that he was close and could talk quietly without risk of being overheard.

He went on, "A couple days ago, we got some calls; somebody trespassing, an Indian, scarin' people at some of the rental cottages over by the east side of the lake. This isn't the first time it's happened. In fact, as soon as I heard about 'em, I coulda practically told you who it'd be." Kellet reached back into his desk drawer and grabbed something. "There's this Indian from the reservation for the Grand Traverse Band in Peshawbestown; Joey Greydog. He's not quite right up here, ya know." The sheriff pointed to his head. "Anyway, I'm pretty sure he was snoopin' around the tourists and I went out there to talk to him and I noticed he was wearin' this." He held the object up so that the

Russels could see that it was a graduation ring. John opened his hand and the sheriff dropped it in. "I think it's your dad's."

Clearly etched in the metal was the Wayne State insignia. John rolled it around in his fingers, to view it closely from several angles. He looked inside and there it was. The inscription read 'John A. Russel'.

"Jesus." John was amazed.

"So it is?"

"Yeah. It has to be. But how did this Greydog get it?" John passed it to Shelby.

The sheriff explained. "It's sorta crazy, but I think it was him who broke into your house." Kellet stood up and walked back around his desk. "See, Joey Greydog thinks that he is some kinda Mohawk chief, part of the Six Nations of Iroquois. He thinks that he 'sees' for the council...that he's the eyes of the departed warriors."

"Wow." Shelby chimed in, acknowledging his insanity.

"Yeah, it's strange. I told you." Kellet continued. "I went to school with him for awhile and even then he was like this."

"So what does this have to do with the ring?" John was becoming impatient.

"Well, John, it's not just the ring. He gathers things. Things that belong to the visitors and takes them. They're kinda offerings. He hopes that if he takes them the people will go away, too. He puts them into..." Bob shrugged, "An arrangement; sort of a shrine, I guess you'd call it, out in the woods somewhere. And usually when we find these things, there's more."

"What do you mean?" Again, Shelby was curious, suspecting where this was leading.

"For years he's been doin' this. It used to be odd things; beach toys and maybe some silverware or something, but in the last few years it's escalated. And what he does is dig a cave, they used to just be holes, and he'll spend the summer collecting and then in the fall, he'll cover it over, hiding the stuff. He says it will keep the visitors from returning."

"So you think that there could be more things that he took from our cottage somewhere out in the woods?" John asked.

"Yeah."

"Maybe he can make that guy in the car go away," Shelby added.

"...guy in the car?"

John stood up and moved to the window. "Someone's been following us. You can probably see him from here." John looked out at the spot where the car had parked, but it was gone. "He's gone." He turned back to the sheriff, "It seems to me that this is robbery. I mean, we've been robbed, the ring is stolen. You seem to take it kinda matter of factly. I think you should arrest this Joey Dog or whatever his name is and we'll get to the bottom of this right away."

The sheriff did not appreciate the accusation and curtly responded, "I did. He's here. Now."

Shelby smoothed things. "I'm sorry Bob. We know you're doing your job. Things have been a little...well, you know, kinda...tense lately."

"Sorry, Bob." John apologized.

"I was hoping that once you got here we could get him to show us where he's putting the things and we could look around a little." The sheriff looked directly at John, "If you want us to charge him, we will."

"Well, it is a robbery, isn't it?"

"I suppose. But you may find that, especially with Greydog, a little leniency goes a long way. But it's up to you. Ready?"

On the way to the cell where the Indian was being held, Kellet explained that for years, when people around the county would be clearing land or hiking, they would occasionally come across one of Joey Greydog's shrines. "Usually we just find out who owns the stuff, if we can, and return it."

They walked down a short hall to one of the county's two cells. Inside, behind the locked steel door, was Joey Greydog. John caught a glimpse through the small window.

The Sheriff opened the cell door. "Hey Joey, how's it going?"

Joey had removed the thin mattress from the lower of two small bunks and placed it on the floor. He was seated, leaning against the far wall, his legs comfortably stretched out across the ticking, reading a magazine. When he spoke, his voice was pleasant, "Just fine, sheriff, just fine."

"These are the Russels; the folks I told you about."

Greydog's dark eyes roamed over them, ultimately coming to rest locked with John's own. He laid the magazine down and got up from his spot. John noticed that he was wearing a dark blue, uniform-type work shirt with the name 'Joey' embroidered in red and white on a patch sewn over his left breast pocket. "Pleased to meet you." He extended his arm to shake hands, first with Shelby and then with John. His hand was rough. It was a working man's hand.

"I told 'em maybe you could take us out to where you been hiding your collection, Joey; that they might be able to look around, you know, just to see if there's anything else from their cottage that you may have...collected."

Joey looked hard at John, "Too many visitors, had to get them to go."

"So you did...take things from my cottage."

"To make the visitors go. I work for the warriors." Then, considerably more lucent, "You gonna press charges?"

Shelby was quick to recognize their leverage. "Will you give us back what you took? Will you take us to see what you have?"

"Greydog can't work in jail."

The meaning of this comment was indisputable. Everybody was looking at John. "Oh, Jesus fine. We won't."

The Indian smiled. "Then I will show you."

Peshawbestown had changed in the last few years. What had been a poor but quiet home for the Grand Traverse Band had now become a destination. Where they once had Pow-Wows now stood several large contemporary structures, the Leelanau Shores Casino. Where once few cars, always in various stages of disrepair, had made the journey from Sutton's Bay, up route 22, along the bay with supplies for the reservation, now came busloads of gamblers.

Joey Greydog, observing the traffic from his vantage point in the back of Kellet's cruiser shook his head. "Too many visitors." He said it several times as they drove. And John, having been here so much as a boy and recognizing the difference had to agree: "Too many visitors."

They made their way up the highway past the casino and the hundreds of cars to the north side of the reservation. Winding through the Michigan woods they could see the water to the right, and every so often in a clearing an old trailer, an Indian home, usually rusted at the seams. There were some now with new frame additions and new cars parked proudly in front, their chrome shining with new wealth. The gamblers had brought money to the tribe and work; jobs John imagined, for these daylight fishermen, now blackjack dealers by night.

As Greydog instructed, the Sheriff turned off the highway and onto a two-track, disappearing into the dense woods. The car snaked around in the dappled hills, climbing upward, until, suddenly the road simply ended. "We walk from here."

Joey led as the foursome dodged swinging branches and climbed up higher, to the top of this small mountain. Through the occasional break in the forest you could see the huge bay cutting in and the Old Mission peninsula that it created twenty miles beyond; and to the south, along the coast road, the reflected flash from a windshield or a bumper from the endless ribbon of vehicles surging northward.

They came to a dark thicket, hidden under the umbrella of tall old pines. "Here," the Indian said, but they saw nothing.

Joey moved a large branch from a bank on the angled edge of the clearing. He brushed the thick piles of pine needles away until a hole was revealed behind the camouflage. It grew three feet wide, then four. John and the sheriff began to strip away the branches until the opening was complete. "There," Greydog said. The opening was large enough for two men to walk in side by side and high enough that only the tall sheriff had to duck. Beyond, Joey had carved a tunnel, about twenty feet in length into the side of the hill. From the edges, thin fingers of pine roots fell like dark hair. In the deepest part of the cave there was light, beaming from above through a chimney-like hole in the earth, illuminating the larger circular room that Joey had dug.

"Wow." Shelby was impressed.

"Pretty nice, isn't it?" Greydog was flattered. "C'mon." He disappeared into the initial darkness, leading Bob Kellet and the Russels inside. Shelby could feel the roots rubbing against her and it gave her the chills. She held on tightly to the back of John's shirt as they moved carefully ahead to the center of the dirt room. When their eyes adjusted to the dim light, details of the den emerged from the darkness.

Joey had carefully excavated shelves which continued around the perimeter, rising like steps in twelve inch increments up from the floor to the widest part of the room where they stopped, the wall continuing upward in a smooth arch to the hole with the light. There were remnants of a fire; scraps of charred wood in a circle of round stones in the center of the room. At the far end, the deepest part of the excavation was a platform which Shelby recognized as a rough bunk. "Do you live here?" She asked.

"I come here sometimes to talk with the warriors."

"Uh huh." As if that would be where she would go for similar conversations.

John scanned the shelves. They were filled with Greydog's current collection of stolen artifacts. On the bottom, were some of the larger items: a beach ball, an array of hubcaps, a bicycle pump, and a couple of brass floor lamps. On the second shelf, the collection contained many smaller things: photographs, books, cameras, binoculars.

Hanging down from the ceiling, tied to roots, were pots and pans, large spoons and spatulas, lamps and mirrors, and an old bicycle frame.

"Do you see anything that could have come from your house?" The sheriff asked.

"No." John was disappointed.

"My cave is your cave. Take your time. Look around." The Indian grinned.

"I thought you said..." he stopped, not wanting to play games.

Shelby was examining some of the things more closely. She had begun systematically at one end of the top shelf and was working her way down the line. Most of the things he had taken wouldn't even be missed; a lot of it was trash. She kept looking. John started at the other end of the same ledge. Nothing.

Joey stood silently at the entrance to the dirt room, smiling widely at the sheriff, watching as the search continued.

So this Indian had one of Dad's rings, so what? John was becoming more frustrated. He had driven all the way up here for nothing. He should be talking to Keenan himself. Instead, he was digging around like a mole, going through someone else's discarded junk. The Indian had probably raided garage sales all over the county. He was surprised not to find handwritten price tags stuck to the lamps. But he had to look.

Shelby had come across an old picture album. She flipped through, glancing at the photos. She turned another page. "Ahhh!" She threw the book to the floor, jumping back, horrified. Earwigs had eaten through the back binding and made a cozy nest in the damp interior. Hundreds of the insects fled, shocked from the drop, and scattered at her feet, running for the roots. "Oh, god!" She screamed, wiping her hands against her clothing to remove any imaginary animals.

John saw what it was. "It's all right, Shel," he comforted her.

"Thanks." She was laughing, realizing how silly she must look. "Let's keep looking."

They had completely gone through everything on the top two shelves and Shelby had started on the third when she noticed a closed shoe box. "John, could you...eh?" She indicated that she wanted him to open the box.

"Sure." He ripped one of the serving utensils from the roots above his head and used it to lift a corner of the lid. Immediately Shelby noticed something, a crumpled paper, newspaper used to wrap whatever was inside. John lifted the top further. No. It was something much more familiar.

"Junior. Look!"

He flipped the cover off completely, and it fell to the floor. They leaned over the box.

"Jesus." John knew immediately what it was. The missing pages from the journal. The equations and formulas covering them were unmistakable. They were written in the familiar stroke of his father. He lifted the shoe box from the dark shelf and carefully placed it into the brightest spot on the floor. "Where did you get this? When were you at my cottage?" There was no response.

Joey Greydog was gone.

"Dammit!" Sheriff Kellet couldn't believe he had let him get away. He ran for the opening, but it was too late. "Shit!" He kicked at the pile of pine needles, sending them flying into the air. There was no sign of him.

When he got back inside, the Russels were peeling away each page of the precious wrapper from the box. John and Shelby were intensely focused on the contents. Was this it? What Christine was talking about? What if it was? There was something heavy wrapped in the paper. Shelby reached in and felt the cold metal. She pulled it out. "Junior..." It was a sculpture; two hands posed as if in prayer; cast as one piece which included the flat base. It was unusually heavy and dark, tarnished except for the slight scratches that reflected the glint of descending sunlight as she passed it to John through the beams.

"What is it?" Bob Kellet asked.

"I don't know, Bob, I've never seen it before." John Russel took the sculpture into his hands."

"There's an inscription," Shelby noticed, "On the base of it."

John rubbed the accumulated oxide from the base. Engraved into the metal it read:

'I HAVE PUT THESE HANDS TOGETHER FOR THE MAN WHO HAS BECOME,

MORE SIGNIFICANT IN DEATH'S DIFFERENCE THAN EVER IN LIFE'S SUM'

And in extremely small lettering under the last word, 'J.A.R.'

John read the words out loud to Kellet and Shelby and pointed out the initials. "And this...John Albert Russel."

"What the hell does that mean?" Shelby asked.

The ride back to the sheriff's office was quiet. Shelby read and re-read the journal pages. John cradled the hands in his lap. He knew when he rubbed the discolored coating from the casting and saw the shiny metal underneath; when he felt the weight of it, that it was made of platinum. And he felt the weight of his discovery, too. He knew there was no doubt now of his father's involvement. What else was there? What next? He didn't really hear Shelby speaking, but he numbly agreed anyway, "Uh huh."

"John? Junior? Did you hear me? It gives a reference number here. To the experiment. It tells which book to look in! It's all right here, John."

"Really," he answered, but did not hear.

John wondered what the Indian was doing with this and when he had stolen it. He knew Doran's men had searched the cabin, no matter how much they denied it. He was sure that Joey Greydog knew nothing about what he had. Was it possible that Doran had actually found the hands, but dismissed them as some kind of religious artifact? He had asked, John remembered, that day in Keenan's office, if his father had an interest in such things. It was an odd question that John never did understand. Doctor Russel was never much for religion. Maybe Doran had what he wanted all along, but didn't know it. Maybe he left it behind in his frenetic desire to tear the cottage to shreds.

Maybe he didn't know what he was looking for.

14

"Shelby?" Christine answered.

"We found it, Chris. What we were talking about, we got it."

"Where are you?"

"In Leland, at the sheriff's office."

Christine cut her off, "Let me have the number. Stay there. I'll call you back." and hung up.

Christine's heels clicked on the marble as she quickly crossed the lobby to the private elevator. She made her way down to the garage and her car. As she drove out, she returned Shelby's call.

"Shelby, sorry to be so abrupt, I think this is a safer phone. We had a guy sweep the place and he said we were fine, but still, I don't trust it. Tell me about it. What did you find?"

Shelby explained about the hands and where and how they had come across them. She told Chris about the equations and the data from the Wayne medical library. "I think all of the numbers refer to dates and specific experiments. And, if that's true, then Dr. Russel's journal pages that the hands were wrapped up in, refer to dates from July fifteenth seventy-five to August fifth."

"Wow." Christine didn't know how else to respond.

Shelby went on, "But the real information isn't recorded in the database, it's in the books themselves…"

"…at Wayne."

"Yup."

"I can go over there later. I'm on my way to see Keenan, now."
Chris paused. She spoke authoritatively as Shelby's counsel,
"Shelby, listen, I called Keenan yesterday to set this meeting and
he told me that I should,…we could expect some warrants."

"What do you mean?" Shelby's heart was sinking.

"He hinted that the FBI might request a warrant for John and
maybe even for you."

"What for?"

"I don't know. It could be anything. But, if it's the FBI, that
means Doran, and he could be dangerous. He's got the legal
backup to make things pretty rough, so be careful. Don't tell
anyone what you suspect. I hope I'll know a lot more after I see
Keenan, but, for now, just go back to the cottage and wait. I have
that number." She paused again. "I know this is going to sound
like spy stuff, but we can't take a chance. Is there a place up there
with a pay phone? Somewhere near the cottage?"

"In town."

"Good. When I call, if it's necessary for us to talk, go to that
phone and call me, I will ask for Dr. Russel. Tell me I have the
wrong number and hang up. If you can't go immediately, let me
know. Just say, 'there must be twenty other Russels in the county',
or 'thirty-five', or whatever. The number will mean the number of
minutes until you call me back. Okay?"

"Okay."

"If, and I wouldn't worry too much about it, there's a real
problem; if you need help, just hang up right away without saying
anything. All right?"

"Sure, Chris."

"I'm almost at the Federal Building. After I meet Keenan, I'll call
and we'll try it out." She gave Shelby the number and hung up. She
turned onto Fort Street. Even from this distance, seven or eight
blocks from the MacNamera Building, she could see the crowd of

media people ahead. There were police cars with flashers on and policemen directing traffic. The hot August afternoon burned down on the sidewalks where businessmen in shirtsleeves, jackets over their shoulders strolled back from late lunches. The last of the secretaries reluctantly disappeared into buildings, ready to squeeze out the last few hours of work on this hazy summer day.

Stuck in traffic, she slowly crawled closer. She kicked up the air conditioning one more notch and adjusted the vent so the cool air brushed her face.

The circus on the sidewalk in front of the building forced pedestrians to cross the street in front of her to continue on their way. She watched this hot parade, waiting for the light to turn. Then, in the crowd, she saw the white shirt and suspenders crossing in the opposite direction, against the flow. She recognized the unmistakable gait of the prosecutor. She pushed the button on the armrest and the window descended. Against the rush of hot air, she called to him as he crossed the street, "Charley? Charley Keenan."

He picked up speed, "No comment, sorry. Nothing to say."

She yelled louder, "Charley, it's Christine. Christine Ferrand."

Charley stopped and leaned down to window height. His seersucker jacket fell from his shoulder and he gathered it up to keep the light fabric from the dirty curb. "Hey Chris," he smiled. "I was just on my way back to the office."

"Hop in."

The cheerful prosecutor obliged, taking up a position in the passenger seat, turning the air vent to blow directly on his face. "Whew, damn if it isn't hot enough to pop the corn where it grows," he said. "How the heck are you Chris?"

The light was green and they moved forward. "I've been better, Charley."

"I was sorry to hear about Henry; a shame really; and I'm sorry for you. I had no idea."

"Thanks." She appreciated his homespun honesty. "Listen, let's get out of here and go to a restaurant or something. You had lunch?" Christine asked, but she guessed from the small, yellow mustard stain the she already knew the answer.

"Had a little something, but I could go. Sure. We can have our meeting early and you won't have to fight those reporters. Turn here," he instructed.

The traffic thinned as they got farther from the federal building. They found a lot, parked and walked the last block to the Coney Island restaurant on Woodward.

The hot air outside was pungent with spices, garlic and thyme, mingling with the smell of shredded beef. When they opened the door, a wave of the seasonings drifted over them from inside the noisy room. Most of the Formica tables were occupied, and many were being wiped to accommodate the constant stream of new customers. Several men were seated at the counter, eating and reading the newspaper. At the far end, past the row of chrome-posted stools was the register. Behind it, a man took money and orders. The area was open to the kitchen where three dark-haired cooks furiously filled the requests as they were shouted across the room.

"Hi, Mr. Keenan." The small dark man knew Charley and his order, "Two up on one. Sloppy," he yelled back to one of the cooks in a broken Greek dialect. "And for you miss?"

Although it was popular, Christine had never been here, but she went along, "Same, I guess." And the Greek repeated his chant to the kitchen.

Almost instantly the food arrived in front of them on polyfoam plates, each containing two hot dog buns filled with loose, seasoned meat, topped with no-bean chili, mustard, and diced onions.

"I tell ya, there's nothing like it." Keenan leaned over the steaming food to inhale the rising aroma, "There's a table, there, by the window. That okay?"

Christine followed him to the spot, dodging waiters and bus boys and they sat down. She could see the city moving by on the sidewalk and across the street, the once busy stores, now boarded up, the customers long since having fled to safer suburban refuge. Charley was already half way into his first loose Coney, "These things are addictive." He wiped his mouth, "Now, what is it you would like to discuss today, Chris?" He continued to eat, waiting for her response.

"As you know, since my fa…since Henry died, I represent the Russels."

"Okay. Then I'm officially warned." he chuckled.

"I'm serious, Charley."

"Do they need a lawyer?" Keenan was sly as ever. "What'd they do?"

"They didn't do anything, but somebody did. And I think we're getting closer to discovering who that is." She took a moment to brace herself for the next part, "I think the Russels are in real trouble. I think my dad was murdered."

"Really." The prosecutor stopped eating.

Christine reached into her purse. This was it. All she could hope for was that he would have an open mind. She pulled out the old photograph of the men at Eastern Market. "Take a look at this." Still holding it she moved it closer so Keenan could see it. "Do you recognize any of these guys?"

"Well, sure." The prosecutor was stunned at the stupidity of the question.

"Have you seen this particular picture before?"

"I don't think so, Chris, but I have been working on this for twenty years, I mean I can see that's Hoffa and Antonio Tenino and the sons..," he said matter of factly.

She interrupted, "And in the back, see who's standing there?"

Charley put on reading glasses so that he could study the images more closely. "That's Domati, Vincenzo Domati. And with him...I don't know. It looks like...but he is young here...it looks to me like Frank Doran." He lifted the glasses from his face and handed the photo back to Chris.

"Right. And that's what I wanted to talk to you about; Doran. I'm not so sure what his motives are in this."

Keenan took an expected tack, "Well, we've both been on this awhile. If he seems a little overzealous, you can see why. We've got the body, Chris. We found it at their place. He's got to start somewhere."

"But why is he so intent on John Russel? I know you've checked him out. And, if you did, I know that you didn't find a thing. So why not drop it? These people didn't do anything. You told me there are warrants."

"I told you, you might expect some warrants."

"It's a small town, Charley, and it's hard to keep secrets. Are there warrants?"

"Doran has requested a warrant for Russel," he admitted, "It'll prob'ly go in today. But it's really just for more questioning. He could get him on assault, you know."

"That's just what I mean. I was there when John took a swing at him. At the house. And I suppose, technically, you're right. But John was provoked. I didn't hear what was said, but he was provoked. And besides, what was Doran doing there in the first place? Is it common practice for the FBI to show up at a house fire?"

"Chris, I think you're reaching, and I don't blame you. If the Russels were my clients, I would, too. But, as far as I'm concerned, Frank's doing his job."

"What about Domati? You gotta believe that he has something to do with Hoffa. Hoffa was supposed to meet him the night he disappeared. Everybody knows that. Can't they find some physical evidence now that they have the body?"

"Look Chris, like I said. Frank's doing his job. If he comes across something that would exonerate your client, I'll let you know. That's the best I can do. What do you want? Do you want me to stop Doran from looking at the Russels? I can't do that. I have to explore every avenue."

"What if Doran doesn't want anyone to find out what really happened?"

"That's ridiculous. He works for the FBI for crissakes."

Christine could tell that Keenan would not be easily convinced, but she hoped she might trigger a small shred of doubt, at least. Maybe she could buy a little time for John and Shelby. She tried the picture again.

"There's Doran all buddy-buddy with Domati, maybe it goes further than that." She could see Charley wasn't buying any of it. Her father, Henry Swain, had told her she could trust Keenan, but she was scared to death. She felt her face go white, the blood rushing away.

Keenan sensed her trepidation. "Are you okay, Chris?" What is it? Tell me."

"Off the record?"

"Fine, Chris."

"And the Russels don't know anything about this. I want you to know that, too." Christine reached down into her purse and pulled out a white envelope. She opened it and unfolded the sheet of paper that was inside. She pushed aside the salt and pepper shakers, the mustard, and the napkin holder, and laid it on the table. Charley was intensely curious, "What's that?"

"It's a list," Christine responded, certain that they could not be overheard above the din of silverware and conversation, but whispering, "Of banks; actually, of bank accounts."

Charley scanned the page, "And those dates?"

"When the accounts were opened." She stared directly into his eyes and went on, "If you check these accounts you'll know what I'm talking about. See the first entry, there, at the top of the list." The prosecutor nodded, "Fifth Third Bank, Cincinnati, September thirteenth, 1975. And there next to it, fifty thousand dollars. The next account, opened in April of the following year at National Bank of Detroit, forty-three thousand, and it goes on right up to this one on August fifth, '95, just two weeks ago, off-shore in St. Thomas."

"And?" Keenan had no idea why this was relevant. But Chris blasted ahead.

"Two hundred and fifty thousand, two days after they found the body."

"You're suggesting this has to do with Hoffa?"

"It's worse than that. Check out these accounts in all these banks all over the country and you know what you'll find? That every single one of them, in one way or another, belongs to Frank Doran; not in his name, but in all different names and DBAs. Check the signatures and the names. You'll see. The last one is Baglia's account. I had our guy check it this morning and guess what, two hundred of it was withdrawn the day before yesterday. Kinda tough to do when you've been dead for a month, don't you think, Charley?"

"Naw." He did not want this to be true. He shook his head like a man who had just been told his son had played hooky or stolen a beer from the refrigerator.

She continued, "My dad knew the guy was dirty. He kept track of him. He called it our 'health insurance'. Every month, our investigators send an updated report and I put it in the file. This is what Doran was looking for at our office; why we were rousted. It didn't have anything to do with the Russels." Christine could see that Keenan was upset. "Charley, I hope to God I can trust you."

"Of course."

Keenan was stunned. "Look at all this money. It must be over a million."

"Two million four."

"Where did it come from? Do you know?"

"Yes. He got it from Domati."

"But there are ways of tracking this stuff. He would've had to have paid taxes. The banks would report the deposits."

"Just check the names, you'll see how they do it. There's always enough left behind for the IRS and you know as well as I do, Charley, that as long as they get theirs, they don't give a damn about anything else. They used Domati's guys to sign the withdrawal slips, but those guys never saw any of the money. It was Doran's. Some of them are guys Doran put in jail himself. It wouldn't surprise me if he got their signatures first. You'll see, Charley, it's true."

Keenan pushed the plate aside and stared at the page, astonished at the implication. "You know, Chris, for all these years, I've been completely immersed in this case. It's all I've done," he confided, sensing now the possibility of Doran's betrayal. "And all along, Frank's been there, too. I can't believe he could do something like this. For so long."

"I'm sorry. I didn't want to tell you. I didn't know what would happen if I did. And there's more you should know, but right now I have to make sure that Doran doesn't get his hands on the Russels. I need your help."

Keenan slipped the envelope with the list into the inside pocket of his sport coat and put the jacket back on for safekeeping. He didn't say much as they walked back to the car. He was consumed by the thought of Doran's involvement.

Many times Keenan's investigation had pointed at Domati, but Frank could never produce any evidence, instead directing his attention toward the Tenino family. They were Hoffa's supporters and allies from the beginning and actually ran the Teamsters Union on his behalf when he was in prison and afterward. They controlled all the money and made loans from various union funds to friendly enterprises in New York and Las Vegas. Tenino's men had remained in positions of control long after Hoffa disappeared, even after Anthony Tenino and his son Michael were executed. It was this that Doran always used as the basis for the theory that some faction of that family, the Tenino family, was responsible for Hoffa's presumed murder. If it had been Domati, surely these men would have been eliminated, too, he argued.

Keenan silently played the facts over in his mind, looking at them now with newfound objectivity. Several inside men who were known to be sympathetic with Domati were killed within a week of the Tenino killings, furthering speculation that this was a retaliatory action, and that, in the war over the Teamster money, the Teninos had prevailed. It had always looked to Charley, or perhaps was it made to look, as if Tenino did it.

The Hoffa case was one of the most unusual in Keenan's recollection, by virtue of its endless branches and dead ends. Usually criminals will eventually, for one reason or another, provide the information you want. As a group, even the Mafia, is not as impenetrable as one would think. But in this case no one had revealed anything; for twenty years. Why? Walking, oblivious to his surroundings, he ran it through his mind again. They always crack. Unless somebody deliberately gets in the way. Someone with authority and access to information. He shook his head, admitting to himself that it was possible that what Christine had told him could be true. It would certainly explain why he had gotten nowhere with the Hoffa case. He felt like a fool.

"Charley?" Chris caught his attention, "Here's the car."

"Oh, Chris, thanks. I think I'll walk back. It's only a couple of..."

Suddenly, thundering down Fort Street, the deafening sound, echo and instant recoil of an explosion.

"My God!" Christine jumped, "What was that?"

Charley tugged her back, closer to the buildings, shielding her, not knowing what may come next.

Smoke, dark, ascending rapidly in the distance. The almost instant cry of sirens filled the city as people scurried around them, not to escape, but to get a better look at what was going on.

"That's the MacNamera Building." Charley could see approximately where the explosion had occurred, "That's the office, Chris, you better go. I've got to see what's going on." He ushered her into the car, and held traffic so she could get out.

After she was safely gone, he made his way through what was now a growing and curious crowd. Ahead on the steps in front of the building, the police were clearing the area, pushing the press back from the positions they had occupied for the last two days. A police truck arrived with yellow wooden barricades and several dozen officers hurried to block the street. The first of nine fire trucks arrived and took up its station on the side street. Charley could see others behind the building. People ran everywhere. There were cameras and reporters, thrilled with their good fortune, having been there already, at the Federal Building, when the bomb went off. The crews from the television stations jockeyed for position at the perimeter, each testing the camera angle to be sure they would get the maximum cloud of smoke in the background.

Keenan cut through, his identification clipped on his jacket pocket, and ducked under the barrier. He could see that whatever had exploded had not caused damage to the front of the building.

The firemen seemed to be concentrating on an area in the rear. What's going on?" he asked a cop, but got no answer. Just as he got to the edge of the steps, Agent Morse came out. She held her hand up motioning to the crowd to calm down. The reporters, sensing information, overwhelmed the police and surrounded her, beginning the volley of questions.

"Take it easy. Take it easy. Quiet. I'll make a statement. No questions will be taken. All right?" The gang quieted. She motioned to the police to let them stay where they were and she began to read from a scribbled page. "I am Special Agent Karen Morse. I am a field operative stationed in the Detroit office of the FBI. There has been an explosion at the rear of the second floor of the building..."

One of the reporters rudely interrupted, triggering similar outbursts from most of his colleagues, "Has this got something to do with the Hoffa investigation?" "Who was the target?" Was anyone killed?" "Were there..."

"Please!" Morse cut them off. "Be quiet and you'll get the information that we have at this time," she read, "There has been an explosion at the rear of the second floor of the building. Damage to several offices seems to be extensive. We can confirm that there have been no fatalities. However, there are some personnel who are wounded and several others suffering smoke related injuries. The cause of the explosion seems to be accidental, possibly a result of an electrical problem in the breaker box on the second floor which may have ignited cleaning materials in a storage closet nearby. This information is preliminary and we will have no conclusive results until a complete investigation is conducted. There is no evidence, at this point, that this is a..."

Her words faded behind him as Keenan moved closer to the entrance. He was recognized by another agent.

"Mr. Keenan, glad you're okay. We were looking for you." He keyed the microphone on his walky-talky. "This is number one door."

"Go," came the response.

"I got Prosecutor Keenan down here. It appears he was out of the building. He's okay. Out."

"10-4," the voice came back.

"Can I get in?" The prosecutor asked.

"You can try. But the thing went off in your office. It's a hell of a mess up there."

"Where's Doran?"

15

At the cottage, John was intently searching through the text of one of his father's chemistry books. The platinum hands sat on the table in front of him. The four missing pages from Dr. Russel's journal, the ones from the shoe box, were spread out flat so that John could easily reference them. He was absolutely convinced that the explanation for this odd sculpture lay in the abstract scientific writings. He was not so sure that 'HS4++' meant 'Henry Swain' at all, but he also figured that with Henry gone, it wouldn't help anyway. So he concentrated on the other formulas.

He didn't notice the news reports on the television, but Shelby was glued to the set. Agent Morse was answering questions about the events at the federal building. Shelby knew that Chris could have been there, that she was going to meet Keenan.

"John, look at this," she interrupted, "Chris might be there. She had a meeting." John put the book down to watch.

The agent continued, "...that there is no way to know at this point whether or not this was an intentional..." Karen Morse went on, "...no, that's correct, no fatalities."

"Thank God," he said.

"Do you think this has something to do with us, I mean, with this Hoffa business?"

John wondered how life could get so fucked up so fast. "Jesus." It was all he could say.

The phone rang and Shelby picked it up. She recognized
Christine's voice immediately and was relieved.

"Is Dr. Russel there?"

"Thank goodness you're..." Then she remembered, "I'm sorry,
you have the wrong number." She hung up. "Junior, I gotta go.
You need anything from town?"

"Beer."

Shelby gave him a quick peck on the top of his head as he sat
dumbfounded, gazing at the news report. "I'll be back soon."

He turned off the set, disgusted with the whole business,
determined to quickly solve his father's mysterious puzzle so his
life could return to normal.

He studied the book. He had confirmed that the compounds
Shelby had referred to while they were driving, represented nitric
and sulfuric acid. He was pretty sure that those formulas did not
have secondary meaning. As far as the 'H does not equal H2'
business, he had not found any corroboration that this was a
chemical or physical reference and concluded that it was possible
that this could be a cryptic message. Maybe Shelby's explanation
was as good as any; that these were initials. But there were
elements of this formula that he was sure were chemicals, the
acids, not to mention the obvious reference to Platinum.

John lost track of time, buried in the chemistry textbook. He
had noticed a reference to something called *aqua regia* in the
notes. He scanned the index. There it was, *aqua regia* or 'Royal
Water'. Quickly, he turned to the specified page and read. Royal
Water. Like a bullet, the description shot into his brain. It was
defined as the combination of the acids, nitric and sulfuric, in a
specific ratio of three parts to one part, and, it explained that, in
this combination, they possessed the peculiar ability to dissolve
platinum, a property neither possessed alone.

It wasn't the hands. It was something *inside* the hands. That's what his father meant. There was something molded within them that was proof; maybe the only proof, of what happened to Jimmy Hoffa.

"Holy shit."

John threw the book down on the table. Those acids were here, at the cottage. He had seen them somewhere. Plastic bottles, labeled with those formulas. Where? Shelby would know. Where was she?

He began to pace, to try to remember. Under the sink. No. In the shed. That wasn't it, either.

The boathouse.

He ran out, skipping the bottom two steps, leaping ahead toward the lake, running past the excavation, carefully skirting the yellow taped border, glancing momentarily into the huge hole, careful not to fall in. "Pricks," he said aloud to no one.

He knew the small bottles were out there, in plain view, sitting on the shelf above the old workbench where John and his dad had made fleets of wooden boats and fixed broken tennis racquets. Where they had wrapped presents for his mother and hidden them, knowing this was a sacred, messy corner of their world where she would never look. They were there, with the gas cans for outboard motors, and paddles, and clutter from quieter years at the lake. Just like so much junk you would never notice. And that was exactly why Dr. Russel had put them there; for John to find.

He pulled open the brown painted door and daylight burst in. A startled chipmunk leapt from the bench, chirping, and ran for his life, escaping under a rotten board. John swept the cobwebs from his face. There they were; two small, brown, dusty, plastic bottles on the shelf. He read the faded writing on the worn masking tape label. H2SO4 and NO3. It was as if his father was talking to him. Here it is, John, he was saying. This is what I wanted you to find.

'BOOM', Holloway's shotgun rang from the distance, and again, 'BOOM'. C'mon, Shelby, John thought, give him the signal, honk the horn. 'BOOM' again.

John grabbed the chemicals and shoved them into his pant's pockets, one each side. He headed down the driveway to the road, walking briskly but carefully, fearing the bottles might leak. If they could melt platinum, there was no telling what else they could do.

He reached the road and turned left, toward Holly's Retreat. Another blast. Jesus, Shel, honk the damn horn, will you. He was close enough to see a car, just beyond the small bend in the two track, dead even with Holloway's driveway.

But it wasn't Shelby. John ducked behind a tree. It was the black Ford, parked, with its engine running and driver's door wide open. It was the car that had been following them; that he had seen at home, on the highway, and earlier today at the sheriff's office. He heard Holloway shout, "You get the hell outta here!" 'BOOM' he let loose another round, slicing a pine branch from above, sending it crashing down beside the car. Something moved. Behind the door. A large man. He slid under the open door to a spot near the front wheel. As John watched, the man with the curly dark hair got to his knees, still ducking down so Holloway couldn't see him. He reached into his jacket. John saw him pull out a large revolver, check the action, cock it, and slowly look up over the hood, to take aim at his assailant. Just as he raised the weapon to fire, John yelled, "Look out Holloway! Get down!" and ducked back behind the birch. Milliseconds later, a bullet, aimed at John, creased the tree bark, no more than six inches above his head.

"Jesus." John could only mouth the word, his fright preventing any sound.

"Go call the Sheriff, John, I got him pinned!" Holloway yelled back.

The intruder lowered his pistol. "John? John Russel? I have to talk to you," he said.

'BOOM', "I got your talkin' right here, Fatso!" and a shower of rock salt dispersed above the man's head.

"No, wait a minute. Russel, I gotta talk to you. It's important."

"Go call the sheriff, John. This smartass isn't goin' anywhere."

"Who are you?" John asked. There was a long silence and then the reply.

"Tenino. Benito Tenino. I gotta talk to you."

John had seen this frightening looking Italian before, at the reception, at Uncle Henry's mansion. "Hold it, Bill, I'm coming out."

Holloway had moved closer to get better aim. "I got him covered, John, c'mon."

Tenino stood up. His breathing was fast. He was heavy and not accustomed to exercise. He brushed the dirt and pine needles from his clothing. Benny Tenino, my God, this just keeps getting worse, John thought. "Leave your gun there," he ordered, sensing at least momentarily, that he had the upper hand, "On the ground."

"Relax, Russel, I'm not gonna do anything. I think we can help each other."

John was adamant. He hated guns. He had gotten rid of all the hunting rifles and shotguns in the cabin long ago. "Put it down or I swear to God I'll let him shoot you." He wasn't about to invite an armed Mafia boss into his house.

Slowly, Tenino removed the pistol again, this time letting it fall into the leaves at the side of the dirt road. "There. Can we talk now?"

John agreed, and Benny drove up and parked near the front of the cabin, across from where the body was uncovered. He commented on the hole, "They did a nice job on you, there, John. Real nice," and followed John inside.

"Why have you been following us?" John asked, hoping the question would distract Tenino and divert his attention while John moved the platinum hands, as nonchalantly as possible, from the table to the kitchen counter that divided the room, returning to stack the journal pages neatly, turning the top one over so that it could not be read. "What the hell is all of this about?" Again, hoping the man wouldn't notice.

Benny surveyed the room. "May I sit down?"

"Sure." John indicated a chair by the stone fireplace and took his seat in another, identical chair facing him.

Benny began, "You know, we have a great deal in common, you and me. Your papa was like a big brother to me, you know, from way back. I remember you when you were as high as this chair. Just this high." He put his hand out, even with the armrest. "I also know that you and I have not spoken since then and I understand. But now this Hoffa thing has got us both back together, you could say, we're kinda…connected." Tenino laughed at the prospect, a joke more to him than to John. "You gotta drink?" He reached for his pocket and John stiffened at the motion. But instead of additional weaponry, he produced a handkerchief. Benny, still a little out of breath, patted the sweat from his forehead.

"Water?" John asked.

"That's fine."

John went to the kitchen to get the drink. He noticed the wrinkles and the age on Benny's tough face and that his dark hair was brittle with years of black dye. He was sixty-one, but he was trying hard to be forty. His reputation as a tough boss was well known, even to John. He was widely thought to have taken Harborside Trucking legitimate. But there were always questions and indictments and issues which resulted in Benny's status as Uncle Henry's best client.

"Here." John handed him the glass.

Tenino took a sip and began, "There's a lot to this that you would have no way of knowing; a lot that happened a long time ago that's gonna come out now."

John knew that this man may be the only person on earth that might be able to finally straighten everything out and bring this horrible occurrence to an end. He couldn't help himself, "You've got to tell me. You have to tell me all of it." And then John remembered who he was talking to. "I won't say anything to anybody, ever." That didn't come out the way he meant it.

"Take it easy. We both want the truth." John listened and he went on, "Back when this started, there was a plan, a good plan and it couldda worked, too." He took another drink. "Now, I'm gonna tell you about it, John, cause you should know. My papa would want that. But I swear on his grave and the grave of my brother, that if you ever repeat it, you will be sorry. You have a nice house and a beautiful wife and I wouldn't want to see anything happen to that. You know what I mean, don't you Johnny?"

He did.

Tenino stood up putting his finger to his lips, "Shhh," he whispered. He started looking around, lifting things. John realized he was searching for microphones and other electronic devices. "You have to be careful," he said. He seemed to know exactly where to look. He went immediately to the counter and reached underneath, feeling along the bottom. His hand stopped, finding something. He pulled out a small black microphone, dropped it to the floor and smashed it under the sole of his shiny, black loafer. "There's one," he said, and continued the search. He positioned one of the tall stools so that he could climb up onto its seat. Then balancing precariously, he removed his hanky and unscrewed one of the light bulbs from the recessed overhead canister. Again he removed a small microphone from inside the fixture, dropped it to the floor, awkwardly climbed down and squashed it into the wooden floor.

John could not help his grin. Maybe it was the raw fear, but he was smiling. As he sat, petrified in his chair, he wondered. Was this the Sicilian James Bond? What other equipment would he produce? The ridiculousness of it was not lost on John. Finally, after locating two other similar devices, and adding them to the broken pile on the floor, Tenino seemed satisfied.

Once again, he sat by John.

"I've been following you because I know eventually they'll come to get you and whatever it is that your father left. They have to. It's the only thing that's keeping them from getting away with the whole deal."

"What deal?"

"Your father and I grew up together. He was like another brother for me. Papa treated him like family. He was a lot like me, though. Some of the things the family did, he didn't want to know about. He had a family of his own; you and your mother, and he didn't want to get involved. It was rough then. We were all getting started. But I didn't want it either. We used to talk about how we would stay out of it and we would be okay, but they killed my father and my brother…" He stopped for a minute, "And your father and mother, too."

"What?" It was an accident. His parents had an accident.

"It was a time when our family was very close to Hoffa and the union, but things were getting hot, they were starting to look at what we were doing with the money. Still, things were going pretty good. But Papa decided that it would be better if maybe Hoffa disappeared. I was running Harborside, taking it straight. So, it was decided that I should not be part of what they were going to do. I knew about it, but not all the details."

"And my dad?"

"Johnny was a big part of it. As a matter of fact, he was the key. It was decided that if they could make it look like Hoffa had been murdered, a lot of the heat that Kennedy and those shits at the Justice Department started would finally go away. We figured they were just trying to make a name and using Jimmy to do it. He's gone, so are the headlines."

John had to agree that so far it made sense. Benny continued.

"If we could make it look like someone else did it, all the better. So, in 1975, we set up the meeting..."

"At the restaurant?" John interrupted. It was one of those things that everybody knew.

"Yes."

For the next fifteen minutes Benito Tenino explained to John what some of the most connected Mafiosi didn't even know. He told him about the war with the Domati Family and how it escalated from the trucking industry to the casinos in Las Vegas. About loans from the pension fund. About the set up at the Red Fox restaurant and how, with Hoffa's help, they targeted Vincenzo Domati, but he never arrived. And he told John the details and specifics of the plan to hide Hoffa and cover the trail forever.

"...that's when Swain brought your father into it. He said Johnny could change a body, make it someone else. They figured if they had to, they could always let it be found."

"...in my lawn?"

Benny began to explain the treachery. "No, that wasn't the deal. My brother had it set up so that one of Domati's men, Dominic Baglia, would pick up the body and take it...well, somewhere else. It was a good plan.

"This Baglia guy thought it was Hoffa?" John asked.

"That's what he was told."

"What happened?"

"When my brother Michael went to leave the van for Baglia, he was ambushed. Nobody was supposed to be there. In fact, we didn't even tell anybody where the van with the dead guy would be. Michael was gonna do that later, after he was safe. But, they already knew. That same morning, Papa and me were fishing over in Mitchell's Bay, across the lake on the Canadian side, when Domati himself showed up with his fucks..." Benny could barely say the words, "...and butchered my father as I watched."

"Oh, my God." John knew that this information would have a price, but so far Tenino hadn't asked for anything and he wanted to know more. "Why is all of this happening now?"

"I couldn't do anything to them. I have my own wife and children and now grandchildren. They threatened to kill them. I run a legitimate business so my kids won't have to get involved in this kind of shit. If you retaliate, it never ends. They would have been sucked in too. But then, a couple of weeks ago, there was a letter from this scum Baglia, that the FBI has. I know. I have people in there, friends. That's what led them to your house here and the body, which, by itself doesn't matter, at least not to me. But when I found out what your dad had done, John, I knew this was my chance. I knew they figured out they could be exposed, and they would come after you.

John glanced at the hands and wondered if Tenino had seen them or knew what they were. "So you've been watching?"

His answer came quickly, "Yeah...waiting for you to find the bum's finger. So we could use it to get to that lying union bastard, and to Domati, who will die for my father, and to that prick Doran who arranged for my brother and for your parents, and who betrayed us all, who can't hide anymore."

Benny smiled, pointing toward the kitchen, directly at the hands, "And now that you have it, we can get on with it."

16

Twenty-five minutes had passed. Shelby still wasn't back. Tenino continued and John's head ached with information and knowledge of the facts of Hoffa's disappearance. Things he never wanted to know. Everything Christine had told him to fear was true, and what she feared most, the threat from Domati, was closer than ever. Benny Tenino explained that there was over seven hundred million dollars at stake in the union pension fund alone and, as they had planned, almost seventeen million more that had disappeared along with Hoffa. This money was to be divided between Hoffa and Antonio Tenino and used to fight the war in the west against the Domatis and drive them out of the lucrative gaming industry. Without it, the Teninos could not protect their own interests and ultimately were driven out themselves.

While it was true that several of the Tenino union people had remained in office, their authority was severely diminished. Many privately alleged that Hoffa's own son and other members of his extended family were excessively cooperative with the Domatis after his disappearance, even to the extent that union funds were made available to them for their operations. This lead to speculation of complicity, but once more, there was no proof.

According to Benny, Hoffa was greedy. He had seen an opportunity to keep all the money and lose costly partners at the same time. He knew he would never run the union again. So he chose to betray the trust of the man who had lifted him up from the beginning, Antonio Tenino, his business partner and friend, in favor of his own singularly selfish ends.

As he listened, dozens of questions were spinning through John's mind, but one was most disturbing, "So, if that's not Hoffa they found out there, where the hell is he?"

"That's what you're gonna help me find out, John." Benny took another sip, emptying the glass.

Wham! Another shot from Holloway's Retreat. The water glass hit the floor. Benny instinctively started to get up, but realizing what it was, sat back down. "That guy's gonna kill somebody."

"At least he keeps the reporters away. It's probably my wife, coming back from town."

"Listen John, there are things we have to do, that I want you to do." This was the price tag that John expected, "You have to get them here, the sooner the better. You have to let them know what you have. We'll have plenty of help, don't worry." He stood up to leave. John could hear Shelby coming up the steps. "You just let them know."

The door opened. The scent of Cuba. "We already know, Benny." Both men were shocked to hear Frank Doran's soft voice, as unmistakable as his cigar smoke, and struck by fear as he began to give orders, "Stay right there, both of you." His command was punctuated by the automatic pistol he pointed at Tenino, its long barrel extended by the silencer. "In fact, why don't you have a seat."

John protested, "Listen, whatever you think you're going to gain by..."

"Sit the fuck down," Doran insisted. He walked slowly into the room, chewing the butt. "Benny, what the hell is wrong with you? You are such a dumbshit. Don't you see what's going on here? If you wouldn't have said anything, I bet I could have gotten Mr.

Russel to give me what I need without having to kill him. But now, what you've done is make sure it won't happen that way."

The reality of this statement was numbing. John prayed that Shelby would not return. His eyes searching the cottage for a weapon, a distraction, something he could do to escape. But there was nothing.

Then Benito Tenino did the dumbest thing of his life, although it may not have mattered. He reached for his gun, by habit, forgetting that it was not there. For an instant, he touched his empty holster. His eyes sad but resolute and somehow peaceful as he faced his destiny. Benny Tenino looked up. He was staring at John when Doran's bullet exploded through the side of his head.

John saw the barrel begin to turn toward him and, more of instinct than of heroism, jumped from his chair, leaping across the space toward the kitchen. He grabbed the heavy platinum statue from the countertop and threw it as hard as he could at Doran's head. Doran fired, but flinched badly, the shot tearing wildly into the ceiling. The praying hands had caught him squarely on his forehead and he fell, groggy, to the floor beside Tenino. John rushed across the room and grabbed Doran's weapon. He was ready to run when he remembered the statue. He leaned down to pick it up and when he did, he heard the faint moaning of the nearly unconscious FBI agent. He felt the gun in his hand and he stopped, frozen at the door. His fingertips played over the machined steel. There, lying helpless at his feet, was the man who was responsible for his parents' deaths. He thought for just the slightest moment of using the gun once more, but seeing its disgusting effects, the blood gushing out of Benny Tenino, and the cold vacant look in this friendly Italian's dark eyes, he couldn't.

Out the door. There was Tenino's car. Take it and run. Before Doran comes after him. He had to find Shelby. They had to get to Christine and tell her what had happened. John jumped into the black Ford. No keys. Shit. He left the gun on the front seat and ran back to the cottage. As he entered, Frank Doran was on his hands and knees. John cocked his leg and kicked him as hard as he could solidly in the midsection. Doran moaned once more with pain, collapsing back onto the floor.

Tenino's blood was everywhere and John nearly slipped as he stopped next to the body. He searched the pockets of the man's jacket and found the keys.

He drove quickly down the driveway and out to the road, a cloud of clay gravel dust behind him. Something in the road. He slammed the brakes down. The dust caught up with him and engulfed the car, making it difficult to see what it was. John got out to take a better look. He gagged, physically repulsed when he realized that it was his neighbor, Bill Holloway, lying face down in the dirt, his salt-filled shotgun beside him. There was one bullet hole in the back of his head and his hair was singed from the closeness of the discharge.

John held back his sickness and, taking a firm hold around each of Halloway's ankles, dragged him out of the way.

He drove north on M-22, speeding toward Leland, looking for Shelby. His mind was filled with mush. He had no idea what to do next. He looked over at the seat and realized that this was the murder weapon, the gun that had killed two people. What the hell would they say. Doran would say that he did it, that he went berserk. The whole damn FBI would be after him. John felt his foot sliding on the pedals. The blood. It was all over the floor. "Jesus."

Ahead, approaching, a car, his car. Shelby. John flashed the headlights repeatedly to get her attention, but it looked as though she would drive right past him. He couldn't let her go there. He had to stop her. He glanced in the mirror. No one. John locked the brakes, throwing the vehicle into a spin no more than fifty yards in front of her. His own tire's squealing joined with Shelby's as she tried to stop. She veered onto the shoulder, sliding to a stop.

John was out of the Ford. He rushed to meet her. "Shelby, you can't go to the cottage. Turn around. Turn around," he called from the middle of the street. She was out of the car, shocked.

She could see the bloody foot prints he left on the pavement, "What's going on, John? What happened?"

He held her tightly and whispered, "You have to go, Shel, you have to go back and get Kellet." He was breathing hard. He heard another car coming and saw it in the distance. He crammed in what he could, "Shel, Doran's there and Tenino, Benny Tenino, and Holloway, he's dead."

"What? Dead? What do you mean?"

"Just go back. Now. And tell the sheriff." He kissed her hard on the lips and pushed her away, "Go now, Shel," he said as the car came closer. He did not want to be seen. He needed this time to think. The Ford was blocking the road. He had to move it.

"Where are you going, Junior?" Shelby was dumbfounded, "What are you going to do?" she called after him. There were sirens in the distance.

"I'll find you," he yelled as he got back into Tenino's car. "I'll call Christine." He slammed the door and spun the car around. He headed south to M-204 and turned toward the center of the county. The siren drew closer. He saw it race past in the rear view. An EMS unit. Thank God.

He realized he would have to get off the main roads. He knew this county. He turned left, heading north into the rolling hills and cherry farms. His mind was a dizzying funnel of unwanted information. A vortex tugging at him, sucking his life down the drain. He would have to get rid of Tenino's car. He drove slowly, zig-zagging through the orchards, traveling on dirt paths that the farmers used primarily to access the most remote sections of their fields. He was careful not to raise too much dust.

The paths were all connected, John recalled, in a large matrix of tiny nameless arteries and, if one knew the way, he could traverse the entire area. He was thankful for many years of summers here and delighted that his memory of the terrain remained so vivid.

He worked his way northward, through the county, until again he came to the road that circled the penninsula, to M-22 between Northport and Leland, and he stopped. When he was sure it was clear, he darted across the main highway and snaked through the woods, to Johnson Road.

Again, after checking carefully, he gunned the accelerator and lunged out onto the blacktop. Sirens. Thankfully, not too close. Not yet. He only had an eighth of a mile to go. The noise was getting closer. Then, there it was. On the right, grown over and barely distinguishable, the gravel access road. He locked the brakes and spun in, bouncing badly over the rough drive. The sirens were close now, coming from the north, from Northport, racing to Leland. John pulled off into the weeds just over a grassy mound where he hoped he would be hidden, and waited. It was only seconds, but they were eternal. He rested his forehead on the steering wheel and drifted. Oh, sweet Shelby, how could this ever happen?

The first car sped past, then another, each with its deafening wail, both lower now and decreasing in frequency after they passed. John could breath again. Certainly, Shelby would be able to convince Bob Kellet that John had nothing to do with the murders at Duck Lake. Christine would be helping. Maybe he should go back there, to Leland, to the sheriff's office.

But there was not much a local sheriff could do, John reasoned, especially when Doran had the resources of the FBI and probably Keenan in his pocket, too. John decided he could not take the chance. He drove on.

He remembered this property. Once, he had even thought of buying it. He also remembered one of the reasons he didn't.

The parcel was approximately fifty acres, give or take. It was high, and at the top of the biggest hill, you could see Lake Michigan and Pyramid Point to the southwest, twenty miles in the distance. Looking east, you could see the bay. There were a couple of old barns and a small cherry orchard down by the road, and a partially excavated hillside where a previous owner had used the part of the property as a small quarry to dig sand and gravel, but that enterprise, like the orchard, had long since been abandoned. The main reason John had decided against this parcel was just ahead, in a pine thicket at the bottom of a natural bowl in the center of the hilly acreage. He had noticed, some years earlier, that this had become what amounted to an illegal dump, its chief attraction inaccessibility and camouflage created by the mature trees. Locals had left kitchen appliances, farm equipment, and, most frightening to John, many unmarked barrels, which had, over time, rusted and disintegrated, leaking their dubious contents into the soil. There were also many abandoned vehicles, John recalled.

Soon, there would be another.

He parked at the top of the hill, gathered the gun and the praying hands from the front seat, and rolled the window on the driver's side all the way down. When he got out, he checked his pockets to make sure the chemicals were there.

He searched the rocky ground until he found a stone of sufficient weight, and, wedged it between the center console and the gas pedal. The large engine began to whine with power. John reached in, snapped the gearshift into drive, and jumped aside.

The thought of explosion never occurred to him, being inexperienced at this sort of thing. But, as he watched the car lunging down the hillside, headed for the pile of junk, he realized it was a real possibility.

Thankfully, there was none. Instead, the old black Ford bounced, dancing to the right and back to the left, ever more violently, moving faster away, until finally, unable to maintain its course, in a last gasp of life, it bounced sideways and up and spun in circles in the air, like a great Olympic high diver, eventually landing on its roof and collapsing in the heap of other cars in the rusty pool of metallic debris. The engine raced for a moment and stopped. And, except for the wind, and a faint repetitive echo of the crash, it was quiet.

Two hundred yards away, in the new silence, stood John Russel. He looked down from the highest point of land, feeling the growing heat from the August sun, his face cooled by the breeze that lifted up fresh from the blue water below; comforted briefly by the momentary peace that surrounded him; forgetting for an instant the sad reality that he now was, by any definition, a fugitive.

17

The explosion at the MacNamera Building had eliminated the wall between Charlie Keenan's front office and the adjacent storage closet where the blast was detonated. From the hall, he could see that the outside wall was also missing. He felt the warm air from the alley blowing in. The area had been cordoned off with yellow tape. Charley ducked under and made his way to what had been the door to his outer office. Only the left side remained, supported by the marble facing. To the right there was daylight and a mound of shattered rock. The contents of the storage closet, the pails and mops had been propelled to the left side of the room and added to a much larger heap containing all of his old office furniture.

He felt the crunch of small debris under his shoes as he carefully entered. He could see that, amazingly, his primary office was intact with the exception of some toppled filing cabinets presumably jostled to the floor by the concussion, their drawers open and papers scattered. There were several wrappers from fast food items lying in the dusty rectangles where they had been. His desk lamp had fallen, as had his phone. He picked it up, and after pushing the button on the cradle heard its tone, still alive. He replaced it on the desk and started to organize other misplaced items, but soon realized the absurdity of his pursuit. He would not be working in this room for some time.

The big leather chair, his chair, stood as it had before, squarely behind the desk, as much a friend as any over the fifteen or so years they had been together. Charley sat. He surveyed the destruction around him and returned his focus to the situation.

He pulled the list that Christine had given him, the list of bank accounts, from his jacket pocket. It was nearly impossible for him to fathom the implications if what she had told him were true. It meant that Frank Doran was indisputably corrupt and, in his position, dangerous. It was easy to understand Christine's concern for the Russels.

All the money. So many accounts. All the time they had been working together outlined so precisely in this parade of dates. He wondered if Frank had been on Domati's payroll all along, back as far as the Eastern Market, when the two men were photographed together. He had never suspected Frank.

Keenan carefully folded the paper and returned it to his pocket. He knew he would have to stop Doran and do it as soon as possible. But how? Domati had a long reach. There was no way to know how far. It was within reason that his influence could extend far beyond Doran to others within the FBI, the courts, and Justice Department.

He rose from the comfortable old chair and walked across to the fallen file cabinets. The first step was to get the files on the Domati family. There were many. Charley knelt down next to the scattered folders scooping documents back inside.

"Need some help?" Agent Morse was standing where his doorway had been.

"Karen, thanks. I'm just trying to get a few things back together, some files I can review at home at least."

She knelt down to help. "It's pretty bad when they start blowing up our own offices."

"So it's no accident."

"Doesn't look like it."

"Where's Frank?" Keenan asked, trying to be as matter of fact as possible, "One little bomb and that Yankee's nowhere to be found."

Karen laughed, "Actually he's up north, in Leland. I've been looking for you. We requested a warrant for the Russels. As a matter of fact, we've already got her at the sheriff's office up there. He took off."

"Oh my God. What happened?"

"Russel; he shot Benny Tenino. Frank tried to stop him. Overpowered him. Took his gun."

"Tenino? What the hell?" Charley was shocked. He stared at Agent Morse hoping for more details. It didn't make sense.

"That's all I know. We've got a special response team on the way."

As quickly as he could, he jammed the papers back into the folders. He grabbed all of the ones he could find that dealt with Domati. Without saying a word he maneuvered his nearly three-hundred pound frame to a standing position, his kneecaps crackling under the pressure.

Before Karen Morse knew what was happening, he had ducked under the tape. "Charley?" she called after him, but he was moving as fast as she had ever seen him move and already at the top of the stairs. "Charley?" she yelled more loudly.

He did not dare alert her to his suspicions. Faintly, she heard the echoed reply, "Call me at home."

He was gone.

He reached the bottom of the stairs and bolted to the pay phones across the deserted lobby. Frantically, he searched his pockets for change and the card that Christine Ferrand had given him. Finding both, he cradled the file folders between his knees and dialed.

"Ferrand, Mascio, Stein, & Swain."

"Hello. Yes. Christine Ferrand, please," he huffed, out of breath.

"Just a moment, sir."

After what seemed a long time, Christine answered.

"Chrisitine, it's Charley, Charley Keenan..."

"I'm glad you called. Where are you? What the hell is going on over there?"

"Nothing really. They've evacuated the building. What the hell is goin' on with the Russels? You're boy John is in a shitpot of trouble."

"I know. I just spoke to Mrs. Russel. She's in custody in Leland. I'm on my way up there. There's a seven-twenty."

"Don't go yet, I'm on my way to your office." He hung up. It was already four-thirty.

As he had since the body was found, to avoid the ever swelling gang of news people at the front door, he made his way down to the basement and out through an unmarked service door into the alley. But this time, he was spotted.

"Hey, it's Keenan," a voice yelled. Seconds later a throng of reporters rounded the corner. He was defenseless and surrounded, but he pushed ahead, fighting them off with terse 'no comments' and 'nothing to say at this time'. Eventually, he pried the door open against the bodies and entered the relative safety of his car. He was dripping with perspiration, this being much more exercise than was usual. He blasted the air conditioning and felt its flow of heated air, wet but still cooling, as the compressor went to work. Slowly, he rolled out through the crowd to the street. Gaining speed he left the mayhem behind.

It wasn't long before he arrived at the Buhl Building and Christine's office. He entered the underground lot and parked near Swain's private elevator. He took the Domati files that he had rescued from his office and secured them in his briefcase. Certain to lock the car, he approached the stainless steel door. To the right, in the cinder block wall, was an intercom speaker and a button. He knew the procedure from previous meetings at the firm and, without hesitation pushed it. Aided by hidden camera, the receptionist confirmed his identity, and the door opened.

The elevator began to move and soon the door opened again to the green marble lobby of the firm and Christine's greeting.

"Is everybody okay over there? I've been watching the news." Her blond hair bounced randomly over the shoulders of her casual button-down shirt as she crossed to meet the prosecutor.

"Oh, don't you even worry yourself for one little moment, everybody's fine." Charley gently took her outstretched hand.

"They're saying it was deliberate, a bomb." She motioned toward the conference room, "C'mon in here. We've got a couple hours before we have to go. Can I get you something?"

"Aw no, Chris, I'm fine, thanks."

There was a hired guard posted at the main door to the hall, where the rumble of the press was growing louder. Occasionally one of the assemblage would courageously attempt to open the door, only to be turned back by the security man.

"Donut?" Anticipating his answer, she nodded to the receptionist who immediately went off to get the pastry.

"Maybe one. Thanks."

In the large room, Keenan found a comfortable spot at the far end of the oversized table. He threw the seersucker jacket over the back and sat where he could look out over the hot city. It felt good to be down to his white shirt and suspenders and cooling in the air conditioning.

Christine had stopped as promised at the Wayne medical library on the way back to her office. And, using the identification numbers Shelby had given her earlier, she located the records and made copies of the pages that seemed significant. She had guessed, correctly, that even if the photograph and bank account numbers hadn't convinced Charley Keenan of Doran's guilt, the deliberate explosion must have. She saw no reason not to share the information with the prosecutor.

She had laid all of the pertinent documents out on the conference table, and, after Charley was served with donut and coffee and the receptionist had left, Christine swung the large door tightly closed, standing at the opposite end of the room, she began.

"I'm glad you called, Charley, I was going to call you anyway after I found out what had happened at the Russel's cottage. I gotta believe that there's no way you can possibly feel that my clients are involved in any illegal activity."

"The FBI seems to have their own opinion," Keenan offered.

"But there's no way in hell you'll ever get an indictment."

"The problem is as far as anyone knows, Russel is a dangerous felon who attacked a Federal agent and took off. Plus they want him on murder, for Tenino. Doran's gonna swear he saw your boy do it."

"Who do you think shot Tenino? From the sheriff's description of the scene, there's one bullet in the ceiling…at the back of the room, away from the door. Sounds to me like someone came in shooting. Besides, if my guy is good enough to drop Tenino with one shot square in the head, how the hell could he miss Frank Doran? If he wanted to kill him, why didn't he? He could have." She was pacing back and forth between the bookcases and the conference table.

"You know as well as I do, Chris, that there's no way to know for sure what happened. I know what you'd like to believe…"

"C'mon, Charley," she interrupted, leaning on her closed fists on the mahogany, staring wide with her deadly blue eyes.

He turned on the southern charm, "…please don't misunderstand me, I think you're probably right. But what we have to do now is get this animal to slow down a little so we can catch up to it. You can't sneak up on a bear when it's runnin'."

Christine took a deep breath, surrendering to the down home metaphor, "What do you suggest?" She sat next to him at the table.

"Well, I think the Leelanau County jail might be the best place for the Russels. At least then we'd have a shot at getting to them before Frank takes them away to God knows where. Until I figure out who to call on my end, the sheriff is prob'ly our best bet. Do you have any way to get hold of John Russel?"

"No. He could be anywhere. But Shelby...Mrs. Russel, thinks he will try to contact me at some point. He has to."

"Good. If he does, let's get him to come in, to the sheriff's office, by that time we'll be up there. Do you think we can trust the sheriff?"

"I had my investigator do some background. He seems real clean."

"Good. Let's give him a call, shall we?" Keenan devoured the better part of a jelly donut. Christine reached to the phone in the center of the table, dragged it closer, and dialed. "What's his name?" he mumbled, still chewing. Christine held up her index finger while someone answered on the other end.

"Hi, this is Christine Ferrand. Is Sheriff Kellet there?" On hold, she responded, "Bob Kellet; county native; ex-marine...Bob, hi, it's Christine Ferrand again. How's Mrs. Russel doing? Good. Listen, I have Prosecutor Keenan from the Justice Department here in my office and I was wondering if you might have a minute to talk to him. Good. Thanks Bob. Here he is, Charley Keenan." She handed the receiver to Charley with an introduction, "Bob Kellet." She listened intently to Charley's end of the conversation as the two men talked.

As always Keenan began with his disarming charm, "Hey Bob, how y'all doin' up there in cherry country? Good. Good. Yes, I know, and it's kind of a tricky situation. Christine will be there tonight, but I'd appreciate it if you wouldn't mention that to anyone, anyone at all. Oh good, thank you. This being a federal case and all, it may be difficult for you to assert yourself in this next area, but if you could try, it would be helpful. I've got pretty good reason to believe that Mrs. Russel may be in real danger and you, by keeping her there if you can, could really help; at least 'til we get the whole picture sorted out." He winked at Chris, "Well that's great Sheriff. We certainly do appreciate it. Thank you." He handed the phone back to Christine.

"Thanks, Bob. Are you going to be around later? Okay. I'll talk to you then. Good-bye."

"Thanks Charley."

Keenan was curious about the papers, "What's all this?"

"They're copies of research records from the medical center library; from Wayne. Pretty much every experiment or study they have ever performed is there. It helps with grants, when they're up for funding."

"And they have something to do with the Hoffa case?"

"They could have everything to do with it. In fact after reviewing these pages, I'm not even sure this is the Hoffa case. Here, let me show you." Christine arranged the copies so they both could easily see them. She slid her chair closer. "It starts here on July fifteenth, 1975, fifteen days before Hoffa disappeared. This one describes a subject, one B.M. Wilson, his initial physical condition, his appearance, sixty-three, Caucasian, etcetera. Then, these other pages, dated sequentially over the next two weeks, clearly document the deterioration of his blood system by way of intense chemotherapy and radiation, the effects on his vital organs, specific drugs that were used, and, at the end, when he was almost dead, a marrow transplant from an unnamed donor." Christine waited to see if the prosecutor had made a connection. He shrugged his shoulders. He had not. She directed his attention to the top of the first page, "Each researcher, the person conducting the experiment, began each log with his initials. Here they are for this one, next to the identification number." She read, "JAR/MD; Dr. John Albert Russel;...John Russel's father."

"Let me see that." Charley's interest was piqued. He examined the page carefully.

"Okay? Now go back here to the end of the section and you'll find that Dr. Russel designated the donor as 'H1' and eventually referred to the recipient, Wilson, not by his own initials, but as 'H2'. And here's the real kicker. On the last page, identified as witnesses are the following initials: HS, AT, MT, and finally FD." Christine paused momentarily, then went on, "My father, Henry Swain, the Teninos, Antonio and Michael..."

"...and Frank Doran," Charley Keenan finished the sentence. There was no way this set of letters, which corresponded so perfectly to those names, could coincidentally show up in one of Dr. Russels logs.

"Look at the date, when the 'experiment' ended." Christine pointed to the bottom of the last page as Keenan read.

"30 July, 1975."

"The day of the Hoffa disappearance."

"Exactly."

"So what do you make of it?"

"I'll tell you Charley, this is a bit rough for me, we haven't even had the funeral yet and I'm already implicating my dad in a criminal conspiracy," Christine stopped briefly, struggling to contain her swelling emotions, "It looks like these men, my father included, conspired with the doctor to fake Hoffa's abduction and create a body that could be mistaken for Hoffa's and that they could produce if necessary. It seems pretty bizarre, if you look through there, there are dozens of references to changing blood type and DNA. I called a doctor I use a lot as an expert witness and asked him. He said that without a doubt, it is possible. In fact these days its pretty well documented; they're doing so many of 'em. And that's what happens, the blood type can change. I also found out that twenty years ago the transplant procedure described here was not approved or accepted as standard medical practice, although many at that time were researching such a possibility using animals. I know Russel was. Suppose one day there's an opportunity to use a human subject. I gotta believe it would be pretty hard to resist. Of course with his obligation to the Teninos, I don't suppose that he could have refused if he'd wanted to, but I can also see where he may not have done it against his will either. But typical of the researcher that Dr. Russel was, he couldn't help documenting his findings. Otherwise, from his point of view the whole procedure would be a waste of time."

"Not to mention, when he figured out what this was really about, it was a damn good way to cover his butt," Keenan laughed briefly, "But Doran and the Teninos? That evidence of yours puts him smack in Domati's pocket. It seems like an odd group, though. It doesn't fit."

"I know." This was one area that still puzzled Chris. "Maybe you could help me piece that together."

"You said that these records are from Wayne? Doesn't that mean that anybody could get ahold of them?"

"Absolutely. But you'd have to know exactly where to look. They're catalogued by experiment numbers *followed* by the dates. If you didn't have the first number you'd be out of luck."

"How did you find them?"

Christine explained the discovery in Greydog's cave and how Shelby had deciphered the numbers from the doctor's journal pages.

"The odd thing to me," Charley began, "Is who benefited most. I mean if the Tenino family was behind the abduction whether real or not, you would think they would have come out better. The old man was killed the next morning, and his son Michael that same night; both executed. It doesn't make sense."

"Unless one of the group betrayed the rest."

"And you think that's Doran?"

"I know the date of the first deposit corresponds to that time frame. I know my dad had no use for him; and never trusted him. Why else would he keep such a close watch on Doran for the last twenty years?"

She made a strong case. Keenan could not refute any of it. He opened his briefcase and handed Christine the Domati files he had rescued from his office. "These are my files on Domati. I've been over them a thousand times. There are notes from various interviews. There's stuff on Baglia. Most of it is there. I can probably tell you from memory what each of them says. You're welcome to look it all over."

To Christine, this was the final proof that Keenan could be trusted. She let down a little. A small puddle of salty tears was rising in her eyes.

"Thank you, Charley. I really needed for you to believe me." She was crying, "I'm sorry, it's not very professional..."

Charlie reached back into the breast pocket of his sport coat and produced a clean white linen handkerchief. Gently, he dabbed her tears from either side of her nose and pressed the material into her hand.

She laughed nervously, slightly embarrassed, "I feel like an idiot. It's just that Henry was my father and to believe he could do this..."

Charley leaned over and embraced her. He knew it could be no substitute for the hugs from a true father, but he tried nonetheless to console her. As her head rested on his large shoulder, he whispered, "I know what its like to lose somebody. It's okay to feel like shit. As far as I knew, Henry Swain was a respectable man; never made me a promise that he didn't keep." He lifted her head and, with two fingers under her tear soaked chin, looked directly into her glistening blue eyes, "Now, let's just forget we ever had this talk and get to the business at hand before anyone else gets hurt. You go on and take care of your clients, and I'll get on with what has to be done here."

"Thank you, Charley."

18

Before the wheels on Benny Tenino's car had even stopped spinning, John realized how ridiculous and dangerous his situation had become. He couldn't stay there in plain view, but he couldn't keep running either. He had no business with an automatic weapon and, if any of Doran's men were to come upon him, they would shoot him without asking many questions.

He walked quickly down the hill, cradling both the platinum hands and the gun in his folded arms. There was a sharp pain that began to prick his right thigh. The acid. Leaking. The seam on the bottom of his pants pocket was soaked. He dodged rocks and brambles as he made his way to the junk heap in the miniature valley at the bottom. Two dozen or so barrels, all decaying to varying degrees, were interspersed throughout the pile. He found one with its top rusted through completely and dropped the pistol inside.

He could hear a crackling sound near him; the unmistakable sound of electricity. Tenino's car. There was a smell. Gasoline. It dripped from the overturned vehicle. There were tiny explosive drops riding down the steel rocker panels, moving ever closer to the hot engine and worse, the arcing battery.

"Jesus," John's eyes widened. He turned away and started to run. More crackling from the Ford. He ran, now full speed, leaping over the tall dry grass toward the road. He was almost to the edge of the property fifty yards from the car, when it blew.

Rusted shrapnel whizzed past his head. Then, as if a hand had tossed him across the field, he was airborne, ten feet or more. The waves of heat from behind him pushed him even higher, flipping completely over himself until he came to rest, prone, on his back, disoriented. The final flame, an inch above the buttons on his pressed, pinstriped shirt, blew over him as he lay motionless and confused. The fire jumped skyward, igniting a half acre stand of eighty year old pine. The trees erupted in a huge orange torch one hundred feet high and sucked the wind from the ground around him up with it .

He shook his head to clear the shock and felt, almost immediately a prickly sensation. The small plastic bottle was leaking more. The liquid burned at his leg. The hands. Where were the hands? He spun to his knees surveying frantically, the blowing, burning landscape. There, several feet from where he had landed, a glint of sun reflected through the smoke. He crawled head on into the artificial squall. The heat was growing unbearable. The field grass had begun to burn in a line, moving toward him and the statue. He raced to recover the sculpture, reaching as far as his arm would allow, until, finally he felt the metal. Crushing it into his palm, he stood up again and ran from the fire, leaving the black petroleum smoke billowing upward behind him.

He made it to M-22 and, without looking, raced across the dark blacktop on a dead run, through several hundred yards of cherry orchard to the relative safety of the thick woods beyond. He could hear the sirens again closing distance. Finally at the edge of the forest, out of sight in the cool shade, he rested for a moment. John struggled to regain his breath and felt what was now searing, sharp pain on the top of his leg reminding him that if too much of the chemical escaped he would not be able to dissolve the platinum hands. He reached carefully into the pocket and withdrew the bottle. Only a small amount had spilled. The liquid burned his fingers and he dropped it to the ground. He grabbed the pocket itself and tore it from the inside of his pants and, kneeling, he carefully wrapped the plastic jar in the fabric.

When he did, he noticed another liquid dripping from behind his right calf. Blood. Fresh and red. His own, mixing with the dried brown stains from Benny Tenino. He leaned back, looking over his shoulder at the wound. Some of the flying steel had caught him in the muscle and ripped a gash of flesh several inches long. He would need to stop the flow.

John tore a long strip of denim from his frayed jeans and fashioned a bandage, wrapping the material around his leg.

He looked back across the highway. Where he had been standing, only seconds before, was now a white hot inferno. Sparks from the pine branches rose hundreds of feet in the air, a huge smoke signal, and John knew the message, "Hey, Doran, here I am. Why not just come out here and kill me?"

In minutes the FBI *was* on the way. The increasing volume of the sirens was joined by a larger roar, its pulsating low frequency building as it moved closer. The ground began to shake and more wind, swirling the tops of the evergreen branches over John's head, sending pine needles flying and dead branches crashing through the timber. His hearing, deadened by the percussive explosion, had barely returned, only to be challenged again by the approaching machine. He covered his head, ducking low in a fetal position. The huge helicopter stormed overhead, then slowly moved away toward the hill on the property on the other side of the road, and descended as if to land.

Four feet off the ground, with engines adjusted to hover, eight men, dressed in full combat gear jumped out into the steep downspray of the blades and hustled double-time to a position on the side of the small hill. John could see the vests with large yellow lettering 'FBI' on their chests. Their black helmets were dull in the late sunlight and their faces were painted dark. In addition to several other weapons, each had a rifle with a scope.

Satisfied the SWAT team had been safely deployed, the huge transport began to rise, mercifully moving away this time to the northeast, over the bay.

The fear was like a blanket, covering John, warm, suffocating, and making it hard for him to breathe. They were after him. He had to move now. He had to get as far away from Doran's men as he could. He picked up the statue and the cloth-wrapped bottle and started walking. Deeper into the woods.

The brush grew more dense, which, though it made for difficult travel, John considered good. It would make it much harder to spot him. He could tell he was moving south, more or less, from the position of the low sun. He could still see, behind him, now far in the distance, a small, flat cloud of smoke spreading high above the trees, bending the sun's waning light into a rich sunset.

He doubted whether he could stay out here all night. They would find him. He knew they weren't far. The best course of action was to try to get in touch with Shelby and Christine. He had to turn himself in. Bob Kellet was a substantially better alternative than being captured by the FBI or worse, by Doran who would surely kill him. His cut leg was throbbing. His feet hurt. Cole Haan loafers were not for hiking. But he dared not stop.

Occasionally, as he walked, he would surprise animals, not accustomed to human intrusion; a pheasant bursting upward at his feet; squirrels scurrying away; and he would stop, listening, waiting for the silence to return. Each time he could feel the instant blast of adrenaline, rushing through him, wasting precious heartbeats.

It was during one of these pauses that he heard a different, rhythmic crunch of dry twigs behind him. Something large was moving toward him, following him through the dark pines. John stood completely still as the sound grew slightly louder. As quietly as possible he slowly knelt into a crouch. He didn't even breathe, so consumed was he with the diminishing distance of the sound, its volume now nearly as loud as his heart. He flinched when, suddenly, hawks in the trees directly above him scattered, sensing the approach, leaving only John Russel to confront this new intruder, realizing that this could be the last moment of his life. And Shelby. He wondered about Shelby.

He turned his head, slowly, hardly moving at all, and rose to peek, just an inch from his crouched position. He could see nothing, but he could hear the twigs breaking not more than ten feet away. It was the only sound left. It could be a deer or a wild turkey, John reasoned, there were many in this part of the county. He lifted his head a little more, but ducked quickly back down. It also could be Frank Doran.

John felt faint and a little sick. He closed his eyes, hoping whatever it was would go away. He felt a warm breeze across the hairs on the back of his neck. Breath. Jesus.

"Hi."

"Aaaaaahhhh!" John vaulted to his feet, screaming. In two giant steps he had traveled ten yards, dropping the bottle and platinum sculpture in the leaves. He spun around to see who it was. "Jesus. Fuck. Why don't you just scare the holy shit outta me?"

"Too many visitors?" Joey Greydog asked, grinning at John through the trees.

"Yeah, no shit. What are you doing? How did you find me?"

"It wasn't hard."

John was returning to a normal metabolism, "You can help me. I have to get to Leland." John moved closer and spoke in a quiet voice, "I have to get to the sheriff's office."

The Indian just smiled. John continued, "What the hell's the matter with you? Don't you hear what I'm saying? What? What do you want?" John could tell that this was Joey's way of bargaining. He was shrewd. The damn Indian knew he had John.

"I want what the warriors want. I want the visitors to leave."

"So, help me get to town. When I'm gone, they'll go, too."

"I could do that." He paused, smiling again, "You know the FBI men are less than a mile behind us. And they have dogs."

This was no more than a shakedown. "Look, I'll give you anything you want," John said.

"You have a boat. I've seen it. Joey Greydog needs a boat."

John would have given him his house, "Fine. Consider it yours. Can we get the hell outta here?" He scooped up the statue again and the bottle of leaking acid and started quickly off into the woods. Greydog stood still and watched for a moment before he interrupted, pointing in the opposite direction.

"We're going this way." He started walking.

It was obvious that the slippery Indian wasn't about to wait. Abruptly, John turned to follow him. They made their way through a quarter mile or so of thick brush, Greydog leading, until they emerged into a thicket. They crossed through the blanket of pine needles to a nearly hidden path which disappeared into the forest on the opposite side.

It was getting darker, but they were making good progress. John wished he had some idea where Joey was leading him. For all he knew he could be marching him straight into a federal prison.

By eight o'clock they had reached a familiar hill. "Isn't this...?"

"My cave. Yes." Joey answered, continuing up the hill to the well disguised entrance. "You can wait here. I will be back before dark."

"Back? What do you mean? Where are going?"

The Indian didn't answer. Instead he brushed back the branches at the entrance and motioned for John to go in. "You will have what you need here. There is water in those jugs." He pointed to one of the rough earthen shelves he had carved in the dirt. Here put this all over yourself." Joey held out a small plastic jar.

"What is it?" John laid the hands down at his feet and put the nitric acid beside them.

"Here. Just put it on."

John took the jar from him and twisted the lid open. The smell made him gag and nearly throw up. "Jesus. Uhh."

"Its wolf piss. The dogs won't come near it. Put it on. Hurry. I need it back."

John held his breath. An Indian must know something about such things, he thought. He began to pour the putrid substance on his shirt. It ran down for a moment over the starch until finally being absorbed, forming a dark yellow stain.

"More," Greydog insisted, "About half of it, then give it back."

John obediently distributed the liquid over his clothing and handed the remainder back to Greydog. The smell filled the small area and lifted up through the hole, Joey's makeshift chimney, taking the mosquitoes with it. They didn't want to go near it either.

Joey drizzled it on the ground as he backed toward the entrance. "You wait for me. I'm going to get a car. I'll be back before dark. But if I'm not, stay here. They will pass you. Be very quiet. I'll cover the entrance."

Before John could respond, he had disappeared again. He heard rustling branches, presumably as Joey tucked him in. The smell of the wolf urine was cloying and sour, and created an almost burning sensation in his nose. He pushed some small appliances aside and sat down on the clay bed that the Indian had sculpted into the far end of the cave. The hole above provided just enough dim light to see across the room. He could see Joey's odd collection of things had grown since the first time he had been here. There were several new garden implements; a new rake and a lawn spreader. At the end of what was really no more than a wide shelf where he was seated, he noticed there was a down comforter, undoubtedly pilfered from an unsuspecting summer resident. He spread it out over the dirt. He returned the hands to very nearly the same spot where they had been discovered in the first place and put the chemical next to them.

The urine smell had diminished or he was getting used to it. It was easier to take in any event. He lay down on the soft quilt. The wound on his leg had stopped bleeding, though it was sore and throbbing. He kicked his shoes off and his swollen feet pulsated with their own pain.

He was hiding in a cave covered with animal urine, an accused murderer, whose fate now clearly rested in the hands of an insane Indian. How does something like this happen?

He looked up at the hands praying, reflecting the smallest light from above, reassuring him that, if he made it through this, there was definitely a God. He closed his eyes, took a slow, deep pungent breath and waited for Joey Greydog's promised return.

19

John must have fallen asleep, but was quickly jarred back to consciousness. He sat up. The dogs. They were close. It was almost totally dark now inside, but he could see a slight circular glow through the hole. He could hear men's voices and branches breaking in the woods. Radios broadcast their distorted messages back and forth to one another, communicating the searchers' progress.

And John sat, motionless, listening.

He looked at his watch. It was nearly nine. Joey should return soon. John just had to hope that the FBI SWAT team would pass. Again his pulse buoyed by the adrenaline, raced. The men were right on top of him now, on the hillside over his head. Their voices were clear.

"Got anything?" one searcher asked.

"Nothing. It's like he disappeared. The dogs are running all over the place. We lost him."

Thank God. The wolf piss worked. Soon they would be gone.

John heard a cry directly over him, "Ahh, dammit." And before he knew what was happening, dirt and leaves fell from the opening followed by a man's booted foot. The man struggled to free himself from the hole. "Shit," John heard him say and another voice getting closer, "What is it? What happened? You all right?" The man was pulling frantically, trying to maneuver his boot back through the opening. "It's just a hole," he heard him say, "I'm fine." But John was taking no chances. If the guy looked down, he might see something. He scooped up some of the dirt and debris that had dislodged from the rim and piled it onto the dark comforter. Then as quietly as he could, John lifted it over his head, carefully so it wouldn't spill, and held it a few inches beneath the wiggling footwear.

John felt a whiff of air as the foot was freed and heard the man again, "There, jeez, fuckin' rabbit hole or somethin'. Let's go."

The two men talked, complaining about the incident, as they continued the search, their voices mercifully fading into the dusk. John shook the dirt from the cover and replaced it on the clay bed. "Where the hell was the Indian?" he thought. The last thing he wanted was to stay the night in Joey's cave. He could only wait.

He heard the occasional helicopter and, every once in awhile, a distant siren. At least for now, he was safe. Again, he checked the time; nine fifteen. There would be daylight enough to make it out of here for another twenty five minutes or so. After that, he might have to wait for dawn. The sooner he could get to the sheriff's office the better, though. He did not want to give Doran more time to find him.

There was rustling at the entrance. John stood, "Greydog?" More noise, "Greydog." A flashlight appeared followed by the Indian, carrying something. He threw the bundle to John.

"Put these on."

John caught the clothes, gray pants with a wide stripe of navy blue fabric stretching the length of the leg, sewn to the outer seam, and a light blue uniform shirt.

"I also brought you this." Joey handed him an official looking policeman's hat, gray, to match the trousers, with a shiny black patent leather brim.

John tossed the uniform on the bed, "Thanks. I didn't think you were coming back."

"You will learn to trust Joey. I have a car. We have to hurry."

John stripped to his underwear, dropping his rank smelling clothes to the ground. "The wolf stuff worked, I'll give you that."

"This will work, too. You'll see. Before you know it you'll be in a nice comfy jail." He obviously was speaking from experience.

A week ago this would not have sounded so inviting. He pulled on the pants and then the shirt. John noticed the patch with the Leelanau Shores Casino logo on the sleeve and another above the left breast pocket which said 'Casino Security' in bright red, embroidered letters over a white field. Searching the cluttered dirt room for a suitably reflective surface, he settled for the lid of a stainless steel cooking pot, which was propped upright on a clay shelf, to check his appearance. His features were exaggerated in the convex metal so that his well proportioned nose was grotesquely large. His dark wavy hair looked like a small fuzzy patch glued to an egg. He adjusted it as well as possible and stepped back to survey the rest of himself. It was hard to see with only Joey's flashlight beam lighting the cave, but he was sure about one thing.

"I hope I'm not supposed to pass for an Indian," he said, and placed the policeman's hat on his head. He gathered the statue and bottles from the ledge above the rough bed. "Let's get outta here."

Greydog turned to lead the way out. When he reached the entrance, he stopped. "Here." He handed John a second flashlight and turned the one he had been using off. Briefly checking the sky, he said, "If we're lucky we won't need them." Again, he was moving, not waiting. But John didn't hesitate, and soon he was only a step behind him.

Luck, he figured, didn't really enter into the equation. If it had, they would have dumped Hoffa's body into the cement foundation of the Meadowlands football stadium in New Jersey instead of his front yard.

The two uniformed men moved quietly through the brush. John could feel the angle steepening as they descended out of the hills. It wasn't long before he could hear traffic speeding by on a nearby highway.

Joey motioned for him to get down and John instantly obeyed. The same fear returned as the top edge of the trees were alternately lit with flashes of red and blue and a large engine raced by.

"You wait here. Watch where I go. When you hear the sound of two quick honks, you follow. I will be there with the car. It's only fifty yards to the road. Stay here."

John watched the Indian disappear and waited. He laid the platinum hands and the acids on the ground at his feet, afraid to move or even breathe that it might be too loud.

If he could get to Kellet's office, he would have a chance to explain what had happened at the cottage. He would be protected by the relative safety of the public eye. He could turn over whatever clue these hands held to the Hoffa case and be done with it.

Wanhh. Wahh. It was Joey's signal; the horn.

John scooped up the evidence, cradling it in his forearm. He shoved the bottles into the dry pocket of his uniform pants, secured his hat to hide the top of his face, and moved swiftly into the near complete darkness, following the same downhill line that Greydog had defined. As he approached the highway, he heard another vehicle speeding past. He ducked to avoid headlights. When it was silent again, he continued. Before long, he was there, standing at the gravel shoulder of the road. He looked left, to the south, then northward. Nothing.

Wanhh. Wanh. The horn, then lights, in his face, from the left. The car, moving toward him, gaining speed. John walked forward to meet it, but stopped, frozen like a deer, unable to move from the beams. He noticed something, there on the top of the vehicle. Lights. A police car. Jesus. John turned away and began to run as fast he could down the side of M-22. He could hear the car drawing closer. Soon it would be upon him. Where was the path?

Where? *Wanhh. Wanh.* The horn again. The car sped to his side. The horn. Wheels locked, half on the gravel, sliding to a stop.

"Get in. What are you doing? C'mon!" Greydog's welcome voice called to him as he pushed open the passenger door. John, stunned, obeyed. Blue and red flashes, behind them, and highbeams, growing brighter and closer. John slid in and slammed the door. In seconds the other car was there and past, leaving only wind and a cloud of dry dust drifting through Joey's headlights. "Too many visitors," Joey lamented, "Too many damn visitors." He pushed the accelerator.

The highway hugs the eastern shoreline of Grand Traverse Bay, winding easily around its many coves. When there is no wind, the water is a still mirror poised to reflect the sun at dawn, and at night, as it was now, eerie with its pale blue-white reproduction of the oversized summer moon. Occasionally, as they traveled southbound John saw the tiny edges of waves on the sand and soon he recognized the area. They were just a few miles north of the casino. There was no traffic at all.

When they drew closer, though, the volume increased considerably. There were tour busses parked in the huge parking lots where they unloaded the seemingly never-ending stream of elderly patrons who arrived from points south.

The opposing lane of traffic became a compressed band of oncoming vehicles, resting temporarily while another soon-to-be gambler made the left hand turn into the entrance. These Indians were making a fortune, but in the process the secluded county had been compromised. Joey had a point, there were too many damn visitors. And the ones that weren't throwing dice were poking around in the wilderness searching for John Russel.

They made it to Suttons Bay without incident and turned right onto M-204 to Leland.

Members of the various media had created what amounted to a campsite in the old library parking lot across the street from the sheriff's office in the tiny Michigan town. There were more than a dozen vans each with tall microwave antennae fully extended. Crew members wearing jackets emblazoned with network insignia played solitaire on the pavement waiting for something to develop. The on air reporters gathered in small groups, leaning on vehicles, talking. Some slept in the seats of the vans or obsessively adjusted their hair and makeup, awaiting the inevitable arrest of the Hoffa accomplice and murderer of Benny Tenino. They were loud, laughing and talking, long after the throngs of tourists had retired. Whenever one of Kellet's men emerged or one of the FBI agents entered, concentric circles of activity spread outward from the building. This had happened so many times that many of the press no longer reacted at all and few noticed when the casino's dark blue security car pulled into one of the spaces in front of the building reserved for sheriff's office personnel.

"Jesus."

Joey shut off the ignition. "I'll go first. You follow." Once again, he hadn't waited for John. He was already at the steps by the time John collected his statue and chemicals and got out. Remarkably, none of the assemblage behind them in the parking lot seemed to care at all about their arrival. To be sure, John held the brim of his hat as he walked, positioning his arm so it would further hide his face. He walked briskly to the front door, unnoticed and alive. Joey Greydog had gotten him there, as promised, and it was worth a damn boat. Maybe two.

"Hey."

John looked up toward the sound and was instantly blinded by several rapid flashes.

"Gotcha." The photographer grinned.

The mob from the other side of the road was instantly mobilized. They rushed toward him. "There he is!" one of them shouted, and another, "It's Russel, he's right there!" John grabbed the handle of the door and pulled to open it, but something tugged at his arm. More photographers. One reporter blocked the door so that it wouldn't open. And there were plenty of questions. "Are you a hitman? Were you hired by the Domatis? Did your father kill Hoffa?" John pulled harder and the door began to move but stopped dead against the weight of the questioner. He could see movement inside, somebody coming. Suddenly the door burst open catching John in the forehead and launching both he and the reporter backwards into the crowd. One of Kellet's deputies appeared. The mass was converging around John, leaning down over him, firing questions, closer, stepping on his arms as he struggled to cradle his evidence, pressing it to his chest.

"Boom! Ba Booom!" Gunshots. Fired into the air. Scurrying. Ducking until several dozen members of the press had joined John and now lay silent, shaking on the pavement next to him.

"Good God," he said aloud. For the second time today there was shooting. He shut his eyes.

"That's enough now," the deputy loudly ordered, holstering his pistol. The press, realizing what had happened got back to their feet and watched as he slowly walked over to John's shivering body. The flashing again intensified, the cameras following him as he leaned down and spoke softly to John who listened intently but could not force his eyes open.

"Mr. Russel," the deputy said, "I think it'd be better if we went inside."

20

Kellet's deputy held back the noisy crowd of reporters so that John could make his way back to the entrance. Inside he was confronted by the sheriff and several other of his men. Joey Greydog was nowhere in sight.

"John Russel. I'll be damned. Well. Where the hell have you been? We've been lookin' all over for you."

John removed his security officer cap and limped to the counter where the dispatcher was sitting. "You don't want to know, Bob. But let's just say this has been a fucked up day and I've had about enough of it. Here." John handed Kellet the platinum hands. "Where's Shelby?" Not waiting for an answer, John headed for the fire door which separated the large front room from Kellet's office and the county's two jail cells at the rear of the small brick building.

"Wait a minute. What's this?" Kellet asked, following John through the door.

"Hoffa's body was not at my cottage. I had nothing to do with killing anyone. That Doran is a fucking psycho who tried to kill me, too. And somehow it's all about whatever's in the middle of that platinum sculpture." He was walking faster. His voice went up a notch. "And you can have the Godamn thing. I don't want it."

A voice from around the corner, "John!" and Christine's perfectly blonde hair. They met, embracing near the brick corner where the hall split into a tee, leading to the doors of the cells; one to the left, the other to the right. John could feel her heart pounding against his own as the hug tightened. "I thought they would kill you."

"They tried." John loosened his grip, dropping his hands to her hips as he moved around her. He could see, standing at the bars beyond, Shelby's hands, holding on. He released Chris and moved closer. Through the iron he could see the shiny hazel eyes and her small grin. He stood there opposite Shelby, on the outside. John reached up and wrapped her delicate white hands in his, surrounding the bars. She silently began to sob as her mouth broadened into a wide smile and his tears joined hers as their foreheads touched. She stared into his dark eyes locked inches from her own.

"Junior," she sighed, "It's been a pretty screwed up day."

They were both chuckling, "Bob, can you open this door?"

The sheriff reached for his keys. "You know John, I have to arrest you. And I'm gonna have to tell the FBI that you're here. But I don't see any reason why you two can't be in there together." He opened the barred door and John quickly moved in. He hugged Shelby tightly feeling her strength around him.

Chris chimed in, "Thank you, Sheriff. You're probably safer here tonight, John, than anywhere else. I don't know what Doran's got in mind, but I spoke to Prosecutor Keenan and I think we're gonna be all right. Tomorrow, I'll see what I can do to get you out of here."

"We have to get that creep put away. That's all there is to it." Shelby was mad.

"What happened out there, John?" Kellet asked.

John let go of Shelby. His leg was throbbing again. He sat down on the small cot in the corner. "I was at home. Shel had gone into town to call you, Chris. I was going through some of my dad's stuff. I heard Holloway shooting; he had a shotgun with salt in it. So I went out to see who was out there."

"Tenino." Kellet interrupted.

"Yeah, Tenino. And he wants to talk. He wants me to help him get Doran. He's at the house. And I hear Holloway's shotgun again and I figure it's Shelby. The next thing I know, in comes Doran. He shoots Tenino and aims at me and I throw that thing at him and take off. I didn't know what else to do."

"You did fine. How'd you get back here?" Christine asked.

"That Indian, Joey. He found me in the woods. He brought me back here."

The fire door opened and the same large deputy that had come in with John called back to Kellet, "Hey sheriff. You're not gonna believe it, but you know that casino car, the one that was stolen. It's parked right out front."

"Jesus." John shook his head.

"And I found these in the front seat." The deputy was holding the two plastic bottles wrapped in material from John's pocket.

"Those are mine; from the cottage."

"I'll take 'em." Kellet said and ordered the deputy to call the FBI.

"Please, Sheriff," Christine was adamant, "You have to keep the Russels here until morning and we can get a judge to listen to us. You've heard what John said. This guy Doran is a killer."

"Ms. Ferrand, I told you, I'll do what I can."

John was back on his feet. He crossed the room so that he could speak more quietly to Kellet. "Bob, listen. The key to this whole thing is in that statue. That's what they wanted at the cottage. That's what all of this is about. Whatever my dad put in there will prove that Hoffa wasn't who they found."

Shelby joined in, "And it may prove more than that. You can't let Doran have it. He knows we're onto him. If he gets that, whatever it is, why wouldn't he just kill us? He's tried it once."

"It's the only leverage we have, Bob." John said.

Kellet looked at the hands. "It's the missing finger; from the body. I overheard Doran talking about it at the hospital."

There was a long pause. They tried to absorb this new piece of information. "What?" John asked in disbelief, remembering Tenino had also said something about a finger.

"The body, it didn't have a baby finger on one hand. It wasn't there."

"Well that's it." Everything was becoming more clear to John. "We have to get it, Bob. I'll bet ya; it won't match. It's not Hoffa's. That's what my dad was trying to tell us."

Christine pleaded the case, "He's right. We can get to the truth, but it's going to take a little time. We need your help."

John continued, "Look, you were out there, you saw what he did to Bill Holloway. The old guy never had a chance. He shot him like some kind of animal. From less than a foot away. His hair was burned. You saw him, Bob."

Kellet had known Bill Holloway and seen how he was killed. He also knew that tampering with evidence in a federal felony case was serious. He had never considered such a thing.

Russel could see he was getting to him and he went on. "Bob, *he* committed the crime, we didn't. This may be the only way to prove that. If he takes those hands out of here, I guarantee you'll never see them again. Then he's gotten away with murder and God knows what else. C'mon. We have to do this now." John was desperate to convince Kellet. "Doran doesn't even know you have the sculpture. The last time he saw it, it was flying at his forehead. He knows I took it, but you could have found it anywhere, at the cave, anywhere. Those are the chemicals we need to get to what's inside. My God, Bob, let's use 'em."

Christine offered a solution that would get him off the hook, "Sheriff, you must know someone you can trust at the state crime lab. Whatever we find, send it there. If it's what you think, screen it for DNA. Then we'll have our proof."

But it was the penetrating gaze of Mrs. Russel that the sheriff could no longer resist. "Please, Bob."

There was another long silence while they waited for his response. Finally, it came. "Brody!" Kellet shouted, "Brody come here!" A few seconds later the deputy leaned in through the steel door at the other end of the brick hall.

"Yeah, sheriff?"

"Have you called them next door?"

"Just about to do it. I'll..."

"Never mind," Kellet instructed, "I want you to hold off on that 'til I tell you. In the meantime, make sure nobody comes back here. And put a couple of guys outside to keep those reporters back from the building. Especially keep 'em away from my office."

With the bottles and the sculpture in hand he motioned with his head for the Russels and Christine to follow him. He walked up the hall halfway to the front and turned through an open door into his office. "Close it please," he said to Chris, who was last to enter. He handed the statue and the wrapped bottles to John and opened a second door to a small private bathroom no bigger than a closet.

"Go ahead." He pulled a long string and the light above went on. John hurried in. While the others watched at the door, he pulled the chrome lever to stop the drain. Carefully, he laid the sculpture of the hands in the deepest part of the tiny porcelain sink. He unscrewed the black plastic top on one of the bottles of acid. He hesitated. What was the ratio? He couldn't remember. He decided to pour the whole thing in over the shiny metal and it rose almost covering it. He added the entire contents of the second bottle. The four of them watched. Nothing.

"Shit." John knew he had read the definition correctly, 'Royal Water.' It dissolves platinum. Let's go. Dissolve. Nothing. "Damn."

Shortly after Benny Tenino and Bill Holloway were murdered at the Russels' cabin, the FBI had descended on Leland's only public school, setting up a command post in the gymnasium. It was a perfect location, providing sufficient parking for the growing number of government vehicles, controllable entry, and convenient access to the sheriffs office, just down the block. The school was situated away from the street and hidden from the throngs of summer tourists, so it would be easier to avoid the curious and control the press.

More than two dozen agents were positioned at long tables that had been set up in rows. Wires ran everywhere, to phones and computers. There were moving blankets spread across the floor to deaden the echo from the many voices speaking at once, but it was still far too noisy to hear Deputy Brody's warning shots.

Frank Doran, his head throbbing from the impact of the thrown sculpture, had spent the hours since Russel's escape pacing deliberately around the huge room. A large bump had risen on his forehead, and the skin, broken in its center, was patched with two beige butterfly bandages.

John had managed to elude the special response team and this made Doran furious. It had been so simple. Kill him and get the evidence. Now he's out there. Domati would not be happy.

His thoughts were interrupted by agent Garnetti who had just arrived. "There's something going on at the jail," he said, "The reporters are right up to the front door. There's a lot of noise."

Calmly, Frank paused for a moment to consider the information. Quietly, almost to himself, he responded, white eyebrows raised, optimistic. "Really." He slowly removed a fresh cigar from the pocket of his sport coat. He clipped the end. "Get a car ready for prisoner transport. And two men. Have them stand by here and wait for my instructions. I'm going for a walk.

"What's that smell?" Shelby was right. There was an acrid aroma rising from the experiment; sulfur. Around the edges of the hands, bubbles were beginning to form. The smell intensified. Then the bubbles, becoming increasingly more violent, erupted into a full boil and the metal began to distort, a thin black layer floating outward to the edges creating a dirty ring. It was melting.

The gas intensified. Christine couldn't stand it. She retreated to the office and opened the only window to breathe. Shelby held her nose and inhaled into her mouth from between her fingers and tried to stay, but the substance irritated her throat so badly that she soon joined the attorney. Kellet and John remained, leaning over the tumbling liquid to see what was happening. John could tell that under the surface the statue was dissolving, slowly. Before long, the liquid was entirely covered with a shiny black skin, heaving in the tiny waves. He couldn't see what was happening beneath it.

Frank Doran, a good hunter, could sense the kill. It filled the August evening with anticipation. They had Russel. He knew it. These locals stick together. They're predictable.

As he walked down the sidewalk in the warm air, he delicately chewed the finely rolled Havana cigar, rolling it in his lips. He reached into his pocket, searching for a match. Then other pockets. None. He continued down the block, growing closer to the sheriff's office. Garnetti was right. It was obvious that something was going on. The crowd was huddled around the front and a man was patrolling near the rear of the building.

Strange. There was a faint odor, too, septic, blending into the clear, windless night.

Doran kept walking. Except for the press, the street was deserted. He could see cars occasionally pass through the intersection ahead in the center of town. There was a restaurant past the jail, on the corner. He could get some matches there.

The bubbling in Kellet's sink continued as they waited. The smell of the reaction was unbearable to all and so intense that they took turns at the open window. After the second time that John had sufficiently cleared his lungs, he returned to the small room and realized that the bubbling had subsided. "Sheriff. C'mere. It stopped."

Kellet took a deep breath, and, followed by the two women returned to the bathroom doorway. Their eyes burned in the chemical laden air.

In the sink, the liquid was calm. A small circle was beginning to clear in the center and they could see the outline of something that had settled at the bottom, by the drain. John struggled to get a better look, but he realized he would have to get it out first. He surveyed the bathroom, looking for something to poke into the steamy, foul smelling substance. He opened the medicine cabinet and discovered, on the metal shelf behind the hinged mirror, a plastic cup. Inside, the sheriff's toothbrush.

Using it as a tool, John was able to reach to the bottom of the sink and by balancing it on the handle of the brush, maneuver the thing up the stained porcelain. The tip first. A craggy, broken fingernail, partially separated from the flesh beneath it. The first knuckle, and the next. John flipped it up onto the ledge at the back of the sink and leaned down for a closer look. The liquid under the skin dripped out leaving trails against the white; a sick mascara crying down the sides.

The bone had been cut precisely, and the tiny muscles that surrounded it, severed cleanly. The skin was white and almost transparent, though spotted from the chemical residue. John lifted the drain lever and the liquid rushed out. He ran the cold water, and after filling Kellet's plastic cup, poured the cool water over the finger. It was amazing how well it had been preserved in its platinum shell. With the exception of the separated fingernail, it seemed as perfect as it had been when it was living.

"Wow." Shelby was dumbfounded. She stood in the doorway mesmerized by the appearance of Devil Bob's little finger.

"There it is, Bob." John Russel said, amazed, as they all were, that the process had actually worked. He prodded the digit again with the plastic handle of the toothbrush, rolling it over to reveal the pad with its distinctive pattern of lines. "Send that to your buddy in Lansing and then we'll find out what's really going on."

Preceded by a puff of smoke drifting upward in the streetlight, Doran crossed the road. He was almost part of the crowd before a technician near the back spotted him. "Hey, Inspector..."

As though they had been choreographed, the media turned as one and converged. Frank, undaunted, continued along his route to the front door, creating a human wake as the curious separated. "Is this a mob war? Are you gonna go for the death penalty? I heard Russel is one of your informants. Is that true? What about the woman? Was she in on it?"

Doran moved deliberately ahead past the deputy. "Evening officer." He went to the door, opened it, and disappeared into the brick building.

Deputy Brody, seated at the duty desk, was taken by surprise. "Inspector. I..."

The fire door swung open and the large frame of the sheriff appeared.

"Where is he, Kellet?" Doran asked him, but didn't wait for an answer, instead walking directly to the hall. He brushed the sheriff's uniform as he passed, leaving a trail of Cuban smoke behind him. Kellet followed.

Christine Ferrand, hearing his voice, turned away from the cell where she had been talking through the bars with John and Shelby and positioned herself between Doran and her clients. She stood firm, not relenting to the approaching federal agent, blocking his way.

"Well, Ms. Ferrand." Frank stopped, facing her, glancing beyond her to the prisoners. "I see the Russels are well represented." He took a long draw on the cigar and slowly walked around Christine and up to the bars. Frank Doran stared at John. "There seems to be quite an odor in here, Sheriff. Plumbing difficulties?" Kellet said nothing. Doran continued, "You know Mr. Russel, I'm sure there's no need to tell you that these murders have created a serious situation..."

John Russel, already standing, moved closer to the steel rods, "You know all about murder, you son of a bitch..."

"John, don't." Chris ordered, preferring to speak to Doran herself. "We know what you're doing and what you've done, all of us, and you're going down for it. This whole thing is bogus, Doran, and you know it."

"What I know counselor is that I can send your boy here to the gas chamber if I want to. You see, I have proof," he said smugly, "I saw him do it."

"Now, if there were some room for negotiation, I suppose that I would have to reconsider my recollection of the details." He puffed again, smiling at John. Shelby held on to her husband's arm and glanced at Kellet. Frank went on, "Let's understand something here, Russel. If you give me what I want, things could go much better for both of you."

John was paralyzed. There was no way he could give this guy the finger and live. Doran would never let him do that. They had to keep it. It was proof and protection. He hoped that Kellet would help. He hoped Kellet had put it somewhere where Doran wouldn't find it on his own.

Doran started to pace, back and forth in front of the cell, "Sheriff, you're not keeping anything from me, are you? I mean if there were some little bit of evidence that you happened to come across that you just maybe, forget to tell me about, that would be obstruction and I'll take you down so fast you won't know what happened." He walked slowly back down the hall and stopped next to Kellet's office door. "That smell seems to be coming from in here. Mind if I take a look?" Doran opened the door and walked into the room. His eyes scanned the area. "It's much worse in here," he said. He was looking for the hands. He lifted papers from the desk. He opened drawers. Kellet, not able to restrain himself any longer, grabbed Doran's shoulder spinning the older man around.

"I want you to get the hell outta here."

Doran pulled away from his strong grip, slowly moving around the room, continuing to search. When he opened the door to the sheriff's bathroom, a wave of pungent gas caused him to pull back, gasping, wincing at the intensity of the cloud. "Whew." He waved his hands in the air to disburse it. He could see that the sink was badly stained with gray lines near the top and others that had dripped from the back ledge.

John and Shelby listened from the back, unable to see what was happening. Christine watched Doran from the hallway.

"There. You see that?" he said, pointing his smoldering butt at the sink. "That's the problem, right there, Sheriff. Someone's been screwin' around with something they shouldn't have." He walked slowly over to Bob Kellet until their eyes were no more than inches apart. "You can smell it. And it stinks." Doran paused for a moment, then increased the level of his voice to give orders. "Have the prisoners ready to travel. We'll be taking them tonight." He skirted past Christine on his way out and she called after him.

"You can't do that. You can't take them like that in the middle of the night." Doran ignored her. She was losing her temper. "Listen you prick," she yelled, "You're the one that better watch it, I've got enough to put you away for good." He was ignoring her. "I know you killed Tenino. I know you killed my father." Doran had just about reached the fire door when she launched her final salvo, "And Keenan knows, too."

Frank Doran stopped cold and turned slowly around. His eyebrows crunched closer together, wrinkling his forehead and causing the bump to throb again. Christine stared at him, her rage passing, giving way to evaluation. The sheriff stood close, his hand in his pocket, holding on tightly to the cold, rubbery finger. John and Shelby listened, unable to see what was happening, but they could hear his footsteps on the cement floor, and knew Doran was coming back.

When he was close to Chris, he dropped the cigar and dowsed it with the heel of his shoe. He exhaled the last smoke over her shoulder and it rose into Kellet's face. He took her gently by the arm, leading her away from the sheriff and back to the steel door so that he would not be overheard. When he was certain that was the case, he tightened his hold on her bicep and leaned to her ear. Chris could smell the tobacco. It blended with the sulfurous remainder of the chemicals, and together with her fear, left her nauseated. Doran's breath, intense and close, vibrated a wisp of

Christine's blonde hair as he whispered, "You're right, Chrissy, your dad did say something about putting me away. He was always spouting off about something, wasn't he? But we haven't heard much from him lately. Have we?"

21

Shortly after eleven PM on July 30, 1975, twenty years earlier, four men had entered the service entrance of the Wayne State University Medical Center, two others remained outside to prevent anyone from following. None spoke as they walked through the deserted corridor to the elevator where Henry Swain waited.

"This way," he directed them.

He removed the fireman's key from the slot in the small panel on the wall and stepped in with the others as the car came to life. The doors closed and the elevator moved downward. Anthony Tenino was upset, his forehead compressed, pushing his gray, curly eyebrows together until they almost touched.

"What the hell happened at the restaurant?" The old man questioned his eldest son, "I thought Domati was gonna show, Mike."

Michael Tenino obediently responded. "It was all set, Papa. I don't know."

"Well, I'll tell you this, after we get this done, I'm gonna find out what happened. You hear me, Michael?"

"Yes Papa."

"If it doesn't look like it was Domati who did this thing...if it comes back on us," he warned, "There's gonna be trouble."

"Yes, Papa."

The conversation was interrupted by a second, older man. He was in his sixties, but the adolescent dialect of an east coast dock worker was unmistakable in his speech. "Hey Tony, maybe you should take it easy. Maybe we didn't make it clear. Maybe Domati just had somethin' better ta do." The tough looking man laughed and put his arm around the younger Tenino. "Right, Michael?" His grasp was strong.

"I guess so."

Michael Tenino was also bothered by the events that evening and embarrassed to be publicly chastised by his father. He had arranged, with Hoffa's virtual stepson, Chuck O'Brien, for the meeting at The Machus Red Fox. It was a perfect venue. A dark restaurant frequented by the upscale elite of Detroit's business community and the scene of frequent clandestine meetings.

The staff had a reputation for discretion so it would seem to Domati that Hoffa had every intention of secrecy when he chose that location. Domati would not suspect that many of the employees were on the Tenino payroll, witnesses paid to fabricate a much more violent conversation than would have actually taken place. A confrontation, they would swear, continued into the parking lot where they would insist a reluctant Jimmy Hoffa was forced into a waiting car.

But Vincenzo Domati never arrived. And Michael didn't know why. It scared him, but there was nothing he could do now. The elaborate plan was in motion.

When the elevator stopped and the doors opened, Dr. John Russel was standing there. Henry Swain was the first out, followed by the older Tenino, whose demeanor became much more friendly.

"Johnny boy, how are you?" Tenino embraced the doctor, kissing him lightly on each cheek. "You probably remember Jimmy here." Hoffa extended his hand.

Who wouldn't know Jimmy Hoffa? John thought. And John Russel knew him better than most. He had seen him as he was coming up, hanging around Eastern Market. He had watched him get deeper and deeper into Tenino's business and watched as the two of them took over the trucking operations, forcing their competitors out of business. Hoffa was always outside of everybody else, beyond the touch of most. He did not command respect, but instead, demanded it, crushing any who attempted to withhold it from him. It was out of this profound fear, and not without a large measure of help from Antonio Tenino, that he built his support ultimately into the powerful Teamsters Union.

"Tony, you sure this kid knows what the fuck he's doin'? Last time I saw him he was loadin' bananas into trucks." The union leader laughed. John Russel reluctantly greeted him, ignoring Hoffa's course attempt at humor.

Michael anxious, answered quickly, "He says it'll work, Jimmy, you gotta trust him. Let's do it, Johnny."

"Sure, Mike." The doctor was all business. "Right down here."

"You stay here, Frank." Tenino ordered Frank Doran, the fourth man, "Make sure no one comes outta that elevator." Disappointed to be left behind, but ever the loyal soldier, he grudgingly obeyed. He took up his assignment, finding a seat in the adjacent waiting area.

Swain took the key from his pocket, inserted it into the wall slot, and turned it to the right, leaving it there, locking the elevator in place. He caught up with Russel and the rest of the group at the end of the hall and followed them through the fire door to the staircase.

"Those elevators don't go all the way down," the doctor explained.

They descended to the floor below on foot. It was cold. There was a smell of medicine and formaldehyde. On the right they passed a door marked 'morgue' and the next one, 'pathology'. Halfway down the hall, a security door. The sign warned, 'RESEARCH DEPARTMENT/ NO ONE ADMITTED WITHOUT PASS'. Emblazoned on the front was the circular black and bright yellow symbol for radiation. To the right, on the wall, was an electronic locking device with a digital keypad and a slot to insert identification cards. The doctor slid his in and entered a series of numbers. The buzz of the release. They were in.

Passing the next door, Hoffa could see rows of animals locked in cages; rats and monkeys, and others that he didn't recognize. And, like them, the life he left didn't matter any more. He had built his own cage, less than an hour earlier, when he staged his abduction, and now, there was no way he could unlock the door and go back. But if this doctor really could do what he claimed, it would be worth it. He would escape the federal government and further scrutiny into his dealings. He would have all the money and none of the hassle. He would be dead.

At the end of the corridor, on the left, was the door to Dr. Russel's laboratory. Stuck to it, a clear plastic envelope containing a card with 'quarantine' printed on it in large red letters. Underneath, in pen, the doctor had written a dangerous sounding explanation of imaginary contamination. He pulled a key from his pocket and unlocked it.

The doctor led them past counters of glassware and other scientific equipment to what had originally been a storeroom, but had been converted, some years before into a surgical area which Russel used to conduct animal experiments. Inside, barely alive, lying motionless on a hospital bed, was what remained of Bobby Merrimac Wilson; Devil Bob. The sucking sound of air pumping in and out of his respirator hose echoed around the painted cinder block walls.

"Here, put these on." The doctor handed out surgical masks, one to each of them. "He's very susceptible to infection. We can't risk losing him now." He noticed his friend's pale appearance. "Henry, you all right?"

Swain had never been comfortable with the sterility of a hospital and this was much worse. The vision of the man lying there dying and the knowledge that they were responsible did not sit well. He was becoming nauseated. "God, he looks like shit, John," he said, tossing his mask in the trash. "I'll be out in the hall."

Even the foul air in the corridor was better than what was inside. Still, the combined chemicals from the various rooms turned Henry's stomach. He decided to go back upstairs.

When he got to the hall, he realized that Doran was not at the elevator as Tenino had asked. Swain walked closer. He could hear a faint voice as he approached. He stopped to listen. It was Doran talking on the phone around the corner. Swain tried to hear what he was saying, but he was too far away. He thought it was strange for the cop to be calling someone, but decided not to confront him. Instead, he walked back to wait in the dark stairwell where he could smoke and watch Doran through the steel mesh in the narrow window of the fire door. For all Henry knew, Doran could be acting on Tenino's orders, and it didn't make sense to question too much around this bunch. About that, he was sure.

Swain's assessment of Devil Bob was accurate. At the hands of John Russel, he was dying. In the two weeks since Michael Tenino had grabbed him from the alley in the Cass Corridor, he had been bound to this bed both at the wrists and ankles. Tubes had been inserted to carry waste from his body and to carry chemicals into it. Four of his ribs had been broken, as was his right leg. The doctor had twice dislocated Bob's shoulder and replaced it into its socket. Injuries deliberately caused to make him more perfect; as close a physical match for Jimmy Hoffa as was possible.

He had been blasted, for eight consecutive days, with such devastating amounts of radioactivity that his blood had turned from a living organism into an inert indiscernible liquid. And, earlier this morning, his teeth had been extracted, the doctor careful not to damage the gums where others would soon be implanted, to bond to Bob's jaw.

Devil Bob could not move. He lay in a dream-like daze, a stupor from the drugs. He could hear men talking in the room, but could make no sense of their conversations.

"Strip down to your shorts, please, and hop up here." Dr. Russel instructed Hoffa, pointing to a wheeled gurney, he had borrowed from the morgue. He held a large needle, about ten inches long in his hand. At the end there was a wide tip, about an eighth of an inch across.

Hoffa climbed up onto the makeshift operating table. "What the hell do you think you're gonna fuckin' do with that thing?" he asked.

John Russel considered Hoffa little more than a bully and a thug, and felt no need for manners. "I'm gonna jam it about five inches into your hip and suck your bone marrow out. How does that sound?" He smiled broadly.

"Fuck you."

Tenino put an end to it. "Why don't you settle down, Jimmy, and let him do what he's supposed to do, all right? So we can get this over and get goin'? Okay?" Hoffa nodded. The doctor continued his business.

"Lie down on your side. This is going to take about a half an hour. Then I'm gonna have to put you under for the teeth."

The old man joked as Hoffa lay down on the table, glaring at John, "Hey Jimmy, this could be the first time a goon gets himself killed and lives to talk about it, eh?" Tenino laughed. "Go over this again, will ya Johnny?"

John Russel didn't find humor in any of it. He had worked hard to become a doctor and a researcher. He realized that it would have been much more difficult without the old man's help but he knew all along it was a mistake to let Tenino give him money for school. He knew what he was doing now could threaten it all, and even land him in prison. But he continued. He did his best to explain the experimental procedure as simply as he could, knowing that these people could not understand.

"What I've done,…what we have, rather,…is a situation where the blood system has been virtually eliminated in the recipient."

"The bum, right?" Hoffa asked.

John glanced briefly at Bobby. "Yes. We've killed his blood system. And what we're going to do is inject your marrow into him. That will become his marrow and begin to manufacture blood cells in his body, your blood. At least that's how it's supposed to happen."

"What da ya mean?"

"It works in rats." The doctor smiled, unable to avoid the obvious comparison.

"And then he's me, right?"

"If he doesn't reject it, and the graft takes before he dies. He'll have your blood, so in one sense, yes. The soft tissue won't change. But if that's gone, yeah, over time, he's pretty much,…you."

"This is fuckin' incredible, eh Jimmy?" Hoffa didn't have a clue. Neither did Tenino, but the old Italian trusted John. He was like a third son.

"…Yeah, fuckin' incredible. This is gonna hurt, isn't it?"

Russel didn't answer. He primed the needle. The reality of his involvement in this act was overwhelming, but he was bound by his promise to Tenino. Still, he tried to justify his actions, rationalizing that what he was doing was somehow scientifically significant. He recorded every detail of the experimental transplant in his journals, using carefully coded references to disguise the true identities of his subjects. What he would learn about the procedure, he reasoned, he might use to help others in the future. So were his thoughts, but no explanation could ever overcome his sense of murder and stupidity.

Before he inserted the needle, he leaned down to the man on the table in front of him and with heightened intensity and quiet outrage, spoke slowly, in an almost silent whisper, directly into the union man's weathered ear.

"I don't give a shit whether you live or die," Dr. Russel said, "Or if these guys take you out behind this building and slice your throat. If the old man wasn't watching, I might do it myself, right on this table." Dr. Russel lowered Hoffa's shorts to take clear aim on his hip, then continued whispering so that no one else could hear. "But I want you to know this, no matter if Tenino trusts you or not, I don't, and don't you ever try to screw any of us over or I go to whoever the hell will listen and blow the whole deal. And don't think I can't do it. I'm the only fucking guy on this planet who can prove it." He stepped back to get an angle.

"Ahhhh!" Hoffa cried out as the doctor slowly inserted the metal, moving it just slightly back and forth as it went in.

The procedure continued with Dr. Russel filling a large vial every ten or so minutes, replacing each with another, until there were four. When he was finished, he pulled the needle out slowly, again moving it unnecessarily from side to side.

Devil Bob could hear the moans next to him and wondered what was going on, but he could not utter more than a dim gurgle, which joined the other sick sounds of the room.

"There." Dr. Russel had finished extracting the dark brown sludge. He spoke to the elder Tenino. "I'm going to put him out now so I can do the teeth." He noticed Hoffa glaring intently at him, "It'll be messy and you probably'll want to wait outside 'til it's done," he hinted, "But you can stay if you want."

As the Teninos watched, Russel prepared a second, much smaller needle with a solution of morphine and pentathol. A deadly combination which could easily kill if the dosage was too high. He tied a piece of flexible rubber hose around Hoffa's forearm and manipulated his arm at the elbow until a large vein rose from the skin.

"Lie still, Mr. Hoffa," he said, piercing the surface, inserting the sterilized steel. Slowly he pushed the small plunger down releasing the drug. "I want you to say the alphabet to me. Go ahead, start now."

Hoffa began, "A. B. C. D....E...G" He was becoming drowsy. "G....F. G."

The doctor pushed more into the vein.

"H." A long pause. "I..."

John Russel felt his thumb trying to stop, trying not to inject the final amount, but he continued to push. He could claim it was an accident. Who would know? He pushed a little more. Hoffa moaned unintelligibly.

"What's wrong? What happening?" Michael Tenino had noticed something.

"Nothing." Russel recovered. He withdrew the needle and tossed it onto a stainless steel surgical tray, the lethal remainder of the liquid inside dripping from the tip. "Nothing, Mike. Everything's fine. Relax." He removed his surgical gloves and threw them away. "I'm going out to have a smoke and get a coffee. It'll take a few minutes for the drugs to work. If you want, there's some vending machines up in the lounge. You might be more comfortable up there."

"We'll wait here, John," Michael said. His father agreed.

"Yeah, Johnny, go ahead."

If nothing else, these men were predictable. John knew they would not leave the room now and it would be difficult to get them to leave at all. Antonio Tenino would want to see for himself everything that was going on.

"I'll be right back." The doctor headed out through the lab and past the security door. Once in the hall, he found Henry Swain, pacing.

"John, what's going on?"

"Shh," he commanded, "Walk up to the lounge with me. Got a cigarette?" Although he rarely smoked anymore, he did not hesitate to light up. Where's Doran?"

"Upstairs at the elevator."

"C'mon."

They stopped in the darkness at the top of the stairs. Looking through the glass, John could see Doran at his post.

"I told them I was getting some coffee. Come with me. I'll handle Doran."

They walked toward Doran who sat reading a magazine in the small lobby. As they passed, John spoke matter of factly.

"Hey, Frank. Goin' down to the machines. You want a candy bar or something?"

Frank shook his head and returned to the magazine.

After the lobby, they reached the lounge and entered. The door closed obediently behind them. John started immediately, speaking quickly, not knowing if they would soon be interrupted.

"Henry, listen to me," Russel hurriedly whispered. "I know we've known the Teninos for a long time, and I'm not saying that the old man hasn't helped me more than anyone, but it's Jimmy Hoffa for God's sake. This is gonna heat up. If I were Jimmy Hoffa, I wouldn't want us around. Would you?"

"Calm down, John. Tenino gave us his word. We'll be all right." Henry attempted to be reassuring, but was not at all convincing.

"Yeah? What if something happens to him? Then what?" The doctor didn't wait for an answer, "If it was just Tony that'd be one thing, but when we got into this, I had no idea. I'm not taking the chance."

"What the hell are you talking about?" Now Henry was getting nervous.

John extinguished the first butt and asked for another. When it was lit, he continued.

"We need leverage."

"What do you mean?"

He spoke quickly, "I don't have time to tell you the whole thing, they're probably wondering where I am already. I don't even want to tell you exactly, 'cause you may not need to know...ever. But if anything goes sideways with this, I want to be able to prove what they did."

"How?"

The door opened suddenly. It was Frank Doran, leaning in with a message. "Tenino's looking for you."

"I'll be right there." The door closed again as he left. Then Dr. Russel dropped the bomb. "Henry, I can't do it without your help. You're gonna have to keep them busy. I need some time."

Swain's fear was instant, and, sensing this John tried to lighten it up a little, "Henry, relax, I'm sure we're gonna be fine." John crushed the cigarette out. "Face it, Henry," he paused for effect, "...What could happen?"

"Is he all right? It looks like he's dead," an anxious Antonio Tenino said as soon as John returned.

Russel examined Hoffa. "He's unconscious."

The old man was getting jumpy. "Let's get goin' with this, Johnny. Okay? That bum's been staring at me. I don't like it."

Russel put on a fresh mask and gloves and prepared the instruments for oral surgery. He clamped Hoffa's mouth open and placed a rubber-tipped tube inside to suck out the saliva and blood which would follow. He moved a high intensity lamp into position. "This is not gonna be pretty, Tony," he warned.

"Do it," the old man insisted, unwaivered.

As the Teninos watched, he began. He reached the dental pliers deep into Hoffa's mouth until he had a firm hold around the right rearmost molar. Moving the instrument from side to side, the tooth started to give way. More movement. And finally, the first was out. Blood gushed through the tube into a canister on the floor. More blood covered the doctor's hand as he withdrew. With a loud clang, he deposited the molar into a waiting metal tray. Not being equipped for dentistry, Russel had filled a spray bottle with cold water and used it to wash inside the mouth, to clean the area where he would be working next. He turned to the small utility sink nearby and washed the blood from the first extraction from the tool. He adjusted the light for a better view and went in again. Back and forth. Tugging. Twisting. A minute later, the second tooth.

The blood was surging down the tube and with the increased volume the gurgling noise from Hoffa's mouth grew louder. It sounded to Tenino like the last sound a man makes when he's being strangled.

Russel methodically repeated the procedure as planned, extracting the lower teeth first, to provide more room to work on the top later. Neither Tenino moved. They were unaffected by the gore. They would stay, as John expected, until he was finished, intently watching every move.

Where was Swain? It was time. He only had three more teeth to remove. After that, the opportunity would be gone.

Dr. Russel worked more slowly, stalling, hoping his audience wouldn't notice. Where the hell was Henry?

"Somethin' wrong?" The younger Tenino had detected the pause.

"Gotta take it easy with this one. Don't want it to break." Michael seemed to accept the explanation, but the doctor knew he'd have to pick up the pace.

The pile of cigarette butts was growing on the linoleum tile at Swain's feet. One after another he smoked, waiting for Doran to move. John Russel had told him how much time he needed. It was up to Henry Swain to get it for him.

For over thirty-five minutes, from this position near the stairs he had watched. Occasionally, Doran had looked up from his periodical. Once their eyes had met and Henry had nodded down the long hall in recognition. But Doran had not moved from his seat in the small lobby.

It was obvious to Swain that he was running out of time. If the planned distraction was to work, he had to get Doran away from the elevator, if only for a second or two.

He decided to take a chance, to lure him away from his position. Henry stuffed another Marlboro under his shoe and started down the corridor toward the elevator. When he was close enough for conversation, Doran looked up again.

"Hey, Frank, can I buy ya a cup of coffee?" Swain asked. "You look like you could use it."

"Yeah, sure. I'll come with you."

Doran threw the magazine on the orange Naugahyde and moved across the room. "Jesus, how long is this gonna take? I thought this was a quick deal."

"Got somewhere to go?" Swain quipped.

When they arrived at the lounge, Henry seized the opportunity. "Pour me one, will ya? I gotta hit the can." He gestured to the men's room directly across the hall. Frank bought it and he continued into the lounge.

Henry Swain surveyed the hall. No one. He raced silently on tip-toe like an Indian, back to the elevator. He turned the key in the fireman's override slot on the wall next to the doors and the stainless beast sprung to life. He pushed the up button and the doors opened. Again he reached for the fireman's key and turning it briskly ninety degrees clockwise, stopped the car. He reached inside to the button panel, pressing every floor, then feeling for the red toggle switch. There it was. Flip it. Instantly the searing volume of the emergency bell belted down the hallway. Doran would be out in seconds. Henry had to hurry. He ran toward the bathroom door, twenty feet away. He only had a yard or so to go when the lounge door started to open. He would never make it. If Doran came out now, Henry realized, the cop would be between him and the door. The lounge door started to open first a crack, then more. Doran was coming out. Think fast Henry. Or be killed. He couldn't look but, for all he knew Michael Tenino could be closing on him from behind, drawing his gun, firing into Henry's back. He saw the tip of Doran's shoe poking out into the hallway. My God. Then, desperate, he reached down with his right hand and pulled his zipper down. He grabbed his belt and pulled. The clasp let go. In one spinning motion, he turned his back to the men's room door, as if he'd just come out. He bent his right leg at the knee and kicked it as hard as he could. The metal swung open, slamming into the tile beyond. Henry took hold of his waistband with both hands and tugged loose the buttons. His pants fell open and dropped slightly. As Doran ran out of the lounge, he reversed direction so that it would appear he too, was heading for the elevator. The two men nearly collided.

"What the fuck?" Doran was in his face. Doran ran ahead to the elevator as Swain pulled his pants up and followed. Doran drew a pistol from a holster inside his sport coat and raced to the small lobby. He ran to the stairwell, efficiently searching the area, ducking low, weapon level, swinging wide arcs left and right. Nothing. This well-trained cop moved deftly to the side of the elevator, and slammed his back flat to the wall, pistol pointed upward, held against his chest.

Just as Swain, now running at full speed, reached the elevator, officer Doran turned low, rotating 180 degrees, leaping into the elevator, sweeping the interior with his eyes and his revolver, his back to the open doors and the hall.

As he shot past, the speeding Henry managed to grab the key again, and barely breaking stride, with one swift twist to the left, energized the car, closing the doors and sending Frank Doran upward and out of the way.

Henry resumed his pace, headed now for the stairs and down to Russel's lab. They would wonder what the hell was going on, he reasoned. They would leave John Russel alone.

At the first sound of the bell, as Henry hoped, the Teninos were on their feet. Michael was already in the stairwell, hurtling up, three steps at a time. He, too, had drawn a gun.

Sweat was dripping from Henry when they met on the landing. He continued the deliberate misdirection, throwing suspicion away from himself, "Where's Doran?" Swain yelled to be heard over the elevator alarm bell, his voice echoing upward "Seen him, Mike?" The effect of this comment was predictable.

Michael didn't answer. He pushed past Swain and leaped up the last of the stairs, bolting out the door. Henry proceeded ahead to the storeroom where John Russel was working. When he got there, he was confronted by the elder Tenino.

"What the hell 's goin' on out there, Henry?" Antonio Tenino was rattled.

"I don't know. I thought Doran was supposed to be out there? Is he here?" He could see the old man's curiosity kick in, so he further fueled the fire. "I can't find him anywhere."

Tenino was moving, heading out to see for himself, allowing John to begin.

When he was gone, John hurried into action. "When he's past the security door punch 787 on the inside panel. That'll lock it." Dr. Russel ordered. "What the hell took you so long, Henry?"

"What difference does it make? It's done now. What are you going to do John?"

"I'm gonna try to save our ass. Just watch the door. When they come back push 787 again to unlock it but take your time. If they ask you about it just make up some bullshit about how it's automatic or something."

Russel moved quickly to a second tray of instruments and selected a medium sized scalpel. He grabbed a large plastic bottle of alcohol from a shelf above the sink, opened it and poured most of the contents over the knife. Shaking off the excess, he hurried to the bed where Bobby Merrimac Wilson was and pulled the sheet up.

"Uhh." Swain was ready to vomit at the sight of the man's withered body.

"Go ahead. Wait outside if you have to," Russel yelled, "Just let me know when they come back." The doctor didn't notice whether Swain had gone or not. It didn't matter. He had to get this done. He took the bum's left hand into his own and, pinching the smallest finger hard at the first joint and began to slice through the tissue. Once he had completed a circuitous incision, he laid the bleeding hand down, resting it on a small white towel. The flow continued while he returned to the counter near the sink and dumped the rest of the surgical instruments out, wedging the stainless steel tray between Bobby's arm and the edge of the bed for additional support. Searching frantically through the pile of equipment on the countertop, he found a small bone saw and returning to his unwitting patient he began. He could not bare to look at Bobby. He could only focus on the procedure. With delicate precision Dr.

Russel moved the tiny teeth back and forth, cutting the bone under the first knuckle until the tip of the finger began to wiggle. Working on one side and then the other, like sawing through a miniature tree trunk, until it cracked and ultimately broke free.

Bobby felt nothing, he was sure.

The ringing stopped. They would be back any minute. Quickly the doctor wrapped the detached end of the finger in the cloth and shoved it into the pocket of his lab coat. He took the final ounce of the clear alcohol and drenched the bloody stub.

The door opened. It was Henry. "John, I hear 'em at the door," he warned quietly.

"Go let them in."

With his teeth, Russel ripped surgical gauze from a roll and wrapped Bob's finger tightly to stop the bleeding. He used the spray bottle to clean the red substance from the rail along the side of the bed and from the scalpel and his hands. Seconds before the Teninos entered, he jerked the sheet back over Bobby and spun around to the examination table and Hoffa. As calmly as he could, he asked Tenino what happened.

"Everything all right, Tony?" He pulled the last molar.

Michael answered for his father, "Fuckin' Frank got stuck in the damn elevator. He swears he wasn't anywhere near the damn thing when the bell went off. I don't like it."

The tension was thick when the door opened again. Michael Tenino, still holding his pistol, instinctively leveled it at the opening and Henry Swain, who stopped dead in his tracks in the doorway, staring at the barrel. He let out a frightened squeal, before his breathing resumed. "It's me. It's me."

Tenino lowered the weapon and grilled Swain, "What the fuck's goin' on?"

Swain walked slowly toward him gesturing with his open hands, as if pushing the tension toward the floor, "Settle down, Mike. Please. I don't know."

Russel could sense Henry's predicament. He quickly formulated what he hoped would be a believable excuse, "The damn elevator…if it's disabled too long, the alarm goes off. I should have warned you, but it happens so often, I don't even think about it any more. I'm sorry, Tony."

Antonio Tenino was running out of patience. He waved off Russel's apology and spoke quietly, taking in a deep breath first, "Let's just hurry this up. Okay, Johnny?"

"I'm finished with him. You can take him in a couple of minutes. Just roll him out on this gurney, if you want. It'll be awhile before he comes around, then you're gonna have to give him these." The doctor handed the old man a bottle of pills. "They're pain killers. He's gonna need 'em."

"Michael, tell 'em to bring the car up. And get Doran down here to help move him. Henry, go out in the hall and keep an eye on things, I want to talk to Johnny."

Before he left, Swain glanced at John. If Tenino suspected anything, he didn't show it.

When they were alone, the old man moved closer to John. Russel could feel his legs weakening under him. At the edge of Tenino's wrinkled mouth though, he detected the beginning of a smile. Tenino spoke softly, reaching up to cradle the back of John's neck in his hand.

"Johnny, Johnny." He shook his head with a father's pride. "I know you don't like this, what we do, I mean. But you have to know that we do what's best, for us, for the family, Johnny." Russel, petrified, could only nod.

Tenino reached into his jacket. He brought out two envelopes and handed them to John. "This is the first of it, for you and for

Henry." John began to protest, but the old man stopped him before he could speak. "Johnny, I know. You're a good boy. You would do this for nothing, I know. But you have a family started and you will need this, believe me. I have sons, and believe me, sons will eat," he chuckled and pushed the envelopes into John's hand. "My boys have not missed many meals, but they're strong and they're good boys." He sensed Russel's remorse. "This is something that had to be done, Johnny. You'll learn, there are things to be done. I know I can trust you and, like I said, nothin's gonna happen to you. You've got my word. This will be fine."

Russel, uncomfortable, changed the subject, "I have to get the teeth in him, Tony."

The old man persisted, "Johnny, take the money and give the other one to Henry later, after we leave. Okay?"

Dr. Russel nodded.

"You guys did good. Real good." Antonio Tenino wrapped his arms around the doctor, squeezing him hard, patting him firmly on the back. "I love you, Johnny, like my own," he whispered, "Thank you."

22

The urgent call from Christine Ferrand, received well after midnight, had rocked Charley Keenan awake. He knew that this most valued activity would be difficult to resume. Many times he had lay on the sofa for hours, after such calls, his body numb with fatigue while his mind raced forward. For weeks at one stretch, he had not slept at all, instead dozing at his desk unable to overcome the weight of his insomnia.

Though months had passed, he could not stop the endless replay of the last days of Anita's horrible pain. His wife's uncontrollable moans had been mercifully diminished by morphine but, to Charley, they were still so emotionally piercing that to remain with her, in the same room, hearing her suffering, was impossible. He had retreated, for sleep, to a couch in the den. But as her cancer advanced, he would be awakened more easily by even the slightest odd sound, fearing it could be her last, and would quietly walk down the hall to look in on his failing spouse.

Since her death, he had not returned to their bedroom, instead moving his clothes to another, and himself to the couch, closing the door forever on the life they had shared.

He had wrapped himself completely in the Hoffa case ever since. It was his demon; the monster that had stolen so many hours away from Anita. He hated it. But now, finally, after twenty years, he would bring it to an end.

Doran was acting quickly now. He insisted that the Russels be taken overnight back to Detroit to await arraignment in district court in the Wayne County jail. Obviously, he was trying to force their compliance. Keenan had known Frank Doran to be a methodical, patient investigator. This impulsive behavior was out of character. He must be feeling pressure, Charley thought.

After speaking to Christine, he tried hard to return to sleep. But after several hours of tiny naps he gave up. The sun was shining brightly across the city buildings, casting dark, long shadows just after dawn. Charley could see the mist rising from the pavement below and he could tell that it would be a hot Sunday.

While the coffee brewed, he opened the door to the hall and retrieved the paper. Others lay in a long row extending in both directions down the long hall of the old apartment building waiting for still sleeping customers.

Charley returned to the kitchen and without looking, tossed it on the table. He knew what had to be done, but it was far too early. He stole a cup from the gurgling coffee maker and sat down to read.

There, again huge, centered on the front page was a photograph of John Russel. Above, the headline, "BULLETS RAIN. HOFFA SUSPECT BEGS MERCY." The shot showed John, his eyes tightly closed, huddled in a fetal position on the cement near the front steps of Sheriff Kellet's office. The tips of the shoes of several reporters surrounded him. The related article comprised the entirety of the front page and was preceded by the subhead, "INVESTMENT COUNSELOR IMPLICATED IN TENINO HIT."

At eight forty-five, Charley left his apartment building and headed east on Jefferson. Ten minutes later, he pulled into the parking lot behind Memorial Church. He waited in his car, watching people as they crossed the lot to the back door. Watching for one in particular. This was his church, though he hadn't been to a service in months. It was also where Judge Easton Witheral, Chief Judge of the Southern Division of the Eastern District, attended services. He had come before Witheral a number of times over the years and the two had developed a certain respect, if not friendship with one another. Keenan spotted him walking with his wife and hopped out of the sedan into the warm air. He had removed his sport coat for the drive but now replaced it, smoothing out the wrinkles as he walked. "Judge Witheral," he called out, "Excuse me, Judge," Keenan's ample frame bounced as he walked, hurriedly to intercept him.

Judge Witheral was much older than Charley, at least seventy, but he had the rugged tan and strong composition of someone younger. His white hair was brushed to a neat part on the left. Together with the white shirt, it framed his bronze face and lent contrast to the pressed blue blazer. His wife, equally handsome, stood quietly at his side. The judge stopped, recognizing Keenan. "Well, Charley Keenan, how are you?" he said sincerely, reaching out to shake hands, "How nice it is to see you here again. I believe you know Helen…"

"Ms. Witheral." Charley released the judge's hand and bowed ever so slightly, "Ma'am."

"We haven't seen you since…" She stopped, uncomfortable with what she started to say.

"It's all right, ma'am," Charley assured her, "Things are getting better. Judge, could I have a minute?" He turned on the long studied charm of his southern heritage, "Please forgive me, Ms. Witheral, I'm not generally in the habit of accosting people in church parking lots, and I would never do so under normal circumstances, but it is a matter of some urgency and importance."

"Why of course, Charley. Don't think anything of it," the judge answered, "Helen, why don't you go on in. I'll be along shortly."

Mrs. Witheral smiled, leaving the two men to talk.

"What is it, Charley?"

Keenan leaned closer to the judge and spoke carefully in low tones, "It's too much to go into out here, but if you could spare a couple hours this afternoon, I'll explain everything."

Christine Ferrand was exhausted. With the exception of her nap on the bench at the Leelanau County sheriff's office, she had been up most of the night. It was nearly two in the morning when Doran's men came for the Russels and she was abruptly awakened.

They burst in, four of them, while two others remained outside. Before she knew it, they had spirited her clients out a side door and into an unmarked cargo van. Two men jumped in back and as they pulled the doors closed behind them, Chris could see that the Russels, shackled, were pushed to the carpeted floor behind the front seats. Doran himself sat in the passenger seat and another of his agents in the driver's seat. As the van was leaving, she ran to her own car to follow. It was over so quickly that most of the press didn't realize what had happened.

She kept close during the entire trip south. Doran was capable of anything, and she vowed, as long as he had John and Shelby, she wouldn't be far away.

The sun was up when Doran arrived with his prisoners at the Wayne County jail just over four hours later. When the back doors of the van opened, she was there, standing not fifty feet away, behind a tall, barbed wire topped fence that surrounded the parking area. When Frank Doran got out, he smiled at her while he supervised the transfer of the Russels. His smug confidence was disgusting.

Shelby blocked her eyes from the sudden wrath of the bright morning, holding her handcuffed wrists to her forehead as she stepped out over the bumper. Both she and John stretched to relieve two hundred miles of stiffness, breathing in the last fresh air before their descent into this frightening urban facility.

"Don't worry, John. It'll be all right," Chris yelled as they were led away. But she was not so sure.

She decided that it was pointless to go home, the press would be all over her. She went instead to her office, into the parking lot, up the private elevator and tucked herself in to what had been Henry Swain's inner office. Many times he had slept on the oversized leather sofa or worse, Christine imagined. Now it provided an opportunity for quiet rest.

On the coffee table in front of her, was a stack of letters and cards, condolences from clients and friends, and even enemies of Henry Swain. It was ironic, she thought, that a man so public in his life would be so shy in death. But his wish was for a true peace at the end, without ceremony. Christine knew that for certain. She had written the will herself. He had also instructed that he be cremated, although it was never intended to be a prediction of the method of his death. Perhaps, Chris thought as she looked through the cards, he didn't want to make a big deal out of his death because he simply refused to acknowledge that romance was no longer a possibility or admit that he could never have sex again. He was not forgotten, though. In fact, Chris was astounded at the volume of mail that arrived at the office each day. As she read some of it, she drifted. Back to high school. To the University of Michigan. She and her father.

She had been sleeping for over two hours when Keenan called to set the meeting. One o'clock. An hour away.

Chris sat up, bleary on the couch. Her cotton shirt was badly wrinkled. She stood and walked across the cavernous office to the bar. In the mirror behind it she caught the first sight of herself in almost twenty four hours. She looked like hell. One side of her hair was flattened, the other ratted in a cascading arch to her shoulder, with random strands falling to her eyes. She had lost an earring somewhere along the way. She removed the one that remained and laid it on the polished marble bar. Underneath, in Henry's small refrigerator, she found a half used can of Maxwell House and dragged it out to make coffee.

This was her office now, although she hadn't had time to completely move in yet. She had brought some toiletries from home to outfit the private bathroom, a luxury afforded senior partners in the firm and, also, now hers.

At first, she had felt a little guilty barging in here so quickly after her father's death. But that was what he wanted, and in fact, demanded, as part of his last testament. Why not? She rationalized. Her name *was* on the door; Ferrand, actually her mother's name. Many years before, Henry Swain, then an associate at the firm founded by her grandfather, had not been married to her mother, but her aunt when she was conceived, the result of ceaseless pursuit and final surrender; of passion and obsession and disgrace. An event so scandalous at the time that arrangements were made. Her mother was sent to Switzerland where Christine had been born. Henry had paid for her education and living expenses for both of them, and had agreed not to attempt to contact his daughter in any way until she had reached the age of majority. Eventually, her mother remarried and remained in Europe. Christine returned to study at the University of Michigan at the suggestion of Henry Swain who had, on her eighteenth birthday, introduced himself as her father. They had been inseparable ever since.

She unbuttoned her plaid flannel shirt and tossed it over the back of the couch. She dropped her jeans and underwear in a heap on the bathroom floor and turned the gold handles allowing the steamy water to flow. Tiny droplets condensed on the cold green marble walls and clear glass door. She could smell the fresh coffee as she stepped into the enclosure and finally, after this horrible night, felt the warmth relaxing her sore muscles.

Keenan had done as he had said. There would be a meeting. If the judge agreed, this would be their chance to get Frank Doran.

As Chris worked the shampoo to a stiff lather she thought about the Russels, prisoners, lumped with the trash of the world, with the hookers and junkies, trapped in that concrete hole. They had done nothing. It was really her father's fault,...and John's father's, she thought...that they were involved at all.

When Charley and Judge Witheral arrived, Chris greeted them in the formal lobby of the firm. She looked every bit a lawyer. Her conservative blue wool suit hugged her perfect form, the hem flowing gracefully at her knees as she showed the two men to the conference room. There, in the large pot, she had made more coffee. On the sideboard next to it, was a tray of donuts and cookies from the bakery across the street, anticipating Charley's ever present hunger.

"Gentlemen, please make yourselves comfortable. I have to run and get some files. I'll be right back."

Keenan immediately went for the food. Judge Witheral carefully removed his blazer and folded it over the arm of a chair and sat down at the far end of the table.

"Coffee?" Keenan asked.

The judge nodded, "Sure. Thanks."

Chris returned, closing the heavy oak door behind her. "Thank you, Your Honor, for taking time to meet with us," she said formally. "Prosecutor Keenan, I'm sure, told you of the urgency of the situation." Christine pulled the chair out opposite Witheral and sat down before she continued. "Your Honor, I represent John and Shelby Russel who have been arrested on a federal warrant and are currently being held pending arraignment in the Wayne County jail. My immediate interest is to obtain their safe release." The old judge listened attentively. "We believe the arrest is bogus."

"Ms. Ferrand," Witheral said deliberately. "In all the time I've sat behind the bench, I've never known counsel not to have argued his client's innocence."

"There's more, Your Honor...we..."

Keenan jumped in, wiping shreds of donut from his mouth as he spoke, "We've got a major conspiracy here, Your Honor, and I mean this thing dates back to when I started, twenty years ago. It's the Hoffa disappearance. I think we know, at least for the most part, what went on. The trouble now is we don't know how far it could go."

"But we do know that it involves officials of the Justice Department," Chris said.

Judge Witheral was listening intently now, leaning forward with his forearms crossed on the conference table. "Who?"

"Frank Doran," Charley answered, then added hastily, "But let's not get the wagon out in front of what's pullin' it. We should lay it out for you from the beginning, Easton."

"I assume you have evidence," the judge added.

"We do." He motioned to Chris.

She opened one of several manila file folders that were spread out on the mahogany in front of her, "It's kind of convoluted, so please bear with me. First, with regard to the charges against the Russels. They were arrested for open murder in this case, and as accessories after the fact. I'm sure though, that Doran will go for much more."

"The interesting thing about this, is that he never contacted me," Charley said.

"Is that unusual?" Witheral asked.

"Yeah, it's unusual, since he was investigating a tip on the Hoffa case, and what supposedly is Hoffa's body was discovered at the Russels' summer cottage. I mean, clearly this is my area. But I think it's deliberate. He seems pretty anxious to get these people charged, and I think we can show you why, so he's probably dealing with someone else in the prosecutors office."

"What would his motives be for keeping you out of it?"

"Because he knows we're onto him," Chris glanced at Charley. "It wasn't smart. I know. But it slipped."

Chris slid the open folder across the table to the judge. "That's a statement from John Russel attesting to the circumstances of the murders of Benito Tenino and his Leland neighbor William Halloway. In it, he insists that it was Doran who committed those murders and actually tried to kill him, too. And only through a bizarre and lucky series of events was he able to escape with his life. I should add, also, that he turned himself in to the local sheriff."

The judge scanned the papers, "Seems to me, Charley, that it's his word here or the word of a career FBI man for God's sake. So far I don't see anything."

"Easton, this murder is the culmination of a much broader situation. Lets start twenty years ago. Suppose, on the day Hoffa disappeared, there was going to be a meeting; a meeting between Hoffa and Vincenzo Domati. Say this meeting was a set-up. It was intended to create the illusion that Domati, the last person to be seen with Hoffa alive, was somehow involved when Hoffa vanished."

"Okay, Charley." Witheral went along, but he was skeptical.

"This meeting was set up by the Teninos, specifically by Michael Tenino. He had all the waiters and valets in his pocket; witnesses to the abduction. It's a good frame. And remember that Hoffa stood a good chance to run the union again, but we were watching him pretty closely then. If he funneled money to his pals in the Tenino family, we'd be all over him, he knew that."

"So what does he do?" Chris asked rhetorically, "He fakes it; his disappearance, it's a fraud."

The judge shook his head, "Even if this were true, and let's assume for argument, that it is. He pulled it off. He disappeared. Nothing ever led to anything conclusive on Domati, did it Charley?"

"No. But that's the point. Domati never showed. Somebody tipped him. According to Benny Tenino, it was Frank Doran. The same person who made damn certain I never got close to Domati. It was Hoffa who betrayed his pal Tenino. And Doran who helped him get away with it. It's all in there." Keenan pointed to a folder.

Christine passed over a second file. "In here, you'll find a second sworn affidavit from John Russel describing his conversation with Benito Tenino on the day he was killed. This conversation took place up until the moment of his death. There are facts in there that he could not possibly know unless they were told to him by Tenino."

"The facts are that Mr. Russel's father was complicit in the conspiracy with Antonio Tenino, Frank Doran, and..." Keenan stopped short of the next name. But Chris went on.

"It's all right, Charley. The fourth conspirator was Henry Swain."

"My God. Go on." Judge Witheral was intensely following the allegations.

"We have evidence that indicates that Henry Swain, Tenino, Dr. Russel, John Russel's father who was a researcher at the medical center, and Frank Doran engaged in an elaborate plot to 'create', I guess, for lack of a better word, Jimmy Hoffa's body."

"And they did it. The procedure is described in these copies of Dr. Russel's medical notes and there's a correlating study that turned up in the archives at Wayne. It's all pretty well documented." Chris pushed a third folder toward the judge. "As long as the body wasn't found before it decomposed completely, the bone marrow could be tested for DNA. It would match Hoffa. It was brilliant."

"If anyone started sniffin' around, they produce a body. End of story." Charley took a big bite of his donut for emphasis.

"So who do you think came up with this?" The judge sorted through the information.

"I suspect it was Hoffa himself," Charley offered, still chewing.

"And the motive?"

"Money. Seventy million dollars. Missing from the Teamster's pension fund. We knew it was gone and we investigated some of the Tenino underbosses, but we could never find out where it went. Somehow we just assumed Fitzsimmons embezzled it, Charley continued, referring to Hoffa's successor as union president, "But now I don't think so. I think Hoffa took the money. Imagine, millions of untraceable dollars in the hands of a guy everybody figures is dead. You gotta admit, it's pretty good."

Christine continued, "The result was Domati's control over the Detroit operation, the union…"

"And plenty of capital to fund his drug operations out of Florida and parlay the profits into substantial control over Vegas as well."

"But," Chris continued the tag team conversation, "Dr. Russel and Henry Swain fouled them up. They were the only ones who could prove what really happened…and it cost both of them their lives."

"So how does that bring us to the current situation?"

Christine and Keenan continued for almost two more hours, explaining how the doctor had left information, how Doran had received large sums of money and banked it under various names, how he had betrayed the Teninos, and Chris' final kicker.

"There is also physical evidence that exists which proves the body that was found on the Russel's property is not Jimmy Hoffa."

This remark left Witheral silent momentarily and neither Charley nor Christine intervened, preferring instead to let him reach the obvious on his own, which of course, he did, "And that's why Doran is squeezing your client so hard."

"Exactly." Chris smiled. "And why we have to nail the bastard now."

"He knows that we suspect him and he knows that we have evidence. So does Domati. My guess is that Domati is squeezing Doran. If he can get the Russels to give up the only physical proof, then all we have is circumstantial and they know that. They know we probably can't get a conviction," Keenan speculated. "But, if we can grab Frank now, we might be able to turn him and get Domati; maybe bring the whole thing down. But we have to do it right away."

"You want a warrant."

"Yes."

"For Doran."

"Yes."

The elderly judge leaned back in his chair, his tanned face wrinkled with contemplation.

"...and Domati."

This was a surprise even to Christine.

"Easton, I think it's time to go after the whole conspiracy. I think, as long as we've got Frank, we can complete the circle, we can follow the money, we can prove it." Keenan reached down and grabbed the handle of his briefcase, lifting it up to the table from the chair beside him. He snapped the brass latches open and removed several pages from a folder inside. "From the way I read it, the Federal Racketeer Influenced and Corrupt Organizations Act is pretty clear in such situations. I think we can prosecute both of them under that act and under federal jurisdiction, your jurisdiction. You can issue a warrant under that statute, I think, based on the information that we have provided today. That means we can lump any state felonies into it, too. That gives you authority to preempt any other action in the murders up in Leland, since we maintain that those crimes are merely predicate to a larger criminal conspiracy." He winked at Chris, "So now you got the whole thing, Easton, airtight as a pork chop in Tupperware."

This deserved another donut, Charley decided. He got up and walked to the platter while the judge considered the approach.

After a long silence Witheral began to chuckle. "Charley Keenan, you are an amazing individual, you know that? Nice try."

Charley gulped his coffee to wash down the dough, "Your Honor, this old southern dog is just getting too tired to spend another twenty years chasing his tail."

"I don't doubt it, Charley. I'll get with the clerk and find out who's scheduled for the arraignment, but I think the Domati warrant, at least until you have Doran's cooperation, is a stretch. You'd have a hard time with that one." He turned to Chris, "I assume that you can produce this 'physical evidence'?"

"Absolutely." Chris figured by the time it would be needed, she could.

"Charley, I'll see you in my office at seven tomorrow morning. I'll have your warrant for Doran. We'll see what happens after that. You're going to need some enforcement help. Is there someone you can trust in the bureau?"

"I think so." Keenan was a bit disappointed.

"Good." Witheral rolled his chair back and, standing to leave, cautioned them both, "This is going to be a mess. Miss Ferrand, I hope you're ready." He put his blazer on and walked to the door, "Charley, I'll see you in the morning."

23

The Grosse Pointe home of Vincenzo Domati was one of the few of its grandeur that remained. It sat on nearly five acres and stretched the entire distance, over a quarter mile, from the entrance on East Jefferson to the lake. Originally it had been built in 1906 for Elijah Slocum Peabody, then president of the Pullman Company, and had been sold twice since; first to Harry Fleisher, the notorious bootlegger and head of Detroit's Purple Gang in 1930, and again in 1964 to it's current occupant while Fleisher was serving a twenty to forty year prison sentence and had no need of such accommodations.

Peabody's penchant for privacy and love of the water inspired the home's location at the extreme rear of the lot. The original high wrought iron fence protected the property from the street and the dense hedges that paralleled it, added by the second owner, restricted the view of the immense front lawn. This landscaping continued down each side of the lot. Another tall hedge had been planted against the driveway, creating a high green tunnel along the right side of the property, extending from the metal gate at the street all the way to the house. At the end, it turned toward the center of the lot and released into a square, stone courtyard which was bordered by the garage on the right, the guest house on the left, and the main house centered between them.

The architecture was decidedly French-influenced and offered views of the grounds on the front, and Lake St. Clair from dozens of windows and small balconies in the back. Over the years, ivy had climbed the brick and surrounded each with deep green, shiny leaves that sparkled randomly as they turned in the late evening breeze to reflect the last of this Sunday's sun.

At the rear of the estate, a huge porch of slate and granite ran the entirety of the building's dimension, stepping down twice to a central slate walk which branched symmetrically through formal gardens, each presenting a unique variety of rose.

Extending out from the seawall, over the water, in matching ivy and brick, was the boathouse. Used frequently by the first resident, a recreational sailor, and to excess by the second, it was also useful to Domati. It provided a second egress from the property. Although he was constantly watched, it was possible to elude surveillance, if he was careful, using his small Sea Ray to idle out slowly at night, waiting to reach the middle of the lake before revving the craft's powerful engines.

This was the kind of evening that Domati cherished. The sun, nearly gone, gave way to the lessening waves which slapped the rusted steel breakwater, their rhythm growing faint as the warm night began.

He would walk in his garden every night, admiring the plantings. Sometimes he would come across one of his gardeners and would ask about a particular variety; its color or scent, the conversation a pleasant relief from business.

But tonight, as he waited, except for Paulo Anguillo, he was alone. The huge Cuban would never let Domati stray from his view. His adoration for the old man was deep, his family saved first from tyranny, then he himself from life in a Florida prison. He believed that without Domati's help he would be dead. It was his pledge to protect the old man.

The fact was that Paulo served not as a result of Domati's compassion, but as part of a business arrangement. Santos Trafficante had brought Anguillo, a top ranked Cuban boxer, and his family to Miami shortly after Castro's revolution. After several professional fights; losses, his trainer alleged that he was paid off by the Miami mob. Anguillo beat him to death. Before he was tried, however, both the trainer's wife and the Dade County prosecutor disappeared. The case was never brought to trial.

This favor was repaid when Traficante permitted Angelo Domati, Vincenzo's eldest son, to assume control of his drug operations, providing a better pipeline to Detroit, with better profits, while further cementing the relationship between the two families.

Anguillo and his sister Maria had worked for Vincenzo Domati ever since.

It was she who broke the peaceful moment with her shrill voice, heavy with accent, "Senor Domati," she called from the back door near the kitchen, "Senor Shapiro has arrived."

He signaled for Paulo, who came immediately. "Paulo, tell her to have him wait in my office." Domati wheezed, shuffling forward, with the help of the muscular fighter, toward the porch. Anguillo shouted back across the yard in Spanish and Maria went inside. Domati appreciated the additional language. It made monitoring their conversations even more difficult.

It took them several minutes to reach the old man's study which faced the courtyard at the front of the house. Once there Anguillo was dismissed. Domati continued shuffling to his desk at the far side of the room. Shapiro, casual in a golf shirt and shorts, stood from the antique leather club chair and watched silently, daring not speak, while the old Italian made his way around to his chair. Before he sat, he stretched his hand out to the younger man.

"Leonard," he said, coughing, "Sit, sit. It's good to see you."

"Thank you, Don Domati."

Once seated, he waited. Over the thirty years that he had represented Domati as his consigliere and his personal attorney, he had learned this was how Domati preferred to begin each meeting. This time he started with a pointed question.

"You said you have something?"

"Yes."

"Would you have some wine, a drink?"

"No, thank you, I'm fine. I…"

Domati held up his hand to stop him mid sentence. He reached into the pocket of his plaid cotton shirt and produced a handkerchief into which he sputtered, coughing up a wad of phlegm. He pushed a switch on the floor alerting Maria.

Soon she arrived at the door. "Wine, please. A little wine. Bring the bottle and two glasses."

"Thank you for your hospitality, Vincenzo. I appreciate it." The lawyer knew that the use of the first name was as close to familiarity as he could get.

Soon, Maria returned with the wine, poured a glass for each of them and left, quickly, closing the door behind her.

The older man took a large drink and it seemed to clear his throat and bolster his voice, "Okay, Lenny, give it to me."

"They've asked for a warrant. For Doran. And for you." Shapiro leaned forward taking his glass, also drinking.

"And for that you come all the way here on a Sunday? What can they do to me? How do you know this?"

"Well, I…"

"Don't tell me." Domati said, shaking his head. Leonard Shapiro had ways of finding things out. He knew people. And people knew who he worked for. But still he could move, as a Jewish trial attorney, in circles where Domati could not. He could broker Domati's favor and did so regularly with the old man's permission, increasingly as Domati grew older. They had built a trust. If Shapiro identified a deserving individual, he would be rewarded or punished. It was how Domati controlled politicians, and policemen, and judges. It made Leonard Shapiro a very powerful man.

"They've got records...of Doran's bank accounts, from Swain, through his daughter. They've had a man inside, too, for awhile I guess, watching him. They're gonna charge him for Tenino and the other guy. They're set up to grab him in the morning, at court."

"I see. And they're gonna grab me, too?" Domati's sarcasm sliced the room.

"Not yet. But Keenan thinks he can turn Franky and bring you in on the Hoffa deal." Shapiro was deadly serious. He stared intently at Domati, waiting for the reaction. Much to his astonishment, the old man began to laugh.

"Well, Lenny...here." He poured the attorney a second glass of the red liquid. "You know what it sounds like to me? It sounds like Franky has let this get a little out of control. People runnin' around thinkin' they're gonna arrest me. Not yet. That's a good one. I'll talk to Franky." His laugh was a sputter, alternating with wheezing coughs.

Shapiro interrupted, "They have some evidence, something to do with Hoffa's body, some proof of what happened...somehow it has to do with the family. They can point it at us."

"Bullshit!" Domati slammed the glass down. "How?" He leaned forward on his desk, "Doran's not gonna say a thing, trust me." Again his foot found the floor switch. "Thank you for coming."

This was his cue to leave. Shapiro stood. Domati did not. Instead, for a long uncomfortable moment, he gazed out through the crisscross pattern of the leaded pane window into the courtyard beyond, his small brown eyes squinting, contemplating the next step. Finally, Maria arrived and Vincenzo apologized.

"Lenny, I'm sorry to rush you, but there are things I must do."
He offered his hand but did not rise. "Maria, please show Mr.
Shapiro to the door and, since I have interrupted his evening wine,
have Paulo load a case into his car. Good bye now. We will talk."

"Thank you, Don Domati."

"Drink in good health, my friend." Again, he was looking out
the window. "When Paulo is finished with that, Maria, send him
back here."

Domati said no more. He barely noticed that Leonard Shapiro
was gone. Now he had business. He lifted the phone and punched
out the familiar number, one of hundreds he had memorized. It
was his habit not to write down anything.

A man's voice answered and Domati said simply, "I want you
to call me," and hung up. It was one more precaution. He would
always call the same number which would be forwarded twice, to
another line and then a third. Even if the first was tapped, the
second and third would be switched regularly, infinitely
compounding the difficulty of locating the phone, and making it
virtually impossible to secure the necessary authorizations for a
legal wiretap. The call would be returned from the third number.

Domati waited, sipping at the wine. Soon his private line rang.
It was his son Angelo, calling back from Miami.

"Papa Mio, you are in good health?" he asked using the
nickname he had used as a boy.

"Yes, Angelo, yes. Thank you for calling so quickly," the old
man replied, "I need you to be here. Tomorrow morning."

"Okay, Mio."

"You should bring DeVera."

"I will."

Carlos DeVera was a fabrication. He was nothing more than an
invention carefully constructed by the Domati family to provide
the necessary cover for Frank Doran. He was a native Colombian,

a businessman. He had made frequent trips, over the last fifteen years, to Miami and New York. His lifestyle was grand, almost legendary in the South American country, though few had ever seen his face. He had been many different men during that time. He was to be interchangeable.

Angelo knew exactly what to do. Immediately, he arranged his flight, a non-stop at 6:10 in the morning, first class, both for himself and for one of his lieutenants who would be Carlos DeVera. They would arrive in Detroit at 8:37. On the return they would connect through Kennedy Airport in New York.

They would be followed, as they always were, from the moment they left the Miami Beach compound. It was Angelo Domati's intention to make sure they were.

The elder Domati had more work to do. When Paulo returned to the study, he was quick to issue orders.

"Paulo, good. Come in and close the door." Obediently, the Cuban entered. "I want you to get ahold of Cappola and have him come here as soon as possible. He will have to stay here at the house and drive me tomorrow."

Paulo nodded. He rarely spoke. He knew that if Cappola was coming, this was serious. The man was a sadistic murderer and so feared that even Domati's other enforcers would not look at him if they found themselves in his presence. It was said that he once accused a valet parking attendant of eating in his car. He slit the man's throat and stood over him until he bled to death at his feet. This, in full view of horrified patrons who never spoke of the incident, insisting that they hadn't seen a thing, and curiously were never able to identify the perpetrator. It was because of incidents like these, true or otherwise, that the killer had received his street name; Joey 'Ghost' Cappola. At forty-two, he was less than half the age of Vincenzo Domati and only Domati himself, in his youth, was said to have been more deadly. The two shared a common bond in that each actually enjoyed the act of murder. It was out of this passion for death that they had developed mutual respect.

Domati kept his Cuban bodyguard out of his business. Indeed, his ignorance was a necessity.

"Have both cars ready by six in the morning. You will be going to the airport to pick up Angelo. Call him. Find out when he is coming." As certain as he was that his own line was not tapped, he knew the regular line to the house would be. Doran made sure of it. The authorities would know that DeVera and the younger Domati were expected in Detroit. "Bring him back to the house. Thank you. You may go."

For the next two hours, Domati was on the phone. It was a courtesy to inform the other bosses whenever a major action was planned. It prevented unwanted interference and allowed them the opportunity to get their people out of the way.

There were many details to cover with his own men as well. It would be a dangerous day.

At eleven-thirty, the 'Ghost' arrived. He was sent directly to the study. Maria followed behind him and, aware of his taste for brown liquor, quickly rushed to the small wet bar and poured him a glass. She was twenty years his senior, but his dark, slender handsome good looks and smooth voice, caused her to giggle like a teenager whenever he spoke.

"Thank you, Maria," she blushed and hurried out. When the door closed, Cappola raised his glass in salute, "Don Domati." The older man returned the gesture.

"Joey, my young friend, sit, please." He motioned for Cappola to sit near him in a large, green, brass-studded leather chair, in the back corner of the large room. It offered a more intimate situation and demanded less volume from his vocal chords to carry on a conversation.

"I am sorry for the late hour," Domati started. "Thank you for coming so quickly."

Cappola settled back into the comfortable chair, resting his legs on the ottoman. He was as always, dressed in black. On this Sunday night, he wore pleated wool trousers and an imported silk shirt. He was well built, slender, tall, nearly six-four. "Don Domati, it is never a problem."

"Help yourself to the scotch."

"Thank you."

After a brief cough, Vincenzo Domati began, his eerie voice barely audible, "Much work must be done tomorrow. Did you bring your things?"

"I did."

"Good. We will start tonight. At around eight o'clock in the morning we will need to secure Kleenco downtown." He referred to the warehouse of the Kleenco Linen Service, located near the river just east of downtown Detroit. It was one of many legitimate businesses that the family owned. He went on as Cappola listened intently. "There will be two packages there about nine. We will need to have one of our trucks ready to take them up to the plant."

"In Mount Clemens?"

"Yes. Make sure they're set for a week. You will drive. Angelo will be here tomorrow. He can help. Paulo will get him at Metro around eight-thirty. They will be coming here. We'll have to take care of those shits who are watching the house, so I can leave. My son will drive me to the plant. There, we switch, and you will drive tomorrow night. I will need you then."

Joey stood and crossed the carpet to the bar, listening to the instructions.

"They have men on Franky, too, and his line may no longer be safe. Someone will have to take my orders to him."

"I will do that personally, later tonight, Don Domati."

"Good."

Cappola walked back to his chair, "I will need some help, a couple of men."

"You can have Nino, I've already called him," Domati said, referring to his other son. "After that, I can only give you girls."

"Your daughters are lovely," Cappola complimented the don.

"But not so lovely that you would have one for a bride, eh?" The old man drank deeply from his glass, choking back laughter.

"I don't think I would make a good husband." Cappola smiled.

Domati finished his wine. "It's almost one and I need sleep," he said seriously, "Here's what has to be done."

24

Christine decided it would better if John and Shelby were not told of the plan to arrest Doran, fearing any slip might jeopardize the operation.

She had spent most of Sunday evening with the Russels, alternating between the women's visiting area on the fourth floor and the men's on the fifth. She could not conceive of a more horrible place. The prisoners were like animals, calling out obscenities from their cells whenever John or Shelby passed. It was not usual for them to have such refined and terrified prey and they enjoyed the sport, relishing the fear they could create. It was one of the few things in their lives that they could still control.

Christine had gone earlier to the Russel house to get clothes for them to wear to court, plus a few personal items that Shelby had requested. When Chris returned to the jail, she was able to convince the duty officer that she required a joint consultation with her clients, prior to their arraignment. The Russels were brought to a consultation room on the first floor where the three of them could talk.

She also brought the newspaper which, as it turned out, was a mistake.

The headlines had sent John into a blind, ranting frustration, pacing like a trapped atom around the room. "Jesus!" he had yelled after seeing his photograph and the headline of the lead story, part of which he repeated, "...'Implicated in Tenino' hit for crissake! I knew the guy for forty-five minutes! I'm the one who was nearly killed! Who was practically blown up and then chased down through the goddamn forest! My clothes are ripped to shreds. I've been bleeding all over two counties and half of my pubic hair has been burned off by sulfuric fucking acid!" John let the paper fly. It bounced off the steel mesh that covered the room's only window, "Fuck this!"

Unfortunately, the commotion attracted two huge black guards who were stationed at the door. They burst in with nightsticks drawn to put the insane criminal in his place. It was only the two women, Christine and Shelby, blocking their attack, standing between them and John, that prevented serious physical injury.

After the outburst, Christine watched, unable to intercede, as the Russels were once again led away to their respective areas. She could hear the catcalls starting, spreading through the incarcerated mass. She hated to leave her clients there, but she had done what she could to comfort them, without being specific, and to convince them that it was almost over and soon they would be free.

Now, that moment was approaching. And on this bright Monday morning, she had already spoken with Keenan several times. He confirmed that he had received the warrant from Judge Witheral as promised and that the plan was in place.

Her adrenaline flowed hard to her heart as she parked in the lot on Lafayette across the street from the Theodore Levin Courthouse, where her clients would be brought. Her anticipation heightened as she pushed through the crowd of reporters and photographers, ignoring questions, and quickly ascending the stairs to the guarded lobby. She had been to this courthouse many times, running papers back and forth for her dad and other attorneys in the firm. She had clerked for one of the judges when she was in law school. She had witnessed the process, but never participated as a principal. Today would be her first time. She was ready.

Once inside the grand structure, Chris recognized Karen Morse. She was standing in the huge limestone entrance hall with several other FBI agents. Christine felt eyes following her footsteps as they echoed from the polished stone. She caught the occasional view of similar groups in the blurry spaces between other counselors and clients brushing quickly past on the way to proceedings of their own. The agents were stationed at strategic points around the building; by the elevator lobby, at the fire exits, at the intersections where each of the long hallways converged on the main room.

The heavy brass doors of the vintage elevator opened and Chris got on. She pushed the button for the second floor. When she arrived, she noticed more agents patrolling the upstairs corridors. She thought it was funny that these obvious men somehow believed that they could go undetected as they lurked about. She smiled and nodded, knowingly, to one of them as she passed, on her way to room 217, the courtroom of Catherine Cody-Putnam, senior judge and the longest to have been seated on the court, having received her appointment in 1964 during the Johnson administration. She was a notorious liberal and overt in her distaste for the American social aristocracy. It was certain that she would look upon the opportunity to incarcerate the Russels as another victory in her crusade to unseat the wealthy, although she herself was well-heeled, having inherited the majority of the stock of Putnam Mining, her late husband's company.

When Christine arrived, the room was already half full. The national press comprised the majority in attendance. She felt her stomach tighten as she walked down the long corridor between the worn oak benches. She could hear the loud whispers behind her. The high ceiling caught the comments and bounced them back, delayed, to the oak floor. The walls were paneled with detailed mahogany to a height of eight feet or so, and above, cream colored plaster. Giant oil paintings of former judges and legislators hung opposite several large multi-paned windows on the high wall. There was a railing supported by milled oak spindles, ten inches across, that extended the width of the room and divided the audience area from that in which the lofty business of the state would be conducted.

At the prosecutor's table to her right, six or seven attorneys huddled plotting their strategy. Just as she reached the swinging wooden gate that separated them one of the men rose offering his hand; Prosecutor Arlan Quinn, tall and perfectly tailored, with searing blue eyes and graying hair, moussed back tightly to his head.

"Ms. Ferrand, I assume? Arte Quinn." He had made no secret of his aspirations toward higher office, and this greeting was, as every move, calculated to attract additional attention from the growing gallery behind them.

"It is." She had no patience for foolishness.

His voice rising to be quoted, "I look forward to prosecuting this case against such a lovely adversary." His phony charm was amusing to Chris.

"I don't think you'll get that far. Excuse me." Chris opened the gate and turned away, leaving the astonished imbecile in her wake, and settled into her own area to the left of the aisle, at the defendant's table. She spread out the necessary paperwork and waited. She could hear the room filling and the voices growing louder. She looked over the assemblage. In addition to various friends of the Russels, and the press, she recognized several other characters from her father's parties. The audience was a curious mix of Junior League women and Mafiosi; of law students, politicians, and the press. Keenan was not there.

At eight-forty-five, the large door at the front of the courtroom, directly across from Christine, opened. One of the Wayne County deputies entered, and behind him, John Russel, handcuffed. A second guard unlocked the shackles. John rubbed the pain from his wrists. He looked up to Chris who was standing as the guard led him to the table. Once there, under the attendant's envious gaze, the two embraced.

"Hey Chris. Good to see you," John said sincerely and quietly, "Really good."

"You too."

John looked exhausted. Although he had managed to shave and get himself into one of his best blue suits, it was clear to Chris that the night had not been easy. His leg throbbed constantly from the shrapnel wound. Whenever he moved, the wool pant legs rubbed against the tender, now hairless area of his inner thigh. He was psychologically spent. He stared blankly at the crowd, at the faces which stared back at him.

"Here John, sit down. This is going to be over before you know it."

"I don't know how to take that." He laughed quietly as he nestled into his chair next to Christine's.

She sat down and pulled her chair tight to John's and whispered, "You may be surprised at how this turns out." Before he could ask, she was studying her papers once again.

"I don't know how many more surprises I can handle. Where's Shel?"

Chris looked at her watch, "I don't know. It's almost nine. She should be here."

"Hm." John scouted the room, careful not to look overly concerned, although he was scared to death. He had shared a cell with two other guys, neither of which, it would be kind to say, was able to relate to John's particular circumstances. One of them was passed out cold from heroin and cognac and awoke only to vomit. The other looked like Mr. Clean with a hint of anti-Christ thrown in for good measure. John had not dared sleep, fearing either to be drowned in oral excrement or transported to hell by the dark, menacing angel. Instead, he had sat awake, his back to a corner of the painted cinder block, inventing a game: guessing when the junkie's next heaving eruption would occur.

It had been emotional torture, worrying about Shelby, imagining her in a cell. His anger had joined his fear and further prevented him from falling asleep. That Doran could do this to her made John crazy.

The courtroom was full, a gang of the curious. John noticed the prosecutor, Quinn, mugging for the audience. What an idiot. If he hadn't been appointed to this job he'd be out at the airport pan-handling for dinner. Unfortunately, he knew John. Actually he knew of John's public support for his opponent, the eventual victor, when Quinn had sought a judgeship in the thirty-sixth district. It was now Quinn who smiled most broadly at John from across the aisle.

At five to nine, the huddle at the prosecutor's table tightened. The suited men seemed troubled and anxious. Quinn issued orders to his staff and one of them broke from the group and scurried away, trying not to be obvious, choosing the perimeter for his exit to the rear.

At precisely nine-o-clock the court clerk, a young black woman, entered from a door on the opposite side of the judge's bench from where John had emerged, and took up her position at the front of the room. Succeeding her, the uniformed bailiff, who stood in the open area between the empty jury box and the tall podium from which Judge Putnam would dispense justice.

"All rise," the young officer commanded, and all in attendance did.

There seemed to be ongoing unrest at Quinn's table, whispering and heads shaking. John leaned to Christine, "What's going on?"

"I don't know." She had also detected the strange behavior.

"Where's Shelby?"

"I don't know that either."

They were interrupted by the bailiff, "The Honorable Judge Catherine Cody-Putnam..." he continued but neither John nor Chris were listening. Shelby should be here; had to be here.

Into the crowded courtroom walked the slight, older woman, draped in the black robes of the profession, the material dragging on the floor behind her as she ascended the wooden steps to the bench. She was intense in her surveillance of the room, actually pausing for a moment to get a better look at the assemblage before slamming the gavel down and screeching in a voice that made you want to throw water on her to see if she would melt, "Courts in session. Sit down."

John did. She looked like his grandmother's evil twin. But where his had the compassionate eyes of wisdom, this one had the stare of a wrinkled vulture peering over her half glasses to read her notes. Her face was drawn, appearing to have excess skin that dripped from her cheeks. She was once much heavier. The pounds had disappeared in proportion to her dwindling appetite as her years accumulated to nearly eighty.

She noticed the prosecutor attempting to get her attention and addressed him without looking up, "Mr. Quinn?"

He rose from his place at the table, nearly pirouetting while fastening the button on the front of his suit coat. "Your Honor, if I may, just for the purposes of..."

"Cut the bull, Mr. Quinn," she admonished, to the roaring delight of the gallery, "What is it that you want?" Her lips bent into an inverted U shape and she lifted her head and stared impatiently at the prosecutor.

"If I may..." he indicated that he wished to move closer.

"Oh, very well." She removed her glasses and with a deep sigh, relented. "Approach." With both hands raised, she beckoned the attorneys.

"What's this about?" John whispered to Chris, who shrugged and joined her counterpart at the bench.

Judge Putnam began in a harsh toneless voice, "Whatever it is you think is important in this proceeding Arlan, I assure you, isn't. Now if you will just step..."

"Your Honor," he interrupted, "Mrs. Russel, who was to be one of the defendants in this case..."

"I am aware of the parties in this case."

"Of course. Well anyway, she hasn't...arrived."

Christine was listening intently, "Where the hell is she, Quinn?"

The judge was equally curious, "Counsel has a point. Are you inferring that she has escaped?"

"No, your Honor."

Judge Putnam, fuming at this waste of time, and consumed by nicotine withdrawal, spoke in short whispered puffs, "Damn...it...all, Quinn, where is...she?"

"We don't know."

"What?" Christine couldn't contain herself. John and several others near the front had heard her outburst and looked to see what was happening.

"Keep it down, honey," Putnam scolded, "I'm not gonna let this turn into a bigger circus than it already is. I need a cigarette. Step back." She waited until they were back in place, then loudly announced, "This court will recess for fifteen minutes to address an administrative concern. Ms. Ferrand, Mr. Quinn, I will see you in camera." She slammed her gavel loudly down and stormed out leaving a confused courtroom behind, instantly buzzing with speculation.

John noticed that Quinn's assistant had returned and now frantically shook his head from side to side.

The large frame of Keenan arrived just as Chris returned to the table. He leaned over the rail to talk to Chris and Russel. "Sorry I'm late. I came down to see the fireworks. What's going on? Where's Doran?" He scanned the room.

"Putnam wants us in chambers. I don't know what happened, but Shelby isn't here. I don't like it."

John was dumbfounded. Charley's demeanor changed.

"Doran," Keenan said seriously, "He knew. Someone tipped him. You go see the judge. When this is over, find Agent Morse. You know Agent Morse, right?" Christine nodded, "I'll see you later. Don't worry, Mr. Russel." He assured John and made his way out, through the crowd, and was gone before John could respond. The deputy was back. John stood. The handcuffs were back on. They took him out and down the hall to the holding area. When he was locked in, the cuffs were removed. The two guards waited at the door.

Christine, as instructed, headed for Judge Putnam's chambers.

Keenan dodging the herd of press, headed down the limestone corridor to the stairway next to the elevator lobby. He opened the metal door and flew down the concrete steps, bursting out on the level below. Instantly, two agents reached inside their sport coats, until they realized who it was and relaxed. "Have you seen Morse?" he called out as he passed.

"No," the answer came back.

"Doran?" he shouted without missing a step.

And again, but more faintly, "Nope."

He kept going, reporters on his heels. He was almost to the front of the building when he spotted Agent Morse and her group, "Karen!" he yelled, and she, recognizing his urgency excused herself from the men and met Charley in the hall. The other agents held the reporters safely out of earshot.

"He's gone. He took Shelby Russel."

"Shit."

"Here's what I need you to do." Charley took a moment to catch his breath. "Check with the locals. Try not to give 'em too much, but see if they've got anything on Doran, or his car, you know, the regular stuff. I don't want a bunch of trigger happy idiots chasing him down, though. You know what I mean. But first, wait for me with a car at the prisoner's entrance in back of the building."

"All right."

"I'm going back up there to get Russel and Christine. You can take us back to my office. I want to stay away from the feeding frenzy. Thanks." Charley heard her behind him, calling orders to her men, as he walked back toward the elevators. He felt confident. She was a good agent.

When Christine arrived at Putnam's office, Quinn was already there. To the prosecutor's continuing astonishment, so was Chief Judge Witheral, who greeted Chris.

"Ahh, Ms. Ferrand...the best laid plans, eh?..." His eyebrows rose, "Please, sit down."

The presiding judge puffed hard at the last inch of a Camel before snuffing it out in her Putnam Mining ashtray. It matched the era of most of the furnishings throughout the drab room.

The judge leaned forward in her red Naugahyde executive chair, resting her forearms on her desk. She spoke her first words in smoke.

"Arlan, this was supposed to be a simple matter," he started to respond, but she cut him off before he could say a word. "The Russels are involved as material witnesses in a larger ongoing federal investigation. All I can tell you at this point is that the purpose of this morning's proceedings had nothing at all to do with the murder charges you sought to bring against them."

"I had no idea."

"Oh course you didn't. Now listen to me carefully. I am inclined to issue a writ of capius. In this case, unfortunately, I can't."

"What?" He was astounded at the threat of such a directive, which required that he personally assume responsibility for producing the subject, as soon as possible, no questions asked, and without regard to any other circumstances, nor the necessity of a warrant.

"…but I'm not sure you could find your own dick if you had to go to the bathroom. Besides, I think you'd trip over somebody else's trying to find her, don't you?" She didn't wait for the idiot to answer, but instead continued like a mother instructing her son, "I've got to admit, Arlan, in forty-six years this is the first time the prosecutor has physically lost a defendant…" She would have said more, but instead lit another cigarette.

Christine timidly used the opening, "Regarding my clients, your Honor?"

"We have five more minutes. Then we'll all head back to court where you will make a motion Mr. Quinn, to dismiss."

He was like a school boy, "Aw, C'mon," he pleaded.

She took two massive draws on the butt, "Surely you can find some high profile child murderer or gang rapist to ride to the mayor's office or wherever you think you're headed. But today, you lose. Now let's get this over with." As the others began to leave, the defeated prosecutor sat, shocked. "Go," Putnam said, shooing him from her desk.

A few minutes later, the court back in session, Quinn stood to address the judge. He exuded confidence, at least publicly, "If it please the court, the people...do not wish to bring charges at this time." He sat down to an additional surge of mumbled speculation. The judge banged the gavel. "Quiet. Quiet please," she ordered. "Assuming, that the defense has no objection, I grant the motion. Will the defendant please stand." John did as she ordered. Christine, standing next to him, reached her hand to his and squeezed gently, leaning to his ear, whispering, "Here we go."

Putnam continued, "Mr. Russel, you are free to go. Court dismissed."

The air was instant noise and total confusion. Reporters ran out to disseminate the new information. No one was more astounded, however, than John Russel; shackled fifteen minutes earlier, accused of murder, now free. And Shelby. Missing.

He saw Keenan making his way back into the room, bouncing from side to side as the press scurried past. Some, however seized the opportunity to confront John, rushing forward, hurling questions.

Charley got to the railing barely a half step ahead of the mob. "C'mon. This way." He grabbed both John and Chris' forearms and led them toward the front of the courtroom where the bailiff stood.

He reached into his jacket pocket, removed his identification and showed it to the officer, "Bailiff, I'm Special Prosecutor Keenan. We need to get back to the holding area."

Without hesitation, the man rushed to open the door. Russel, Chris, and Keenan scooted through. When they had disappeared, the bailiff returned to his position, guarding against the surge of unwelcome interviewers.

The trio proceeded down the long hall past the two holding cells and down a flight of stairs. At the bottom they turned into a second long corridor, retracing their path now a floor below.

"What the hell is happening, Keenan?" John asked as they walked, "Where's my wife?"

"Mr. Russel, I don't want y'all to panic," he smiled, "I want you to know that we have a handle on this. You'll know more soon."

"I want to know now, dammit!" He jumped directly in front of the prosecutor, causing him to stop abruptly to avoid running John over. John's eyes burned at Keenan's, inches from his face as the anger tore the tone from his voice until all that was left was a gruff whisper. "I want to know now," he said.

Christine touched his shoulder, "John. Please."

John struggled to control himself. He backed away from Keenan, shaking his head. "I'm sorry, Charley. I apologize. You've gotta understand, I..."

A voice called from the end of the hall, "Prosecutor Keenan," it was agent Morse, "I'm right outside."

"Thanks, Karen," Charley called back. "I know this is horrible, John," he said quietly, as they started walking again.

"Doran has her, doesn't he, Charley?" Christine asked, but Keenan dodged the question.

"We'll talk more when we get back to my office." He was businesslike with most of his convenient drawl gone.

John looked hard at the prosecutor and for the first time since they had met, he detected something less than the jovial disarming southerness and easy going charm that was the usual menu of the man's demeanor. John witnessed the transformation and he knew.

Chris was right. Doran had Shelby.

"Jesus."

25

The quiet Monday dawn belied the intensity of the calculated activity at 810 Wilton Street in the comfortable northern Detroit suburb. Inside the brown brick bungalow, while the rest of Royal Oak slept, Frank Doran was hurriedly making preparations. He had been since Cappola showed up on his doorstep, hours earlier. This was the end. They knew, all of them, what he had done.

He had anticipated this day. He had planned for it. He was prepared to disappear, and actually would have done so anyway in less than a month, after his retirement from the bureau. But Frank had hoped to avoid the scrutiny and pursuit, which would now undoubtedly result, and simply vanish quietly. As pragmatic as he was, though, he figured this was as good a time as any.

In any event, it didn't matter now.

Shortly after three, he had been jarred awake by the ringing doorbell and Joey Cappola's loud knocks in between. He only stayed a few minutes, just long enough to explain to Frank what was planned at the courthouse and to convey Domati's instructions. There was very little time.

Immediately, Doran went to his basement, and with a cold chisel started to work on the mortar joints between the cinder blocks on the back wall of his furnace room. In less than fifteen minutes, one was loose. He pushed in on each end alternately with his hands until it pivoted out enough to grab. He removed the heavy gray block and put it behind him on the cement floor.

The opening behind it was deep and dark. Years before, he had dug it out of the hard clay soil. The smell of damp earth filled the room. Doran grabbed the flashlight from the top of the water heater, and scanned the hole with its beam. Insects scurried to avoid the light, running away on tree root bridges, slipping through tiny gaps in the hard walls. There it was. He reached in and removed a plastic bag. The twist tie, badly rusted, fell apart in his hands as he opened it. Inside there were two envelopes. He ripped the first one open. It contained a new passport, birth certificate, and driver's license; more than perfect forgeries, actual documents, complete with Frank's picture over a new name; Carlos DeVera. In the second was a stack of bankbooks wrapped in a rotted rubber band. He opened the one on top, checking to make sure it contained the necessary identification, another driver's license, also with his picture, but with a third name, signed in his hand at the bottom. He checked them all and each had similar modifications, all corresponding to the appropriate names on the various accounts. Inside the back cover of each one, folded neatly in half, was a rubber surgical glove, with a single numeral written on it in black marker. A matching number, also in marker was written on the last page of the thin book.

Doran searched deeper in the hole, this time retrieving a second clear plastic bag containing a pistol, ammunition, and twenty-tree banded piles of currency of assorted denominations, mostly hundreds and fifties.

Frank scooped all of it up into his arms, carried it upstairs and dumped it on the table in the kitchen. He went out the back door, down the steps of the small wooden porch, and followed the long concrete driveway that led to the garage which separated his modest house from his neighbor's.

Inside, in an old coffee can, stored on a high wooden shelf, he got the wad of plastic explosive. He brought it inside and dropped it on the table next to the other items.

He made coffee, and while it brewed, he found some cold cuts in the refrigerator and slapped together a quick sandwich which he, more or less, inhaled. The sun was up. He had to hurry.

Upstairs, after his shower, dressed as he always did for court, in his best gray suit, he looked around his bedroom for the last time. He came downstairs and walked through the other small rooms. This had been where he lived since he joined the FBI. It was where he could blend in. Where no one really knew him, though many would occasionally wave. He paused for a moment to absorb the inside of this place for the last time; this house, his house.

He opened the front hall closet. On the floor at the back, partially hidden behind his overcoats and raincoats, was Swain's briefcase. The one that Henry's last wife had filled before she killed him. Doran brought it to the kitchen table and opened it. Without sitting, he leafed through the contents. One file contained information on the Tenino family and its business operations. Doran removed it and laid it on the counter next to him. Another was personal information. Another dealt with Domati and included surveillance photos of the Capo and various underlings; two taken at the Red Fox restaurant. Then there was Dr. Russel's file. Doran opened it and looked through the pages, stopping to read John's father's will. There it was, among the things he intended to bestow upon his only son..."*Additionally, my complete history of experiments as represented in my journals, and, lastly my platinum statuette of praying hands in the hope that my son will search deep to find their true meaning...*"

It was so damn obvious. Frank felt stupid. He'd always suspected the doctor and Swain had something. There it was. The damn document had gone through probate. He had even seen it before, but never picked up on this obvious reference. Stupid.

Frank threw the file back into the case and closed it again. He picked up the pistol and secured it in his empty shoulder holster. He threw the savings passbooks on the counter with the Tenino file. From under the sink, he grabbed a white plastic trash bag, then swept the countertop clean, dumping the papers, bankbooks, into the bag. He tucked the explosive putty in the palm of his hand and grabbed the handle of the briefcase with the tips of his fingers.

Again he went down to the basement, this time to his workroom, and removed the top red metal shelf from a large toolbox. The entire bottom area was filled with the money he had taken from Swain's garage; the money that Carla had stolen from the safe at the lakefront mansion; over six-hundred thousand dollars. He shoved the bills by the handful into the kitchen trash bag.

It was almost ten after seven. He walked back to the furnace room, still carrying the nearly full bag in one hand and the leather briefcase in the other. He put them both on the floor and replaced the cinder block. That done, he once again opened Swain's case. He lifted the top file, took the matches from his pocket and lit the corner. Quickly it was surrounded with flame. When he could no longer hold it, he tossed it back in, lighting the rest of the documents. Before the container itself caught fire, he slammed the lid shut, reducing the fuel inside to embers. He stuck the clay-like wad to the outside and touched the warm case with his fingertips, testing it's temperature. Satisfied, he slid it across the floor, under the gas valve of the water heater. He turned the knob clockwise and watched the pilot light sputter and die. When it was out, he reopened the valve.

He took the bag with him as he vaulted the steps to the first floor. He darted from room to room checking each window to be sure it was closed. Before he left the house, again in the kitchen, he turned the kitchen faucet on, full hot, about one quarter of the way, so the stream was little more than a steamy trickle. He had rehearsed this many times and he knew that the water heater, now fully reheated after his shower, would continue to supply the tap, at this rate, for about an hour. After that it would demand more, and the main gas valve would open, filling the house with explosive vapor.

He had walked to the stove, turned one of the gas burners on low, lit his De Christo Capo cigar, shoved the plastic bag into his own briefcase spinning the combination to lock it, and left to pick up Shelby Russel at the Wayne County Jail.

Frank had seen the surveillance car behind him as soon as he left the house. He noticed another ahead as he drove south, down Woodward, toward downtown, the two cars leapfrogging, alternately following his, in a silly attempt to avoid detection.

When he arrived at the jail, shortly before eight, he parked in the center of the lot behind the building, where there were many open spaces. He wanted to be sure that he could be seen clearly as he left his car and walked slowly across the parking area. It was important that those who were watching him would take note of his whereabouts.

He entered the large back lobby of the building, and stopped at the first security point. It was manned by two deputies who recognized Doran, but he flashed his FBI identification anyway, more of habit than necessity, and clipped his badge to the breast pocket of his sport coat.

"Morning," Frank greeted the first guard, removing the untraceable weapon and sliding it down a long table next to the metal detector to a second deputy beyond.

"Morning, sir," the second man said, handing the gun back to Frank who replaced it without losing a step.

He headed toward the sergeant at the duty desk in the central reception area. He also knew Doran.

"Morning, Inspector," the man said.

Frank smiled, "How are you, Sam. Looking for a prisoner, Russel, Shelby Russel." Doran waited as the deputy looked through his release log.

"Yeah. Right here." He pointed to an entry, then to his right, "Number three lockup. Down there."

"Thanks."

Doran walked to the doorway indicated and opened it. Inside, a wide hallway. Identification out. Another deputy checking it and handing it back, reaching out for Frank's pistol and briefcase, as he handed them over.

"Russel. Shelby."

"Number three on the right," he responded, then raised his voice, shouting his command to an operator, "Gate open." Instantly, Frank heard the whirring electrical sound of a motor. The first of two steel mesh fences began to roll out of the way and Frank passed as it closed behind him. Only after the first was secured, would the second move. He felt uneasy for the brief time he was contained between them. Finally, it opened and he moved out into the hall. On each side several cells with prisoners locked inside, staring, waiting to ride to the courts and their own destiny; as dressed up as their wardrobes would allow, wearing the camouflage of the innocent, men in business suits and ties, women in dresses, each hoping to hide at least some degree of guilt behind these extra layers, smiling at Frank as he passed.

Shelby was alone in the number three cell on his right. She paced impatiently, her heels clicking rhythmically on the hard concrete floor. The gabardine fabric of her business suit shifted from side to side as she walked. She had done her hair as well as possible without benefit of a mirror and sponged her chest and underarms with a wet paper towel, during the last of her supervised visits to the ladies' room.

As the FBI agent approached, she looked at him, confused. Frank Doran was the last person she expected to see this morning, at least not before court. Her eyes widened. Her temper uncontrolled, "You bastard. Get the hell away from me, you murdering bastard." She started to cry, "How could you do this to us?"

Doran walked deliberately to the edge of the cage. He spoke in a calm, quiet voice, "Now Mrs. Russel, there's no need for all that. Just come along with me. You'll see, everything will be fine." He raised his voice and yelled down the hall, "Guard."

One of the uniformed deputies unlocked the door and stepped into the cell. He pulled handcuffs from the leather strap on the back of his belt and snapped them in place around Shelby's shaking wrists.

"I'll help you take her out, Inspector. There's a van waiting," the man offered. But Doran quickly shut him off.

"That's all right, Deputy, let me have the key, I'll take her myself. I don't want her talking to her husband. Thanks." Obediently the guard handed it over.

Doran held on tightly to the upper part of Shelby's arm, squeezing hard when she protested, "No. I'll go with the deputies. Officer, don't let him take me. Please. You don't understand!"

All of which was ignored by the deputy and met with a chorus from the other cells.

"I think he undistan plenty, honey, yo white ass is goin up!" and whistles from the men and the women, one of whom shouted, "I'll see you in Jackson, sweetie an' I'll give you sompin you can really love!"

The mesh gates slid open again, leaving the disgusting monologue behind, and Doran, holding Shelby firmly by the chain that connected her wrists, led her out to the central area. The tears streamed down her cheeks to her long neck leaving faint dark trails of makeup residue behind. Frank collected his gun and briefcase as he made his way back out through the steel door.

Terrified, she could only whisper, "Please, no. Please."

Doran walked quickly pushing her along beside him, ignoring her pleas, this time, not to the back door where he had entered, but to the main entrance, fifty yards down the hall on the opposite side of the duty desk.

The hall was busy with traffic, attorneys, sheriff's deputies, and other prisoners. It was easy for Doran to blend in with the hectic pre-trial crowd and the noise level was sufficient to mask Shelby's desperate attempts to get help. He was often in the building and his presence there this morning would not seem strange.

Nobody paid any attention to him as he led Shelby down the steps and outside to a large parking lot filled with government vehicles. Several signs warned, 'PARKING FOR AUTHORIZED VEHICLES ONLY. ALL OTHERS WILL BE TOWED'. He kept moving at a brisk walk, not wishing to appear rushed, navigating between the rows of dark colored Fords.

When he got to the third row, he reached into the side pocket of his tweed blazer. He pulled out two rubber surgical gloves and, satisfied that he could not be seen, slipped them over his hands, juggling his briefcase between them as he did.

The black Ford LTD was parked where Cappola had said. It was unlocked. Frank opened the passenger door, tossed the leather into the back, and pushed Shelby, still protesting, into the passenger seat. He held her against the back with his left arm, opened the glove box with the other, and there, as he expected was a small bottle filled with clear liquid and a washcloth.

Shelby, afraid of what would happen next, began to squirm in the seat, trying to get free. She drew in as much breath as she could and used it to propel one final scream. But before it could reach full volume, Doran had soaked the rag with chloroform and pressed it to her mouth. She held her breath as long as she could, resisting the growing necessity for fresh air, until finally her body insisted and she involuntarily sucked the vapor into her lungs, instantly lifting her into a peaceful fog.

Doran felt her muscles relax. She fell sideways toward the steering wheel. He slammed the door, again checking to see if he had been observed, and then hurried around to the driver's side. He slid in, pushing Shelby upright. He reached across her lap searching for the seatbelt on the other side of the car. When he felt the buckle, he pulled it back over her and connected it in to the latch in the center of the front seat. He opened the ashtray, inside, the keys to the car.

He backed out of the space and soon, while four other agents watched his car on the other side of the building and waited for him to return, he was gone.

As he drove, he could not help glancing at Shelby's strong legs. One of her shoes had fallen off as she struggled. He noted the perfect curve of her ankle and foot, smooth behind her sheer stocking. Her head, tilted backwards swayed from side to side as the car turned, and the brown waves of her hair alternately touched her pink cheeks. Her neck filled the car with the fresh scent of her perfume as it led his eye to the buttons of her silk blouse and the rise of her breasts beneath it. Her blue wool skirt, pushed upward revealing her thighs.

Frank Doran, felt the adrenaline rushing through him, and could not help reaching for Shelby across the seat, touching the top of her leg, rubbing his gloved hand farther up, pushing the fabric of her skirt until her entire leg was exposed.

When he was just east of the Renaissance Center, he turned toward the river, winding his way through the deserted back streets, between the crumbling brick buildings to an alley. He slowed and parked.

Reluctantly, after a final stroke, he removed his hand from Shelby. There was no time.

He reached into the back seat and grabbed his briefcase, bringing it up onto his lap. He worked the brass dials to release the lock, opened it and poured its contents onto the front seat beside the unconscious Shelby. He emptied the plastic bag and shoved it back inside, closing the case. When he was sure no one would see him, he jumped out, walked several feet down the alley to a large steel dumpster behind a building and threw it in. On the way back to the car he stopped and opened the trunk. From inside, he removed a second briefcase, empty, which had been left for him as he instructed. He quickly slammed the trunk lid closed and got back into the car. He opened the new case, rested it on the hump in the center of the floor, scooped the pile of money and bankbooks inside, and locked it.

Gradually he was eliminating anything that could lead to him. By now his house would be burning furiously, nothing more than rubble. He hoped that the agents would still be watching his deserted car, that they weren't onto him yet. But still, he had to hurry.

He drove in circles around many blocks until finally turning down St. Aubin, across the railroad tracks, and past abandoned factories and vacant lots overgrown with twenty years of weeds and rough grass. When he was almost at the river he turned left again and headed east down a narrow street. At the end, a gate, open and unguarded as planned. He drove in past the small unoccupied gatehouse and high loading docks which protruded from brick buildings on either side. At the far end of the short block he turned right and stopped a few feet away from a large metal garage door. He honked once, then twice quickly and the door began to rise. When he could clear it, he drove in and the door reversed direction. Joey Cappola approached the car as Frank got out. He was dressed completely in white, the uniform of Kleenco company drivers, a dramatic change from the black wardrobe he preferred.

"Hey Frank."

"Joey."

Just ahead of the car, there was a large, white stepvan. The Kleenco Linen logo was painted in green lettering on each side. On the back, also in green, it asked, '*How Am I Driving?*', but provided no phone number. There were two rough-looking men standing quietly against it. With a wave from Cappola, they hurried into action.

One opened the passenger door, and dragged Shelby out. The other took the wheel and, without waiting, jammed the shifter into reverse. The first pushed the button that activated the door as he hauled Shelby to the back doors of the van. The car sped out of the building and disappeared from sight. Cappola closed the garage door and walked back to help load his cargo into the linen truck.

"Hop in, Frank."

The inspector obliged without hesitation. Inside, he sat on soft bundles of tablecloths. Above him, on both sides of the truck, uniforms hung on long racks. Shelby Russel was thrown onto several bundles across from him. And the door closed them both into near darkness.

Gradually it grew lighter as the garage was opened again and Cappola backed out. The clean smell of starch combined with exhaust fumes. The clothes above them swayed from side to side, their hangers banging with each bump.

Out, past the gate, into the city, they drove, to the freeway and north. The prisoner, Joey 'Ghost' Cappola, and now, Carlos DeVera, who would, as had been planned, live the remainder of his years at his estate in Columbia where he was well known.

Frank Doran lit a fresh cigar. It was a hell of a way to retire.

26

The confusion at the Detroit courthouse added more fuel to the ever growing media firestorm that began under the front lawn of John Russel's Leland home. Many of the press had settled into comfortable headquarters in the designated area across the street where the television networks had stationed their giant tractor trailers, motorhomes, and vans. All had assumed that the trial of the Russels would be an ongoing event and the cornerstone of the evening news. At nine-thirty, most were still milling around in front of the building in an attempt to determine exactly what had occurred inside. A few of the more curious, however, after hearing that the charges against John Russel were surprisingly dropped, had wandered several blocks to the MacNamera Building seeking more information.

While Charlie Keenan, Christine Ferrand, and John waited upstairs for the FBI briefing to begin, Karen Morse addressed the small crowd in front of the building.

"At eleven o'clock there will be a press conference in the main conference room on the second floor. That's room 2111 for those of you who do not know. At that time..."

"Is Messing here?" one of the reporters yelled.

"I can offer no comment on the whereabouts or schedule of the Assistant Attorney General. At eleven, though..."

The interruptions continued and grew louder as more reporters sensed news and joined the gathering, "What happened to Russel? Where's Mrs. Russel? There's a rumor that someone from the FBI is missing, is that true?"

Agent Morse cut them off with a terse closing remark. "You will know more at eleven. Thank you." She reentered the building without confirming that Stanley Messing had indeed arrived earlier this morning. His general title was Assistant Attorney General of the United States. But specifically he was in charge of the Federal Racketeering Unit and Charley Keenan's immediate superior.

He was sixty-two and as intelligent as he was street smart. He had grown up in New York City. In fact, many of his closest friends had chosen crime over school. But Messing worked hard, saved the money and eventually put himself through college and then law school at Georgetown University in Washington, D.C. He never left. His passion was politics. It was said that he had even retained a public relations firm to publicize his high profile cases, though he vehemently denied that.

When Messing entered a room he was noticed. This entrance was no exception. He was followed into the third floor conference room by his assistant, Jack. Both were dressed impeccably in dark suits. Messing's tie was slightly more colorful and flamboyant. He smiled broadly, his face wrinkling into his gray temples.

Immediately, Charley Keenan stood to greet him and make introductions, though none were really required. He started with Chris.

"Stan, This is Christine Ferrand, Mr Russel's counsel. And Mr. Russel..."

"John." John said, standing, as the two men shook hands.

Keenan continued, "You know Agent Garnetti, of course. This is Attorney General Messing."

"Please, sit down. Thanks Charley. We have a lot of work to do." He spoke directly to John, "Mr. Russel…John, I am aware of the situation with your wife." He paced back and forth at the front end of the room, addressing all present with a clear, deep speaking voice. "I should first tell you, that Bob Garnetti here, Agent Garnetti, is directly assigned to my office and has been working here under my authority, specifically maintaining surveillance on the director, Frank Doran…"

"You mean, you knew about Doran?" Chris was flabbergasted, "And you just watched him. He murdered two people. What the hell were you thinking?" She was angry. "For how long?"

"Well Ms. Ferrand, I think the prosecutor can fill in some of the spaces. Charley."

John Russel could feel his heart rate rising, "Wait a minute. If you're watching that prick, you know where he is…where Shelby is, right?"

"We are waiting for information now. Charley, go ahead, start at the beginning."

"Yeah," John said indignantly, "Start at the godam beginning, Charley, but make it fast 'cause you guys are gonna go get my wife and arrest Doran or shoot him or whatever it is that you do when you're not standing around 'watching'. Jesus. What the hell is this?"

The full drawl was back, "Now John, I want you to hear me out. There are things you should know." Keenan spoke in his most soothing southern tone, "This started with Dominic Baglia."

"No, it started when you dug up my lawn. Ever since then my life has turned to complete shit and I want it to end. Give Doran what he wants. Get my wife away from him. He's gonna fucking kill her."

Christine touched his arm and John sat back listening once again to Keenan.

"There was a note. Sent to my office. It was intended to light a fire under Doran. And obviously, it did. I had talked to Baglia many times at Milan where he was a prisoner. His name actually came up originally when I first started investigating Hoffa's disappearance. He worked for the Domati family. I'm sure you have heard of Vincenzo Domati?" Chris and John nodded and Keenan continued, "We were looking at him for the Hoffa case but we could never get anywhere. But I kept working on Baglia."

"How did you get on to Frank Doran?" Christine asked.

Messing jumped in, "He walked right into a banking investigation. In St. Thomas. We got him on tape. He deposited over a hundred thousand in cash into an account that had been opened eighteen years before. Under the name of Dominic Baglia."

"I pressed Baglia on it and finally he caved," Charley said.

"And the note?" John asked.

"That's something that I'm very sorry about, but I'm going to ask you both to try to understand that we are in the business of prosecuting criminals and sometimes we employ some different..."

"You sent it. To yourself. Didn't you Charley?" Chris felt a tight knot growing in her stomach.

"Baglia wrote it. He was dying. At that point, he had nothing to lose. He told us that he took the body to your cottage and told us where he buried it. I told him what to say and I had it sent."

"He also implicated Doran," Messing added, "It was then when I authorized the operation."

Charley continued to explain, "I think we were all shocked at the speed and severity of the events that followed."

"No shit," John offered.

Chris was starting to piece it together, "The fire...He killed my father, didn't he?"

"We know he was there that night. But Domati and two of his men were also there earlier."

Bob Garnetti spoke for the first time, "We checked on your father's wife. We believe she may have been under contract, a killer."

"Chris," Charley was sympathetic, "It's hard to say for sure."

Christine fought to hold back the welling pain. She looked at Keenan, her eyes foggy. At first not able to speak, but then summoning her most professional demeanor, said simply that she understood.

John was growing impatient. He really didn't much care how any of this started, only how they proposed to make it end.

"That's terrific. Now let's get Shelby back. Where the hell is Doran now?"

Messing responded, "Shortly we will have a complete update. He was last seen at the Wayne County jail." He moved closer to John and leaned down to his eye level, "In situations like these, we have found, Mr. Russel that it is best to wait until the perpetrator contacts us, and, I assure you that Frank Doran will...and soon would be my guess. We know what he wants." He walked back to the front of the rectangular room, "And he knows we want Domati. He's not stupid. He'll deal."

John was becoming more uncomfortable with the way the conversation was drifting.

"Wait a second. You are going to leave my wife in the middle of this just so you can get this guy Domati. I don't think so." John stood up and walked over to Messing. "He's going to deal all right. He's going to deal with me. I'm going to get that disgusting finger and give it to him and after that you can do what you want."

"Just hear me out, Mr. Russel. Maybe we can all get what we want. Bob."

Garnetti took the cue, "We can 'provide' a human finger of similar characteristics. We don't think he'd be able to tell the difference. It would even be possible to insert a tracking device that would be virtually undetectable."

Messing's assistant was writing furiously, taking notes of everything that was said. The agent went on, "We feel that after the exchange and your wife has been safely returned we would be able to grab him. That's about it, Stan."

"You can't do that. What if he has the damn bone that attaches to it. He has access to it doesn't he? I mean he is an FBI agent. Jesus. No wonder you guys can't find Jimmy Hoffa."

Messing was mad. "Oh, we found Hoffa, Mr. Russel, now it's just a question of who's going down for the murder."

Christine was curious, "Found him? I thought you understood. That's not Hoffa. The body you dug up isn't him, we can prove it. Charley, help me out here."

"Sir, Ms. Ferrand is…" Keenan tried.

Messing slammed his fist down on the heavy table, "As far as I'm concerned, it is. We've got the forensics to back it up. That's it. That's how we're playing it." He stood up straight, adjusting his hair, which had fallen out of place. Once again he spoke in a low, calm voice, "Now, we're going to arrest somebody for it. Right, prosecutor Keenan?"

Before Charley could answer, there was a knock on the conference room door. It was Karen Morse. "Excuse me, sir. Prosecutor Keenan, may I see you outside for a moment?"

"Certainly. Excuse me, gentlemen."

John returned to his chair. He half listened as Agent Garnetti and Stan Messing defended their illogical scheme. He noticed that Jack, the assistant and silent accomplice, wrote down what he no doubt assumed would be quotes of some future biographical significance. Occasionally, John would question some aspect of the plan, but they would ignore him and continue. Finally, John blocked it out.

Fuck this. He already knew what he was going to do.

When Keenan returned, John could tell instantly that something was wrong. "What? What happened?"

The room was silent. "They lost Frank. He's gone."

Garnetti was defensive, "That's impossible."

"What happened?" Chris asked, pressing for more information.

"Apparently Doran went to the Wayne County jail about an hour and a half ago and never came out. When Agent Morse's men went in looking for him, he was gone."

"And no one saw him? That's bull."

"Bob, I just know what I was told. He entered the building, checked in...even talked to several guards. He got Mrs. Russel and that was the last of him. He never signed out. Nobody saw him leave. His car is still there."

"Oh, my God." John was paralyzed. "We gotta find him."

"They checked his house?" Chris tried to be rational.

"What's left of it. Explosion, a half hour ago. Natural gas. Karen's got men there already. No one inside, best as they can tell."

John slowly stood up. He could not believe what had happened. Shaking his head, desperate, "Now what?"

Bob Garnetti was quick to answer, "He'll contact us. Soon."

"It'll probably be you, Mr. Russel, that he calls," Messing added, "Charley, have Agent Morse set it up. Bob, you run it from here."

"What do you mean?" John asked, "What's going on?"

Again Garnetti responded, "Agent Morse will go with you, back to your house. Your phones are wired already. When Doran calls we'll take it from there."

Stan Messing attempted to reassure him, "We'll do the trade. You'll see, everything will be fine."

John looked at him with disbelief. Based on recent events, he was less than confident. He walked toward the door, his posture sagging, the weight of his growing depression tugging his shoulders toward the floor.

Christine jumped up, "Wait, John, I'll go with you." She joined him at the door.

John looked around the conference room first at the assistant attorney general, then at Keenan, searching for something more to say. Nothing would come. He was getting cold. Shock. Chris supported him, her arm wrapped tightly around his waist. She felt the fear shiver through him and felt him wobble slightly.

Into the long conversational void, Charley Keenan dropped his suggestion, "Go home, John," and his personal promise, "I'll let you know what's happening."

"Go home, John."

27

It had been hours since they had pulled into John's driveway in Chris' black Mercedes convertible. As he waited for her to open the garage door, curious reporters had surrounded him, banging on the car and the dark tinted windows. It had blended into a whirling dream, a horrible fog. He remembered the police pushing the press away so that they could drive in, but that was all. The rest of the day was blurry.

The television in the cabinet across the family room had been muttering hypnotically for hours. The evening sun, still deep yellow and warm, burned across the light wool carpet. He heard Karen Morse talking endlessly on her cell phone behind him in the kitchen as he gazed out into the green stretches of the large yard. Occasionally, a pair of arms would emerge above the fence, holding a camera as high as possible to snap a photo. Usually a pair of police hands would descend on them and haul them away. John grinned at this silly drama and tried to predict exactly where along the perimeter the next incursion might occur. He was alternately hot and then chilled. He used a small knitted afghan that Shelby kept folded over the back of the sofa to fend off the waves of cold. The perspiration had permeated John's expensive wool suit and it had become badly creased from the moisture.

Hours passed. The phone rang constantly and, thankfully, Chris was there to answer it, pleading for the inquisitive to leave the line open, but never offering any explanation.

It was her firm hands, massaging the tight muscles in his shoulders that brought him temporarily out of his catatonic funk.

"Thanks, Chris." The rubbing helped ease his tension. He knew what he would do. He had been going over it a thousand times since he got home.

He felt her release and heard her steps moving once more toward the incessantly ringing phone in his nearby office. Again he drifted off.

"John." He recoiled instinctively, startled at Chris' touch on his forearm and her strong voice, "It's Keenan.. He wants to talk to you."

John instantly came alive, bolting into his office where he picked up the waiting receiver. He was suddenly alert. "Charley, what?"

The voice at the other end began, "He called."

"What?"

"Just now, for me. He wants to meet."

"Where? Tell me."

"I don't know. He didn't say. He 's smart. He called here on a secure line so we couldn't trace it."

"When?"

"I don't know that either. He said he'd get back to me. John, I think he wants to make a deal. He knows there's no way out of this."

"And Shelby? Did he say anything about Shelby?"

"He assured me that she will be fine, that's all. He wants to meet me."

"I'm going with you," John said decisively.

"You can't, John. It has to be me. Alone."

"Do you really think that Messing will allow that? C'mon. You heard him. All he cares about is solving the Hoffa case. You can bet your ass he's gonna want you to carry a tape recorder or camera, or some other high tech shit that's gonna screw the whole thing up."

"I won't let him. We've talked. He understands."

"Right. He'll have half the Justice Department following you around. He doesn't care about you or Shelby or any of us."

"Look, I know Frank Doran better than anybody. I believe he called to make a deal. He trusts me. He knows I'll level with him. I think I can get this resolved. Try to hang in there. I just called to let you know what the status was, that's all."

"I appreciate that, Charley, but I've gotta go with you."

"I can't let you do that. I'm sorry. I have to go. I'll call you."

"Charley. Wait." The dial tone hummed in John's ear. "Damm it."

"What did he say?" Christine asked, "What happened?"

There was a long pause while John absorbed Keenan's words.

"John?"

"Yeah....I'm sorry. It's Doran. He called Keenan," John answered, but offered no details. Still talking, John went to the powder room to splash water on his face. He called out to Chris, "Keenan wants us to hang here. He'll let us know if anything else happens. At least they're talking. And apparently Shelby's okay." John dried his face and stared at his image in the mirror. He wanted to believe it. He wished he could let it go; that he could trust Keenan to pull it off. But he had seen Doran in action. The prosecutor was no match for him. It was becoming impossible to stay home and do nothing. As he returned to Chris and the family room, he heard Karen Morse in the kitchen concluding her conversation on the mobile phone.

"I need a drink. Some wine, I think. Chris, you'll join me?"

"Of course."

John headed into the kitchen. He knelt at the wine storage rack under the counter. Agent Morse wrapped it up with Garnetti and pushed the button to hang up.

"He called Charley, eh?"

John found the bottle he was looking for, "Yeah." John noticed the agent's jacket hanging on the back of a kitchen chair and under it, he saw the leather strap and shoulder holster. Her service revolver was snapped inside. He stood up, got a corkscrew from a drawer, and opened the Merlot.

"Would you like a glass?"

"Can't. Thanks."

John nodded and returned to the bar in his family room, pouring two goblets, for himself and Chris. He handed her one of them and sat down next to her on the couch.

"Thanks."

"We could use a belt of something. I can't believe this is happening; that we can't do anything."

Morse was on her phone again in the kitchen.

"I know."

"It's frustrating, sittin' around watching these news bozos with their damn speculation about everything." He gestured to the news man on the television, "We're supposed to be waiting here for Doran's fucking call, like they said, and what does he do? He calls Keenan. I don't think any of those guys have a damn clue what they're doin'." John stood up again, pacing, looking out in the yard. Another flash went off at the back fence. "And we're surrounded by these assholes. It's unfucking believable."

"John, there's nothing we can do," Chris calmly reassured him. "Nothing."

He wasn't so sure of that. He had seen Chris put her car keys in her purse after they got home. Where was it? He put his empty glass down on the coffee table and went back to the kitchen. There, on the counter by the door. But first he had to get rid of Morse.

"Want some ice water?" he shouted loudly to Chris in the other room. Without waiting for her to answer, he lifted the brass handle and the water burst in a hard stream from the tap. He saw that Morse was having trouble hearing the person on the other end of her call. He got a couple of tumblers from a cabinet and pressed the first against a lever in his refrigerator door. The cubes began to drop in as the ice maker roared to life on the other side of the door. That did it. She was gone. Just to make sure, he set the control to 'crushed', which was even louder, and filled the second glass to the top, which drove the FBI agent deeper into his family room and the TV.

With the cold water still running, he moved quickly to the purse. He found the keys to Chris' car and shoved them into his pant's pocket. She would understand.

When he got back with the water, agent Morse had disappeared completely into his office where it was quiet. He could still hear her talking.

John, standing, refilled the wine glasses.

"Thank you, John. It's very good."

"My pleasure." He took a long drink, finishing the whole thing. "It is good." He took a deep breath, stretched, and let it out slowly. "Chris...I don't want you to take this wrong, but I need some time...you know...to be alone; to put things into...I don't know...some kind of order, I guess."

"John, of course. I can go. Give you some privacy. It's no problem." She started to stand.

"No!" That may have sounded too frantic, but he didn't want her to look for the keys. "I mean...please, no. Stay. Please. I'm just going upstairs. Get out of this suit. Relax, if I can."

"I don't blame you. You could use some rest, John. It's been hard. But we're here if you need anything. At least I can answer your phone." Chris reached out and took John's hand firmly within her own. She looked at him, piercing him with blue, "Are you going to be okay?" she asked softly.

"I'll be fine. Thank you, Chris. I'll see you in the morning. If you hear…"

"Don't worry, I'll keep you posted," she interrupted.

John smiled and went upstairs. He had the keys to the Mercedes. That was the first step. Better than Shelby's Jeep. The press would be looking for that.

Quickly he changed into blue jeans and a tee-shirt, white socks and running shoes. They would all have to realize that he had to do this; that, as far as he was concerned, there was no choice. The gun. He hated the damn thing, didn't even want it under his roof. Now he needed it. Open the door slowly, quietly. Listen. Downstairs, television channels changing. Christine. And Morse. Her voice, still talking on her cell phone in the office. This was it. As lightly as he could, John descended the carpeted steps, careful not to step in the middle where the boards, worn over the years, might squeak and betray him. Quiet, like a bowlegged cat; left edge, right edge, until he was down. Around the end of the banister, down the hall to the kitchen. The chair. Damn. It was bright. He should have turned the lights off. Stupid. Get the thing and get out. That was all there was to it. Unsnap it. Grab it.

"John?" It was Christine. She had heard him in the kitchen. Shit.

"Gettin water. Good night." He hoped she would buy that. Lights off. But now he would have to go back upstairs and start over. Up again. Close the door with a loud, I'm going to bed now slam. There.

He had managed to undo the snaps on Karen Morse's holster, so it should go fast. No time. For all he knew, Keenan may already be on the way to meet the bastard.

The bowlegs again. Down the stairs. This time through a much darker hallway. Reach into the leather. There it was. Heavy and cold.

Out then, to the garage. No lights. He peeked out from the dark through a small window in the garage door. He could see in the descending pool of the streetlight, the now diminished and unsuspecting press, kept at bay by the local policemen, out on the street, away from his house.

Quietly, he got behind the wheel of Christine's dark convertible. He put the key into the ignition and started the engine. He felt the rumble as it came alive. John took a deep breath. He looked at the gun on the passengers seat. Leaving the door open, he ran around the back to the button next to his garage door. One push and the door started up. By the time he was in the driver's seat again, it was high enough to skirt under. He pushed the gearshift into reverse and blasted out of the garage.

The two policemen at the end of his driveway stood motionless, stunned as the man in the vehicle backed out directly in front of them, reversed direction and sped away down the street. The various reporters and photographers, taken by surprise, rushed to follow. Only one car, though, had any chance at all of catching John as he raced toward East Jefferson and the lake. John saw the headlights behind him and drove even faster.

When he reached the major road, he waited. When the other car was in the same block, he turned left away from Detroit, driving more slowly. As soon as the headlights turned to follow he accelerated again. The lake appeared on the right as the road became a wide boulevard with beds of low flowers planted artfully in the center of the short cut grass divider. It was almost ten and the Monday traffic was light. There were groups of vehicles cruising in both directions though, catching a last glimpse of the calm lake and the mixed fragrances of fresh water and mowed lawns. Neighbors on the way home to the serenity of a night much more certain than his.

When the reporters following had closed to within a quarter mile, John slammed on the brakes, turning left at an opening in the manicured center and sped out, timing his U-turn to be just a few feet ahead of the oncoming traffic. He heard horns sound behind him, but didn't look back, instead pushing the accelerator pedal down hard to the floor, gaining speed, leaving his persecutors stuck in the gap between opposing lanes. It had been since high school that he had pulled this move. Then, it was merely to avoid the Grosse Pointe police when he and his friends would cruise this same stretch of Lakeshore, racing each other in stodgy cars that belonged to parents; Buick station wagons and Cadillac sedans. Then it was fun. Tonight, it was more serious.

When he was convinced he was no longer being followed, John slowed. Soon, in Detroit, the pristine protection of his suburb gave way to the demolished eastside ghetto; the buildings along Jefferson boarded and broken, the road cracked and uneven.

John could see the lights from downtown offices burning high in the night sky ahead. He checked repeatedly in his rearview for other cars following him. There were none.

He passed what used to be Woolworth's, the dime store, now nothing more than a shell, a pawn shop, criss-crossed with steel mesh to protect its filthy windows, covered with signs advertising 'loans for jewelry' and 'highest prices paid for gold'. He remembered that, as a boy, he and his friends would ride bikes here and spend hours inside, buying squirt guns and balsa wood airplanes. Until one day a group of ghetto kids chased them away, racing after John screaming at him. He never went back.

Now it was frightening even to drive here.

He came to Van Dyke Avenue and the bridge to Belle Isle, a public park, an island, in the middle of the Detroit River. It was the bridge where a gang of teens had forced a woman to jump to her death after she refused to have sex with one of them. He wondered what could drive people to such extreme action, to such violence. But as the streetlights passed, each casting a long moving shadow across the black metal of the pistol on the seat beside him, he knew that it could escalate. He could never forgive the others, but in this moment he began to understand desperation.

He reached for the weapon and pushed it out of sight under the passenger seat and continued toward the center of the city, checking again to see if he was being followed.

When he reached the MacNamera Building there were dozens of reporters crowded together on the street out front. John drove past them around to the rear, where the employees parked. It was a large lot, well lit, and encircled with a high cyclone fence, topped with barbed wire. He drove past, scanning the area. John went around the block several more times, until he feared he might be noticed and changed his route. Finally after his fifth pass he came across an empty parking space on Washington Street, far enough away from the federal building, but where he still had full view of the sliding metal gate and the lot beyond. He pulled in and shut off the engine. And waited.

Each time a car approached, he scrunched down in the black leather seat, leaning sideways to hide his face, until it passed.

As the minutes and eventually hours drifted past, he thought of his wife, and Doran. The man was capable of anything. He had witnessed it himself, how easily he would kill. He wondered if Shelby may have been killed already. It was a question he had prevented all day, not wishing to contemplate the answer. He was more convinced than ever that what he had done, what he was doing, was the right thing to do. He had to do something. He had to do it now. He would be forgiven in the end, he was sure. So he waited.

John Russel was scared to death.

28

A car turned the corner slowly behind him. At the sight of the headlights, John assumed his position, ducking low. The rumble became louder. This car was different from the others. Suddenly the light, a spotlight swept the interior and John tightened into a dense ball. The beam cut across the headrests and the mirror. The car stopped next to his. It was the police. He could hear their radio. Jesus. Again, the spotlight. A radio call.

Then the noise. A siren. Its incredible volume causing a reflex action as John bumped his head on the steering wheel, "Ahhh." He quickly silenced the scream, but he felt the throbbing above his left temple as he heard the car rev and speed away. Thank God for crime.

He sat up cautiously and looked again at the parking lot. Charley Keenan's Lincoln was still there. John rubbed his head and waited.

It was almost midnight before the prosecutor appeared. As he left the parking area he turned east, away from John. When John felt Keenan was far enough ahead, he started the Mercedes and pulled out to follow. He was not alone. Ahead of him, a black Ford, did the same. One of Garnetti's agents. John had warned Charley not to trust Messing. Of course they would follow him.

John had to get closer.

As the three cars traveled to Woodward and turned right toward Jefferson and the river, John was directly behind the FBI agent. When Keenan turned right and entered the tunnel under the convention center, the entrance to the northbound Lodge freeway, John increased his speed, passing the Ford. Once ahead of him, John began to slow down, forcing the man to slow down behind him. Several times, the man tried to pass, but each time John veered into his path, slowing even more, allowing Charley to disappear around the curve of the brightly lit tube. When he was sure Charley could no longer see him in the rearview mirror, John scooted to the right lane. The agent gunned his car again trying to pass. But when he was just about even with the convertible, John pulled down hard on the left side of the wheel and slammed into the side of the Ford. The agent swerved wildly, regained control and tried again. Again John slammed into him. Again and again.

Finally the man lost control and John watched in his mirror as the car went from side to side, crashing into the cement walls, until it spun, disabled, sideways, stalled in the road, the agent unconscious behind the wheel.

John sped up. He was going almost a hundred miles an hour when the light blue Town Car came into view and he slowed to match Keenan's speed. He followed the prosecutor through the interchange and onto Eastbound I-94. There was enough traffic for John to remain hidden from Keenan's view a few vehicles back. John continued to follow, eastbound through East Detroit and St. Clair Shores, where he merged onto Interstate 696. At the first exit, Gratiot, he got off and continued along the service road to Groesbeck Highway and turned right, northbound.

For several more miles John followed Keenan, out into the more rural Clinton Township, past small tool and die shops, bars, and auto repair shops. Gradually the road was becoming more deserted. It was late and most of the blue collar population was sleeping. As they got farther out, the retail businesses gave way to overgrown acreage, gravel pits, and junkyards.

Well into the country it was dark. John and Keenan were the only two vehicles on the road and John had to drop back. But the highway was mercifully straight and he could see ahead for miles. He kept the Lincoln tail lights just barely in view.

On the horizon on the left was a bright blue-white glow. John saw Charley Keenan's brake lights. He accelerated. The light was becoming brighter. He saw the prosecutor turn in up ahead. When he got closer, John could tell that the brightness was coming from tall halogen light towers that surrounded a monstrous scrap metal operation. He could see the conveyors and the piles of rusty metallic debris as he approached. He watched as Keenan disappeared through the open front gate. John continued, speeding down Groesbeck to avoid suspicion. As he passed the entrance he read the sign, 'MICHIGAN SCRAP METAL'. It was almost two stories high, painted with red letters on a yellow field and lighted with spotlights.

It was an odd place for a clandestine meeting, John thought, but then as his car returned to the darkness of the highway, he realized that it would be easy to spot anyone who may have followed. It would be difficult to enter the facility undetected.

When he was about a mile down the road he pulled off into an old driveway and turned off the headlights. It looked as if it had been some time since it had been used. Tall grass grew in between the gravel troughs in the area closest to the road and completely across it further in. He drove in a quarter mile with only his dim parking lights to guide him. His eyes adjusted slowly to the darkness, but when they had, he could see the path outlined by light from the three-quarter moon. He turned into the field, the car hidden by the grasses, and shut the engine down. In the distance he could hear the low rumble of heavy machinery almost drowned out by the sound of thousands of crickets. When he stepped out, they stopped, creating a silent circle around him.

The quickest way back, along the road, was also the most dangerous. But, not knowing the terrain, an attempt to go directly cross-country would be unpredictable. He decided to take the road. He grabbed the revolver and jogged back through the weeds. At the shoulder of the road he ducked down and checked for traffic in both directions. Nothing, He walked out, skirting between the pavement and the drainage ditch, picking up speed until he was running along the road. John's previously wounded calf and his head, throbbing together as each step landed. Headlights. He dived into the grass and lay still until they passed. Then up again moving swiftly toward the sound and light. Jogging. The pistol held tightly in his hand, swinging at his side. Another car. Back in the grass. Running again.

When John was a few hundred yards from the entrance to Michigan Scrap Metal he cut deeper into the field, cutting a line directly toward the loud noise. He ran up a small hill, falling to his knees near the top and crawling up to the edge of the tall cyclone fence to see what was beyond. It was no wonder they chose this property. The decibel level at this distance was earsplitting. The monster that filled the night with this inhuman sound was six or seven stories high. At one end was a tall crane. At the other a huge crusher which was used to compress cars into four by three foot steel cubes. From the end of the crane arm dangled a circular electromagnet, six feet in diameter. It would descend on a pile of rusty stripped vehicles, attaching itself to the one on top, haul its prey to the end of a conveyor belt, and drop it. The lump would move on the belt to the far end and higher, where it fell into the compartment to be crushed. Far away, on the other side of the device, through the superstructure, John caught a glimpse of Keenan's Lincoln. He had to get inside. He walked along the fence looking for a way to get through it. Five hundred yards later, he discovered a pole where the metal linkage had rusted. He kicked hard at the spot and the fence tore away.

He slid through, and hiding behind the small hills around the site, he was able to maneuver to another hill, higher still, where he could see the entire area around the car. He could see Charley Keenan sitting calmly behind the wheel, waiting. The area where he had parked was wide open, over three acres John estimated, and all gravel. It was flat and well lit and would be almost impossible to cross without being seen. It was hidden from the road by distance and piles of scrap metal. It was also situated where the crane operator would be unable to see it, although he could clearly see the front gate and watch for unwanted intrusions. Several other of Domati's men patrolled the fence.

Soon, a new set of headlights approached from the south. The car turned into the entrance and drove past the machine to the back of the lot where Prosecutor Keenan was parked. The black limousine pulled up beside Charley and stopped between John and the Lincoln.

John had an excellent view from his high vantage point. The passenger door at the rear of the long car opened. Frank Doran emerged. Bastard. John felt the incredible urge to charge down to the plateau. He felt the blood pumping through him. He couldn't. Where was Shelby. Was this the exchange? He hoped that it would be. He prayed she would be the next to get out. Instead, the driver was next. He was dressed completely in black, a tailored black sport coat and slacks, but not in any uniform. He was slender and tall. He quickly walked to the passenger side of the car and helped Vincenzo Domati out.

Doran walked deliberately over to Keenan. Domati and his driver followed behind, the older man shuffling over the loose sand and stone.

Charley Keenan was frightened. He slowly opened his car door and eased out. The man with Domati pulled on a pair of black leather gloves and a pistol from a shoulder holster. He pointed it directly at Charley's head.

This wasn't good. John was torn. He had absolutely no idea what to do. Shelby might still be in that car. Maybe he could get a little closer and, while the men were preoccupied, get a better look. He slid down a few feet from the hilltop and retreated around the next mound moving farther from the road. There was a small valley between them that afforded some cover from the area where the cars were parked. John crawled closer. The crane and conveyor slammed away behind him. The lights cast long shadows from the cars and hills. If he could stay within them, he could hide. He hugged the hill, rolling even closer. He could hear the men yelling over the noise.

"Charley," Doran began, "Glad you came." He let a puff of smoke escape into the dusty air.

"Frank, what the hell are you doing?"

"I'm not going to waste your time Charley. There's evidence that was missing when we dug up that body. I want it."

"What about Shelby Russel?"

"She's fine. I've got her. She's fine."

The prosecutor looked over Doran's shoulder at Domati, What's he doing here? Charley wondered, "I thought this was between us. I thought we could make a deal, Frank." He saw Domati lean over and say something to Cappola, presumably so that he could take advantage of younger lungs. And Cappola reiterated what Domati had said, shouting over the racket.

"Mr. Domati says that there will be no deal. That first he will send a message and you, Mr. Keenan will be the message."

"Frank, listen," Charley tried desperately, "What are you going to gain? We can work this out. At least release Mrs. Russel. She has nothing to do with it."

Frank Doran moved closer to Keenan so that the other men couldn't hear what he said. "It's not my decision, Charley. It's never been my decision, not since the beginning. You are as close a friend as I have ever had. But in a strange way, I'm glad you know the truth. I'm sorry."

Doran stepped back and stood with Domati. Joey Cappola handed him the gun. Frank dutifully held it on Keenan as Joey led the overweight lawyer to the far side of his car. Joey opened the passenger door and reached across to the ignition. He turned the key partially, activating the electric windows. He pushed a button and the right front went down. Without a word he methodically produced handcuffs from his pocket and used them to fasten Keenan's left wrist to the car's window frame. Then he slammed the door tightly shut, forcing it to close, anchoring the handcuffs and the distraught attorney in place.

While John watched from the shadows, seventy-five yards away, Cappola started the Lincoln, and began to move forward slowly. Charley, having no choice, walked along with it. Cappola increased the speed. Keenan had to move more quickly to keep up. Joey drove in a wide circle around the area, maintaining his pace, about five miles per hour.

John could see the sweat dripping from Charley's face, soaking his collar. He saw him reach over with his free hand and rip the shirt open allowing air to flow inside, cooling him temporarily.

John had to do something. He had to help him. He had no doubt that they would kill Keenan. They had already started. His grip tightened on the pistol handle. He crawled in closer. He was tense with fear. Could he actually shoot a man? What if he missed? The thoughts raced through his mind. And if Shelby was in that limousine, she may not be alone. They would kill her, too. John decided he couldn't take the chance. He could only watch, horrified.

The car was moving faster now and Charley was running to keep up, begging Cappola to stop, gasping at the dusty air.

Don Domati motioned for Frank to come closer, so he could hear him over the equipment, "You see Franky, this is an important lesson for you. No one will listen to you unless they respect you." Doran had heard this lecture many times before, but Domati enjoyed sharing further examples with him in case the point had been forgotten.

"You have to earn that respect, Franky. So this is a message to them, that we want what we fucking want and we are not going to play games to get it. No deals. Capiche?"

Doran watched as Keenan clutched at his chest, screaming, unable to breathe. His heart fighting to pump his blood, to satisfy his body's increasing demand. But it could not.

John turned away, unable to witness Keenan's last convulsions. A few moments later, when he did look, Charley Keenan's limp body was hanging by his arm from the door, and from the waist down dragging along the hard packed gravel.

Cappola pulled up to the original position and he asked Frank Doran to help him load the heavy, lifeless Southerner back into the car.

This was John's chance. If he had one. He got up from the grassy hill, but just as he did, he heard a voice behind him, "Hey. You there. Don't move!" It was one of the guards.

John turned around and in a split second realized the man was pointing a long automatic pistol at him, raising it. He was going to shoot. John felt his own weapon in his palm and he made a choice.

John Russel pulled the trigger. Twice.

The explosions from the smoking barrel seemed enormous. The recoil sent his hand straight up as the man fell in the opposite direction and lay writhing in the grass and dirt. He was sure the others must have heard the shot, but none of them even looked around. Now, he was grateful for the noise the giant machine was making.

He had shot a man, another human being. An act he despised more than any. The man groaned, and struggled for breath, then silence. John felt a sick heaving in his stomach, and then, without warning, he threw up on the ground in front of him.

He had to get himself together. He had to go now, while Domati and Doran were out of the car. It was his best opportunity.

John bolted as fast as he could to the limo, dashing across the open lot and diving onto the gravel near the car for cover. He took a deep breath and poked his head up to see in the driver's window. The front seat was empty. Hidden by the long black car, he crawled to the back door. Checking that the gun was still in his hand, he tugged the door open, fully expecting to find Shelby in the back seat. He waved the gun back and forth, fearing she might be guarded. No one. Empty space. What now, John thought, what now?

He should have tried to save Charley Keenan. He should have done something. Shit. He heard voices. Quickly, he ducked out of the door, closing it as quietly as possible and crouching beside the car. The men were yelling to be heard over the equipment.

First Joey Cappola, from the driver's window of Keenan's Town Car, "Frank, you take the limo. I'm gonna take him a couple of miles up Groesbeck. Why don't you follow me and…"

John realized that if he ever wanted to find Shelby, he had to stay with them somehow; follow them. He slid back along the car to the driver's door and opened it. Stretching his body across the front seat, he managed to open the glove box. He felt around inside until his fingers landed on a button. The trunk release. He lifted his head up just long enough to confirm that the men were not facing him, he took a deep breath, pushed it, and heard the latch pop.

As fast as he could, he closed the small compartment and the car door and ran to the back end of the Cadillac. The trunk lid was moving up. He had to hurry. He ran. Please don't turn around now. Jesus.

With the dexterity of a teen-aged high jumper he scissors-kicked his body over the bumper and into the space, landing square in the center of the wheel of the spare tie. The end of the bolt that held it jabbed him hard in the lower back, sending another sharp pain racing to his already throbbing head. John grabbed the cross member on the underside of the lid and yanked it down tight, locking himself in the trunk of one of the most dangerous men in North America, hoping he had not been seen.

As he lay there waiting though, he felt comparatively safe. He held the revolver tight in his hand. If anybody opened the trunk, he would shoot. He heard Doran's voice muffled, yelling something, coming closer. Shit.

But the voice passed. The door opened and Don Domati slid into the back seat of his car, leaning back in the leather about a foot from John Russel's head which was twisted behind him in an effort to conform to the available space. Another door. The engine started. The car beginning to roll faster over the rough area. Each bump plunged the metal bolt deeper into John's backside and he cringed in silent agony. Each turn contorting his body with centrifugal force.

Fumes spinning around in the dark cavity were making John sick as he bounced from side to side; carbon monoxide from the exhaust, making him tired. Voluntarily getting into the trunk may have been a mistake. But, if it was a stupid move, it fit nicely with what had happened over the last three weeks. Until then, his days, for years, had been filled with life and Shelby. And now all piled up in death. He could see the look on Charley Keenan's face. And the sad eyes of Benny Tenino as he bled on the floor at the cottage. Those visions played like an old slow motion movie, over and over again, each time more exaggerated and grotesque. If this was the end, he had tried, he had done what had to be done.

The hot gases made his thoughts swirl in a dazed, convoluted mess as he tried to reason with himself. He needed oxygen. He felt around the interior of the compartment, finally locating the rubber weather-stripping at the bottom edge. He yanked a section of it free and, although it wasn't much, it allowed a slight stream of fresh summer air into the poisonous metal tomb.

John's fuzziness began to clear immediately. And with the clarity came the realization of the new horror of the situation.

As they rolled down the highway.

With Frank Doran at the wheel and Don Vincenzo Domati, seated comfortably in the back seat of the Cadillac.

While less than two feet away, John Russel, reduced to a painful grain of human salt, was being rubbed into his recently wounded life, and tossed violently in all directions inside the deadly shaker.

Gradually suffocating in the dark.

29

If Vincenzo Domati's intent was to send a message, there could be no doubt on this gray Tuesday morning, that it had indeed been delivered.

The scene at the Federal Building was more frenzied than ever. Even the pounding sheets of warm rain had not dissuaded the crowd. The death of the Hoffa prosecutor had actually caused an opposite effect. There were now more reporters than ever jammed together, umbrella to umbrella on Fort Street. And Stan Messing was in the middle of it all, basking.

Upstairs, in the FBI offices, it was chaos. When Morse and Christine Ferrand arrived, agents were scurrying in and out, the phones were ringing out of control. Agent Morse presented her identification to the agent behind the bullet proof glass in the office lobby. He conveyed Garnetti's instructions.

"Agent Morse. Good. You're here. Briefing in the conference room. Miss?" he addressed Christine.

"She's with me. Christine Ferrand."

"Just a moment, please." He called someone on the phone, and after a pause, "In the conference room. It's fine," he said, reaching under his desk, buzzing them into the locked interior.

The hectic morning continued inside. Garnetti had mobilized the entire office and all hurried to the main conference room, leaving only clerical assistants behind. Karen Morse and Chris went directly there. Inside, next to the long permanent table with its comfortable reclining chairs, fifteen metal folding chairs had been added along the sides and rear of the large room to accommodate the overflow. Morse and Christine worked their way to two of them near the back.

Agent Garnetti began, "Sit down, please. Please, find a seat." The last of two dozen or so did and, except for the occasional cough and whisper, the room became quiet. Garnetti strolled to the windows that stretched the length of the wall and looked down at Messing and the crowd outside gathered in the strong rain. "What we have this morning is a hostage situation which began yesterday. Many of you know personally and certainly all of you have worked for Frank Doran, the agent in charge...formerly in charge, of this office." A buzz went through the room.

He continued, "Yesterday morning, at the Levin Courthouse, an operation was underway. Many of you were involved in that so please bear with me while I explain to the others. Frank Doran was scheduled to appear at the arraignment of John and Shelby Russel. They were arrested on federal conspiracy charges and predicate murder relating to the death Saturday of Benito Tenino and another man." Garnetti crossed to the front of the room. "Bottom line, they had nothing to do with it. In fact, we believe, that John Russel may be the only witness to that crime. The operation yesterday was to apprehend the actual perpetrator, whom we believe to be Frank Doran."

The conversations among Doran's former subordinates rose in disbelieving tones.

"Agent Morse, who was in charge of that operation will fill us in on the particulars. Agent Morse."

Karen Morse stood up from the folding chair to address her peers, "Yesterday, at approximately seven twenty-five AM, surveillance reported that Inspector Doran had left his Royal Oak residence. Our men followed him to the Wayne County Jail where he arranged for the release of Ms. Russel. It was from that location that he was able to allude two teams which were on site. Anticipating his arrival at the courthouse, we had an additional seven teams in place at that location in preparation for the arrest. As Agent Garnetti indicated, there was none."

"Thank you, Karen." Morse sat. "I should mention that, seated next to Agent Morse is Christine Ferrand, counsel to the Russels." The agents turned to see who he was talking about. "Ms. Ferrand may be helpful as we develop a profile of her clients."

Garnetti went on, describing John's disappearance and theft of Morse's weapon. He discussed Shelby's abduction and Doran's probable motives. Christine considered seriously, for the first time, that her clients may indeed have already been killed.

She was jarred from her thoughts by Garnetti, "Ms. Ferrand?" He was calling her.

"Ms. Ferrand, regarding the physical evidence, without being too specific..." Clearly he didn't want her to describe the exact nature of it, but she understood why it would be important.

"Of course," she said, raising her voice, "Certain physical evidence exists which, I believe, is the prime motivation behind the kidnapping of Mrs. Russel. It is that evidence which is key to the recovery of the victim and also what Mr. Russel will exchange, given the opportunity, for his wife."

"And where is that evidence now?" Garnetti asked.

"It is, I believe, undergoing forensic testing at the state crime lab in Lansing."

"Thank you, Ms. Ferrand. As far as John Russel is concerned, we believe that he followed Prosecutor Keenan to a meeting with Frank Doran, but we have nothing solid after that. We have pictures." He walked to the corner of the room and pulled a small white rope. The curtains began to close. One of the other agents turned on the slide projector which had been hastily set up near the front of the table, while another pulled down a movie screen from a metal cylinder near the ceiling. The first advanced the slide tray and the bright white rectangle was replaced by a recent photograph, taken at some charity event, of Shelby Russel dressed in a tight formal dress. "This is Mrs. Russel. Next slide please."

The room broke into laughter as the picture of John, jumping from the front porch of his cottage, swinging the telephone, his eyes wild with rage appeared on the screen.

"Please. Please everyone. It's the best one we've got. Duplicates are printed for you. Pick one up as you leave. Now, Agent Stoddard, status on Domati."

The man stood as the other agents shut off the projector and opened the drapes, "The team on his house reported that Joey Cappola has been there several times, beginning late Sunday. Also, Domati's son Angelo and a Colombian, a Carlos DeVera, arrived from Miami early yesterday morning." The man was clearly nervous. "As nearly as we can tell, sir, none has left the premises since that time."

Garnetti picked up on it, "What do you mean, as nearly as we can tell?"

"The men on Domati's house have not reported in yet today," he answered.

He was obviously frustrated, "Get someone out there and find out what's going on," he ordered, and proceeded with the briefing. "I want the usual coverage immediately; airports, buses, everything. Specific assignments. Agent Morse, take two teams. See what you can do to track Russel's movements from the house. Stoddard, I want you back on Domati. Obviously there's something up. It may not be related, but I want it checked out anyway. The rest of you will be given your specifics later. Those of you who are on the taps, stay with them. Doran will be calling. That's all."

The room filled with noise as the agents dispersed. Bob Garnetti motioned for Karen and Christine to stay. When it was just the three of them, he shut the door and sat down near them on the edge of the conference room table.

"I'm not gonna lie to you, Ms. Ferrand, this doesn't look good."

"You blew it." Christine answered. "It was all that bull about switching fingers and trying to fool Doran that sent John over the edge. If anything happened to him, as far as I'm concerned, it's your fault; yours and Messing's."

He avoided the accusation, "What I'd like to do is try to piece a few things together based on anything your client may have told you before he took off. Could we do that?"

"Sure."

"He got the call from Keenan. After that what did he tell you?"

"Not much. Nothing really. But I heard him ask Charley Keenan if he could go along. I heard him tell Charley not to believe your guys wouldn't follow."

"Let's try to retrace his activities. You said, Karen, that your man at the Russel house lost him, where?"

"On Lakeshore."

"And we picked him up again as he was following Keenan onto the Lodge. The next place we can put him is out in Clinton Township. That's where your car was found, Ms. Ferrand. It was near a scrap metal yard that is definitely tied in with the Domati family. It's only four miles from where they found Keenan."

"You think they killed him don't you?" Chris asked.

"Yes."

"What about Russel?" Morse asked.

Garnetti started pacing again, in front of the window. He was perplexed. "He wasn't out there."

"And he should have been?" Chris wondered.

"If they knew he was there, that he followed Keenan, I think they would have killed him, too. He may have seen something."

"What about the finger?"

"I don't know. I think we'll have to assume that they know everything that we do; that they know it's at the lab." He returned to his seat. "I've worked the organized unit for a long time. It's gotten to the point where I know what they think. Keenan was a message. Domati just wants us to know that he will do whatever he has to, to get what he wants. He wants us to know that the family is serious. I wasn't so sure before, but I am now. This is the key to the Hoffa case."

"And Charley Keenan knew it," agent Morse offered.

"That's why they killed him."

"As for Mrs. Russel?"

Garnetti paused momentarily losing his words, "They used her to...to get the prosecutor's attention....I...I would doubt..."

"You think she's dead, too, don't you?"

"Yes."

30

John had passed out from exhaustion and fumes hours earlier, long before the rain. His body was pounding with pain from every direction. It was black. There was no light at all. As he awoke he began to remember where he was and what he had seen. He listened for several minutes, but heard nothing. The fluorescent hands on his watch read ten after five. He had been out for at least three hours. But where the hell was he?

He had to get out of the car trunk. He searched blindly in the blackness feeling around for the tire iron. Finally in the recess behind his head he touched the forged metal tool. It was held in place with a plastic clip and it took several attempts to free it. He contorted his body, twisting to the side so that he could gain leverage on the latch. He listened again, heard nothing and began to pry apart the fingers of the latch. The tool slipped, crashing against the metal. John's heart raced again. They could have heard that.

He lay still. He listened. Not a sound.

Again working on the lock, but it wouldn't release. Eventually after four of five more attempts he gave up on finesse and took the straight, sharp end of the iron and hammered it into the back side of the lock itself.

With a loud metallic ripping, the entire cylinder hurled outward, landing on the cement. The sound echoed.

Immediately, without coaxing, the trunk lid opened and John could see in the light from the security flood lights that streamed in through the row of small windows, that he was in a garage, Domati's garage.

He grabbed the stolen pistol from the trunk and crawled out, breathing the fresh air deeply as his hands and knees hit the floor. It was a fairly large building, big enough to house three more vehicles, but there was only one other parked inside, an identical, black Cadillac limousine. His eyes, accustomed to total darkness, quickly focused in the partial light. He could see the lock cylinder under the other car. He crawled along the floor and grabbed it. Crawling back, he did his best to replace it, but when it wouldn't stay in, he gave up, leaving the trunk open.

With a crack of thunder, it started to rain. And water flowing. Wait. Footsteps. Above him in the carriage house. A toilet flushing. Jesus, someone was coming downstairs. Someone had heard him. Closer from behind the plaster of the side wall. From the steps. Shit.

Just as Paulo's large hand reached around for the light switch, John leapt back into the trunk. There was no time to push the lock back into its hole, so he yanked the lid down over him, careful not to slam it, and held it tightly in place with his hand.

He heard the man's footsteps approaching. His shadow crossed the back of the car.

Boom. Thunder. He flinched, terrorized. The man walked on to the garage door. John heard him test it to make sure it was locked and listened while he checked each of the others. Apparently satisfied, he shut off the lights and went back upstairs.

John out once again. But now what? He decided to wait and watch from here. Eventually, he reasoned, they would leave. They would lead him to Shelby. They had her somewhere. He would follow Doran.

He took up his position in the corner nearest the house and watched as bolts of lightning struck the water and the trees in Canada across the lake.

The rain poured down for more than an hour before anyone appeared.

Then, he saw lights, first on either side of the front door followed by others in bedrooms above. On his left, far away, a sound, the motorized front gate, and a car coming closer, splashing down the driveway. Leonard Shapiro's dark green Jaguar. The lawyer passed John and the garage and parked hastily in the middle of the courtyard. As he got out, Maria appeared at the front door. He was expected.

"Good Morning, Senor. Senor Domati will meet you in his study."

"Thank you, Maria." He bounded up the granite steps two at a time.

John knew of Shapiro and his reputation. He had seen him at the club. He knew he was the Domati family attorney.

Soon there was more activity. The Domati brothers, Angelo and Nino, appeared on the front porch, and then Joey Cappola. They lit cigarettes and talked under the main portico, fifty feet away. John could barely make out their words, muffled in the driving rain.

"I'll take you over. Tell Paulo to get the boat ready. As soon as Papa is finished, we will go."

Nino obediently followed his older brother's orders, walking to the side door of the garage. John heard him through the wall. "Hey Paulo, we need the boat."

Shortly afterward, John again heard footsteps upstairs. They came down and left, walking out into the rain which had now settled into a steady downpour.

Inside, in Domati's study, Shapiro paced, impatient with information, waiting for the old man to arrive. Soon, with Maria preceding him and Doran on his arm, he shuffled in. He was wearing an embroidered silk robe and slippers. Doran wore gray sweats. Both men, had recently awakened.

"Maria, coffee please." Domati ordered and she hurried away to get it. "Lenny, come in, have a seat."

"Thank you, Vincenzo. I apologize for the intrusion at such an ungodly hour."

"I know it must be important. Here, Franky, sit next to me." He motioned to the leather chair beside his desk as he slowly moved around to his own. "Sit. Sit," he insisted and Shapiro followed his instructions, seating himself directly in front of the don. "Now, what is it?" Domati noticed that Shapiro was reluctant to speak. "Don't worry, Frank can hear everything that is for my ears. And, Lenny, if I were you, I would think that Franky was not here at all, that you did not see him this morning."

"Of course, Vincenzo. I understand." He leaned forward and began. "One of the men...at Michigan Scrap, was shot last night, and wounded."

"Where is he now?" The don asked.

"I have taken care of it and, with all respect, it is better if you do not know. They called me after it happened. I handled it. But, this is why I'm here. I spoke to him. He's a guard out there and he described the man who shot him."

Frank Doran listened intently. "May I?" he asked Domati, who nodded and Frank removed a thick cigar from the box on the old man's desk.

Shapiro continued, "Whoever it was saw what happened out there."

"Shit. For fucking crissake. Don't I pay so that I can not have to worry about this?" Domati said, "How does that happen?" He was angry.

Maria returned with cups and a pot of freshly brewed coffee. The men waited silently until she left to resume the discussion.

With a puff of blue smoke, Doran speculated, "It wasn't a cop. Or they woulda been all over us by now. PI...maybe."

"Possibly. But from the description, I think it could have been that Russel guy, John Russel. I wanted you to know, right away."

There was a long silence as Domati coughed newly dislodged phlegm into his handkerchief and poured a cup of coffee. "Is that possible?" he asked, but didn't wait for an answer, "I suppose it is. He's got some gonads, doesn't he?"

"He must have followed Keenan somehow. He knew that Keenan was coming to meet me." Doran speculated, "But I can't believe that little shit would be able to pull it off."

"They found a car. Out there. No one around. I checked it out. It's his lawyer's. They didn't touch it. The FBI found it about an hour ago."

"So," Frank started to piece it together, "He follows Keenan out there in that car. We know he's not in Keenan's car. So that puts him on foot, or..." he paused, thinking out loud, "He wants his wife. He knows we've got her. And if he had the balls to go out there last night, there's no telling what else he could do. He may have saved us some trouble. With your permission, Don Domati." Again the old man nodded. Doran stood and quickly left the room.

A few moments later, John saw him on the front porch. He spoke quietly to Angelo and Joey, and to Nino who had returned after helping Paulo ready the Sea Ray. John noticed that Frank seemed to look over the shoulders of the other men, surveying the yard.

When he was finished talking, the men split up, each going in a different direction. Angelo walked quickly toward the front gate. Nino returned to the boathouse. And Frank Doran and Joey Cappola walked directly toward the garage doors, crossing the courtyard, moving toward John, then separating and disappearing from his view, one on either side of the brick building.

John heard the door open at the side, by the stairs to the carriage house above. Jesus, They were looking for him. He scurried back into the trunk of Domati's limo, holding the lid down over him. The shaft of light sliced past his finger in the hole where the lock had been. Trembling, unable to take a breath, he saw the first cloud of white Cuban smoke drift through the beam.

He held the pistol tightly.

There was a tugging upward on the trunk, slowly but steadily increasing, until John could no longer hold it down. He let go and shut his eyes tight, still gripping the hand gun.

When the trunk was up, he opened his eyes and looked up into the faces of the two men; into the silence and cigar smoke; at Joey the Ghost, near the hinge at one side of the car, and Frank Doran at the other. Both with automatic pistols pointed directly at his head.

Doran chewed down hard on his cigar, smiling at his discovery, "Good morning, Mr. Russel."

Cappola was not so affable. "Get out," he ordered, "Leave the gun there."

John loosened his hold on the pistol, letting it fall gently on the carpet of the trunk. He slowly climbed out, flanked by the men.

"Frank, go get the old man. I'll watch this asshole."

Doran put the gun away and left. Joey, with one hand still aiming the pistol, grabbed John's arm with the other and wrenched it behind his back. John felt the cold metal close around his wrist. With the same handcuffs that had attached Keenan to his car a few hours earlier, Cappola fastened John's together.

When they were locked, he put his weapon away, stuffing it into the waistband of his black, pleated slacks. "Sit down, shithead," he said, shoving John to his knees in the corner of the damp building.

More pain, rising from the concrete floor, through John's shins adding to the sharp waves from his injured back, moving up to his head. His arms, crushed behind him, sandwiched between his body and the brick wall, throbbed with dull stress.

Joey Cappola stood over him, turning occasionally to look out one of the small windows.

A few minutes later, Frank Doran appeared with Domati. He helped the old man shuffle across the courtyard, guiding him around the puddles.

John heard the door hinge squeak open at the back of the garage, just over his shoulder, and then coughing and wheezing as Domati slid toward him, Doran at his side. Before he knew it, the don hovered over him. He replaced his handkerchief in the top pocket of his robe.

"Well, Mr. Russel, it is as if I know you already. And even though I have not invited you here, I am more happy than you know that you have come. I am Vincenzo Domati. Welcome to my home."

John said nothing.

"I'm sorry that the circumstances could not be different, but I am glad that you are here, believe me." He turned to Joey, "Bring him to the study."

With that, the old man shuffled away. Cappola lifted John to his feet and pushed him in front of him as they followed Domati out.

John was not entirely unfamiliar with the Domati family. Thirty years earlier, when both he and Domati's son, Nino attended the same grade school, John had a run-in with him. The ten year old Mafiosi had been bragging about his family and his family's activities. And John, with a small toy tape recorder he ordered from the back of a comic book, recorded the comments. The next day, behind the swing set on the gravel playground, Nino beat the shit out of him and smashed the machine to bits. Wisely, John had avoided him ever since.

But oddly, as he was being shoved toward the front door of the French mansion, this incident played over and over in his mind. He remembered every word of the fifth grader's bragging, much of which had to do with torture and murder.

While Domati was still negotiating the steps, Cappola dragged John past him, into the house, to the study and threw him into a chair, again crushing his arms behind him. A few minutes later, Doran and the don slid in, the old man again seated at his desk, Frank standing at his side.

The daylight was coming, a dull, light gray in the courtyard. John stared out at it wondering what would happen now.

The chilly silence was broken by Domati's wheezing voice, "Mr. Russel, I think you know what this…all of this…is about."

"Where is she? Where's my wife?"

"She is alive, Mr. Russel, at least for now." He coughed, "And, if you help me get what I want, you will both stay that way. If not, I will kill you. It is a simple proposition. You know I mean what I say, don't you Mr. Russel?"

The image of Keenan's murder shot through John's head, "I do. I don't know if I can get it back. I think it's too late."

"Oh, Mr. Russel, you're being too modest. You managed to find your way last night. You even shot one of my men. No, no, I think a man as resourceful as you will find a way. I have learned that desperate people are very effective."

"I don't think I can do anything. But Please. Don't kill her."

The don shrugged and sighed.

"Wait." John was scrambling. "I'll try. I'll try. Let me talk to her." He spoke definitely, sitting up as much as he could, glaring into Domati's small eyes, "Let me go. I'll get the goddamn finger, I could care less about it."

"See, now you are thinking, Mr. Russel. I have great confidence in you. I will give you a chance. One chance, but only one. If you are not stupid like your father, things will come out all right."

"I want to talk to her first."

"You insult me. Why? If I tell you she is alive you must believe me. If you doubt what I say, there is no point in doing business." He pulled his soaked handkerchief from the breast pocket of his robe and blasted it once more with loosened phlegm. Wadding it into a wet ball, he went on, "Here's what you will do, Mr. Russel. You will get the finger, I don't care how. I will even help you if you need it, but you *will* get it. You will give it personally to me. I will make arrangements."

"But how will I..." John was confused. What arrangements, he wondered.

"We will find you. You have the rest of the day. And tomorrow, until noon."

John's blood was pumping furiously through his body. There was nothing he could say. But that was so little time. Still, he could tell from the tone that Domati would not be swayed further and that this was the best deal he could expect.

"Thank you," he said, not at all sure what he could possibly do to get what Domati demanded.

"Joey, take him down to the boathouse. Take him somewhere and dump him. I want to talk to Franky."

When Domati and Doran were again alone, the don spoke.

"Well, Franky, this is the day that we planned. You are all set?"

"I am."

"Angelo has a car waiting for you on the Canadian side. He has your ticket. On Friday you will go to Kennedy. You will become DeVera as we planned. You will go with Angelo back to Miami and then on to South America. You have three days to collect your money, that should be enough."

"I'll be fine, Vincenzo."

"It is too bad that we are forced into this now. It was my wish to keep all of this quiet. Now time is important. Come over here, Franky." The old man motioned for Frank to come to him as he held out his arms and stood up. The two embraced as a father and son. "I don't know if I will ever see you again, Franky. But I want you to know that I appreciate everything that you have done for my family and no matter what happens, you have my thanks."

"And you have mine, Don Domati." Doran extracted himself from the hug, smiling sadly.

"Good-bye, Franky."

31

Shelby had heard the rain, too, earlier in the night, when she regained consciousness. It took awhile for her to realize what had happened. Images of Doran and the courthouse slipped in and out of her memory, crystallizing a little more each time. It was dark, black, in the room. And loud, like a factory. Her body ached. When she first tried to move it wouldn't cooperate. When it did, she felt the tightness around her right wrist, handcuffs. She had yanked hard and from the clanking sound assumed she was tethered to a pipe or steel bar of some kind. For what seemed like a long time she attempted to free herself, but couldn't. Ultimately, exhausted, she collapsed, passing out into sleep.

Now the morning, flat and colorless as it was, began to fall through the high windows, three stories above her. In the light, she could see that she was in a large, square storage area. Raw, paintless cinder block walls rose fifteen feet high around her and were covered on top with steel mesh. There was a metal light fixture dangling over her and all along the walls, sometimes stacked three high were fifty gallon containers marked with chemical formulas and names too long for her to pronounce.

She could hear the heavy machinery, liquids moving, steam escaping from valves. And heat. Unbearable heat.

She was soaked through her light blouse and suit jacket. The bottom of her skirt was stuck with perspiration to the cement floor.

The other end of the handcuffs were secured to what she saw now was an electrical conduit. She realized she was probably lucky she didn't break it, given the buzz of current that vibrated through it.

God. John must be going crazy. That prick Doran. If he's capable of this, he could do anything. Why was she alive? Why not kill her?

The answer was obvious. She was part of the deal. The leverage they would use to extort the finger from the authorities.

Then they would kill her.

She took a deep breath and the fumes nearly made her vomit. They were acrid, like nail polish remover, but ten times more potent. She blew out the foulness and tugged as hard as she could at the pipe. It was futile.

"Ahhhhh," she screamed, shaking her head with anger and frustration, "Ahhhhhhh. Somebody! Help me. Hey, Doran. Doran! Unlock me, you prick."

Two men, her guards, were perched in the plate glass office, high above the dry-cleaning plant, watching television, drinking coffee and eating. They couldn't hear Shelby screaming, but they could see that she was violently writhing around on the floor of the store room, kicking at the pipe.

"Looks like she's awake.," one of them said through his food. "Better go down an' see if you can shut her up."

"Why don't you do it?" the other said, though his words were barely discernible, muted by custard and chocolate.

"I got the fuckin' donuts. That's why."

He was a fat man, disgusting in his tee-shirt, too tight for his rolls of body blubber. He reached down to his crotch with his left hand while he shoved the last of the sweet dough between his bulging lips. He tugged up on his privates. "I got somthin' right here that'll keep her quiet."

The other man shook his head. "Just see what she wants, will ya? Take her a donut or some water or somethin'."

The fat man stood. He wiped the crumbs from his belly where they had landed. He grabbed another donut from the box.

"Hey, don't do anything stupid. Remember what Ghost said. One piece. I fuckin' mean it."

"Yeah. Sure." The fat man's neck and cheeks rocked as he left the air conditioned room. Instantly the swell of fumes and heat hit him and he began to drip from his forehead. The metal catwalk flexed and grunted under his weight as he made his way to the elevator cage. He couldn't hear Shelby's voice over the dry cleaning equipment, but he could tell she was yelling. He got in the car and pushed the down button.

"Godammit to hell! Shit. Let me go!" It was the last of her energy and once again Shelby lay still. "Damn," she sighed. There was no one to hear her.

The latch on the steel door scraped open on its supports. The door swung out. What entered was monstrous and covered with powdered sugar. He was chewing and dripping sweat from his fingertips, the drops landing with tiny splashes on the concrete. She stared at the hideous man.

"What?" he asked, "What the fuck do ya want?"

Shelby hesitated a moment. "Uh, I'd like to get a drink, if I could."

"You ain't gonna be gettin' anything. But, if you're gonna be real good, I might take it upon myself to get it for you." He wiped his mouth with his hairy forearm. "First, you gotta shut the fuck up, 'cause no one's out there gonna hear shit anyway. You got it?"

This was like playing with explosive material and Shelby wanted to be careful. "Of course. I'm sorry. It's hot, though, and I'm thirsty."

"Yeah. You look hot."

Shelby looked down at her sheer blouse. She could see her lace bra and the dark circles of her nipples through the wet material. The fat beast was staring at her chest. "Please."

He waddled closer and leaned into her face, the smell of yesterday's digested garlic still on his breath. He touched the disorganized strands of her hair with his moist fingertips. "You're hot, eh? I'll tell you what. I'm gonna help you cool off. Then, if you stay quiet, you can have a drink. How's that?"

"That's fine. Thank you." Shelby felt the shiver come over her entire body. There was nothing she could do to stop him from doing whatever it was that was on his mind. She flashed to everything she had ever read about rape; don't fight, keep quiet, cooperate. It was repulsive. She gagged, but held the vomit down, breathing through her nose and swallowing. She covered her chest with her free arm. The man reached into his pants pocket. He pulled a black, shiny object out and with a single movement threw his wrist forward, releasing the blade of the straight edge razor. He awkwardly knelt on the floor, straddling her legs. He pinched the fabric of her sleeve and slowly lifted it from her body, revealing her breasts through the transparent bra. "Leave it there," he said pushing her arm to the floor. "Now we're gonna take care of this."

He inserted the tip of the blade into the end of her jacket sleeve, near the handcuffs and began an incision, slicing the wool fabric to her shoulder, then down, from the armpit to her waist.

He was breathing more heavily and stale garlic surrounded her. Shelby closed her eyes and waited, trying to stay calm. He peeled the jacket from her body and threw it across the room. Then, surprisingly, he pushed his way up clumsily to his feet. He closed the razor and put it back into his pocket. And stood mesmerized by her perfect body.

"There."

Shelby was stunned. She didn't know what to say, but she knew better than to cover up. If this was all the guy wanted, let him have it. At least that was all he wanted now. With her relief came nervous laughter. She couldn't help it. "Thank you," she said calmly, but she had never been more frightened. She knew that this man was capable of anything.

John wasn't sure exactly where he had been deposited. It was definitely not the safest place to be. The Sea Ray had simply bumped up against an aging wooden breakwall and Joey Cappola had thrown him out. He landed in the grass in what was apparently somebody's back yard and watched as the speedboat vanished into the rain and gray haze over the Detroit River.

His wrists stung from the handcuffs. His upper arms were numb from being stretched so far backward. His lower back was badly bruised from bouncing on the long bolt in the trunk of Domati's limousine. If there was any good news, it was that his head no longer throbbed. Banging into the steering wheel while he waited for Keenan, was only a memory. His problems now were more urgent.

At the first intersection, he looked at the rusted street sign; Freud. And Marlboro. The heart of the eastside ghetto, one of the most dangerous areas of Detroit. Fortunately, it was early enough and nobody was around.

He walked fast, toward Jefferson where he was certain he would find a phone. He had to reach Sheriff Kellet. At this point he didn't know exactly how, but he was determined to hold up his end of the deal.

His shirt and blue jeans were soaked. His brown waves straightened as the drops fell down his forehead from the strands of his hair.

The rain was as steady as his footsteps as he replayed the dreadful scenario. The FBI would certainly be looking for him as would the Detroit police. Domati family men would be watching him, too. That's what the old man had said, *'they* would find *him'*. Giving him until tomorrow at noon. Jesus. God himself took longer than that to make a person. And he had a few ribs to work with already.

Walk faster. Shit. A car. Behind him. Don't look. Duck in between these houses. Run. Over the fence. An alley on the other side. Trash cans.

He crouched down behind the metal cans, looking back at the street between two other flats, and saw the car, an old Oldsmobile, pass quickly by.

John got up and began walking again, this time down the alley.

From behind a falling down wooden garage, two Rottweilers bounded to the fence next to him. Panicked, he ran from their angry barking, away from the river, past several side streets, dodging puddles and cracks in the trash strewn path. Finally ahead, at the end of the next block, he heard traffic. Rush hour. Everybody headed toward downtown. He knew there would be a gas station or a store; a phone where he could call the sheriff.

Finally, Jefferson. John stopped at the intersection. To his right, some kind of collision or tire shop, to his left a beer store. In front of it, a group of young black men were talking and drinking beer, standing under a torn canvas awning. John ignored them and went inside.

The clerk was an almond-skinned man wearing a turban. He never looked up from the magazine he was reading to see who had entered the store, apparently secure behind the inch thick, bullet-proof glass. The back wall featured a walk-in cooler, and two aisles of merchandise filled remaining space. There was a magazine rack with most of the material wrapped in brown paper, displays with floormats for cars, free materials from liquor companies and, behind the counter above the clerk's head several rows of multi-colored lottery tickets. On the counter were stacks of daily racing forms and a cardboard display containing 'Love Machine' condoms.

John walked up to the rotating lazy susan style cylinder in front of the clerk. "Pardon me," John said, noticing his own image, large, in the black and white monitor near the man. The man did nothing.

John raised his voice. "Hey, excuse me buddy, is there a phone here that I can use? John looked at himself in the small television. He was a mess. No wonder the guy couldn't break himself away from his motorcycle bondage magazine, he figured John for a vagrant.

"Listen, pal, I just need to make a call. It's important." John reached into his back pocket a pulled out his wallet. He opened it and produced a twenty, shoving it into the plastic slot in the window. "I just need some change." In the monitor John saw a figure standing behind him. One of the guys from out front.

Now the Arab looked up and in some barely decipherable dialect he said, "You want cigarette?"

"No, I don't want cigarettes. I want some change. For the pay phone. You've got a pay phone right?" This was ridiculous.

"You buy!" The man shouted, "Or get the hell out. Go!"

"Jesus, pal, settle down." John backed away from the counter and turned around, staring into the jaundiced eyes of the other customer. "Excuse me," John said, heading for one of the aisles. At the candy rack he grabbed a couple of Nestles Crunch bars, then went straight to the cooler for milk. On his way back to the magazine reading fascist, he stopped at a large display erected by a suntan lotion company, offering free sunglasses and ball cap with the purchase of the product under the headline '2kool2fry...Nubian Guy'. John noticed the pile of cheap red caps with the Nubian Guy logo printed on them in day-glo green, and similarly enhanced plastic sunglasses behind the counter. John selected a large metal tin of the waxy preparation, and returned to the counter, placing all three items in the cylinder where they disappeared momentarily behind the 'food stamps accepted' sign before reappearing in front of the Arab.

"Fifteen ninety-seven," he said, throwing three pennies and four dollar bills in the container and spinning it back to John.

"No, no. I need change, all change," John insisted, completing the spin, glaring at the counter clerk. The Arab finally relented, replacing the currency with quarters.

"Is there a phone?" John tried again, but the man in the turban was pouring over a picture of a buxom woman on a Harley and didn't reply. The junky did.

"Right down da coener, by the tire place. Say, man, you don't have no use for dem smokes, do ya?" he asked, pointing at John's bag. John didn't. He handed them over, put on the sunglasses and cap, and left.

He walked to the phone booth, his pockets jingling with coins. The Nubian Guy hat kept the rain off his face and, together with the glasses, disguised his appearance, though not subtly. Inside, John put his paper bag on the small shelf. The booth was about six inches from the front of the tire store and John could see activity inside. It was nine twenty. They were getting ready to open. He turned his face away from the large window and pulled the cap low to his eyebrows.

There were no phone books, the metal wire that once held them dangled uselessly and only the numbers scratched into the paint provided any directory at all. John picked up the receiver and dialed the number for information. When the operator answered he said,

"Yes. The number for the Leelanau County Sheriff's office please."
He waited. In a moment he had it. He hung up and dialed again.

"Please deposit one dollar and forty cents," the robotic voice
instructed. John shoved eight quarters into the slot and the call
was connected. One of Kellet's deputies answered.

"Sheriff Kellet, please."

"Is this an emergency?" the deputy asked.

"Well yeah, I guess. I've got to talk to him," John insisted.

"Where are you calling from, sir?"

"What difference does it make? I have....."

"Please deposit eighty cents for an additional three minutes."
The voice interrupted and John dropped another dollar in the slot.

"Are you calling from a pay phone, sir?"

"Godammit, put Kellet on now. I'm running out of time." There
was a pause while John was on hold and then a familiar voice.

"Kellet."

"Thank God, Bob. This is John Russel."

"I just got something on you, on the computer. You're a very
hot property. What the hell's going on?"

"I don't have time to go into that now. Did you take the
fing...the item...to Lansing?"

"I'm going today. I've got it here in my refrigerator. T' be
honest with you, I'd just as soon get rid of it."

"Don't. Don't do anything." John leaned deeper into the corner
of the booth and spoke in little more than a whisper. "I'm coming
to get it. Today. Don't tell anyone I called. Not the FBI, no one."

"John, I..."

The damn voice interrupted, "Please deposit eighty cents for an
additional three minutes."

"Bob, you can't tell anyone. Shelby's life could depend on it.
Please. I'm on my way." John hung up. Now the bank.

He turned around, ready to leave, but the door to the booth was blocked by the junky and his friends. One of them had a knife.

"Jesus."

The junky pushed the door and it folded inward on its hinges. "Git yor white ass out here and gimme the money or Lee here is gonna cut you."

If there was one thing that these guys definitely didn't want, it was the police. John didn't either. But he had to take the chance. Within a second, he kneed the junky in the groin and, as he buckled over, pushed him backward into the knife wielding Lee. John vaulted through the hole this created, at the same time winding up and hurling the heavy can of Nubian Guy tanning cream through the plate glass window of Fast Jack's Tires.

Instantly a loud alarm began to ring and John Russel took off, running down Jefferson. By this time the junky and his three companions had recovered. They raced down the sidewalk after him, shouting.

"You better run you honky ass bastard, 'cause if I git you, you gonna die!"

John summoned every bit of muscular strength, struggling to stay ahead of the much younger mob. If they weren't so blasted on dope, they would already be stabbing him to death, puffing away afterwards on the cigarettes John had given them.

He remembered this neighborhood. He had raced for his life here before. In fact, this was the first time he'd returned since. The storefronts were flying by on his left. The traffic headed downtown though, was barely moving. As he ran the rain subsided and the tips of his wavy hair dried from the breeze. Up ahead the blue sign. NBD. National Bank of Detroit. On the other side of the street. He heard sirens. And horns. The commuters, sick sons of bitches, were cheering him on, the white man in the red cap and sunglasses pursued by a gang of ghetto hoodlums. He dodged a group of women waiting at a bus stop and then made his cut, using them to block his assailants. One more block.

He was out in the street running against oncoming traffic and the horns from the cars that nearly missed him joined the rising chorus of those who were enjoying this near death experience. Shit. A police car, lights flashing, siren blasting speeding directly toward him. The gang behind scattered. Had they realized that the cops were more interested in him they probably would have helped them make the arrest. Probably get some kind of civic award.

John cut through, between cars, to the opposite sidewalk, running like hell toward the bank. He heard the police car slide to a spinning halt on the wet pavement behind him, but kept going without looking, turning into the side street to the right, then a quick left up the ally, behind the buildings. He could see the back of the NBD at the end of the block. His heart pounded. He could hardly breathe. More sirens.

When he reached the end of the block, he stopped. There was a large blue dumpster against the building and John used it to discard the hat and sunglasses, so the tellers wouldn't think he was holding the place up. He also threw in the paper bag and candy bars, his appetite gone. He brushed his hair back with his fingers, looked both ways, and walked briskly to the front door of the bank and went in.

They had just opened. He was the first customer. Some of the tellers were still counting cash in their drawers, also, like the Arab, protected from reality by bullet proof plexiglass. In the center of the room, under its high ceiling were two tall tables where one could stand and fill out forms. At the rear past a short wooden railing, two desks, and behind them the private office of the manager. John aimed for that. But before he had walked three steps, a guard confronted him, standing in his path. John smiled as widely as possible and said, "Morning. Nasty weather out there."

He side-stepped the man and continued to the railing at the back. By this time, each of the tellers had a finger on the silent alarm button. The middle aged woman who had been seated at the first desk stood up terrified, as John approached, soaked and panting. He was sure they had all recognized him.

"Mr. Winston. Mr. Winston could you come out here please. Quickly!" she yelled back.

Within seconds, a portly black man, in his fifties, John guessed, appeared in the doorway.

"Thank you," John said politely to the woman as he passed and extended his hand to the manager. "Mr. Winston, if I could have a moment of your time?" They shook hands briefly but John never stopped walking, "In here. Privately?"

Winston shot a look of disbelief at the woman who now silently mouthed the words, 'Should I call the police?' He signaled, 'not yet' and followed the crazy white man into his office.

"What can I do for you?" He was obviously suspicious.

John tried to diffuse the situation. "I am terribly sorry for my appearance and impatient entrance, but as you may have guessed my business is somewhat urgent." Winston glared at him, saying nothing, and John charged ahead. "My accounts are with another branch, but I must make a rather large withdrawal. Here. This morning."

"I see." Winston, intrigued but cautious, motioned tenuously for John to sit. And he did the same, relieving his feet from the burden of his nearly three hundred pounds. "How much?"

"A hundred grand."

Winston sat, catatonic, for about fifteen seconds, before the rolls began to jiggle, before erupting into a full belly laugh. His laughter was so loud that the woman peeked in to see what was happening, but Winston shooed her away. When he was able to assemble words he said, "This is a joke, isn't it? Who sent you in here? It's Cohn, isn't it?" referring to another vice president at the bank and convulsing with more jiggling disturbances. "It's Cohn."

John watched patiently and waited for him to stop before he responded, "No," he said seriously. "This is no joke." He wanted the money. Cash. For the same reason he didn't use his telephone credit card; it would take longer for the FBI to find him.

"You're serious?"

"Yes. And I need it right now." John reached into the back pocket of his jeans and got his wallet. Out of it he produced his driver's license and a business card. "You may verify my balance if you will call him. He will authorize the transaction."

Winston read from the card, "John Delancy?"

"Yes."

He was a client, a friend, John Russel's personal banker, and the current president of the National Bank of Detroit. While he was probably aware of the circumstances surrounding John, there was no way he would refuse John's request. John counted on it. "Please, call him."

Finally, Winston did. John himself had to get on the phone, too, but eventually all of the details were arranged and he was about to get his money.

Winston's demeanor had improved considerably since the call, "Is there anything else we can do for you, Mr. Russel?"

"Actually, yes. I'd like a cab."

The previously terrified woman took care of his request while one of the tellers counted out various denominations and put them, as John had also requested into a canvas bag. When the amount was reached, she folded it over, wrapped it with a large rubber band, and handed it to John. "Thanks," he said, turning to the manager who was supervising, "And thank you, Mr. Winston."

"Your taxi is here, Mr, Russel," one of the other tellers announced.

Winston looked out the front window. As he did, a police car whizzed by and he commented, "Must be something going on."

"Break-in, I think...at the tire store," John answered.

"Good luck, Mr. Russel." Winston extended his hand, shooting John a small wink as he did. He knew exactly what was going on.

"Thanks again." They shook hands. With a quick wave to the tellers, John was out the door and inside the waiting vehicle.

"City Airport," he instructed the driver through the bullet-proof shield, before relaxing into the ripped plastic seat, his hand clutching the bag, as the car rolled away from the curb.

32

"He's got a plane," one of Garnetti's men announced as he entered the conference room, "Charter. Out of City."

Christine Ferrand, at Bob Garnetti's invitation, had remained at the FBI office, awaiting news of John or Shelby. This was the first in over two hours. She looked out at the other downtown buildings. The rain stopped. She could see the crowd of reporters, growing more numerous, on the sidewalk below.

This was good news, hearing that they had spotted John. She feared the word on Shelby may not be so positive, "Anything on Mrs. Russel?" she asked the agent.

"Not yet, ma'am."

As quickly as he had appeared, he left. Agent Garnetti was seated at a large Formica table at the front of the room behind where the projection screen had been. Rows of empty, armless chairs, arranged schoolroom style, filled the rest of the area. The inside wall was cork, and, to enhance the elementary classroom motif, Garnetti had pinned to it photos of the cabin, John's house, the scene where Keenan had been found, and Christine's abandoned car in the field near Michigan Scrap. There were also huge maps of Michigan, Detroit, and Leelanau County. Many agents, in the time Chris had been there, had come and gone, updating the status as they did. The next to arrive was Agent Stoddard, the man who had earlier, at the briefing, run the slide projector and conveyed the unwelcome news of the failed surveillance at the Domati residence.

"Sir?" he asked timidly, peeking his head in.

"Come on in, Stoddard," Garnetti ordered, "What have you got?"

"From Morse, sir, at City Airport. The subject has chartered an aircraft from Sureflight Aviation and filed a flight plan for Cinncinati."

"Do we know his current location?"

"We'll have it shortly."

"Thanks, Stoddard. Keep me posted. I want to know where he is." He pondered the new information, tossing the possibilities around in his head.

"That doesn't make sense," Garnetti said, half to himself and partly to Christine. Then it was obvious. He was doing exactly what he said he would do. "He's going to get the finger." Garnetti stood up, pushing the intercom button on the telephone on the table, "Have Stoddard get ahold of Morse. I need to speak to her."

He walked over to the map of Michigan, staring at it. "He's going to Traverse City."

The phone beeped and a voice came over its small speaker, "I have Morse, sir."

"Put her on, please," Garnetti instructed.

"Bob. Karen." She was on the speakerphone.

"Christine Ferrand is here with me."

"Hi, Christine. We know he's okay."

"Thank God." Chris was relieved.

Garnetti jumped in, "Listen, Karen, his flight plan, does it make any sense to you? Cinncinati?"

"No."

"Where do you think he's going?"

"I'm in the tower now. We've had him on radar for awhile from Bay City. I'd say he's heading north."

"That's what I thought. Alert the team in Traverse. And Karen, see if you can get Detroit to loan us one of their choppers. Stay there. I'm on my way." He disconnected the call. "Ms. Ferrand, you may join me if you wish."

By the time they arrived at Detroit City Airport, Karen Morse had arranged for the helicopter. The pilot was ready, the blades slowly turning as the engine sputtered at idle. She had spoken with her team in Traverse City and they were on the way to the airport there to wait for John.

Garnetti and Chris parked on the tarmac next to the police hangar, about fifty yards from the waiting chopper. As they got out of the car, Morse met them. It had been her intention to make the trip north also, but unsettling news caused her to change plans.

"Bob," she said to Garnetti as he got out, "Stoddard just called...the St. Clair County Sheriff's office reported a body...a woman...in the lake at Anchorville."

"Oh God..." Christine feared the worst.

Karen continued, "They've sealed the scene. I'm heading up there. They're waiting for us."

Garnetti's response was measured and professional, "Okay, Karen, check it out and let me know." Then, softening some, "Ms. Ferrand, if you don't mind, I'd like you to go along with agent Morse...for identification purposes?"

Christine shook her head affirmatively. After a few final words with Morse, Garnetti walked away. The most horrible thoughts spun through Chris' mind. It was not logical to assume that the woman they found was Shelby, but it was clear that Morse thought so, and so, apparently, did the authorities in Anchorville. She was dazed with disbelief.

"We have to do this, Chris. You know that."

"Sure."

The two women rode in silence most of the way. Agent Morse did provide some details, though. Two fisherman, at dawn, discovered the body floating in the reeds just offshore. The description was familiar and frightening; the business suit, similar to the one Chris had brought from the Russel's house, the hair color, hazel eyes, age, height; it all matched. Then there was the timing. The initial opinion of the county medical examiner was that the woman had been dead only a few hours, twenty four at the most, a time frame that unfortunately corresponded to Shelby Russel's abduction. Frank Doran, she thought. He murdered her. He was a cold blooded killer. She would kill him herself if given the opportunity. The bastard.

She watched the hillside rolling by as the sunken freeway turned northbound through Mount Clemens, following roughly, at some distance, the western edge of Lake St. Clair. The distance north of the city is marked by mile roads; Eight Mile, Nine Mile, and so forth. Before she realized it, they had passed Sixteen Mile.

"What do you think, Karen? Is it her?"

"It sounds like it."

"What would Doran have to gain by killing her."

"It's more likely that, if it is her, it's Domati trying to clean things up quickly." Morse sensed that she may have been too direct. "I'm sorry. I don't know how else to put it."

"That's all right." Christine had become accustomed to such overt discussions in the past few days. Now, to her, it was clinical. They had to get Doran or Domati, or whomever, and bring this to an end. "Let's hurry," she said pragmatically, "The sooner we know, the better."

When they got to Twenty Six Mile Road, they exited, heading east toward Marine City, then south on Church Street to Anchorville. Christine had never been here before. She was surprised by the general rundown condition of the area. Small houses with overgrown lawns were nestled right beside the road. Occasionally, in a field, there would be a trailer, around it, a collection of children's bicycles, old cars, and broken appliances.

There was really not much to Anchorville, not much town, not many people. Its primary attribute was cheap lakefront property, a place where you could dock a small fishing boat or go water-skiing on the weekend. Marsac Point, where the body was actually found, is nothing more than a small intrusion into Anchor Bay at the northern tip of the lake.

The road ended at the center of town, at the water. Agent Morse turned right onto Dixie Highway. It followed the edge of the lake, out of town, twisting along the marshland. The sun was burning through the haze left behind by the morning rains. Steam rose from evaporating puddles as the surface heated. The small clouds separated, pushed aside by the Ford as they drove. The town vanished as quickly as it appeared, and soon the last trailer was left behind.

It was less than ten minutes, though it seemed like more, before Morse spotted the flashing lights of the sheriff's cruisers. There were three of them and two unmarked cars parked off the road on the left, the water side. There was a crowd gathered. When they were closer, Chris could see that the area had been cordoned off with tape. A man in a uniform, presumably the St. Clair County sheriff, was talking to a group of local television reporters at the far side, further down the two lane road. Agent Morse pulled in well short.

"Stay with me," she said as they parked. She got out and with Chris just behind, presented her badge to the officer at the perimeter, motioning Chris to come with her as she ducked under the tape.

On the ground ahead, Chris could see the blue blanket spread over the corpse. There were officers taking pictures. Another wore a navy windbreaker with the unmistakable white FBI on the back in large block letters. He was interviewing two men, the fishermen. As the two women approached, he turned, recognizing Morse, and excused himself from the conversation. "Agent Morse, good morning."

"Morning. Those the guys that found her?"

"Yeah."

"They see anything?"

"No."

Christine stood still, like a stone carving, staring at the covered body. She had the most sickening feeling building inside her, acidic and sour. She was white.

"Chris?" Agent Morse noticed Christine's hesitation and took her by the arm to a police car, opened the door and guided her into the front seat, leaving the door open. "Why don't you wait here for a few minutes. I'll let you know when I need you."

Morse returned to the other agent and soon they were joined by another, Jack Rouse, a forensic pathologist.

"Jack, I'm glad you could get here so fast. What have we got?"

Rouse thumbed back to the first page of a small spiral notebook to review his earlier scribbles. "Caucasian female. Thirty-eight to forty-five. Shot point blank." He raised his hand to illustrate, "Right here at the base of the neck. Once."

"Pro?"

"Looks like it. She's been dead maybe eight, nine hours."

"How's she look? I mean, I've got someone here for a possible ID."

"It came out the top. Most of it is gone. Her face, though is pretty much fine. It should be all right if you leave the blanket over the top of the head."

"Anything else?"

He looked over the notes, "Not really. Her mouth had been taped, at least at some point. And she'd been bound, probably handcuffs. Oh, there is one thing; I found what appears to be semen…"

"She'd been raped?"

He paused for a moment,"…in her mouth, and on her chin."

The thought of Shelby Russel perhaps being forced at gun point into some unspeakable act made her insides churn. But her training overcame such personal thoughts. "Thanks." Morse walked over to the woman's body followed by the first agent. "This is where those men found her?" she asked.

"Yes, ma'am"

"You check them out?"

"Yeah. Nothing. They were coming down here to put their boat in and they came across the victim."

"Okay. Let 'em go. Make sure we can find them."

Karen stood for a minute, looking over the scene. There were footprints in the muck, from a large man's shoe she guessed, leading to the body. They were much deeper in one direction than in the other. She reasoned the woman had been carried and dumped here after being murdered elsewhere. There was no reason to wait any longer. She headed back to the car where Chris had been waiting.

"Ready?"

"I guess," Chris responded, though she was not at all sure that she was.

When they got back to the corpse, Morse leaned down, and careful to leave most of the top of the head covered, removed the navy blanket, pulling it up from the bottom. The first thing Chris could see was that the feet were bare as were the legs. They were slender and well formed. Then the skirt. Dark, and wet. Was that the one? Chris couldn't remember. The blouse? It was hard to tell.

She could not remember exactly. But it was close. She knew that. Finally the face and Karen Morse looking up at her for her answer.

Christine looked hard down at the woman laying in this unnatural and uncomfortable looking pose and she began to cry.

Then almost convulsively, she laughed and shaking her head from side to side, she said, "No. That's not her."

33

There had been a car, as promised, waiting for Doran on the Canadian side of the lake. He had been dropped off at the dock of a lakefront home and walked across the yard and between the houses. Parked, running in the street was a blue Chevrolet. The driver, a French Canadian, barely spoke English, but he did seem to understand instructions. Frank had no idea who he was and theoretically the kid didn't know Frank either. He jumped in and soon, they were driving east on the 401, toward Toronto.

After a silent hour on the road, Doran inventoried his supplies, rummaging through the overnight bag on his lap. He had given his briefcase with the money and most of the bankbooks, to Angelo Domati, keeping only a single set. Angelo would return it to him on Friday, at Kennedy Airport in New York. He had some things to do before then.

Before touching anything, he had pulled on a pair of surgical gloves so there would be no fingerprints. He looked at the passport and Ontario driver's license, both of them flawless, the signatures, his own, matching the signature on the bank account.

"I want you to get off at London," he ordered the young driver without looking up. "It's another thirty miles or so. And slow down. I'm not in any hurry." Nothing more was said until the specified exit, when Doran directed the driver to a branch of the Royal Bank of Canada.

They had followed the rain as it moved east and it poured most of the way. "Park close. I don't want to get soaked."

The young Frenchman nodded and pulled into a space near the front door. Frank Doran took a deep breath. This was dangerous, the first time he would be in public since the courthouse. He pulled the passenger visor down and opened the mirror on the other side. He looked carefully at his pictures on the new identification and alternately at his live image, comparing the two. Satisfied that he looked as much like the photographs as possible, he closed the mirror, pushing the visor back into position.

"Wait here," Doran ordered, reaching into the bag to find the passbook. He opened it and checked the balance. Attached to the back cover, wrapped with a rubber band was another pair of surgical gloves. He laid them carefully on the seat next to him and reached back inside the leather bag. He felt the small plastic cylinder nestled in the bottom corner and pulled it out. Super Glue. While the driver watched, Doran removed the first pair of gloves and threw them on the floor. He opened the tube of adhesive and placed a small drop on the fleshy pad at the tip of each of his fingers. He pulled on the new gloves tightly, squeezing each finger where it met the glue drop, and held it firmly until it was attached.

Again, in the bag, this time for a razor blade. Frank using it with practiced precision to cut delicately around each of his fingertips, separating the tip from the rest of the glove. First the left, then, carefully, the right. The discarded remainder on the floor. Frank held his hands out palm up and looked them over. Perfect. He was Thomas Belland, complete with fingerprints to match.

As he got out of the car and rushed through the rain to the door, Doran smiled. It was easy really and he'd done it for years. He didn't even remember who Belland was, but it was certain he had once fingerprinted him, and then, as he had done many times, pressed the man's fingers into a another ink pad tin containing soft paraffin, where a second set of impressions would be taken, and from which as many additional sets of prints as necessary could be made. This was the second time he had used Belland's.

Inside the bank, there were only two positions for tellers and a small seating area with one desk. Frank walked to the first window. He was the only customer.

"Morning," he said politely to the young woman, "Kinda wet out there."

"It is. How may I help you?"

Frank handed over the passbook. "I'd like to make a withdrawal, twelve hundred dollars, and wire transfer the remaining balance to this account number, if you would please." Frank handed her a slip of paper on which he had written the account number and bank ID for Carlos DeVera's Colombian account, which he had set up and maintained for years, waiting for the day, now soon coming, when he would become DeVera.

"One minute, sir." She left the window and walked to the man seated at the desk.

Doran had deliberately chosen a small amount to withdraw. When he crossed the border back to the states on Thursday, he couldn't afford to be caught with too much. If he could get the rest, over two hundred thousand, transferred without incident, this part of his escape would be complete.

"Mister...Belland?" The man was at the teller's position. "There is a fee for transferring, if you will just fill this out." He handed Frank a form. "Oh, and I will also need some identification."

"Of course." Doran took the form. He reached into his pocket, found the bogus driver's license and handed it to the man. He took the pen from its holder and began to write on the paper. He saw the man comparing the signatures on the license and the original signature card, but restrained himself from looking up. Name. Address. Frank remembered it all and wrote it down. He signed the form with a flourish, replaced the pen, and slid it back across the counter to the teller. Both she and her boss compared all three signatures. Finally, the man spoke.

"All right, Mister Belland, we will take care of this immediately." Frank smiled. The assistant manager reached out to shake his hand. He never felt the rubber tips on Doran's fingers.

Frank loved Canadians. They were so simple and straightforward. They lacked suspicion. He watched as the teller counted out his cash, less fifty-two dollars for the transfer. That done, he was on his way.

"Okay, buddy, let's go," he said as he returned to the blue Chevy.

"Jean," he corrected him indignantly.

It was all that was said for another hour and forty minutes on the road, when they reached the rest area at exit 312. The driver did as he was ordered and pulled off, parking at a rest area about fifty yards to the side of the restaurant, near several picnic tables. The rain had stopped, at least for the moment, and other travelers were taking advantage of the break to walk dogs in the grassy area. While most vehicles stopped only for a few minutes, some stayed longer, allowing the drivers to nap before continuing. This was where the Frenchman was told to park and where Doran was told he would meet the second car.

In the drug trade this method of transfer was typical. Dealers referred to it as 'double blind', since it provided the opportunity for the second driver to watch the first one arrive; to detect any surveillance and to simply move on without contact if there was a problem. Usually it was drugs and money being exchanged. Today, it would be Frank Doran.

"Want coffee?" Frank asked his driver.

"Oui, black," the young man said, his heavy accent blending languages.

Doran walked to the building. It was crowded, mainly with truckers who had parked their rigs on the opposite side. He walked through the common area, past the restrooms and phones to the cafeteria on the far side. He followed the line, eventually ending up at the coffee dispenser. He filled two styrofoam cups and secured lids onto both. There was a table with cream and sugar, napkins and various other condiments just beyond the cash register and, after paying, he stopped there.

Cautiously, Doran removed a small vial from his pocket. He pulled one of the cups close, hiding his actions with his body, removed the lid, and poured the contents of the bottle inside. Quickly replacing the top, he threw the tiny vial into the trash and walked out.

Frank handed the lethal coffee to the Frenchman and sat back in his seat sipping his own, waiting. In less than five minutes, the deadly chemical began to have an effect. Jean winced as a cramp developed in his abdomen, then another. He realized what was happening and attempted to lunge at Doran, but only managed to turn slightly, dropping the coffee, the hot liquid spilling in his lap. Death was fast. At first his body stiffening, then falling limp.

Doran calmly balanced his cup on the dashboard and reached over to the motionless driver. He slid his hand over the dead man's face, closing the eyelids. Frank reached further and found the lever for the reclining seat. He let it fall back slightly. He turned Jean's head so it looked as if he were sleeping.

Doran looked outside. Everything seemed normal. He removed the false fingerprints and wadding them into a tight ball, threw them down on the floor with the other gloves and glove trimmings. He pulled on a fresh pair before picking up the pile, his cup, the overnight bag, and leaving. Doran tossed his half empty cup into a nearby trash can and, with the debris tucked securely in the palm of his hand, went back to the building and into the men's room. He went directly to a stall and closed the door behind him. He dropped the wad into the toilet and flushed it down. While it spiraled out of sight, he ripped the bankbook into pieces and when the bowl was again full, he let it fall, together with the passport and driver's license, into the waiting water. Another flush and there was no more Thomas Belland.

On the way back to the parking lot, he stopped at a box near the door to buy a newspaper. He tucked it under his arm and walked across the pavement, passing the Chevrolet without a glance. A few spaces down, he saw the car he was looking for; a dark, green Lincoln, exactly as Domati had described. He continued at a brisk walk to the passenger side and got in.

While he waited for the driver, he scanned the paper. There, at the bottom of the front page, was his picture, taken at least ten years earlier, and a headline reading, 'FBI MAN SUBJECT OF MANHUNT'. Doran read on. Basically, he concluded, it was standard procedure. Press release. Get the photo out. They had no details and the article offered little information, other than he was wanted for questioning as a suspect in a series of felonies. There was no mention of Russel, or Hoffa, or the Domati family. Still, with his picture published, he knew he had to be more careful now. This development was not unexpected and when they got to Toronto and stopped for the night, he would disguise his appearance.

This was all going pretty much as he and Vincenzo Domati had calculated, and having his picture on the front page, while somewhat disconcerting, was not yet cause for panic. It would make it difficult to drain the other bank accounts, though, at least for now.

He had waited about fifteen minutes, reading the rest of the paper before the driver's door opened. It startled him. He couldn't see who it was, but he heard a familiar voice.

"Looks like your Canadian pal is taking quite a nap, Frank." Nino Domati leaned in the driver's side. His dark straight hair and puffy cheeks smiled in a broad grin. He plopped his short overweight body behind the wheel and slammed the door. "Good to see ya."

"Nino? What the hell are you doin' here?" His presence was a total shock to Doran who expected another hired soldier. "You could have been followed. You shouldn't be here."

"Change of plans, Frank. Papa needs you to do something for him." Nino slipped the car into reverse, backed out, and slowly accelerated onto the highway, again heading east. "Papa wanted me to come personal. Said to keep this shit in the family, know what I mean?"

"Sure." Doran knew exactly what he meant, that Domati thought things were getting too hot to involve anyone outside the immediate family. It meant he was feeling pressure. It was a move to circle the family wagons.

They drove for about thirty minutes before the buildings on the outskirts of Toronto came into view. Nino continued on the freeway into the city, getting off at route 400, northbound.

Where are we going, Nino?" Doran was curious and a little miffed at the change. The original plan was to stay the night here. He didn't like not knowing.

"You'll see, Franky." Nino said, staring straight forward, driving the big Lincoln through the hot morning, heading north toward the Canadian wilderness.

34

Bobby Merimac Wilson's life ended as it was lived, without ceremony or recognition on a July night in 1975. Death came quickly after Dr. Russel removed the ventilator. The easy rhythmic pumping had stopped and the storage room was alive with new activity. Frank Doran had returned as Antonio Tenino had ordered, and now helped the doctor slide Devil Bob into a black vinyl body bag. Russel held the sheet over Bob's left forearm until the last minute, and when he was certain no one could see it, or the hand with the missing finger, he pushed it into the dark bag.

Hoffa, sedated and unconscious, still lay on the gurney. Henry Swain covered him with a blanket.

While Michael Tenino held the door, Swain unlocked the wheels and pushed the sleeping union man out into the hall. Doran and the doctor followed wheeling the second man behind. And Antonio Tenino followed. When Henry reached the security door, he again entered the code on the keypad and the lock buzzed open. He led the odd parade to the end of the hall and waited.

"We'll have to carry them up from here," Dr. Russel instructed, "Those legs fold up. There's a lever here." Russel demonstrated, grabbing the gurney at the same time. "Henry, do yours, let's go." The two men hauled Hoffa to the next level and locked the legs back into place. Doran and Michael Tenino repeated the procedure. When they were all in the hall, Swain again led the way. This time to the elevator. They ascended to street level.

They moved quickly down the main hall until they reached the electric doors at the service entrance and stopped. One of Tenino's guards surveyed the empty pre-dawn parking lot then signaled it was clear.

Outside, parked and running, the back door open, was a white Chevrolet cargo van. Next to it, Tenino's black Lincoln limousine. Michael gave orders.

"In the van. Hurry." He pointed at the dead man's body. Dr. Russel wheeled it to the back of the Chevy. Doran joined him and muscled the bag into the back, sliding it along the channels in the corrugated steel floor. He slammed the door shut.

Swain, wheeling the gurney with the semi-conscious Hoffa, started for the limo, but Michael yelled, "No, this one," and gestured to an old Ford Country Squire station wagon that was parked idling in the shadows to the side of the door. Henry changed course. "Wait there, Henry," Michael instructed, then to his soldiers, "You two," he shouted, "Take Papa's car back to the house. Now! Go!" He knew that there would be constant surveillance there and that those who were watching would assume that Tenino had returned home. Michael had planned this well, he thought, only the most trusted of the family would ever know what happened. When the limo was gone, he walked to the drivers window of the Ford and spoke to the man at the wheel, his brother. "Okay, Benito, back it up."

Benny Tenino put the car into gear and quickly backed up to where Swain was standing with Hoffa. Michael opened the back door. The rear seat was down. "Let's get him in here." Doran and Dr. Russel helped Henry slide Hoffa in, leaving the blanket and gurney behind. "Hop in, Papa." Michael opened the passenger door for his father.

Antonio called back to Russel, "Thank you, Johnny. Go raise your children." He smiled and disappeared into the wagon.

"Go Benny. And be careful." Michael slammed the door and pounded his hand twice, lightly on the sheet metal roof. He watched as the car with his father and brother and Jimmy Hoffa sped out of the wide drive into the warm night. "We'll talk, John," he reassured Russel as he got into the driver's side of the van, closed the door and drove away.

He would never see any of them again.

Michael was the first son of Antonio, the first of the family ever to be born in the United States. He had worked side by side with his father at Eastern Market since he was walking. He had learned the business of his family, first the legitimate and eventually all of the other enterprises. He had been a good soldier to his father and was now a good lieutenant. It would not be much longer before he would lead the family.

He was striking, thin and tall, with the strong profile of a movie star, and dark eyes set wide under his nearly black waves of hair.

He lit a cigarette and rolled the driver's window down. This was a moment to relax, to let his heart slow after weeks of heavy palpitation. He blew the smoke and it swirled lazily around the dashboard until it found it's way to the opening and was blasted invisible by the gushing air. He was almost to the expressway. He had to think. Domati didn't show. Why? Hoffa himself had made the call. He set it up. There had to be a good explanation.

Michael wound his way onto I-94 and drove east to the Van Dyke exit. He got off and headed north. The ghetto was vacant, no traffic at all, its residents asleep or dead. He lit another cigarette. Domati. That was the only missing element. Everything else, the difficult stuff, went fine. It was the easy part, getting Domati to the restaurant, that got screwed up. Who could have tipped him to the setup? Why would he pass up any chance to get his hands on a piece of the union. He had to figure that's why Hoffa wanted to meet him. So where was he? Michael did know for certain that it would be much harder to stick the bastard with this now. But the plan had to continue. There was no way to stop it. And nothing he could do now but drive. Drive to the lot where he would leave the van and the body for Dominic Baglia.

Benito was driving, too, just as his brother had planned, carefully watching his speed, cruising unnoticed in this old Ford eastbound on Jefferson, the same route his father's usual transportation, his limousine, had taken ten minutes earlier. But even as Tenino's car, under the watchful eye of the Justice Department was arriving at his eastside estate, Benny was turning south, down a side street toward the Detroit River. He could hear moaning from the back. Hoffa was coming to.

"Uhh. Uhhahh." the low sound of his pain. "Uhhhah."

Antonio reached into the pocket of his gabardine slacks and finding the bottle of pills that Russel had provided, opened it and held one out to Hoffa over the back of the seat. "Johnny said you were gonna need these. Here."

"Uhhh." Hoffa lay still. Only his eyes moved voluntarily, the rest of him rolling at the whim of the road causing him to moan more loudly at the turns and bumps. "Ahhhhhh!"

"Sorry, Mr. Hoffa." Benny was trying his best to avoid the inconsistencies of the pavement, but the county crews didn't usually fix many problems in this part of the city, feeling it was too dangerous for the wages they were paid.

"Here," the old man insisted, "And take a drink of this to wash it down." He had produced a flask. When it was clear that Hoffa wasn't going to take the pill on his own, Antonio dropped it into his mouth, "Hey, c'mon Jimmy, it's for the best. We got a ways to go yet." Tenino reached back, lifting Hoffa's head with one hand and with the other pouring the liquid in behind the pill. The alcohol stung badly and Hoffa coughed and screamed. But the medicine was taken and as far as Tenino was concerned, that's what counted. He turned around and faced forward, smiling. "Good Jimmy, you'll see, that will help you...Johnny knows what he's talkin' about."

The car continued winding erratically through the neighborhood of rundown four family flats and trash filled lots. Even before the first light of the August sun, the heat was building and the garbage was beginning to release a sick, dead smell. Later it would be worse. Benny checked the rearview often. When he was positive that they were not followed, he drove to the waterfront, to A.B. Ford Park at the foot of Lakewood. There was a playground. Most of the equipment was rusty and broken, having gone years without attention. Benito entered the deserted parking area and drove to the far end where a small concrete ramp, a boat launch, descended at a soft angle into the water. The area was hidden by elm trees on either side. Less than fifty yards out was Harbor Island, a once popular residential neighborhood, fallen now from grace. The canal created in between was interrupted by aging wooden docks and sporadic rotten pilings of various heights.

There was a dock next to the park's launching area and, just as Michael had said, tied to the last piling was a dark green, eighteen foot wooden boat. Inside, there was fishing equipment and supplies, a blue wool blanket, a sleeping bag, and a large red tank filled with fuel for the outboard motor.

Benny drove, as planned, to the ramp. He turned the headlights off and backed up until the rear bumper was almost submerged. With the car in park, and running, he opened the door and got out, stepping up to his ankles in the murky water. It was difficult to see where he was going in the dark early morning, still he found his way to the dock. He noticed the first hint of light peeking over the river as he walked toward the boat. He had to hurry. He grabbed the rope, untied it, and pulled the wooden craft back with him to where the water was shallow. Firmly holding the line, he jumped in and dragged the boat to the back of the station wagon. Benny unrolled the sleeping bag, laying it out to cushion the inside of the boat. He opened the back of the car and reached in, grabbing the leg of the union leader and shaking it. "C'mon Mr. Hoffa, we gotta hurry."

The pills were beginning to have an effect, though his mouth still throbbed with pressure. Hoffa inched his way out aided by the angle. Benny held the boat steady against the rear bumper as Hoffa tumbled in turning over to his back. "Auhh." The sudden movement of his bleeding jaw reinstated the sharp pain. "Uhhhhahh," he quietly moaned, allowing his body to rest on the padded fabric.

Benny covered him with the blanket and quickly hauled the boat to the dock, securing it with the line. He walked to the idling car and sat behind the wheel, "Okay Papa, this is it. Get in the boat. I'll be right back." The old man got out and quietly closed the door.

"Hurry, Benito."

Benny drove out of the park and left on Riverside to Port Street. Halfway down the block was a vacant lot where residents had dumped appliances and furniture and other stolen vehicles.

Benny drove over the curb and the sidewalk, through the tall weeds, dodging debris, finally stopping in a clear area near the center of the lot. He shut off the engine and reached behind him. The second seat had been folded down so Hoffa could stretch out fully. Benny lifted it and felt around near the floor until he found the handle of the full two gallon gas can. He hauled it to the front and unscrewed the top. As he got out of the car, he splashed the volitile liquid over the dash and passenger seat. With the can dripping, he walked to the back, opened it and dumped the remainder of the contents inside, followed by the empty metal can. Stepping back twenty or so feet, he reached in his pocket and produced a Zippo lighter. He spun the tiny wheel against the flint and with it lit, threw it into the open back of the Ford, running as fast as his large frame would travel, back toward the park.

The explosion was loud. And powerful, sending pieces of discarded appliances flying into the trees. Halfway down the block, Benny slowed to a brisk walk, not wishing to attract unwanted attention. Lights were coming on in several homes, but no one had come outside. He reached the corner of Port Street and Riverside and turned right. Soon he was at the entrance to the park.

He started running again, full speed across the empty parking lot. He could see his father in the boat waiting. When he got closer he noticed that Hoffa was awake and the two men were talking. Antonio looked up as his son returned.

"Benito. Good. Let's get the hell outta here while the fire keeps 'em busy."

Hoffa grunted his approval.

Benny released the line and used one of the oars to push them off. With a final thrust the boat moved out into the small channel and began to drift downstream with the river's current. They could see the black petroleum smoke rising up over the houses. They heard the sirens approaching. Antonio looked back, scanning the park. No one. "Good work, Benito. Good boy," he complimented his son and, happy the long night was over, finally began to relax.

When they were several hundred yards offshore, Benny pulled the cord to start the motor. With a couple of scant blue wiffs of smoke it choked to life. He turned the control on the handle and with increasing speed started upriver.

We've done it, Michael thought. It was almost over. They would get what they wanted. They would have the union without the pressure from the Justice Department that Hoffa attracted like a lightning rod. They would have all the money. And they would put the heat on that prick Domati at the same time. Michael went over the plan again and again. As long as Doran's assurances were correct and they had paid the right guy to betray the Domati family, they would all be fine. They had managed to create the illusion that Jimmy Hoffa had disappeared. Soon, if all went as planned, the duplicate body would be picked up and on its way to northern Michigan; to Charlevoix Sand and Gravel, one Domati's businesses, where Dominic Baglia would bury it. One phone call to the authorities, and it would be found. And Baglia, believing it was Hoffa, and carefully selected by Doran for his stupidity, would loyally take the fall, thinking, as he had been told, that he actually had disposed of Hoffa on Vincenzo Domati's orders. The murder would be linked to that family. If Michael had to, if something went wrong, he could dispose of Doran, too, distancing his family, the Tenino family, even further from the crime. It was a good plan.

But Baglia never followed it. He had been given different instructions by Frank Doran, and would, instead, without Michael's knowledge, deposit the body of Devil Bob squarely in the middle of the front lawn of a cottage in Leland; the cottage of Dr. Russel, who never knew it was there.

Michael was still sorting out the possibilities in his head as he drove. He had smoked almost a pack of cigarettes since he left the medical center. He passed Seventeen Mile Road still heading north on Van Dyke. He was almost there. Ahead, on the left, he saw the entrance. There was a small guardhouse flanked by IN and OUT driveways. The entire compound was surrounded by a high fence topped with barbed wire. In the ground near the road was a sign identifying the premises: STERLING HEIGHTS TRANSPORTATION, DIVISION OF GENERAL MOTORS.

Michael Tenino pulled in. No one was at the gate, the guards, as he had ordered, were told to stay away. He drove across the paved parking area to a huge windowless building which rose four stories above the cement. This was the principle distribution center for small parts for the giant automaker. Hundreds of employees worked here loading parts into the dozens of white Chevy vans, each identical to the one Michael was driving, to distribute parts to various manufacturing operations around the city. On this night, however, they were idle and parked as planned in designated numbered spaces nose in, in a long row against the building.

Normally, these shipments would come and go at all hours so Michael's arrival at dawn would not be unusual. The facility was union controlled and the Tenino family controlled the union. So access was not a problem.

Michael planned to park the van with the body in a predetermined space beside the building and then leave immediately in another matching vehicle. When he was safely away, he would call Frank Doran, who would in turn contact Baglia. Baglia would then enter the facility in a third white van, park in the space that Michael Tenino had vacated, and leave, with the body he believed to be Hoffa's, in the van Michael had driven there from the medical center.

Mike went over this again as he drew closer to the cinder block building. The space, number eighty-seven, was vacant. As planned. Good. Once more, he mentally dissected the plan for flaws, but found none. He tossed his last cigarette butt out and rolled the window closed. He glanced quickly in back. The door was closed. The body bag was there. Everything was in order. With his handkerchief, he wiped the steering wheel to remove his fingerprints. He got out and did the same to the outside door handle and the handle of the back door. He looked up, scanning the empty lot. He walked briskly, checking the descending numbers painted on the pavement. When he got to sixty-three and the vehicle he was to take, he turned in, walking along the driver's side to the door.

The air inside was stagnant and he immediately rolled down the window. The key was in the ignition as he expected. He started the engine. And reached out to adjust the outside mirror. But there was movement, a reflection. Something beside him. In the passenger side window of the van in space sixty-two. He jerked his head to the left. The window in the other vehicle was also down. That wasn't right. Then the shock of a familiar face, not friendly as he had always known it, but threatening, holding a weapon, aiming it at Michael's head.

"Oh my God. No." Michael shook his head. Then everything went into slow motion and the crystal clarity of betrayal became obvious. This was why Domati never showed. He had no control over what would happen next.

"Good bye, Mike," Frank Doran said softly and opened fire, his semi-automatic pistol quieted by the long silencer. The impact of the first two bullets forced Michael's head away from the shots, but almost immediately recoiled as the force from another flurry of bullets fired from the opposite direction, from the driver's window of the van in space sixty-four, by Dominic Baglia.

In seconds it was over. Antonio's eldest son lay dead and bleeding in a layer of shattered glass on the front seat. Doran jammed his vehicle into reverse and sped out, backing up in a wide arch from the building. The rubber squeaked forward when he shifted again and raced out of the lot turning right, southbound, heading back toward the city.

Baglia ran to space eighty-seven, to the original vehicle. He too, checked the back. He saw the body bag. He knew it was Hoffa.

That's what he had been told. He started the Chevy and left, heading north on Van Dyke, away from Detroit.

From the time Michael had arrived to the time Baglia left, only six minutes had passed. The sun was up sending its first long shadows across the lot. The van in space sixty-three was running, but no one would hear it for almost two hours. Just as no one would see anything. No one would dare enter the facility until eight A.M. Those were Michael Tenino's orders. And no one would find him until then.

The same warm rays found Antonio nodding with sleep in the bow of the small boat, Hoffa staring up at the cloudless morning, and Benny at the helm. They had emerged from the river and were well into Canadian waters in Mitchell's Bay on the other side of Lake St. Clair. This was a popular fishing area and many other similar small boats were already in position, their lines cast in the shallow water.

Benny had slowed to about five knots and they casually approached the outer marker of the inlet. It was no more than a pole with a red diamond shaped board nailed to the top. Another pole with a green diamond marked the far side. Benny maneuvered the craft between them, slowing the motor to a crawl. As they got closer, the reeds that grew from the sandy bottom became more dense and eventually created high swaying walls on either side of the boat.

There was, extending from the land a series of islands. They were separated only by a dozen yards or so and only a hundred feet from the shore. They were only accessible by boat. Cabins had been built on most of them and when taken collectively, comprised a Venetian style neighborhood. Many of the cabins were owned by American corporations and were used frequently by executives for long weekends of meetings and skeet shooting, or trysts with secretaries or prostitutes. The one the Teninos used was deeded to The Harborside Trucking Company. Before that, it had belonged to Illinois Vending, Inc., which was controlled by Sam Giancanna, the Chicago mob boss. It's hidden location and proximity to Canada provided an ideal transfer point for bootlegged liquor shipments during prohibition. Later, Giancanna used it to elude process servers during the increasingly more frequent federal investigations into his activities. It was a hideout.

The three men were nearly there. They were completely hidden from the shore on the starboard by the tall marsh grass as they meandered down the waterway. They passed several cottages each built on its own small island. None looked inhabited.

Antonio Tenino remembered the first time he had ever come here. He was eighteen and hungry. It was easy money. Take the boat. Meet two guys. Load the booze. Bring it back to the American side. For this he was well paid. It was how he got started with Giancanna. Since then, Tenino, as head of the Detroit operation, and he, had met many times. Sam had become a good friend to Hoffa, too, and had given his blessing to the planned disappearance. Giancanna did not want Domati to run Detroit. He was not an ally. Domati had aligned himself with the Miami faction run by Santos Trafficante, a man Giancanna considered loose and dangerous.

As a result of this alliance, Domati had gained considerable stature and power. He resented Tenino's control in Detroit and felt that he could do a much better job. To him Antonio Tenino was soft and conservative and now, with his ties to South Florida, Domati felt he could dominate Detroit's lucrative cocaine and heroin business. But Tenino and Giancanna had strongly resisted, preferring instead to generate revenue from more traditional and less risky means. They had the unions wrapped up and saw no reason to attract additional attention to their businesses. Neither Giancanna nor Trafficante wanted to be involved in a war in Detroit, and they refused to intercede. It was clear that eventually the tension between the Tenino and Domati families would come to a head. The position of the other bosses of La Cosa Nostra was to leave it alone. And see what happened.

Benny turned left and navigated the boat to a position alongside the dock at the cabin. He shut off the outboard.

"Well, Papa, we made it."

"That we did, Benito." Papa Tenino smiled, "C'mon Jimmy, I'll show you the place." Antonio stood up and stretched. He stepped over the gunwale and onto the water-stained wood of the lower dock. The lake had been low for several years and this section was added when it became impossible to climb up to the original dock, now more than six feet above. Tenino hurried up the steps. "There it is." His eye caught the first glimpse of the cabin. "Benito," he ordered, "Help Mr. Hoffa up here, so he can see."

Antonio loved the cabin. He came here often to fish and relax. Over their lifetimes he had brought his boys here hundreds of times. "I'll go see if we have a cold beer. We could sure use one, eh, Benny?" he called back as he crossed the green lawn to the dark brown wooden cottage. He arrived at the door to the screened porch and disappeared inside.

Hoffa, with Benny's help, had managed to get himself out of the boat and up the dock and the two of them walked together toward the cabin. Hoffa was groggy from the medication, but the oral pain had diminished somewhat. It would be a week, he remembered Dr. Russel telling him, without teeth, before the holes from the extractions healed enough to wear dentures. He reached to his cheek, rubbing the sore area. The saliva and blood were building in his mouth and he spit it out, red on the lawn.

It was, except for the song of an occasional bird, an unusually still August morning. Tiny waves, the wake of faraway boaters, gently surged against the seawall that surrounded the island retreat. As they neared the cottage, the sun, warm and comforting, dodged the dense leaves on several cherry trees and dappled the ground ahead. Finally, Benito thought, they could relax.

Benny reached the screened porch slightly ahead of the union boss, who was lagging behind. He opened the door, "After you, Mr. Hoffa." But he didn't move. Instead, he stood motionless. He was staring at something. Benny turned to see what it was. His breath was gone, sucked away as he witnessed his father, held by two of Domatis men, being pushed from the cabin back out onto the porch. He lunged forward, "Papa!"

"Hold it, Benito. I don't want you to get hurt. I need you to remember this day." Domati himself emerged from the building. Dressed, as always, more for a business dinner than a murder. "I need you to send a message." Domati's voice was flat, without emotion. He aimed a large pistol at Benny, frozen, a statue shivering with cold shock.

"No. Mr Domati. No." Benny didn't notice that Hoffa had walked past him and into the screened area.

"C'mon, bring him out here." Domati waved the weapon, indicating the direction he wanted his men to go. One of them grabbed Antonio and dragged him out into the yard, the other brought Benny.

Tenino stared hard at Hoffa and shouted, "You, bastard, Jimmy. What are you thinking?" But Hoffa didn't even turn around. Instead, he disappeared into the dark cabin.

Tenino knew what had happened. He knew what would happen now. He knew why Domati never showed up at the restaurant. And he suspected the worst for his eldest son. Still, he had to ask, "Michael?" Domati shook his head. Antonio felt the small moist pressure building behind his eyes. And he saw his second son collapse limp, falling to the grass, before the tears obscured all vision. "I love you Benito," he whispered. "Don't ever forget that I love you."

Domati handed the gun to the man who had been holding Benny. He moved closer to Tenino. "You think you are such a big goomba, don't you vegetable man? Well, I'm going to show you...show everybody that you aren't." When he was face to face with Tenino, he held his hand out. His lieutenant drew a large hunting knife from the sheath on his belt and slapped the handle squarely in Domati's upturned palm. He called to the other man but never stopped staring at Antonio Tenino. "Make sure that one watches," he said, and then, "Undo your belt and drop your trousers down." Tenino did nothing. With a bob of Domati's head, the man with Benny swung his foot kicking at the young man's head, catching him in the cheek, and rolling him backwards. He grabbed Benito by the hair and pulled to align his eyes with his father's.

"Drop them."

Tenino undid the belt and zipper from his khakis and they fell easily from his large belly in a heap at his ankles.

"The shorts." Domati smiled, snapping at the waistband with the tip of blade and then swiftly tearing the knife through the fabric, scratching the surface of Antonio's skin in the process, and causing the boxers to fall. "You better grab that thing." The man freed Tenino's right arm and he instinctively grabbed his penis, hauling it upward against the bottom of his protruding stomach, covering it with his hand.

Domati stepped back, "Hey, Benito, I want you to look at your father." Benny couldn't. "Look at him!" Benny felt his head jerked by his hair. "You see him? That's what he is. Nothing. Nothing at all. It takes strength now to make it. Not some bullshit vegetable van. It take balls to make it." Domati was pacing, turning the knife in his hands. His voice was growing louder. His adrenaline building. "Balls! And does your Papa here have balls enough to be a boss of bosses? Does he?" Domati, with two quick strides, was a breath from Tenino. He plunged the blade between his left leg and his scrotum and in one motion, sliced through the tender flesh to the opposite thigh, at the same time taking hold of the sack and its contents. Tenino sucked in all the air he could. The blood was gushing from the opened area, running down his naked legs. "No!" Domati yelled lurching toward Benny, holding the amputated testes in his hand, squeezing them in Benny's face. "But I do."

Benny, on his knees, his body heaving, threw up on the lawn. He felt the grip on his head release and he fell forward crying, "Papa..." in the vomit.

Domati hurled the disgusting body parts in the water and raised his finger, pointing at the terrified man, "Benito, you tell anyone who asks that this is my operation now, that I am the one they have to deal with. You understand? Do you? I know you will do this, Benito, and if you do, you will live. Your family will live. Now go. Get the hell out of here. Save your own little life, before you can't."

Benny wiped the foul liquid from his face, got to his feet and waddled to the dock, sobbing. In the boat, started the motor and loosed the lines. As he pulled away he reached down over the side of the boat bringing water up to him, splashing it over his head and body. He was praying, saying the Latin words he learned as an alter boy. He couldn't look back, only ahead. He kept the water flowing, more water, the lake mixing with his tears. Now, the last of his family, he was hoping to wash the evil from his life.

He would deny to himself forever that he had heard it; the splash, the sound of his father's body falling into the water. He swore he had no memory of these events; nor a vision of the men rolling Papa to the wooden breakwater, the edge of the island and dumping him over. Or imagine Domati laughing as he washed the blood from his hands. Or the treason of Jimmy Hoffa. Or that on the day he lost his father and his brother, when they most needed him, he had been completely helpless.

But in the bright sun that beat at him from above, in the reflections that sliced at his eyes from below, in the sputtering sound of the outboard as he crossed the lake, he knew in the darkest, saddest part of his heart that it was all true.

35

"Cessna November 3-4-7 Tango. Traverse tower." The radio voice filled the cockpit of the two seat aircraft. John Russel didn't like small planes in the first place and this constant, crackling electronic drone added to his misery. The seating area was uncomfortable enough, without being squeezed further into it by the noise. "Cessna November 3-4-7 Tango. Traverse tower. Respond. You have entered Delta class air space without authorization. Turn back. Repeat. Turn back."

"Turn that damn thing off," John ordered the pilot.

"I have to respond. They want to know what we're doing here."

"Screw 'em. Turn it off," John demanded, "I paid for this damn plane, didn't I? Now do as I tell you, please."

John had paid dearly for this flight, fifty thousand dollars in cash, but Randy the pilot, (John was never told his last name) was not above further extortion.

"Well, if I don't talk to them, they're gonna wonder...and then there's my license." He had already seen John's bag of money.

"Cut the shit, Randy. How much?"

"Ten."

"Five to turn off the radio. And another five to go where you tell me to."

John figured the guy's license was probably in question as it was. But he reluctantly agreed.

Randy reached up to the radio switch and flipped it to the off position. He took his headset off and smiled at John.

John grabbed the bag, growing lighter from these repeated extortions, from the floor between his feet, and produced a tightly wrapped stack of currency; ten thousand dollars in hundreds. He had already dished out three thousand for the phony flightplan, another five to take off while thunderstorms were still in the area around City Airport, and two more to fly illegally low in hopes of avoiding radar detection, something John had seen done in the movies, so it seemed possible, and he came through with the cash. So this 'Randy' was up seventy grand and the flight wasn't even over, but John didn't care. He was almost to Leelanau and the damn finger. He still had twenty four hours to get it to Domati.

"There's Traverse." Randy pointed ahead.

The southern end of Grand Traverse bay was directly in front of them. It looked like a giant double U with the Old Mission Penninsula jutting up in the middle, separating the east and west bays. At the bottom, the city itself, small by almost any standard.

They were low and John could see the airport at the bottom left part of the letter, near the water. "Keep going. Straight. Follow the shoreline north."

"We've only got enough fuel for about another hour at this speed."

John could see where this was headed and he cut him off. "We've got plenty. Just keep flying. We'll be down soon enough."

At least the weather had begun to cooperate. The first forty-five minutes out of Detroit were brutal. They had dodged huge thunderheads and the winds that swirled around them had thrown the Cessna around like a roller coaster car, battering John against the side window, and once against the ceiling, adding additional wounds to his gradually mutilated body. The smooth air now was a blessing. The even drone of the engine was relaxing. Just to have a moment of relative peace was appreciated. He rested his head on the back of the seat and wondered how this would all come out. He felt a twinge of sadness, a pain cutting through him, when he considered Shelby. For the tiniest interval, he was not able to suppress the thought of her death, an event so unbelievable, he could not conceive it in any real sense. He drifted back. There were so many great memories of summers. Childhood at the cabin at Duck Lake. While dad was busy sawing off fingers.

"Hey. Hey pal. Wake up. We're running out of land."

John felt Randy shaking him back from sleep. He shook his head awake. And the familiar throbbing began, mostly from new places, but still some from others. "Where are we?"

"That's Charlevoix on the right. That's about ten miles. Directly up ahead is the tip of Leelanau County. And after that, nothin' but water."

"Okay. All right." John was still trying to get his bearings, "Hang on a second. There's an airport. Private. Right near here." The canvas bag from the bank was still lodged between his tennis shoes and looked undisturbed. "It's near Northport, near the tip."

Randy pulled out a stack of maps and scanned through them until he found one that matched the terrain below. "Here?" He pointed to two crossed lines. John leaned over the paper.

"Woolsey Airport. That's it. That's where we're going." He sat up straight to get a better view of the ground through the high window. Where the county came to a point was the lighthouse, beyond it Lake Michigan, reflecting gray from the clouds. He traced a line down from the point. There it was. "There."

The pilot looked at the spot where John was pointing, "That's just a field."

"It's an airstrip. Put it down."

Without saying a word, Randy took the controls, disengaging the auto pilot, and the plane lunged slightly. He descended from three thousand feet to two and flew over the area to take a closer look.

"See. That's what I told you. An airport." John said smugly, although he was sure that the remark would cost him. "Can you do it?"

"Yeah."

Randy banked steeply, decreasing the altitude even more as he did. There were two runways, if you could call them that, perpendicular to one another, which roughly marked the compass points. Randy chose to land to the west, against the prevailing wind. He began a tight circle to the right, two hundred and seventy degrees over the water, lower still. The engine whined, working hard. John watched the view out his side window change as the horizon lifted away. Straight down and nothing but water. Jesus. His body pressed deeper in the seat.

Finally the force subsided and the horizon came back into his sight. They leveled off from the turn, which John guessed was much more severe than it had to be, and headed for the landing sight.

The pilot was right, Woolsey Airport isn't much more than a field; two short areas of mowed grass, cut out of the thick pine forest, intersecting at the middle. It sits near M-629, the only road to the tip of Leelanau. There is no tower or gate or metal detectors. The terminal is the size of a small house, mainly a single story, rectangular, except for one end where it is two and lifts up in a round turret. On top of that, a flat, open rooftop, used as an observation deck. The building is entirely constructed of stones, not square building blocks from a quarry, but round rocks polished smooth by the Lake Michigan waves, and this gives it a look of some troll's miniature castle, tucked away in the woods.

As the plane flew over it, ready to touch down, John could see it clearly. It appeared to be deserted, as it usually was. To the left parked in a row were three cars, likely left there by flying owners. Further off to the side, two planes, similar to Randy's Cessna were parked and tethered to the ground. The engine reverberated loudly from the cement roof then diminished as the grass rose to meet them. The power cut and they sunk the final three feet to the ground. They bounced. Once, and again on the undulating green surface, which was anything but flat. Hurtling from mound to mound, the plane gradually slowed, coming to a controllable idle fifty feet before the edge of the forest.

"Jesus. Drive over to the building," John said when he recovered from the jarring.

Randy turned around and, absent a taxiway, scooted back down the runway. When they were near the end, he turned off into a parking area and cut the engine.

"Now what?" Randy asked.

John looked around. No one. "You stay here." He unfastened his harness, opened the door, and jumped to the ground. It felt good to sink into the grass and to be standing on something solid. He ached from everywhere and, stiff, John hobbled toward the stone building. There was a pay phone inside, John remembered.

There were no doors or windows, only openings in the architecture. John chose one and entered the empty, round room. His footsteps echoed as he walked. There were three other window size openings evenly spaced around the wall, and a fresh breeze blew in circulating small bits of discarded paper and dust on the cement floor. As far back as John could recall, this room had been empty and he wondered what it had ever been used for. He turned left, a few steps down the short hall, to the square part of the structure. Directly across from him, secured to the wall, was a public telephone. He noticed, as he got closer, that callers had written numbers on the exposed rock around it. He also caught a distorted reflection of himself in the shiny metal coin box at the bottom of the phone. He leaned down to it to take a closer look at his face. Jesus. His hair drooped in twisted strands across his forehead. Just above his ears, where the Nubian Boy cap had

rested was a circular depression that surrounded his head. He had
grown what was becoming a quite substantial beard over the past
two days. Basically, he looked like shit. Make the call. Get it over
with. Screw the FBI. He would give the damn finger to Domati or
Doran or whomever and they would give him his wife back and
that would be it.

John had no more change. He picked up the receiver and dialed
a long string of numbers, waited and dialed a second bunch to use
his calling card. After the electronic woman thanked him, his call
rang through.

"Leelanau County Sheriff's office." It was one of Kellet's deputies.

"Sheriff Kellet, please."

"Is this an emergency?"

"No."

"And what is this about?"

"Just let me talk to Kellet, please?"

"The Sheriff is…"

"Look, if it makes you happy, it's a goddamn emergency, okay?"

There was a long silence until, finally Bob Kellet got on the
phone, "Kellet."

"It's John Russel, listen, have you got the…you know…the thing?"

"Yeah. But John this is a big deal. The Feds have called me
twice in the last hour."

"I know it is. But this may be the only way to save Shelby. If
you could…" John heard a noise. Loud. The airplane's engine.
"Hold on, Bob. Please stay on the line. Hold on."

John ran out of the building, "Hey! Hey, come back here." The
Cessna had taxied back onto the grass runway and was gaining
speed for takeoff. John was running as fast as his legs would
move, chasing the aircraft, screaming. There was no way he could
catch it. "You prick." It was all he could think of as the plane, a
good hundred or so yards ahead of him bounced up into the air.

He saw Randy wave as he ascended. John stopped, completely out of breath, bent over, his hands on his knees, struggling to recover.

"Shit. Shit. Shit. Shit and fucking hell," he yelled to the ground, now kicking and throwing his arms, punching at the air. The bastard Randy had taken the rest of the money.

He remembered Kellet. John started to run again, this time back to the building. He made it back to the phone. "Bob? Bob, are you there?" Again there was a pause.

"Hello?"

"Yeah, Bob?"

"I had to take another call. Them again. Where the hell are you?"

"It doesn't matter."

"Was that a plane?"

"Was is right. Listen Bob, you know where the Markum farm is?"

"By Peterson Park?"

"That's it. Bring the thing and meet me there in ten minutes." John hung up. He learned a long time ago not to give people a chance to say no.

The FBI would be here any time. He had to hurry. He went back out to the parking area and checked each car. One, a maroon Mercury, was open. He looked around at his feet and in the area in front of the car until he found a rock large enough to smash the ignition. After a few minutes of hammering, it gave way. He ripped it from the steering column and threw it to the floor. Now he needed something to stick into the hole, to turn the switch. The trunk. He pulled the lever at the left of the driver's seat and it popped open. He ran to the back. There, in an old bag, a set of golf clubs. He yanked one out and swung it hard, breaking it against the bumper. The head flew off under the car, leaving in his hand the rest of the broken shaft. He held it on the ground and stomped it as hard as he could with his heel. The broken edge collapsed flat. He hurried back into the driver's seat and jammed the flattened end into the hole in the column, turning it clockwise. The starter whined and the engine came to life. John slammed it in gear and, with tires spinning in the loose gravel, spun around, onto the road. Slow, he thought. Drive the speed limit. Blend in.

The next minute and a half was surprisingly relaxing. It would be hours before the owner reported the car theft. He cracked the window and the clean air brushed the side of his face as he drove south toward Northport. On his left, the woods opened to a small bay and the water glistened just feet from the road. There was no one else around. It was what he loved so much about this part of the county; few tourists ever ventured this far. It was peaceful.

M-201 curved to the right just ahead. It went uphill through the cherry orchards, barren of fruit after the recent harvest. The area was hilly and John enjoyed winding through the curves, each revealing a new vista. In the distance green fields. And a car, approaching fast. A black ford. Damn.

In an effort to look as inconspicuous as possible, John stretched his right arm over the back of the passenger seat. In seconds, the car was on him. It was going eighty as it roared past. Thank goodness. There was no way John's car could have been much more than a reddish flash at that speed, but, just to be cautious, after it passed, he began to accelerate, to get as far away as quickly as possible from the other car. He watched it vanish in his rear view.

Still a mile from town, he turned right, heading for Peterson Park. The next road led to the Markum farm, again to the right. There was no sign, and to the uneducated, it looked to be nothing more than a dirt driveway. John drove to a spot just over the first small hill, pulled off under a cherry tree, and stopped to wait for Kellet.

It didn't take long.

He heard the gravel shift in the distance as Kellet's cruiser turned onto the road. He heard the engine racing toward him. He opened the door and stepped out. Soon the rack of red and blue lights came into view. John walked to the back of the stolen Mercury and when the windshield of Kellet's car was visible, John waved. Instantly the sheriff slowed to a crawl, pulling to a stop near John. As he got out, he shook his head slowly from side to side.

"Mr. Russel, it's good to see you...almost in one piece."

They shook hands. "Thanks for coming Bob. We've got to make this quick."

"You said they had Shelby. Who has her?"

"Doran. Frank Doran. They'll kill her, Bob. They want the finger."

"But John, I don't see why you don't just let the FBI handle this. It's probably your best shot. Giving you the evidence in a federal case could cost me my job, you know. This isn't going to be easy to explain."

"Bob, I know, but I can't. You've just gotta trust me on this one. Sometimes you have to do things yourself. I have to do this. I don't have a choice. You've got to give me the finger. I gotta go."

"How the hell are you gonna get out of here? They're everywhere."

John's frustration rose and started to pace back and forth behind the car, "Fuck, I don't know. I *had* a goddamn plane." He kicked at the loose stones. "I don't know. I don't know anything." He stopped, slamming his fist down hard on the trunk, then leaning against the back of the car. "But, Jesus Bob, I have to try."

The tall sheriff looked sympathetically at John. "Lemme see what I can do." He walked back to his car, reached in through the open window. John watched him talking on his radio, but couldn't hear what he said. When the short conversation ended, the sheriff returned with a plastic sandwich bag full of ice, and inside, among the cubes, the tip of Bobby Merimac Wilson's severed baby finger.

"Here." Kellet handed it to him. "But I still don't see how this is going to help. What are you gonna do with it?"

"I have to get it back to...well, to someone...by tomorrow."

The sheriff looked at the Mercury. "Where'd this car come from?"

"At Woolsey. It was parked. I..."

"All right. All right. I think I know whose it is. Here." Kellet held out a set of car keys. "You take my car. No one'll mess with you. You better get out of here."

"Thanks Bob. Thank you." John hurried to the waiting cruiser as Kellet yelled after him.

"I hope you know what you're doing."

Jesus, John thought, so do I. He jumped behind the wheel, adjusting the seat for his shorter legs, and turned the key. The big LTD roared awake. He put it into gear and was almost moving when two other county cars sped by, sliding to a stop near the sheriff. Four of his deputies got out. Kellet waved for John to go and he did, waving back.

Overhead, in the sky a thunderous sound. John was back on M-201 when he looked up to see what it was; a huge helicopter approaching from the south. He could see, as it came closer, the unmistakable blue and white markings of the Detroit police department on its underside. It shook his car as it passed directly over, speeding north.

John worked his way slowly through the village of Northport, winding back out onto M-22 southbound toward the Indian reservation and the casino. Traffic was light at first, but increased quickly. There were several black Fords that passed him in the opposite direction as he continued to make his way toward Traverse and ultimately, Detroit.

Bob Kellet, in the meantime, had sent one of his men back to the airstrip to return the Mercury. He had joined another in his car and the four of them headed to the main road to take positions just south of Woolsey Airport, where the Jet Ranger had landed. They watched from a driveway as three FBI cars passed, and waited.

"Here they come." The voice came over the radio from the deputy in the stolen car. "They're just pulling out now, sheriff."

Kellet gave the order and his two cars pulled out forming a roadblock across M-201, just south of the big curve away from the bay. The men got out and ducked down behind the vehicles, poised with loaded shotguns, and waited for agent Garnetti and his men.

Less than forty seconds later, the FBI cars raced around the bend. The first slammed on his brakes when he saw the parked cars. The second did the same and the third slammed hard into the first two, pushing the second into a tight spin. The collection of steaming metal slid to a stop about twenty feet from the roadblock and, Garnetti, who was riding in the third car, jumped out stomping, with his gun in one hand and his ID in the other, screaming.

"This is a goddamn federal investigation that you and your hick ass bastards are getting in the way of! Now move!"

Sheriff Kellet calmly got to his feet, his ominous six foot three frame towering over the hood of the car. "I'll need you to drop your weapon, sir."

Garnetti charged on, "Fuck off and get the hell out of the way."

The three deputies cocked the shotguns as they also stood, aiming at the FBI agent. The other agents drew their pistols but before they could even get out of their vehicles, two more county cruisers boxed them in from the rear. The deputies leapt out and more shotguns were pointed.

"FBI." Garnetti shouted, "FBI."

"Please drop your weapon, sir."

Surrounded, Garnetti gave up, tossing his gun down on the road and his other agents followed suit. "Look sheriff, this is ridiculous. Check the ID. I'm Special Agent Garnetti with the Detroit office of the bureau. You damn well know it, too."

Kellet motioned for his men to move in and collect the weapons. "Detroit office. uh huh."

"Check it out."

"Let me see that ID."

Garnetti handed it over and the sheriff took it to the side window of the car where he apparently was comparing it to some other document. He returned with both. "It says here on this hot sheet that one 'Frank Doran', head of the FBI office…in Detroit, is wanted for murder. Then, when I look at the picture they faxed up here, I gotta say, there's more than a slight resemblance."

"You're shittin' me."

Kellet ignored him and went on, "It says he should be considered armed…and certainly that seems to fit," Kellet surveyed the pile of collected weapons, "And…dangerous. Now, judging from the way you stormed up here to my little roadblock, I'd say that fits, too."

"Sheriff, can I talk to you…privately, for a second."

Kellet motioned to let him through, between the cars, and the two walked from earshot.

"What are you doing? You know damn well I'm not Doran. This is obstruction," he said quietly. "I could have your ass."

"I have a reasonable suspicion, that gives me the authority. I'm sorry. Do what you want, but right now, I have to do this." Kellet raised his voice, turning to his men, taking Garnetti by the arm at the same time. "Take 'em in. Give 'em their rights." And then, louder still, "Frank Doran, you and your men are under arrest on suspicion of murder."

Kellet handcuffed Garnetti himself, but before the deputy came to get him, he whispered, "Sorry."

John decided that the main road past the casino would be too dangerous, so he cut into the heart of the county, heading to Traverse on county road 641. He wound his way through orchards and past farms as the road followed southern Lake Leelanau on his right. Every now and then someone out working would wave or a passing car would honk, thinking he was the sheriff. Once, John waved back. He didn't know what else to do. He was moving quickly now. There are few intersections in this part of the county and very little traffic. For most of the way he had the road to himself. He was slowed for awhile by a cruising motorhome ahead of him, but after passing that, the way was clear.

The clouds had blown across the bay and melted in the warming late summer air. John, with the window down, felt the heat blowing by his ear. He smelled the sweetness of freshly cut alfalfa. The wind sailing by the opening simultaneously whistled and roared as he sped along between the swaying grasses that covered the green hills.

He bathed in this comfort for what seemed like an endless time before he noticed another car in his rear view. It was gaining, slowly. He looked at the speedometer; seventy. John watched as it came closer. It hovered for a mile or so about fifty yards behind him. If he sped up, the other car did too. If he slowed, it slowed. He could see that there were two passengers, two men. The car didn't look like one that the FBI would use. Instead, it looked more like a rental. And it was a deep burgundy, not at all like an official vehicle.

He decided not to worry about it. He had bigger problems. It was probably a damn reporter. That's who the FBI should hire, John thought, those sons of bitches could find anyone. He sped up.

When he got to Cedar, which is little more than a couple of butcher shops and a stoplight, he slowed the cruiser to the thirty-five mile per hour speed limit and then to twenty as was posted through the town. The car followed. At the only other road, which made a 'T' between the shops, John turned right, suddenly, and parked, expecting the car to do the same. But, instead, it continued on 641 out of town.

John circled back on the road and watched it vanish ahead of him. He drove on, toward Traverse City, alone, once more, on the road.

A flash. Behind him in his mirror. The reflected glint from shiny metal. And a dusty cloud as the burgundy rental spun out onto the pavement from the gravel drive where it had been waiting. It raced now as fast as it could go passing John in the sheriff's car at well over ninety, then braking to slow him down. He stomped down hard on the pedal. The other car slid to a stop. John was sure he would crash into it. He pushed even harder on the brake and his own car began to skid, first left then right, each movement more severe than the last, then spinning to the left, until the passenger side of his car slammed to a stop against the rear bumper of the other car, and buckled in toward him.

The two men ran toward him. John, dazed and shaken with shock, was frozen in place. The finger. He looked around on the front seat next to him, where he'd left it, and on the floor. He felt around under his seat. Then, he saw it, lodged between the dashboard and the far side of the windshield, thrown from the impact. The men were almost on him. He reached out to grab the Ziplock bag, but before he could, they had opened the door.

"Hold it," one of the men said. John heard the unmistakable click as the man cocked his automatic pistol. John froze, holding his hands in the air, "Jesus, don't shoot, please."

The other man spoke. John had heard his voice before.

"Get that thing and let's go Russel."

John slowly picked up the bag and slid out the driver's side. The first man grabbed him by the arm and spun him around, then pushed him toward the other car. He managed to turn his head to look back over his shoulder to see the face of the other man, the man wearing black, the familiar voice; Joey 'Ghost' Cappola. The man from Domati's garage.

While Cappola's partner shoved John into the back seat, Joey ran to the front seat and got in the passenger side. The other man got behind the wheel.

"Go. Go," Joey ordered, and turned to John. "Give it to me. And lie face down on the seat."

John did as he was told. He heard the bag open and the melting ice cubes rattling as Cappola poked around inside. "Good, Russel. Good. Put your hands behind your back."

Joey closed the bag. He reached under the seat for the roll of duct tape. He pulled off a strip about two feet long, leaned over into the back seat, and wrapped John's wrists tightly. Twice more, he did the same. When he was satisfied, he opened the glove box, took out a bottle of chloroform and a rag and soaked it with the chemical. He ordered John to turn over and when he did, he shoved it into John's face.

John struggled, out of instinct, shaking his head back and forth to escape from the foul fumes and he noticed as he did, the area of cloth that was red. Red from his blood, from the crash. From a gash on the left side of his forehead. But it really didn't hurt at all. It should. Jesus.

He was out.

The rented car disappeared from view, leaving Bob Kellet's car steaming in a heap, sideways, in the center of county road 641. When the last sound of it had faded, there was movement in the tall weeds at the side of the road. From out of the camouflage, a dark-haired man emerged, carrying a screwdriver and moving quickly toward the wreckage, wearing the grease-stained uniform of a gas station attendant with a name emblazoned on the front. With the stealth of his heritage, the plundering Indian, Joey Greydog, moved in. In less than thirty seconds he had pried the police radio loose from its metal moorings and ripped it from its wires.

Before he was seen, he vanished, running as fast as he could with the radio tucked under his arm, across a field and into the thick elm forest, panting, mumbling almost incoherently, "Too many visitors,...

...too many damn visitors."

36

"I wonder if you can feel death."

It was an odd remark, Morse thought. "I don't know."

Christine wandered to the window of Charley Keenan's office while Karen went through his files, gathering them into a growing pile on the prosecutor's oak desk, as Assistant Attorney General Messing had ordered.

"That woman, the one this morning, could she feel it?"

Morse looked up briefly from where she stood at the filing cabinet, but did not respond.

"Who are these people? And what makes them do something like that? I just can't fathom that."

"They're sick bastards, that's what." Morse tossed another file on the pile, then continued her digging in the open drawer. "You can't figure them out or what they're thinking. They just do it, that's all."

On the floor, at the bottom of one of Charley's long dark drapes, there was an old paper napkin, wadded up in a tight ball, an errant shot at his wastebasket, Chris guessed. She picked it up, walked over to his desk and dropped it into the steel container.

"It's sad that because of someone's greed or anger or whatever possesses them, other people, people like Charley...and my dad, die. And God knows what they may have done to Shelby Russel."

"I wouldn't give up yet, Chris." Karen tried to be positive. "We think Frank's already surfaced. We're waiting for confirmation. If we get him, we're that much closer to finding her. He'll make a deal." She closed the file drawer and grabbed the stack of folders from the desk, balancing them on her forearm. "Let's get back upstairs, Messing's waiting."

Christine took one last slow look at Keenan's office before she turned the light out and followed agent Morse into the marble hall.

Upstairs, in the FBI offices, Stan Messing had parked himself in Garnetti's office, preferring that to the conference room. Jack, his assistant, was seated at one of the secretary's desks in the common area just outside his door.

"Jack," Messing shouted, "Find out what happened to Morse, will ya?"

"They're here now, sir."

Karen and Christine stopped at his door.

He stood, out of deference to Ms. Ferrand, the voter. "Come in, please. Have a seat Ms. Ferrand," he said politely, then much less so to Morse, "Let me see those."

She handed him the files and both women sat.

"What's the status?"

Karen began, "We're waiting for a positive on Doran; should have it any time. He hit one of the accounts on the list. Royal Bank of Canada in London, Ontario. Looks like he might be headed for Toronto."

A secretary knocked on the frame of the open door, "Agent Morse, this was faxed to you." She handed Karen the paper and left.

"This is confirmation from the Mounties. One of the tellers ID'd Frank. He was there earlier this morning."

"Was there anyone with him?" Chris asked.

"No. One of the other employees said there might have been another man waiting in the car, but he wasn't positive."

"So, what's next?" Messing leaned back in the desk chair.

"He wire transferred most of the money. We're checking on the other account now. We gotta stay on him. He's the key."

Messing abruptly leaned forward, put on his reading glasses, and opened the file on top of the stack, forgetting at first that Chris was in the room, "Keep me posted. That's all." When he remembered, he looked up smiling, "Ms. Ferrand, I hope to see you later."

As they walked back through the open area and down the hall to the conference room, Chris could hear Messing shouting to his assistant. She whispered to Karen, "What an asshole." And an insubordinate Morse agreed.

Just as they reached the room an agent called out, "Hey Morse, Garnetti's on the phone."

"Put it in here." She entered the room and punched the button for the speaker phone as she sat down at the end of the long table.

"Bob, what's up?" She said.

"I'm calling from the sheriff's office up in Leelanau. I need you to help me."

"Shoot."

"I need you to get Messing or somebody to talk to this guy Kellet."

"Bob Kellet?" Christine asked.

"Who's that, Karen?"

"Ms. Ferrand."

"Oh." There was a pause. "I'm under arrest. All of us…"

"What? For what?"

"He brought me in on the Doran warrant, if you can believe that. It doesn't matter. It's bullshit. Now just…please, get me outta here."

Garnetti's frustration was obvious, but the idea of him in jail was funny and both Chris and Karen Morse had to fight from laughing out loud, fearing he would hear them.

"Lemme see what I can do, Bob..." She was beginning to convulse, "...stay there."

"Very funny." He hung up.

It was as if the tension had finally broken the dam and neither of them could contain the flood of hysterical guffaws. There had been little to laugh about since they had met. When Christine recovered enough to talk, she offered to help.

"I'll call Kellet. I think I know what's going on."

Morse could only nod. The tears streamed down her face and her breathing was reduced to shrill, sporadic bursts of suction.

Christine, pulled her small cell phone from her purse and dialed the number, which was memorized. She held the receiver to her ear. She wanted this to be a private conversation; private even from Karen. She wasn't certain of the circumstances, but she knew Kellet must have had a conversation with John and she felt it was her responsibility as John's attorney, to review whatever new information there was first, before sharing it with the FBI. The last thing she wanted was to endanger her client.

"Sheriff Kellet, please," she said, more serious now.

After a moment, he was on the line.

"Bob, it's Christine Ferrand, how are you." She waited for his response, then went on, "What's the deal with the FBI guys?"

"Can we talk?" he asked, wondering about the safety of the line.

"I'm at the FBI office in Detroit...I am on my cell phone."

"Fine. I understand. I talked to John. We met. I gave it to him; the...you know."

"Really." Christine responded, matter of factly.

"He told me about Shelby. I bought him some time. That's all. That warrant made it easy, being the hick sheriff and all...I guess I must have misidentified the suspect. That's all I can do though, we're dangerously close to obstruction."

"I know. I appreciate it, Bob. Do you have any idea where he might be going?"

"No, not specifically."

Karen Morse, Christine noticed, had stopped laughing and now listened carefully to her side of the conversation. Kellet went on.

"He's got my car, the cruiser. He's gonna try to make the trade."

"How'd he look?"

"Like hell."

"Bob, if you hear from him again...he's gotta call me. He's gotta come in. They'll kill him if he..., well, you know."

"Sure."

"I don't think there's any reason to hold Garnetti now, do you?" Chris shot a smile to Karen.

"Probably not. He's gettin' a little pissed anyway. I hope it helped. Let me know if I can do anything else. I hope Shelby's all right."

"So do I, Bob...and thanks...for everything."

They hung up. Karen Morse was curious. "He had contact, with Russel?"

"Yeah."

"Where is he now?"

"He doesn't know." This was true. Chris wrestled with herself, trying to decide whether or not to tell Karen that John had taken Kellet's police car. She desperately wanted to help him, and she was pretty sure that Morse felt the same way, but after listening to Messing and Garnetti's ill conceived plan, she decided that John might have a better chance on his own. She changed the subject. "He's going to let Garnetti go."

"Good."

"What's the next step?"

"We have to find out where everybody went. Domati's gone, or at least no one has seen him, or Russel, and Doran, he's in Canada. He's running. He doesn't know we have the bank information, though, so it's likely he'll try one of the other accounts. I've got the Mounties on it, that's about the best we can do at this point. If we can get Frank, I think we're halfway there."

"What about Shelby?"

"We wanted to search Domati's fronts, his businesses, I think there's a chance they would hide her at one of them, it gives us somewhere to start, but Messing won't ask for warrants."

"Reasonable suspicion."

"Right. Without being able to tie Doran directly to Domati, Messing says there's no way."

Chris thought for a second. "What about Witheral?"

"Yeah, I thought about approaching him. But he wouldn't issue the warrant for Doran that Charley requested. Something's wrong there."

"What do you mean?"

Morse leaned toward Christine, her eyes wide and her eyebrows raised, "Think about it. You said he was the only one who knew that we were waiting to arrest Doran at the courthouse. Somebody had to tip him off."

It took a moment for this possibility to sink in. "Shit." The prospect that somehow Domati had gotten to the old judge was unbelievable. "Yeah. I see what you mean."

"Between you and me, we're checking those places anyway." Morse leaned back, "Now...we have to get Doran."

A young agent, a man, twenty five or so, entered the room, "I've got the bank information you wanted."

"Thanks, David." Morse took the paper from him and looked it over while he waited. "The money was transferred to a Carlos DeVera, in Bogata.," she read aloud, then issued further instructions to the agent, "See what you can get me on this DeVera. Oh, I want a picture, too."

"Yes, Ma'am." He left as quickly as he arrived.

Morse was lost in her thoughts, scanning the paper and quietly repeating the name, DeVera.

"You've heard that name before?" Chris interrupted.

"I don't know. It's just a chance. It's familiar." She pushed the intercom button, "David?"

"Yes, Ma'am."

"I want you to get on the computer and cross check DeVera against the Domati files. Also, check with the DEA."

Over the next half hour, Morse talked again with Garnetti, who was on his way back to Detroit, and coordinated information provided by other agents involved in the investigation. It wasn't until David returned that any clear picture began to evolve.

"Well?" she asked him, "Let's have it."

He walked to the table. "This is from the DEA." He laid a sheet down in front of her. "Carlos DeVera. Recluse. Colombian citizen. Here's his estate from the air. Big time connected through Miami. But this is interesting…" He turned to the next page, "He's never been arrested for anything, ever. There's no sheet on him. The DEA has him on a 'must watch' and they say he's here now."

"He's in this country?"

"Well, yeah…he's…here. In Detroit."

"What?" Morse was astonished.

"They've got him coming in with Angelo Domati, on Monday, commercial."

"Get a record of the ticket. What about a picture?"

"This is all they had. We've got nothing." He handed Morse a very grainy black and white surveillance photo showing a man walking along a sidewalk in front of a brick building. The shot was taken from above and across the street. He was wearing a hat and dark glasses and only the lower part of his face was visible.

Morse shook her head, "That could be anybody." She dropped the picture on the table with the other papers, stood up, and walked over to the corkboard wall and the map of the United States.

"Ms. Morse?" The young agent interrupted her thought.

"Yes, David."

"I did find something else that I think is strange. I don't know if it means anything or not, but when I ran DeVera through the main fingerprint files, this showed up." He handed her another sheet of paper while Christine sat and listened.

"That's odd." She shared it with Chris. "It's a full set of prints."

"Does that mean something?" Christine was puzzled.

"You can go, Dave. Good work. Thanks."

Morse leaned down close to Chris and asked, "How does someone with absolutely no criminal record get his prints into the FBI computer? I'll tell you how. He puts them there. C'mon, we're going down to the computer room."

Again, Christine followed Morse through the common area and down the opposite hallway. At the end was a large technical room. It was filled with machines, recording equipment, and a half dozen computers set up in a row on a long bench-like table, separated by dividers. Several agents were busy at the workstations, but Morse found one that wasn't being used and sat down. While Christine watched, she accessed the main database at the FBI in Washington. She maneuvered into the section which contained fingerprints and typed DeVera's name.

"You already have those, don't you?" Chris didn't know what she was doing.

"Yeah, but I've got another idea. Watch." She typed in the name, 'Doran, Frank' and waited. Soon a message flashed on the screen, 'NO FILES FOUND'.

"Son of a bitch."

"What?"

"He's not there. Doran. There's no record of him. C'mon." Morse was up and headed out of the room with Christine close behind. "I've got another guess. I'll bet that third set of prints on the body bag, from the Russel cottage, the ones that didn't match up...?"

"Yeah."

"I bet they do now."

"With DeVera?"

"That's what the computer will say. I'll put money on it."

She went back to the conference room. A second later, Dave was back.

"I've got the travel record."

"Good. Let me see it." Karen Morse studied it. "That's it," she exclaimed, "Look," She grabbed a red marker from the rail at the bottom of the bulletin board and drew a long line from Miami to New York, and another from New York to Detroit. "That's DeVera." She drew a third from Detroit to London, Ontario. "That's Doran." She circled the open area in between, the area which contained Buffalo.

Chris looked at the lines, "So?"

She started to pace in front of the board, "Here's what I think. Why, if you could take any of a number of non-stops, would you take a plane that stops at Kennedy? If you were loaded. Why not a private plane? You would have to know that you would be watched, right? Or, is that exactly why?"

"What do you mean?"

Without answering the question, Karen called the young agent on the intercom, "David, please come in here." She disconnected. "I think it's too damn coincidental that this guy shows up here, traveling with Domati's son at the same time Doran disappears. And not having any record of him is impossible. Every one of us has his prints on file, we have to. I think Doran is DeVera. What could be better? If he's stopped, they check his prints. He comes up DeVera. For all practical purposes, that's who he is. And how do you prove somebody isn't who they say they are, when every record confirms that they are?"

"He must have been working on this for years."

"Exactly."

Christine was beginning to understand. "And, with his position, no one would ever check. Wow. He erased himself."

"Pretty much."

The young agent returned.

"I want you to get in touch with New York," Karen ordered. "Tell them it's possible that Doran may show up at Kennedy on Friday, possibly to board Delta 280 to Miami..." Dave was writing furiously on a small pad, "He may use the name DeVera. Go."

A voice came over the intercom speaker, "Agent Morse, Garnetti on three."

Karen picked it up, "Yeah, Bob." There was a pause. "I see."

Christine was intensely interested. Another agent arrived and waited silently for Morse to finish her short conversation. "Yes," she said when she did.

"There's very little activity at the Domati house, and we still haven't located the first team. I have men there now, though, and they report that no one has entered or left all day."

"All right. Stay on it. If Domati shows, I want to know about it."

"Of course." He left the room.

"They found the sheriff's car, abandoned. No sign of Russel," she said to Chris, "There'd been an accident. There was some blood."

"Oh my God. John."

"It doesn't look that serious. But we're running out of time. I've gotta brief Messing. But don't worry, Bob's good. If there's a trail, he'll find it. We're pretty sure Russel's on his way to meet someone, to make the trade. That narrows it down."

Chris thought about Kellet's abandoned car. She was worried, "Looks like John may have met someone already."

Morse walked closer to the table, leaning down, "You should have told me about the car, Chris. Maybe we could have stopped him first."

Chris knew now she probably should have, but she didn't speak.

The agent was up, leaving, "I've gotta see Messing." Morse was nearly at the doorway when she stopped. "Why don't you go home and pack a bag."

The suggestion shocked Chris. "Where are we going?"

"To the last place anyone saw Doran," she called from the hall, "...to Canada."

37

John's body recoiled, suddenly awakened from the bizarre chemical dreams, and he nearly gagged. He opened his eyes and when they finally focused, he could see the face of Joey Cappola. He was leaning over the seat, waving a small cylinder under John's nose; amyl-nitrate. The strong fumes jarred him into consciousness. He could hear talking.

"Wake up. C'mon." Cappola was shaking him, "C'mon asshole, wake up."

John came around. He worked his way to a sitting position in the back seat of the car, his arms still bound behind him. The chemical caused an instantaneous migraine and he winced at the pain.

He was sick in his stomach. His head pounded relentlessly. His arms, numb from being crushed behind his back, tingled as circulation returned. He leaned to his right and caught a glimpse of the gash on his forehead in the rearview mirror. It had scabbed. There was no more bleeding from the two inch cut. He was dizzy. He moaned as he fell back to the side, resting against the door, his eyes closing.

"C'mon, pull it together." The Ghost was unsympathetic.

"I'm trying."

The amyl-nitrate again. "Wake up."

"Jesus. I'm up."

From out of nowhere, Cappola produced a knife. "Turn over."

Again, John obeyed. He felt the sharp point of the blade prick him once before it ripped through the tape that held his wrists together. His arms, now free from restraint, turned red from the increased flow of blood. His fingers felt like they were vibrating and reverberated with shock waves when he bumped the seat.

John was coming around. He saw signs for eastbound Interstate 69. They were merging with I-94 north, through Port Huron, toward the Bluewater Bridge, heading for the Canadian border.

Joey Cappola was talking on his cell phone. The driver said nothing. They must have stopped for fast food while he was passed out. There were crumpled wrappers on the seat and the car smelled of french fries and Joey's pungent cologne.

John saw signs for Canada; four miles ahead, then three. The car arrived at the line for the toll booth, where two lanes of heavy traffic compressed into one, moving at a turtle's pace up the incline, sandwiched between tractor trailers. When they got to the booth, the driver paid, and the car moved out onto the bridge. Joey Cappola finished his call and issued final orders to both of them, "When we get to customs, go to the third booth from the left, no matter what, even if another one is open. Got it?" The man nodded. "And you," he said to John, "When the guy asks you where you were born you tell him, 'Harper Hospital'. That's it. Nothing else. Do you understand?"

"Yeah." John replied, staring out at the huge lake that stretched beyond the horizon. It was the deepest blue, and swirling in whirlpools several hundred feet below the high bridge as the volume of water was compressed into the narrow river. He could see the Sarnia harbor at the far end of the span, and the small city itself just ahead when they reached the peak of the rise. As they started to descend, John could see that many vehicles were backed up waiting to get through. There was an officer directing traffic to various lanes and, in particular, to new ones as they were opened.

There were seven open currently and it looked as if two more would open soon.

When they were almost to the traffic cop, the green light on top of the eighth went on. The cop, pointing directly at the driver, waved him toward it.

"No." Cappola said. "Don't do it."

The driver slowed, but made no effort to turn in the direction indicated. The cop waved even more violently and started to walk toward the car. Joey reached, with his left hand, to the ignition and shut it off. "If he asks, tell him it stalled. When I tap you, start it up and head for number three." He glared at John. "You, remember what I said."

The driver began to roll down the window as the customs officer came closer, still directing other traffic to the newly opened booths. Before he was close enough to ask anything, Cappola tapped the driver. He turned the key and waved at the policeman as he drove past.

They pulled up to the third opening just as the car in front of them left. The driver rolled his window down. Joey leaned over and ducked low to make eye contact with the uniformed customs agent who asked, at least at first, what seemed to be the usual questions.

"All citizens of the United States?"

John didn't say anything, nor did Cappola's accomplice. Joey answered, "Yes, sir."

"The purpose of your visit?"

"Fishing."

"I see." The agent seemed nervous. "Have you...I'm sorry, I heard the fishing is good in Leelanau?"

"Yes, it is." Joey paused, "And it's good in other places," he said.

The customs agent looked curiously through the back window at John. He motioned for him to roll it down. When it was open, he asked where John was born. John didn't answer right away, but instead looked to Cappola for permission. Joey nodded.

"Harper Hospital."

The guard retreated into his booth, "You may go," he said. And that was it. They were across the border.

They drove for several minutes on the expressway before Cappola broke the silence. "Very good, Mr. Russel. Here. I saved these for you." He laughed as he passed a small white bag of cold french fries over the back of the seat. "In case you were still with us."

John's appetite had returned, somewhat, and he managed to hold down the food. He watched out the window as Sarnia gave way to open fields of alfalfa and corn almost ready to harvest. After several exits they turned off onto Highway 21, northbound. There was little traffic on the two lane road and John watched as the speedometer climbed to over sixty. The weather had subsided and the sky was filled with patches of blue. Occasionally, they would fly through a bright splash of sunlight. It was warmer now. John rolled his window down all the way and the rush of air brushed his wavy brown hair flat backwards. On the left, water, the eastern shore of Lake Huron, and small towns; St. Joseph and Bayfield, Goderich and Port Albert.

They rolled along like this for over an hour, and aided by the motion of the car, John relaxed enough to drift off for several minutes at a time, but he was repeatedly jarred back to the realization of the situation.

This time, a new voice, the driver's voice, caused him to wake up.

"Uh, oh," the driver said, looking behind him in the mirror.

"What is it?" Cappola was nervous, but extremely focused.

"OPP," the driver hurriedly responded, referring to the provincial police.

"Shit. Has he got his lights on?"

"Yeah."

"Were you speeding?"

The man lied. "No."

"You sure he's after you?"

"Looks like it."

"Okay. Slow down, but do it gradually. Is he by himself?"

The driver glanced in the rear view and nodded.

"There's a road, or a driveway, or something coming up. See it?"

Again the man nodded. John could hear the siren wail behind him and he closed his window to cut the approaching noise. But he didn't dare look around.

In the front seat, Joey was pulling on thin, black gloves. The driver was almost at the intersection. The car was only going about twenty miles an hour. The trooper killed the deafening sound as both vehicles turned right into the dirt road.

"Pull up a little farther," Joey ordered, "When I say now, you duck. Roll your fuckin' window down." He looked at the driver, "And, for fuck sake smile, will ya?"

The man pulled in another twenty feet and stopped as Cappola requested, and the OPP car parked about six feet behind them. John could see the uniform in the side mirror as the officer walked up to the car. He was alone. Joey reached into his jacket, retrieving a pistol from the holster inside. He shoved it down, inside the white bag from the restaurant, so it was hidden from view. And he too, smiled.

The fields on either side of the road had grown tall and provided cover from the main road. The officer had already run the plates, Joey figured, and discovered that this was a rental car from northern Michigan. He knew the name of the person who had rented it, the man who was driving, but that's all he would know. He was at the driver's window.

"Afternoon. May I see..."

"Now." Cappola yelled. The driver ducked forward, out of the way, as Joey lifted the bag and John Russel dove for the floor. John heard the shot. The bag instantly ripped open sending french fries flying over the driver's back as the bullet ripped through the front of the policeman's head, tearing the right side of it off at the back and hurling the loose flesh into the man's cap, launching it across the ditch at the far side of the road, where it landed more softly, but at the same time, as the rest of his body fell backwards on the pavement.

"Jesus!" John yelled, his eyes wide with horror.

"Shut up," Joey said calmly, pointing the weapon at John before returning it to the holster and opening his door. "Stay here," he shouted to the driver while he ran to the idling police cruiser, got in, and drove it through the ditch and into the field, twenty or so feet. The dispatcher's voice on the radio inside blurted out more information. "Possible subject of FBI search. Consider dangerous..." Cappola ripped the wires from behind the box until the racket stopped. He ran back to the man's bleeding body in the street, unsnapped his holster, and removed the officer's forty-five. Just as John summoned the courage to lift himself up, Joey was at the driver's window. The driver started to speak, but a second blast, this time from the other weapon silenced him before he could.

John recoiled instinctively away from the gun and buried his head in his hands, waiting.

Without a second's hesitation, Cappola opened the driver's door and hurled the driver to the ground next to the cop. He knelt down and put his own weapon in the dead driver's hand, then curled the officer's fingers tightly around the forty five.

He stood up and looked at John. "C'mon, asshole, you're driving." He held the back door open. "Let's go."

John quickly got into the bloody driver's seat while Joey ran around to the seat beside him, slamming his door shut as John slammed his.

"Go."

John put the car in gear and maneuvered carefully, avoiding the two men in the road. He backed around the corner, put it in drive and they were back on the highway. John took in a deep breath, the first he could remember, since Cappola murdered the patrolman.

He could see out of the corner of his eye that Joey had wadded up what remained of the paper bag and was using it to wipe splatters of blood and tissue from the dashboard. John gagged at the sight of it and fought the temptation to throw up. The air blowing in from the window helped.

John was disgusted by the brutal act, "Jesus. Why the hell did you do that? God."

"Shut up," Cappola said quietly, finishing his cleaning, and pushing the bloody wad under the seat. "We need another car. There's gotta be a rental place in one of these towns."

Shocked at how easily the man dismissed the murders, John couldn't let it go, "It means nothing to you, does it? You just kill people; people who have nothing to do with this? Jesus." He knew he was pushing it. He was angry, and very much afraid, not only of the killer next to him, but also of being mistaken as a willing accomplice and possibly shot himself. "Jesus." He pounded his open palm on the steering wheel.

Cappola said nothing. He reached into the glove box, took out his cellular phone, and dialed. After a few seconds, the call went through. "Yeah. Is he there?" There was another long pause before he continued. "It's me. There's been a problem. I had to take care of a cop. We're hot." He waited for the response. "The guy at the border. It had to be....I'm doin that now. Yeah, it's here. I got it....Him, too. Yeah, he did." Cappola looked at John as he spoke.

"He'll cooperate....I will." He pushed the button to end the call and dropped the small phone on the seat. John stared ahead, watching the road as it turned inland. There were rich green fields on the left and gentle hills rising on the right to the edge of the thick pine forest along the top. There was a sign 'AMBERLEY, 3 KILOMETERS', and a bait shop, and a truck stop, its lot full of cars in front and eighteen-wheelers lined up at the back. The smell of chili and burning hamburger drifted across the road.

A few minutes later, two Ontario Provincial Police cars raced past them from the opposite direction, lights blazing and sirens slicing the summer air. The rural countryside became dotted with houses as they approached the town. Ahead on the left, Cappola noticed the tall 'ESSO' sign. "Stop there."

John slowed.

"Pull up over by the cans, over there, kinda outta the way."

John drove to the side of the white brick building and parked at the edge of the blacktop lot near the restrooms.

Cappola reached under the seat, pulling out the baggie, "This thing's startin' to stink. See if you can dump it out and get some more ice." He threw it at John and it landed in his lap. "Ask them in there if we can rent a car somewhere around here. I'm gonna look in the phone book for a place." He opened his door, looking around before he did. There was only one other car in the station. "Don't do anything stupid," he warned.

John watched him walk over to the public phone at the front corner of the paved area. He left the baggie on the front seat while he went inside the office of the small gas station for a key to the men's room. When he came out the other car was gone. Joey was thumbing through the yellow pages that hung from the flexible cable at the bottom of the exposed booth. Several cars sped past, but none stopped. The loud sounds of a semi, braking and downshifting came closer and more deafening as the truck turned in, and crept toward the pumps, releasing loud hisses of compressed air as it stopped. John walked to the car. Cappola was still searching in the book. John reached in through the open driver's window, picked up the baggie and carried it, sloshing, to the bathroom. He unlocked the door and entered the tiny room, flipping the light on. Cappola was right. The finger was beginning to smell. Strongly. John held his breath as he opened the bag. He gulped air through his mouth and poured the yellow, rotten liquid into the sink. When it was gone, he shook the final drops into the drain and resealed the top. He rolled the flat plastic around the severed digit and shoved the cylinder into his pocket. He couldn't hold his breath any longer. Quickly, he turned the knob and pulled. He stuck his head out, drawing in the welcome breath of outside air, replenishing his lungs.

As he took a step out onto the sidewalk, he stopped, frozen. A trooper, his gun drawn, was making his way along the side of the truck, hiding from Cappola, moving in. John ducked back into the bathroom. "Shit," he whispered, then leaned around to see what was happening, peering through a small crack between the door and its frame. Cappola, with his back turned, had no idea that he was being surrounded. "Shit," John whispered again. He realized he had no idea where they were going. This guy was the only connection.

The roar of car engines; one, then two more cruisers sliding to a stop. Officers jumping out, some with shotguns, some with pistols; all aimed at Joey 'Ghost' Cappola.

Joey spun, looking up, wild-eyed from the phone book, and instinctively ran, out into the field. The police shouted for him to stop, but he kept on going as fast as he could, parallel to the highway, edging slightly deeper into the overgrowth, the pursuers closing the distance. Another car, cutting in, from the road ahead. Two more cops, ahead of him, flanking him.

When Cappola was about a hundred yards away, John made his move. He came out of the rest room, walking fast, not running, to the car. When he was close, he ducked down, hiding behind it, reaching in through the window, patting around on the seat until he felt the plastic casing of Joey's mobile telephone. Grabbing it, he turned quickly, and, unnoticed in the commotion, made his way behind the station and up, through the tall grass and weeds, to the top of a small hill a thousand yards away. He stopped, exhausted, and collapsed on his stomach. He heard the shots. Dozens of them. All at once, like the finale on the fourth of July. Then silence. He got to his hands and knees, slowly, and he could see, from his high vantage point, the motionless figure, Joey 'Ghost' Cappola, lying on the ground surrounded by police. His body, covered in black, contorted and twisted from the force of the bullets, began to turn red as the liquid gushing out of him flowed over his silk shirt.

Jesus. John collapsed to the ground, rolling onto his back. Trying to explain who he was and what he was doing with Joey Cappola would be useless. He would be arrested at the very least. He wondered if they knew he had been in the car; if they knew he was here. They had made no attempt to search for him, not yet. He had to find out where Cappola was headed, where he could find Domati.

For over an hour, he waited in the weeds, occasionally peeking to see what was happening below. Eventually, most of the officers left. John watched as they towed the rental car away. It was beginning to get dark. He was hungry and tired. He thought of going back to the gas station, but he couldn't take the chance.

Clutching Cappola's cell phone, the only link to the Domati family, tightly in his hand, he rolled over once again on his back. Above, the stars were beginning to pierce the growing darkness. Jesus, this is bad, he thought.

As he lay on the hillside, the weight of his body crushed the grasses underneath him into an ad hoc mattress, which supported him slightly above the cool dirt. The crickets joined in a monotonous, hypnotic song. And, in what only seemed moments, the wetness from earlier rains evaporated, leaving only dry breezes behind them on this hot August night. If the circumstances were different, it would be beautiful.

He took this moment to relax, still squeezing the phone with his fingers. All of the aches returned, having time now to be perceived. He was not in good shape. Although the shrapnel wound on his calf had pretty much healed, the others, including the cut on his head had not. He reached up to it and bringing his hand into view, saw the blood again. He wiped it off on his pants, too tired to move. His lower back, he was sure, was badly bruised, and his upper arms, the muscles strained from hours of unnatural contortion, sent dull, throbbing signals to his brain.

Occasionally, he heard the sound of a car speeding by in the distance. The first few caused him to tighten, fearing the return of the troopers, but eventually he was able to ignore them.

He closed his eyes and the stars disappeared. He breathed deeply through his nose, letting the air escape slowly.

It was like a night in Leelanau, what would have been a much better night, at Duck Lake. Surrounded by the sweet smell of pine.

And the natural orchestra of the forest.

38

The sudden, pulsating thunder descended from overhead, louder and louder. John was jarred to consciousness instantly. The ground was shaking from the noise. It was dark. Before dawn. He had fallen asleep.

There were lights, bright and moving, scanning the hillside. Shit. His hands empty. The phone. Where was it? He felt around on the ground, sitting up. There, in the dirt. He grabbed it, and crawled farther up the hill toward a grove of trees. The police helicopter had passed low over his head, out beyond the road and the flat fields on the other side. But he saw it turning, coming back again, searchlights blazing from it's underside. He ran through the dark, up the hill, almost on all fours. The grass slapped at his face as he pushed through it. The sound coming closer. He looked momentarily over his shoulder. The lights scoured the area behind the gas station as the craft hovered above it. The pilot turned even with the road, and systematically zig-zagged from one side to the other, flying away about a half mile, then returning again. The next pass would be across the hill.

John ran as fast as his wounded body would move to the trees. He felt the dust and dirt behind him start to blow. Only a few more feet. He dove, landing square on his sternum on a large boulder on the uphill side of the mature pine, just as the light swiped the area. He winced from the new pain, but managed to roll off the huge rock into the dark space between it and the tree, and froze. The sharp white light descended through the branches casting hard, splintered shadows on the brown needles below. John crouched against the main trunk and waited for the monster above him to pass.

When it disappeared over the treeline at the top of the ridge, he took a breath. He dared not move. The helicopter again returned, this time scanning the higher area above him and made several more passes, each farther away. When John felt the distance sufficient, he stood up between the branches. He lifted the cellular phone and pushed a button to redial the last call. A number glowed on the display and he put the device to his ear. Nothing. He tried again and again the number glowed briefly and the phone went dead. "Dammit," he said out loud, "Shit."

He'd left it on overnight and the battery was nearly dead. He had to memorize the number. He pushed the button once more and three more times until even that function failed. He went over the digits repeatedly in his mind pushing everything else out until he was certain that he had it. He threw the mobile phone as hard as he could into the woods.

He could still hear the helicopter, now far away, and realized that the area they were searching was large and that they probably had no idea where he was. He had to get to Domati.

He remembered the truckstop they had passed earlier on the road. The police would have been there hours before. No one would suspect that John would still be in the area or recognize him. It was his best shot.

Moving along the trees at the top of the hill, he worked his way back in the direction of the restaurant. From the horizon ahead, the first tinges of pink light were emerging. It was about five in the morning, he figured, a good time. The diner would be busy. He went over the number again and again as he walked. He checked in his pocket. Good. A few bills. Enough to get something to eat and a drink. Even if the Ontario Provincial Police arrested him, he could, with Christine's help, get out of it. Then again, they didn't seem to want to hear Cappola's explanation the night before. He kept walking, a little faster. It would be better to get there before daylight.

When he did, it was brighter, but the full sun had not yet appeared. He stopped on a hill about five hundred feet behind the building. He could smell bacon and grilled steak in the smoke rising from the exhaust fans over the kitchen. He knelt down, observing the activity below. It had been some time since he had heard the helicopter. And the search, he guessed, had moved east, the direction they were originally headed, so doubling back would put even more distance between them. He was starving and beginning to dehydrate. He felt lightheaded. But, at least he had rested.

Behind the restaurant, more than a dozen tractor trailers were parked, idling. Most of the drivers had slept overnight in their cabs and now had gone inside to eat before leaving on the day's journey. John could see the large painted sign beside the highway, 'ROSE'S 21' it said in bright red letters and underneath, 'FOOD, FAX, SUPPLIES, SHOWERS...TRUCKER'S WELCOME'.

Showers. John looked down at his jeans. They were soaked from the knees to the top of his tennis shoes from the dew. He pulled at the shoulder of his shirt and stretched to see the back. It was soaked and dirty. The front was stained from blood, both from the wound on his forehead and from the murdered driver. The right elbow of the wrinkled button-down was ripped and two buttons were missing. He had to clean up, to blend in.

He looked once more. No police. No troopers. He was up and at first walking, then running, half falling down the incline to the parking lot. He stopped behind a trailer and surveyed the area. A huge diesel revved, puffing black smoke from its chrome pipes above the cab as the driver pulled one of the rigs out onto the highway. There was a rear door for the truckers, and John watched them come and go, and timed his approach for a lull. He walked quickly, navigating between trucks. Up the sidewalk.

Just as he reached the automatic sliding door, it opened. Two large men, who had been talking, stopped dead in the doorway, staring at John Russel. He kept up his pace, passing them without a glance, and as he did they began to laugh, catcalling, "Oooee. Big night, eh sport?" and other comments that he chose to ignore. Inside, in the dark, tile lobby, he had choices. To his left, restrooms, ahead the dining room, and to his right, open to the lobby, a combination gift shop, post office, drugstore, and newsstand. He marched in, leaving behind wet footprints from his soggy Reeboks. As he entered, the other customers backed out of his way.

He sloshed past the counter, startling the clerk, who turned, staring at him, her overly blue contact lenses barely visible beneath the teased bangs, dyed flame red. He headed for a rack of clothing and several shelves filled with imprinted tee-shirts, sweatshirts and caps. He searched through the rack first, grabbing the first shirt he found in his size. It was black, synthetic, and it buttoned up the front. It had short sleeves with elastic around the bicep, circling the arm with a white herringbone pattern. On the back, in glued-on gold glitter, the word 'Toronto' was written in script above a four color silk-screen of the city's skyline. Screw it. It was dry. He found a pair of navy blue sweatpants and a green baseball cap. It was dark corduroy and, emblazoned on the front with shamrocks, printed in light green ink. He was almost finished. He walked to the far corner and grabbed the first small duffel bag he saw from a hook on the wall, and returned to the counter. The red-headed witch rang up the purchases. She asked him how he would like to pay and was noticeably astounded when he slapped his American Express card down on the glass.

The whole shopping trip had taken less than a minute. John grabbed the bag of dry clothes and hurried across the open lobby to the restroom area. Inside, the men's room was divided into two sections; the sinks and toilets on the left, and to the right, on the other side of a tiled wall, the showers. He headed to the right. The room was large and bright. At the entrance, at a long table, stacked high with clean white towels, was an attendant. He was wearing a tight, orange tank top over his well developed frame, and, except for his excessive gut, looked like a body builder. He leaned back in his chair, with his feet propped up on the corner of the table, reading a magazine. "Towel?" he asked John, "Five bucks. Shower's free."

John dug in his pocket for his money. Water was running in one of the many stalls around the perimeter of the room. Steam rose from above the fuzzy glass door. John tossed a rumpled five dollar bill on the table and took a towel. The water stopped. The stall opened and a large man, pushing three-hundred pounds, stepped naked into the common area. He had long dark hair over most of his body, including Elvis-like sideburns and a carefully trimmed goatee. He got his towel from a hook on the wall and started to dry off and get dressed. John found a vacant shower on the opposite side of the room. There were benches that ran around the perimeter and he dropped his new duffel at the end of one of them. He had started to get undressed when he noticed a second figure, a much younger man, emerge from the same stall as the first. The attendant smiled at him, slyly, while staring perversely at his genitals. The big man dressed and left, and, after a few moments so did the younger man, but not before he slipped the attendant a folded bill, a fifty, on his way out. John pretended not to notice.

John threw his shirt in the duffel. He sat down and took off his wet shoes and threw his wet socks in with the shirt. He stood to remove his jeans and as he unzipped them he felt the gaze of the attendant on him. He took the finger, still wrapped tightly, out of his pocket and clutched it in his palm. He looked up at the smiling pervert as the denim fell to the floor. Fuck it. At least the guy would be too busy to notice the baggie. John hauled his briefs to his ankles and got into the relative privacy of the stall. He turned the handles and a hard stream of hot water blasted out. It took a few seconds to get used to it but when he did, it felt wonderful. He put his mouth into the stream and drank deeply. He dropped the bag on the floor and, sealed, it floated near the drain. As the heat poured over him, he surveyed his damaged body. A large blue bruise had formed in the center of his chest. At the top of his thighs, the skin was blistered and peeling, still recovering from the spilled acids. His right calf, where the sharp metal from Benny Tenino's exploding Ford had torn his flesh, was beginning to heal, but John could see that it would leave a large scar. He let the water pound on his lower back and down to his tailbone, trying to ease the soreness left by the bolt in Domati's trunk. He turned and the water hit his forehead, causing him to recoil with stinging pain. The cut started to bleed, but only slightly. John could see in the reflection in the chrome shower head, that it, too, was healing. The rest of him was a collection of additional bruises and bumps and scrapes. But it didn't really matter now. Soon, hopefully this nightmare would end. Shelby would be safe. He pushed the lever on the dispenser on the wall and his palm filled with shampoo. This was the most comfortable moment he had spent in a week.

But he couldn't afford any more time. He shut the water off and stepped out, again with the finger concealed in his hand, fully aware that the man was watching him. He used the towel as a shield and dropped the wrapped digit in the duffel bag. He noticed that his underwear was not on the bench where he had left them. What a sick world. He got the navy sweats out of the shopping bag and pulled them over his still dripping legs, followed by his new

Toronto shirt. The pants had no belt loops or pockets, no place for his wallet or money so he added both, along with his jeans, to the growing wet heap in the duffel. He tucked in the gaudy shirt and tugged the white string at the front of the pants, tying it to tighten the waist. He sat down on the bench and slipped back into his cold, damp running shoes. There was a full length mirror near the entrance and John stood in front of it, adjusting his hair with his fingers, brushing it back. He looked like a jerk, but he figured it was an improvement over his previous impersonation of an alcoholic bum. Again, fuck it. It was time to eat.

He picked up the new duffel and noticed for the first time, the silk-screened 'Montreal Canadians' logo on the side. A nice touch. On his way out, he stopped at the towel table, and waited for the tattooed pervert to look up. When he did, John winked. The man grinned hopefully. John smiled back, then slowly raised his middle finger, silently mouthed, "Fuck you," and left.

John slid into an empty booth in the far corner of the restaurant. There was a public telephone mounted on the wall not six feet away. Almost immediately his waitress appeared. He ordered his breakfast, plus a large styrofoam cup of ice.

When she was gone, he got up to make the call.

39

The lodge at Naganosh Lake had once been not much more than a wilderness logging camp, located centrally within the 1.7 million acres that had been bequeathed by King George to Henry Loring after the French and Indian War. He and his descendants had used it as headquarters for their thriving fur and lumber businesses until 1874, when the property was purchased by John D. Rockefeller, who valued the location for entertaining business associates. In the years that followed it had evolved into a compound of fourteen buildings, including a main lodge with its massive common room containing two stone fireplaces, one on each end, each large enough for a man to walk into, the original building, which was converted into kitchens and a dining hall, a screened pavilion built on pilings at the end of the dock, and sleeping cottages of varying sizes. For his personal accommodations, Rockefeller built what he considered a modest Victorian home an eighth of a mile down the lake. Its twenty-seven rooms filled most of an acre and offered spectacular views and the additional privacy of location, accessible only by footpath through the woods.

At the time, the only way to get to Naganosh Lake was by boat, traveling out of Victoria Harbor, at the southern tip of Georgian Bay, and hugging the craggy coast for nearly a hundred miles, north, to the Still River, where travelers would transfer onto flat barges and be pushed upstream to the lake. It was one of northern Ontario's most remote and primitive areas.

Rockefeller preferred the inconvenience to what he considered the pretentious social habits of his Canadian peers, who had built their summer mansions further to the south on Rouseau Lake.

There were near legendary stories of philandering and drunkenness which supposedly took place at Naganosh and much social speculation as to why, suddenly, he allowed his company, Standard Oil of Ohio, to buy it for a dollar in 1911.

The company's directors continued to use the lodge until the second world war, when it was closed.

It did not reopen until 1958, when it was purchased by Southern Capital Corporation, one of the Domati family holdings. After extensive renovation, it became inhabitable two years later, in 1960. The main home was sold, in a private sale, in 1974.

The primary attraction for the mob was obvious. Still hard to reach, no road had ever been built, the preferred transportation was by float plane, which could land easily on the calm inland lake. The flight from Lake St. Clair was slightly more than an hour and a half, and, if the pilot was crafty, most of the journey would not be detected by radar.

This was where, at the request of Vincenzo Domati, the heads of the families met in the spring of 1975, and where Domati received permission for his move on Antonio Tenino, which occurred later that year.

After he murdered Tenino at Mitchell's Bay, Domati came here, protected from retaliation. And Jimmy Hoffa went with him.

Domati had not been back since. Until now.

The cell phone on the bar was ringing. Angelo, who had been playing pool with his brother in the common room of the main lodge, leaned his stick against the wall and crossed the cavernous hall to answer it. It would be Cappola, he knew that. He was the only one with the number.

It was just after dawn, earlier than they expected, and Angelo guessed Joey must have made good time through the night.

He flipped the mouthpiece open, "Yeah," he answered matter of factly and was greeted by a voice he didn't recognize.

"Your guy is dead." The caller was barely audible over the noisy background of conversation and dishwater.

"What?" Angelo was curious, "Speak up."

"I can't"

"Who the fuck is this?" He was getting mad. Nino put his cue stick on the green felt table, sensing a problem, and listened as his brother talked.

"This is…John Russel….I have it."

"Hang on." Angelo held the phone at his side. Nino followed him across the room and out through French doors to the screened verandah where his father and Frank Doran were having breakfast. "Papa," he said quietly, "…on the phone…he says it's…Russel."

The old man stopped eating and looked up slowly, "Where's Joey?"

"He says he's dead. It could be bullshit. I don't know."

Domati motioned to his son to hand over the phone, "Give it to me." He cleared his throat, "Who is this?"

"This is John Russel. I want to make the trade. Shelby is…she's still okay, right?"

He coughed weakly and swallowed the loosened phlegm, "As I told you…she is safe. Where is Cappola?"

"Cappola?"

"The man I sent to get you."

"Oh. He was shot. By the police. He's dead. He killed a cop. And they got him. And they're going to get me too if we don't get this over with soon." John leaned deeper into the mouthpiece, "Mr. Domati, listen..."

"Don't say that name."

"Sorry. No one will ever know about this. I'll give you what you want and you let her go and it's over. As far as I'm concerned, I don't know anything. You gave me a chance, I got what you wanted, now let's get this done. Please."

"Hold on." Domati covered the microphone. "Nino, we're gonna need the plane. I want you to tell him to be ready." The fat son said nothing, but vanished to follow his father's order. Domati again lifted the phone. "Where are you?" he asked.

"In a truck stop. Near..." he struggled to recall the name, "...Amberley."

"Amberley?" Domati repeated to Frank Doran, who was busy finishing the last of his breakfast.

"Yeah. I know where it is. Ask him if he can get to Thornbury." Doran washed down the final bite with coffee.

"I want you to get to Thornbury. Can you get there?"

"Yeah. I guess so."

"Good. And don't call this number again until you're there."

John heard silence. Domati had ended the call.

Quickly, he stuffed in the remaining bites of his meal, bought a map in the gift shop, and left, again through the back door. The hat shielding his face from the curious, he walked briskly across the cement parking lot, leaving wet shoe prints behind. He dodged in and out of trucks, making his way to the field. When the grass was tall enough to hide him, he crouched down, opening the map. His finger continued up the paper, tracing the roadway, stopping briefly while he read the name of each town, up the coast of Lake Huron, east, inland toward Toronto and back north to Georgian Bay, along the shore. And there it was; Thornbury. A tiny black circle at the edge of the water to the north. Good.

He folded the map into something that resembled its original shape and zipped open the duffel bag. The smell exploded out polluting even the outside. The finger was decomposing. He had forgotten the ice, but he certainly wasn't going back inside. He threw the map in as fast as he could and zipped the bag closed.

The sun was out. The heat was building. He stretched his legs out straight and pointed his toes so the maximum area was exposed to the sunlight to dry. John was starting to feel the positive effects of the meal. His head was clearing and the hazy dehydration gave way to more succinct streams of logical thought. He surveyed the lot. Someone had to be going that way, after all, from what he could tell on the map, this was the only decent highway around. And being in the middle of nowhere already, there were only two ways to go; toward Thornbury or away from it.

There was nobody in the first truck he approached. The driver of the second, a lumber hauler, was headed south. John asked several more before he had any luck.

As he neared the livestock carrier the scent of cow manure was so strong he could barely breath. It was parked nearest the building and he had to stay close to keep from being seen. The engine was running and John had to raise his voice to be heard over it.

"Excuse me. Anybody there? Hey."

Immediately came the response, "Who di hell wants ta know?" The voice behind it was pitched high, almost falsetto, and definitely southern. "Who is it?"

"I was wondering if you were headed north." John yelled upward, pointing his mouth at the open window.

He saw the edge of a man's red plaid forearm, then the rest of the man appear in the opening, his long hair falling over the flannel collar of his shirt. Then, as the driver leaned downward, John recognized the goatee and sideburns; the hairy beast from the showers.

"Weyil, that would depend..." He stopped cold, "Ain't you from the shower? Sure you are! I'll be tarred and damned. Heee. hee, hee, hee. Shit."

Obviously, he thought something was very funny. John didn't. "Are you?"

The huge beast opened the door, revealing his entirety, most of it covered with blue denim overalls. He leaned down so they could talk without yelling, but his voice remained oddly high and cartoon like, "I sure could be, ya know it. Where ya tryin ta git to?"

"Thornbury."

"Thornbury? Ain't nothin' in fuckin' Thornbury. You want some good action, we'll head to Hull," he said, referring to the small Quebec city, notorious for its seedy nightlife. "Git a piece of ass from one a them Frenchies. Heee, hee.." His teeth were grotesque, pushed in from either side, overlapping and converging in the middle.

John said as politely as he could, "I just have to get there. If you're going, I'd like a ride." The man kept laughing, his sick high squeal joining the chorus from the pigs in the back. "I'll pay you."

Now, the driver got serious, "How much?"

"Fifty."

"Hun-derd. Cash."

John succumbed, "All right." He walked around to the passenger side and climbed up on the step. He was about to open the door, when the hairy giant's head popped out of the window.

"Now, honey." He wanted the money first.

"But I..."

"There's a cash machine right over there." He pointed to an enclosed area adjacent to the rear entrance of the building. "I'll be waitin' right here for ya, sweetheart." He banged his hand twice on the sheet metal door and winked.

Great. John hopped down. Could we just get the fuck away from here. He pulled the shamrock cap down low to his eyes, grabbed the duffel and got the cash from the machine; three hundred dollars, the maximum it would provide. He kept a hundred in his hand and shoved the rest into his damp shoe. He returned to the foul smelling truck, paid the guy, and got in. The engine revved, the gorilla put it in gear and they rolled out, at last, onto northbound 21. John let out a sigh and tossed his hat on the seat beside him.

The high voice started, "What you runnin' from?"

"Nothing." John answered dryly.

"I seen the way you ducked around goin' for the money. I ain't stupid, ya know." The husky monster released the wheel with his right hand, reached over his head between the visor and the roof and pulled a thirty eight caliber pistol out of the holster where he had hidden it. He pointed it right at John's head, about four inches away from his left ear. He cocked the hammer and slid his index finger to the trigger, and grinned. "You ain't thinkin' about robbin' me, are ya?"

John was frozen, motionless. It was impossible to get used to people trying to kill him. "No. Please. Put that down."

The man erupted in sick laughter, "Heee. Hee, hee hee. Shit." He lowered the hammer and put the pistol back. "Had ya goin', didn't I? Hee, hee."

You sure did, pal.

You sure did.

40

Before leaving with agent Morse for Canada, Christine Ferrand had contacted Joseph Delahunt, a former FBI agent himself, and one of the investigators her father had used frequently. She instructed him to search any properties or businesses that could be identified as Domati owned or controlled; to do whatever was necessary to locate Shelby Russel. He'd have a better chance than the authorities, she reasoned, not necessarily having to comply with the law.

She had also called her office and learned that, in addition to the merciless assault from the press, Domati's attorney, Leonard Shapiro had called. She had called him back and left a message. Chris was certain he would know all about what was going on. She figured it was probably he who had gotten to Judge Witheral and, in turn, alerted Frank Doran to the waiting trap at the courthouse. But if anyone might offer a deal or a shortcut which could end the situation, it would be him. And Christine had no qualms about circumventing the FBI to save her clients. She was still waiting for the return call.

The two hour drive had been uneventful, without significant conversation. Morse had been busy on her phone coordinating support from the Provincial Police. They were there when Karen and Christine arrived. As soon as the quick sequence of introductions was complete, Morse went to work, interviewing the staff at the Spencer Street branch of the Royal Bank of Canada in London, Ontario. She was very good at it.

She had just started talking to the teller who had, earlier that day, completed the wire transfer for the man claiming to be Welland. Chris stood silently, watching, as Karen Morse showed the woman Frank Doran's photo.

"Is this the man?"

The teller looked carefully at the old picture, "He was older, with whiter hair, but...yeah, I'd hafta say that it's him."

Did you notice if he was alone? Was any one else with him?"

"No."

"Did you happen to see what he was driving?"

"No. But ya know Hank might of. He's usually right there, watching, for such things, ya know," she responded in her over enunciated dialect, pointing to the front of the building where a uniformed man about sixty was gazing out the glass doors, watching the policemen in the parking lot.

"He's the guard?" Karen asked the obvious.

"Sure, eh, fourteen years, December."

"Thank you. We'll talk to him. Thanks."

It turned out that the guard had seen another man in a car; a man that he thought might have been with Doran. And recalled that it was a blue General Motors product but little else.

"And the other man, the one driving?"

"Didn't see him. My eyes...well, they really aren't that good, eh."

That could be the car. That was something. Chris followed as Morse went outside and asked one of the Provincial Police officers to check, to see if any similar vehicle may have been reported recently...for anything. It was a long shot that she really didn't expect to pan out. She was stunned when he returned, moments later from his squad car.

"Ms. Morse. We *do* have a report of a blue 1993 Chevrolet...and a suspicious death."

"Where?"

"It's only about thirty miles from here. Right up the 401."

"Show me. We'll follow you. Let's go." Morse knew that, if Doran had a driver, as would have probably been the case, it was possible, even likely that he would kill him to cover his trail. She was surprised though that he may still be in Canada. It would be much easier to disappear for a couple of days in New York and wait there for his Friday flight to Miami with Angelo Domati.

The police cruiser raced down the freeway ahead of them. Christine and Morse followed in the FBI car. In less than twenty minutes they came to the exit. She followed the police car up the ramp and slowed to a stop, parking behind it. Most of the area had been cordoned off. There was a blue car parked in the middle with the driver's door open. Inside, with his head falling awkwardly backwards against the headrest, was a man Karen presumed had been Doran's driver. Police technicians swarmed around the body taking pictures, measuring and checking for fingerprints.

The scene didn't surprise Karen at all. She had worked enough drug cases to recognize the situation immediately. It wasn't unusual to find couriers killed.

They got out and ducked under the police tape, Karen showing her identification, introducing herself to the detective in charge.

"Morse. FBI. And my associate, Christine Ferrand. What have you got?"

He explained the circumstances, the discovery several hours before of the dead man's body.

"Who found him?"

"Right over there, with my men." He pointed to a man who looked to be about fifty, who was sitting on the hood of a police car. He was dirty and unshaven, a vagrant. "We guess he was trying to rob the guy."

"Thanks. Back in a second." She went back to her black Ford and got the photo of Frank Doran.

Chris met her at the car. Once again, she showed the picture.

"Sir, have you ever seen this man?" Morse began, struggling to keep the man's wandering attention.

The bum grabbed the photo and pulled it close to his face, obviously trying to focus on the image. It took him several seconds to respond. His voice was wheezy and broken. He closed his eyes to slits as he looked up at Morse slyly, "It could be...and then...well ya know my mind is not as clear right now as it could be."

Morse was impatient. "Sir, we just need a simple answer. If you did see him or not, we'd like to know."

Chris realized what he wanted. She opened her purse, found her wallet, and succumbed to the shakedown, handing the man an American twenty.

"Ya see now *that's* a real good memory jogger." He folded the bill into a small rectangle and pushed it into his torn high-top tennis shoe. "There. now lemme take a closer look." He scrutinized the picture, carefully; slowly. Then he threw it to the pavement and announced, "Yep....was riding with the dead guy. Got a couple a coffees. When they got done drinkin' 'em, he walks back in...When he comes out again...this is funny...he just walks right by his own car."

Karen knelt to retrieve the photo, "That's it?"

"That's all I remember." He put his head down.

Morse sensed this was not true and called his bluff, leaning into his face until their noses almost touched, whispering, "Do you want me to tell the police that I think you murdered that guy, trying to rob him? Do you?" She waited for his response.

"No." He started to cry softly, scared to death. "No, please."

"It's okay." She touched his shoulder, "Just tell me if you saw anything else. Then you can go, all right?"

He nodded. "I don't want to get in no trouble. I saw...there was this big guy an he came back...to the..."

"Take it easy. Lets go through it slowly, for me, okay? The man in the picture, he came out..."

"Right."

"And he walked past the blue car."

"Uh, huh."

"And where did he go then?"

"He walked over to this big green car and got in."

"Big green car. What kind?"

"I don't know. I think it was a Lincoln maybe."

"Good. A Lincoln."

He was becoming excited now anxious to help, "An', an'...he sat down in there readin' the paper. Then this other guy, big guy, came an' got in too. An' they left. That's it."

"Okay," Karen reassured him. "Just one more thing. You wait here, then you can go. Okay?"

He nodded again, exhausted from the struggle to remember so much. Morse went to the car again and came back with other photos; photos of Domati and each of his sons. She fanned them out.

"Any of these guys?"

He hesitated for a second before pointing to Nino Domati.

"Agent Morse?" It was one of the officers, "Your car phone...it's ringing."

"Thanks." She jogged back to the Ford. Christine smiled briefly at the vagrant, and returned to the car herself. The door was open and, when she got closer, she could overhear Karen's conversation.

"...yeah, on Doran and a positive on Nino Domati." She waited for the voice on the other end, then continued, "I've got a description of the car but it's not very reliable. I'll put it out, but I don't have anything else to go on."

Bob Garnetti had called from the FBI office in Detroit. "Well, here's something. I traced Russel to a rental car out of Traverse. Ended up somewhere in Canada too; Amberley? On Lake Huron."

"Let me get the map." Agent Morse thumbed through the glove box found the wrinkled map of Ontario, and unfolded it on her lap. She scanned around the province. "Got it."

"Joseph Cappola was with him, but he's dead. Shot a cop. Russel never came back to the car. He did use his Amex card, though, a place called 'Rose's 21'. It's some kind of truck stop."

"Okay."

Garnetti went on, tracing the same path on his own map in the atlas that was folded open backwards on his desk. "Now, if you follow the road along the water, you'll come to a town called Southampton. Find it?"

She did as he asked, "Yup."

"Apparently Russel used his credit card again at a bank there…" He read from his notes, "The First Farmer's Trust…to get a cash advance less than two hours ago."

"I can get up there pretty fast. There's really nothing more I can do here. Doran could be anywhere."

He leaned forward to look again at the map, "Well, maybe not as far as you think. We got another match from Keenan's list, used the name Cross, at another Royal Bank…in Barrie."

"Where's that?"

"About 50 miles north of Toronto; I'm on that now with the Mounties. You should go to Southampton. I'll have one of their men meet you there." Another agent appeared at the conference room door signaling to Garnetti, "I gotta go. I'll talk to you later." He hung up and waved the man in. "What is it?"

"It's Mr. Messing, sir, he wants to see you."

"Oh. All right, David." He knew what he wanted, "Tell him I'll be right there. And ask Agent Forester to come in, please."

Garnetti rose and put on his sport coat. What a pain in the ass, he thought. First, to be arrested by some hick sheriff, and now to come back to discover that Messing had taken over his office completely; to the point of moving furniture out to make room for an additional desk for Jack, his assistant. That left the conference room.

While he waited for Forester, Garnetti walked over to the window. The press was entrenched below, crowded around the front steps of the building, as they had been for two days. He knew that's where Messing was headed, and that he wanted an update before his inevitable mid-day news conference. Bob looked at the clock on the wall above the bulletin board; eleven forty-five, fifteen minutes before the noon news.

"Sir?" It was Forester.

"Oh, good. Follow me. We can talk while we're walking." Garnetti passed him, headed for the door. Fill me in on Domati's surveillance."

The agent caught up, "Not a thing sir. It's quiet."

"And Mrs. Russel?"

"Nothing."

"...we getting anywhere with Keenan?"

"No prints, other than his; so far it looks like a heart attack."

"Yeah, right. What about the marks on his wrist?"

"Nothing definite yet."

They were nearing Garnetti's office and he slowed, "Okay. Just stay with it. Oh, and see if you can get ahold of Sam Baylor, I need to talk to him when I'm finished here, okay?" He was referring to his contact at the Canadian Mounted Police.

"Yes sir." Agent Forester was off.

Garnetti continued to what, until a few days ago, was his own office and stopped by the door.

Stan Messing stood up. "Bob. Good. Come in. What have we got?" The assistant, Jack was holding a suit coat while the assistant attorney general slid his arms into the sleeves. "Fast. We're only seven minutes from the news. I've got to get down there." He liked to show up during the time when the news was actually being broadcast, that way there was less chance his comments would be edited. "Go."

"Doran. He transferred more money to the Colombian account, this time from Barrie, in Ontario."

"Barrie?"

"Canada, sir."

"Of course. What else?"

"John Russel…" He was interrupted by the alarm from a clock radio that Messing had put on the desk and set to go off at eleven fifty-five.

"We gotta move," he said, brushing his hair into a final perfect wave. He lowered his voice, nearly whispering to Garnetti, "This Hoffa thing is just what I need, but you'd better step on it, I think it's getting tired. We need something big. As soon as possible."

Garnetti watched him hurry through the office and out. He took advantage of the opportunity to grab a few things from his own desk, a yellow pad and appointment book, to take with him back to the conference room. He laid them out at the far corner of the large table opposite the door, so when he sat he could see people as they entered. He could also see the bulletin board, plastered with maps and notices and pictures. He walked closer. "Why Canada?" he wondered. Where was Doran headed? And Russel, now with the finger, was he going to meet him?

Agent Forester reappeared, "I have Lieutenant Baylor on five, sir."

"Thanks." Garnetti walked to the speakerphone and pushed the flashing button as Forester left. "Sam, how are you?"

"Fine, Bob, what can I do for you?"

"I just wanted to bring you up to speed from our end. And I've got a couple of questions."

"Sure. Not a problem."

"We've got an agent on the way to that bank in Southampton, agent Morse, Karen Morse. I was hoping you could get someone to hook up with her there."

"Okay."

"What's the word from Barrie?"

"Well, we've positively ID'ed your guy Doran as Cross, but no one saw him come or go. We ran the prints we got from the paperwork...came back Cross. I had 'em sent to your lab in D.C."

"Good."

"That's about it to this point."

"Listen, I was wondering about something...I'm looking at the map...what's up there?"

"At Barrie?"

"Yeah. And around there. I mean is there someplace that it would make sense that they're going? Or is it just woods or what?"

"Well Lake Simcoe isn't far, but a lot of people are up there, it's pretty touristy."

"How 'bout farther out?"

"With the exception of the area right around the shore at Georgian Bay and the mansions on Rouseau Lake, it's wilderness. If you didn't want to be found, it'd be a great place to go."

"Is it mostly government land? I see Algonquin Park, but what about the rest of it?"

"No, there's a lot of it that's private; mostly owned by mining companies or lumber companies..."

"Is there a way to check? You must have records."

"Sure. I can get it, but it might take awhile. It'd be a lot faster if I knew what you were looking for."

"I'll fax you a list. I want to see if any of the names or companies pop up."

"Not a problem. I'll run it through Revenue. Anything else?"

"Not that I can think of, thanks."

"All right, Bob. We'll be talking."

Garnetti pushed the button, disconnecting. He was willing to bet that Vincenzo Domati, his family, or one of his businesses owned something in northern Ontario. And that's most likely where Domati himself would be, too. And maybe Frank Doran. Although he couldn't understand why he'd want to be anywhere near Domati now that the department had the heat on him.

He leaned on the edge of the table, staring at the map. His eyes fell to the picture of John Russel jumping off his porch and to the picture of Shelby. He speculated that she could be there as well.

He walked back to the phone and called agent Forester on the intercom.

"Yes sir," he answered.

"I want you to get a list together of every business that Domati or any family member owns. I don't care if it's his father-in-law's cousin, you understand?"

"Yes, sir."

"Include any known aliases for any of them, too. Do it right away. Then fax it to Sam Baylor. Oh, and add any names from that bank list of Keenan's too, the one's that Doran's been using."

Bob Garnetti returned to the bulletin board and stopped directly in front of Frank Doran's photograph, and, even though he was alone in the room he said out loud, "You thought you had it all figured out, didn't you? But you're greedy Frank, you should have let it go.

But you didn't. And now, we're going to get you."

4I

John Russel was walking quickly. It wasn't smart to be out in the open like this. Soon, he hoped, there would be a phone. Thankfully, there wasn't much traffic. Just in case, he kept the brim of the hat pulled low, almost to his eyebrows.

The trucker had deposited him where the highway forked off toward Quebec in one direction and to Thornbury in the other, but not before relieving him at gun point of another three hundred dollars from an ATM. He still had another two in his shoe.

The sun was high in the early afternoon sky and it pushed its heat down on top of him absorbing into the black Toronto shirt. It didn't take long before the sweat was pouring from him, soaking him once more. He was thirsty again, drained. He kept walking.

He could see there were buildings ahead. And a sign. Thornbury. Good. He walked another half mile. On the right, ahead, he could see a sign, a gas station. The short white pillar rising up along side of it clearly displayed the large white shield outlining the letters 'BP' in yellow. It abutted the roadway itself, without two feet to spare between the three green gas pumps and the traffic lane. The building was painted white, wooden and square, with a gray shingled overhang jutting out from two sides, along the road, over the pumps, and over the front door, on the side facing John. It was only a story and a half and it had small square windows, outlined in green, above the small roof. There were two old love seats, red and blue, on either side of the entrance, against the building on a raised concrete slab. Above them, under the gutter, three signs, 'GROCERIES' on the left, 'HAP'S CORNER in the center, and 'GAS BAIT SODA' on the right. A second road intersected with Highway 21 at the corner of the gravel parking lot. As John approached, he could see that it was lined with tiny frame ranch style homes.

There was an older man reading a newspaper, seated in one of the odd chairs that dotted the cement verandah. John turned his face away from him as he crossed the lot. He could hear voices, children playing in the neighborhood behind the store. Beyond the gas pumps, against the wall, there was an ice machine, and beyond that, a pay phone, mounted to the building.

John kept walking, his pace quickening as he neared the building, until he was safely around the corner, out of the sight of the old man. He jumped up the eighteen or so inches to the slab and went directly to the public phone. Without hesitating, he dialed the number, stored now forever in his deepest memory. It had barely rung when the harsh voice of Angelo Domati answered.

"Yeah."

"It's me. I'm in Thornbury."

"Hold on."

John heard the hand slide over the microphone and muffled conversation. Then the clear voice. "Go to the water. In town. At the marina. There's a bar, 'Captain Hanscomb's'. It's right there on the main drag. Go there and wait. Sit alone at the far end, near the bathrooms…"

"And then what?…hello…"

The call had been disconnected. Shit. There was a noise. Gravel. From the alley. He looked up. Two boys sped around the corner, racing, their bicycles fishtailing momentarily into the road, then speeding straight through the opening between it and the gas pumps and sliding to a dusty stop at the corner of the building. John pressed his back against the wall, startled by the sudden approach, then relaxed when he realized what it was.

He had to get something to drink before he could walk any farther. And some food. It seemed fairly safe to get it here. In the time since John had arrived, no one had even driven by the place. Aside from the boys on bikes and the old man, it was deserted. The main door was open, held in place inside the store by a stop, leaving only a green wooden framed screen door for protection against the flies. John reached for the handle, but lunged back, again startled by the bike riders as they burst back out, each with a soda and some sort of candy in their hands. The door swung its complete course, slamming into the outside wall before its tense spring pulled it back.

"Sorry," one of the boys yelled as he passed, followed by another, "Sorry," from the other as they bolted past, leaping from the cement edge to the loose stone and dirt.

John caught the door before it closed, and walked in, cushioning it from an additional slam behind him. The warped wooden floorboards squeaked under his feet.

A man was seated on a tall stool behind the counter, "Afternoon," he said, studying his latest customer, "Something I can help you with?"

John removed his sweaty green corduroy cap and brushed his wet brown hair backward with his fingers, "Something to drink. Maybe a sandwich." He put the duffel down on the floor near the counter and noticed the faint odor of rot. "And some ice. I saw the machine out there."

"Two dollars. Pay here."

This must be Hap, John reasoned. He was tanned and rough looking, as if life before this boredom had been anything but. Probably a retired cop. He had that look of the street. "Thanks." John tried to be calm. He checked the back of the store where there was a large cooler, and removed a submarine sandwich, wrapped in cellophane. Against the wall next to the cooler, there was a red metal Coke machine, the old kind, about waist high with a door on top that opened like a washing machine. He lifted it and inside between the familiar steel rails were small bottles, held up by the caps. There was a box with a slot for coins and '$1.00' written on it with red marker. John had no change. He put the sandwich on the counter. "I'll have this, and the ice, and some change for the pop machine, please." John passed him an American one dollar bill.

Hap rang the old manual register and the drawer sprung open, "You get up here much?"

"No."

"Fishing?"

"Sort of."

"Got some crawlers there in that fridge, there if you're interested." He pointed to an old white Hotpoint in the back corner.

"Yeah," John said, "That'd be good." Just what he needed, more decomposing flesh. But if Hap wanted to think he was a fisherman, fine.

"Get your license, here too, if you want," Hap offered.

"That's all right. Thanks." John inserted the coins into the cold box and slid a bottle out the end. He opened it in the opener on the side and drank the entire contents in one swig.

"Hot out, eh?"

"Yeah." He handed the man a single, "Change, please."

John got another bottle and opened it, but saved the contents for the journey to town, wherever that was. He paid for the ice and the sub.

"Don't forget your crawlers."

John hoped Hap might have, but it was obvious he was not going to let John leave without the dirty worms. He took a small white container that looked more like leftover Chinese food than bait, from the refrigerator. "Okay. That'll do it," he said, and then, trying to be as matter of fact as possible, "Oh, could you tell me how to get to the marina? I'm meeting someone there."

"Yup. Straight up 21. Second light, about a mile and a half, take a left. It's a little over a mile down to the water. Looking for a boat? I can put you in touch with a guy down there."

"No. Thank you. That's fine."

"If you got good tires and you don't mind a bump or two, take Kirkland Road through the marshland. It's not much more than a trail but it'll save a few minutes. Comes in on the left just before the first light."

Jesus. Two and a half more miles. John grabbed the sandwich and duffel and container of worms and headed back out into the searing afternoon heat. The screen slammed behind him. Hap returned to his stool and opened a magazine.

When John reached Kirkland, he turned left. He tossed the bait container into the cattails in the ditch at the side of the road. When he was far enough from the main highway, he stopped near a large tree. It provided one of the few genuinely shady areas that he had seen. His submarine sandwich was warm and soggy. Condensation had formed inside the plastic. But John was starving. As long as it was food, it didn't matter. He sat by the side of the road and opened the clear wrapping. He started eating. Slowly at first, then ripping huge bites out of the tough white bread, following each with a gulp of soda. He hadn't realized how hungry he had been. In less than a minute, he had devoured the last crumb, chasing it with a shred of warm lettuce that had clung to the wrapper.

He wadded it up in a ball and finished the last of his drink, tossing both the bottle and the Saran wrap into the marsh grass next to the road. Now down to business. Taking a deep breath, hoping to keep the food down long enough for digestion, John unzipped the vinyl duffel. With another deep breath, held securely, he lifted the clear baggy up to take a closer look at the finger in the light. There was green mold growing at the point where it had been severed from the hand and a murky yellowish liquid had accumulated along the crease at the bottom. It too, had a covering of some different, but quickly growing spore. He took out the five pound bag of ice cubes and ripped a hole in it. He could barely look at the baggie, but did glance back long enough to undo the top and quickly jam seven or eight ice cubes into it. The air exploded from him as he gasped and drew in more. Thanks a lot, Dad. Unable to look at it any longer, he zipped the top closed and tossed it into the Montreal Canadien's bag.

The rest of the ice was already melting in its bag and John lifted it, took off his green ball cap, and poured the freezing water over his head, shaking it off at the same time. He dumped out most of the remaining cubes, then tied the plastic into a tight knot, creating a softball sized, makeshift ice bag. He jammed it inside the shamrock hat and pulled it back onto his head. He stood up and stretched, feeling much better, getting used to the various pains.

He'd only been walking about five minutes when he heard a faint crushing sound behind him. Stones. Gravel under tires. Big tires. A car. Damn. The car was coming closer, but slowly. He didn't dare turn around. The heat was melting the ice pack on his head, causing strange wisps of condensation to appear around the headband of the green cap, like breath on a cold day. Water and perspiration was dripping down his face and neck and soaking the top of his black Toronto shirt, almost to the tip of the silk-screened CN Tower. He had a bag filled with dirty underwear and amputated body parts. It would be difficult to explain that.

As the car got closer, John sensed the worst. First the black fender entered his periphery, but he ignored it. Then the white hood. Finally the passenger door emblazoned with an official looking emblem. A cop. Shit.

The car moved slowly alongside him. The man inside, a deputy, studied John carefully. John turned and smiled, but kept walking. The deputy stared back, seriously evaluating this stranger. After almost a minute, he increased his speed and moved on, leaving John inhaling his hot road dust. Sooner or later, the cop would figure out who he was. Time was running out.

Mercifully, the town itself was only three quarters of a mile farther, and in a few minutes, he had emerged from the marshes and stood at the top of a hill. John could see the majority of Thornbury ahead, descending down to the water; the marina, and the docks, and several parallel streets, each lined with small, nicely kept homes. There were sidewalks and curbs and green lawns. There was at least one church near the water at the center of the town, and possibly another at its edge, but it was hard to tell through the dense foliage of elm. The gravel turned into pavement and the random road became a straight street. Soon, a sidewalk appeared and John, not wishing to attract any further attention, quickly got out of the street. He decided that the hat should go, and at the first large tree, he ditched it along with the now empty ice bag, pushing both into the untrimmed grass between exposed roots. His hair was soaked and, without the hat to contain it, it jutted out in odd pointed, brown clumps around his head. John did what he could to brush it into place with his fingers, pulling it together at the back, slapping down on the sides, but the result was less than perfect.

He headed for the water, for the marina, where Angelo Domati had said Captain Hanscomb's, was located. He walked quickly, nervously looking from side to side. There was no telling how long it would take the local authorities to discover that he was wanted by the FBI, but they would.

Soon.

And the deputy would be back.

42

On the way to the bank in Southampton, where they suspected John, or someone using his card had made a withdrawal, agent Morse and Christine Ferrand stopped at Rose's 21 in Amberley. The agent had interrogated most of the employees and some of the truck drivers, but no one could remember seeing John Russel, at least not from the photograph the women had circulated.

They had been back on the road for an hour when Christine's cell phone rang. It was her investigator, Joe Delahunt.

"I may have something."

"On Mrs. Russel?"

Karen Morse listened intently, hearing only Chris's side of the conversation.

"Not exactly." Delahunt continued, "But this is interesting. I was checking Domati's businesses, currently under his family's controls, I checked out some former holdings, too, I mean these guys change businesses like underwear…"

"And?" Chris wanted him to get to the point.

"Margate West."

"What's that?"

"It's a convalescent home in Dearborn. It belongs to Nino Domati, so I went out there to look around."

Chris hated the way Delahunt refused to get to the point. It had driven her crazy for years. "C'mon Joe, please…"

"Okay. It's the same nursing home that Hoffa's mother lived in before she died. I think that's a little coincidental, don't you? Being that..."

"Yes."

"But here's the kicker; every year since Hoffa disappeared, they get a check, to cover her expenses and then some, which is odd in itself, but then after some digging, and this cost me a few bucks..."

Chris raised an eyebrow in frustration, "I'll reimburse you."

"Thanks. I find out that the checks came from some company in Canada; H.L Holdings Ltd. and the guy who controls it is up there, right where you are, pretty much."

"Who? Where?"

She could hear the investigator sorting through notes, "His name is Loring, Harris Loring. He's some billionaire, I guess, lives somewhere called Naganosh or Naga-something, I'll check it out if you want me to."

"No. Just keep looking for Mrs. Russel and if you find anything, let me know. Do whatever you have to, Joe, we may not have a lot of time. Call my office tomorrow. They'll have a check for you. Thanks."

"He got something?" Agent Morse could tell he did.

"Yeah," Chris answered, "Harris Loring?" She continued, explaining what Delahunt had told her, hoping it would ring a bell, but neither she nor Karen Morse had any idea why he would be significant, or if he was at all.

While Chris called her office to get the check cut, Morse called Garnetti in Detroit.

"Karen," He answered through the speakerphone in the conference room, "Where are you?"

"Almost to Southampton."

"Good. I talked to Sam Baylor, he's got one of his guys up there already. When do you think you'll get there?"

"Probably no more than half an hour or so, maybe less. Any word on Shelby Russel?"

"No...not yet." His tone was more somber, "I'm not real confident that we're gonna find her alive at this point."

Karen saw that Chris was watching for a reaction and she shook her head, 'no' before continuing the conversation. "Listen, Bob, Christine Ferrand's investigator came across something. I think we should check it out."

"Shoot."

"Harris Loring. Canadian. Millionaire."

"Doesn't sound familiar. I'll get someone on it. Stay near the phone. I'll get back to you. That it?"

"For now."

Karen Morse tried as hard as she could to place Loring and determine why he might have something to do with her investigation. The two women batted around various scenarios all the way to The First Farmer's Trust in Southampton, Ontario. Here, they were more successful. Not only did the teller remember John, but so did the security guard. But it wasn't until she went door to door through the neighborhood behind the bank, that she learned of the truck.

The woman who lived in a small frame house, across the street, four down from the bank had seen it. She was older and lived alone. Morse got the impression that, out of boredom, she spent a considerable amount of time looking out the window. Her account of events was vivid, if not eloquent, "They was a squealin 'ta beat the band, eh, them hogs, and he parked the damn thing right there. Right out in front of my house," she told agent Morse who was interviewing her on her front porch while Chris looked on.

"I think its awful what them truckers do. I watch 'em all the time."

"Did you see anyone? With the truck?" She showed the woman the photo of Russel, "Did you see this man?"

The woman studied the shot. "I don't know. I don't think so...but...well, it couldda been him, the one that went to the bank. Them hogs stunk up the air so bad, though, I had to shut my door. That's how bad it is, eh. I'll tell you."

"You wouldn't happen to remember the license number, would you ma'am?"

She disappeared into her house, still talking to the agent through the screened door, "Heck, I report 'em, they're wreckin' the damn neighborhood...course I got it. Wrote it down."

The door opened and she handed a small scrap of paper to Morse.

"Thank you ma'am. You've been very helpful."

With the help of Corporal Eppen, the man Baylor had sent, it was easy to run the plate. It only took a few minutes to discover that the truck had been located. The owner, claiming to have been robbed by a man he identified as John Russel, had filed a report with the Provincial Police. He said the incident occurred when he insisted the man get out near Thornbury. There were also additional reports of a man, somewhat resembling Russel, who had been seen by authorities in that town.

"Let's go, Chris." The lawyer followed as agent Morse hurried back to the car. Soon, with Corporal Eppen leading the way, they were racing north on Route 21, up the coast toward Thornbury.

At the FBI office in Detroit, Garnetti had just finished his daily meeting with Stan Messing. He was returning to the conference room when agent Forester called out from his desk in the center of the common area of the office. "Agent Garnetti, I have Inspector Baylor on the line. Line three. Oh. And I've got the information on Loring."

"Good. Bring it in. I'll take the call in here. Thanks." He gestured to the conference room. Forester followed him in, handing over a manila file folder. Garnetti sat down at the end of the long table and pushed the button on his speakerphone, anxious to hear what the Mounty had discovered. "Garnetti."

"Hey Bob, Sam Baylor."

"Sam, whatdaya got?"

"I don't know exactly. I don't know what you're looking for. I went over the lists you sent me, and I found some marginal things that don't really seem like any big deal, but I also found something that might be."

While Baylor was talking, Garnetti opened the file on Loring, "Go ahead."

"There is one property...a huge property, that's owned by one of the companies on the list, Charlevoix Sand and Gravel. You got your map?"

"Yeah." Bob looked up from the papers to the bulletin board.

"Okay. Off of Georgian Bay, about half way up the eastern side, you'll find the Still River. Got it?"

"Hang on a second." Garnetti crossed to the map, tracing upward with his finger, "Got it."

"Follow that inland. It ends at a lake..."

"Yeah, Naganosh Lake, I found it." Garnetti paused for a moment. There was something familiar. He had just seen that name. In the Loring folder. He rushed back to the table.

"Well there's a lodge there and that whole area, a couple thousand acres is part of it. It's all owned by that company. Does that help?" Garnetti was pouring over the information in the folder. "Bob?"

"Oh. I'm sorry, Sam...yeah, that helps...a lot. Listen. I've got something here, too. Have you ever heard of Harris Loring?"

"Sure. Rich guy, kinda strange. Recluse."

"Well according to my information, that's what he lists as his home address...Naganosh."

"Yeah. He bought the old Rockefeller mansion a long time ago. Why? You think there's a connection?"

"I don't know. What's the best way to get up there?"

"It's pretty remote. I don't know. A plane maybe. Helicopter."

"Listen, Sam, thanks. I might need some help. Can I call you back?"

"Sure. I'll be here."

Garnetti hung up and immediately dialed Karen Morse in her car.

"Morse," Karen answered and left him on the speaker.

"I got something on Loring. I don't know what the deal is, but it's going down up there. It's probably the exchange."

"Hey Bob, it's Chris," she interrupted, "You think that's where Russel is headed."

"That'd be my guess, Chris. Karen, what'd you find out at the bank?"

Morse told him about the hog truck, "We're on our way now to Thornbury."

"All right. When you get there, stay. I'll meet you as soon as I can, within the next two hours." Just as he hung up, the assistant attorney general arrived, followed by his assistant, Jack. Messing had overheard part of Garnetti's conversation.

"Thornbury? Where's that?"

"Oh. In Canada, sir."

Messing indicated that Jack should make a note. "Is that something I should mention? Sounds like you're about to wrap this up."

"I wish you wouldn't, Stan. Give me until tomorrow."

Messing walked to the window and looked down. Again, on the steps below, the press was gathering. "You know, they're expecting something, something big. I don't want to disappoint them, Bob." He turned back to the agent, "Is that where Frank Doran is?"

"I don't know. It's possible."

Stan Messing looked down at the crowd, "I sure would like to get that son of a bitch."

His assistant, Jack, was writing every word the attorney said in a small notebook until Messing gave him permission to leave, "Jack, will you please excuse us for a moment?" The man laid the pad on the end of the large table and, without saying a word, left the room, closing the door as he did.

Messing caught his own reflection in the glass, and used it to adjust his white hair and straighten his wide floral tie. He turned away from the windows, toward Garnetti, "You know, we've got a real opportunity here, Bob, I mean as far as anyone knows, we've solved the Hoffa case." Garnetti tried to figure out what Messing had to do with any aspect of the investigation. He watched as Messing rolled a chair out from the oak table and sat comfortably, with his feet propped up, his shoes pointed at the agent, leaning back fully, talking half to himself. "Think about it, Bob. We've got the body..."

"But you don't really think it's Hoffa's...do you?"

"Whose to say any different?" He wasn't expecting an answer. He continued to think out loud, "I don't really care. You're gonna get Doran, sooner or later, as far as I'm concerned, he's the perpetrator."

Bob Garnetti was growing uncomfortable with the direction the conversation was heading. He shifted in his chair. "Yes sir, but we know he didn't do it alone. There were others; Swain, Russel's father..."

"They're dead."

"The Tenino family was part of it, Russel told us that. Remember what Benny Tenino told him?"

"Like I said, Bob, they're dead." The assistant attorney general leaned forward, closer to Garnetti. "Look, Bob, how'd you like to run the whole fucking FBI? You could, you know. This could be a step in that direction." Messing slid his feet off the polished tabletop, stood up and started to pace slowly back and forth in front of the windows, occasionally looking out at the crowd of curious news people. "This is something the people want to know...what happened to Jimmy Hoffa. So, we'll tell them."

"Stan, we've got a long way to go before we can tell anybody anything. What was Doran's motive? They're gonna want to know."

"Money. He was paid, wasn't he? We've got all the bank accounts."

"Yeah, but from where? It had to come from somewhere."

"Bob, with the way they did it, at least from what you told me, it's going to be hard to prove that it came from Domati."

"Not if we can get Doran to testify." He could see that the attorney, distracted by the crowd below, was not paying attention. "That's why I need some time...before we say any more to the press."

"What?"

Garnetti stood up facing Messing. "I would like to have an opportunity to pressure Doran. I think we're close to something...this thing in Canada, whatever's going on, is gonna happen soon. I want to get up there." Garnetti looked down at the reporters, "Can you just hold them off for another day?"

Stan Messing again used the reflection to check his appearance. He sighed, disappointed that, at least on this day, he would not have his moment in front of the cameras. "I guess so, Bob. What's another day?" He slapped Garnetti on his upper arm and started for the door. "I'll let you get on with it. Just keep me posted, all right?"

"Yes, sir. As soon as I know any more, I'll let you know."

Messing pulled the door open, and knowing his assistant would be dutifully waiting close by, he called to him without looking, as he came out into the hall. "Jack, tell them that we're close; we should have something soon, whatever...You know the drill. We'll schedule a press conference later."

The two disappeared down the hall and Garnetti, frustrated by the interruption, had wasted more time than he wanted to. He quickly got on the intercom and called agent Forester.

The agent was there almost immediately, "Sir?"

"We're gonna need an aircraft. Line it up. We're heading for Canada." Bob Garnetti crossed the room to the large map on the wall and pointed. "We want to get to Thornbury, Ontario as soon as possible. I'll need you and one other agent. We'll be picking up Agent Morse and Christine Ferrand there." Forester, bright and serious, made mental notes of what his orders were. Garnetti continued, "I want you to coordinate the effort with the Mounties and the Provincial Police. We'll need authorization, warrants...whatever, and backup...here." He pointed to the Still River, tracing his finger east to Lake Naganosh, as Forester came closer to get a better look at the map, nodding affirmatively as he did. "Call Baylor back. Buzz me in here when he's on. Let me know when we're ready to roll. That's it." Bob concluded dismisively and Forester obediently left.

It wasn't thirty seconds later that Forester's voice came over the small speaker in the phone, "I've got Baylor, sir."

Without answering, Garnetti picked up the flashing line. The activity level in the main area outside the room was increasing, with agents scurrying to accomplish the new orders.

"Sam, hi. I'm on the way to Thornbury."

"What do you need?"

"I've got three agents coming in from this office, plus Morse and another person up there already. We're gonna want to get to that place on Lake Naganosh as soon as we can, so we're gonna need a chopper or something."

"Not a problem. What else?"

"Well, that's a good question. I don't know what to expect up there. It could be nothing. But it could get nasty. We're going to need some manpower. Agent Forester'll work out the details as soon as you authorize the operation. We'll need some shooters."

"I can give you a team. How many men do you figure?"

"Oh, I don't know, twenty maybe."

"Sounds like helicopters. There's really no good way to get cars in there. It'll be tough to get to the lodge unnoticed, Bob. I don't know if that's a problem or not."

"What if we dropped a team in at the other end of the lake? It looks like a couple of miles. How long would it take them to get into position?"

"I'm looking at the map. It's been awhile since I've been there, but it seems to me that it's pretty rough going...I'd say, maybe two hours, three tops, to get to the lodge."

"Okay. Can we do that right away?"

"Sure. Anything else?"

"No. If you can get that started, I'd appreciate it. If your men can get into position, near the lodge and wait for orders, that'd be great. I'll brief everybody when I get up there. All right, Sam?"

"Glad we can help, Bob. We're on it. I'll see you in Thornbury."

Garnetti replaced the receiver in its cradle. He sat down again at the end of the long oak table, and collected the dozens of files and other documents that were piled everywhere, scanning each briefly as he did.

There were twenty years worth of Charley Keenan's work on the case, summarized in one folder, the list of Doran's bank accounts in another. There was John Russel's statement, where he had paraphrased the conversation he had with Benito Tenino just before Frank Doran shot him. There were pages copied from Christine Ferrand's files, which contained the many formulas from Dr. Russel's journals; all of it, every answered question resulting in a dozen more.

His concentration was interrupted by Forester's voice over the intercom. "We're ready to go, sir."

Garnetti tossed the last of the files onto the top of the pile next to the phone. "I'll be right there. Thanks." He stood up and again went to the window, this time looking over the city beyond. It's amazing, he thought, who really controls things. He knew it wasn't the government, not when Messing could go downstairs to that mob of idiots and fabricate anything, and millions of people would end up believing whatever he said. Worse, he had every intention of doing just that.

And what about the truth? Nobody really seemed to care too much about it. Sure he would like to run the FBI someday, but it would be a lot more meaningful if he actually could find out what happened twenty years ago. He knew it was much more complicated than the way Messing had expressed it, just a few minutes earlier. Based on everything he had learned in the past two weeks, he was leaning toward the idea that the body that was dug up at Duck Lake, at John Russel's cottage, was not Hoffa's. There certainly seemed to be substantial documentation to the contrary, not to mention a pile of evidence describing a conspiracy, and implicating Henry Swain, Dr. Russel, Doran, and the Teninos. Somehow Vincenzo Domati and even Hoffa himself were involved. They had gone to a lot of trouble to create a body that could pass for Hoffa's.

But, unless he could intercept John Russel, there would be no physical evidence, it was all circumstantial, and Messing was right, with the exception of Doran, everyone involved was dead. Maybe that's how Messing wanted it.

Domati was smart. Nothing actually connected him or his family to any part of the Hoffa disappearance. Even the money that Doran was paid was once removed, having come from many different sources; criminals, people that Frank Doran had arrested, dead men.

Bob Garnetti looked at the reporters below. He could understand their curiosity, his own having grown. Originally sent to Detroit to investigate Doran's banking improprieties, the ensuing investigation had become intriguing. He was beginning to understand how a man like Keenan could devote nearly his whole career to it. It was too bad that Charlie, like so many other innocent people, got in the way.

He turned back to the table, leaned over to reach the phone, and pressed the intercom button.

"Forester." The voice responded.

"Do we have anything yet on Shelby Russel?"

"Nothing yet, sir."

Garnetti disconnected, "Damn," he said to the empty room. He had hoped, perhaps unrealistically, that they would have found her by now. At least she hadn't turned up dead as he had feared. Not yet.

He changed his focus back to the case and what had to be done now. He pulled his sport coat from the back of a chair and put it on, checking that his shoulder holster was in place, and that his weapon was secure. As he hurried out into the hall and the elevators, gathering Forester and one other agent along the way, his thoughts were again consumed by the ever-present, nagging question; the same question that had first surfaced when there was some doubt about the identity of the body that Baglia had dumped in Leland.

If that wasn't Hoffa, where the hell was he?

43

Harris Loring had been watching the activities at the Naganosh Lodge for most of the day. He had a perfect view from his porch just a few hundred yards away. He had known for twenty years that this day was coming, and dreaded it. He knew this would be his last day at the lake.

When he bought the house at Naganosh in 1974, very little was made of it. In fact, to those close enough to be considered neighbors, those living within a hundred miles or so, it seemed that his ownership was somehow in keeping with the natural order of things, being that he was, so it was said, a descendant of the original Loring family to which the entire area had once belonged.

There was, nonetheless, considerable mystery surrounding the transaction. While the name was well known, the man wasn't. He had purchased the monstrous Victorian mansion with cash, and according to revenue documents, his annual investment income was in excess of fifty million dollars, over half of which he contributed to the government by way of income tax. His generosity had become legendary, donating almost six million a year to various charities, including a hospital in Toronto which now bore his name, although no one there had ever seen him. He also, again according to the scant records that were available, participated in many businesses from large overseas corporations to small import companies, and in industries as varied as tennis shoe manufacturing in Taiwan to convalescent facilities in Michigan; all while never depositing a significant amount in any Canadian bank.

He had never allowed himself to be photographed, although many attempts had been made. He had never appeared publicly and, no one could recall him having ever left the property.

He was, by definition, a hermit. And this carefully crafted impression of his innocuous lifestyle deliberately lacked controversy and therefore held little fascination for the media, who now simply left him alone.

Reality, however was much more interesting. The huge antique home that John Rockefeller had built for himself more than a century before, had become a palace. It lacked no amenity, nor was any cost spared in its construction. Once simple in its furnishings, the current resident had spent millions trading on the black market to acquire rare art which was smuggled into Canada and now adorned each of the twenty-seven rooms. One rear wing of the home had been equipped as a state of the art medical facility, and served as support for the doctors who were flown in as necessary from around the world to attend to Loring's various health needs, the visits becoming more frequent as he advanced into his eighties.

Harris Loring commanded a full time staff of thirty-seven, most illegal aliens from the Pacific rim and South America, many non English speaking, and all with a reason not to be found. It was part of the deal; safe haven in return for secrecy. Money for silence. Death for betrayal. His power was absolute.

While the press portrayed him as a miserable, lonely miser, he was, in truth, anything but. He had traveled extensively, usually to Europe, sometimes to Asia, always by private jet, varying his point of departure and often his passport as well.

His trips became less frequent, though as his body, once strong, had gradually become frail. His legs could no longer support his weight, and their failings caused him to spend most of his time now, at eighty-six, in a wheel chair. His arms, though, with the constant pushing on the wheels, remained strong. His wide shoulders remained upright, his posture square, his upper body significant while the lower wasted away.

It was from his wheelchair that he had been watching earlier, from less than eleven hundred yards away, when the white float plane had come to life, its engine echoing across the still water, moving slowly away from the dock at the lodge, eventually roaring skyward, and disappearing. He knew where it was going. He knew who was there, and what was going on at the Naganosh Lodge.

To Harris Loring none of it was a mystery.

"He wants to be here, Mio." Angelo informed his father, "He says he wants to see for himself." He could see that he had interrupted the old man's cribbage game.

Vincenzo Domati paused. He laid his cards face down on the table and wheezed, "I see," followed by a half cough.

Frank Doran, increasingly nervous at the prospect, crossed the wide porch to where the men sat, near the door of the great hall. "Vincenzo, is that a good idea?" he asked, "It seems to me that we're just asking for more trouble." He puffed on his cigar in short spurts, causing it to glow bright orange before he sucked in the hot smoke. "I don't like it." What he wanted to say was that he didn't like the whole idea of confronting Russel at all; that he'd rather be comfortably in South America, but Don Domati had decided otherwise, and that was that. Frank released the smoke, blowing it through the screen, outside where it rose in the still warm air into the pine trees overhead.

The old man coughed briefly, "Franky, you should relax. I'll take care of this. You don't worry," he instructed. "Angel, if the old bastard wants to come, he can...but you keep him back there." He pointed to a pair of doors at the far side of the immense hall, just beyond one of the huge stone fireplaces. It was a large commercial kitchen, although it hadn't been used for that purpose in years. "And Nino, stay by the door, in there with him...until this is over with."

"Okay, Papa."

"Franky, I want you and Angelo here to stay with me. When Miguel calls, Nino, you can go to the house and bring him back. But no one else. You make sure they stay over there 'til we're gone."

"Yes, Papa," Domati's obese son answered.

Frank Doran continued to pace along the outside perimeter of the screened porch, while Angelo went inside to play pool. Domati calmly returned to his card game. This would be it, he thought. The last connection between the family and Hoffa would be erased. He had planned it all. Now, there was only the wait.

Frank Doran was uneasy with the upcoming confrontation. "Why bring Russel here?" he asked, "Why not just kill him and take the damn finger? I'll know if it's the one. If it isn't, we still have the girl."

Domati didn't answer. There would be no reasonable explanation for why it was necessary. But Frank was there. That's what he wanted. And he wanted Russel there with him. He went over the details in his head. Miguel, the pilot, was to dock the plane in Thornbury, go to Captain Hanscomb's and call when John Russel showed up. There was no question as to whether the man could be trusted. He could be. He had lived on the property for almost fifteen years. He was theirs. After the call, he would bring the finger and Russel back.

They waited for most of the day. It wasn't until almost three in the afternoon when the cell phone rang. Angelo answered. A few minutes later, he returned to the porch. "He's there."

With no hesitation Domati replied, "Okay. Do it."

Angelo flipped open the portable telephone as he walked back inside. He pushed a series of buttons and held it to his ear as it sent out the signal.

The old black desk phone jiggled the bottles on the bar next to it as it rang. John didn't even hear it. He was barraged instead by Merle Haggard blasting him from behind, across the black and red linoleum dance floor, from the jukebox on the other side of the room. It was the fourth time he had heard 'Okie from Muskokie' since he got there. But if it weren't for the music, he might not have found the place at all, hidden as well as it was behind the buildings. It was near the marina as he'd been told, in fact, in was *in* the marina, tucked between storefronts in a block long brick facade that faced Front Street. The only entrance, however, was in the rear, on the water side, from the boardwalk that stretched along the waterfront.

Thornbury's small harbor extended out from Captain Hanscomb's front door. It was bordered by a main wooden dock, about twenty feet wide on the left, and by a grassy point, contained by a rusted steel breakwater on the right. On the water side of the large dock was a chest high steel seawall and both pushed outward about two hundred yards before making an abrupt right to form the outer wall of the harbor. The closest point was directly across from the end of the landscaped point on the other side, creating the entrance. It was marked with red and green wooden markers nailed to pilings on either side. Similarly marked pilings protruded from the water every five or six hundred yards into the bay to mark the channel. Several fingers of smaller wooden docks lay in between. From where John was sitting, as far away from the door as possible, he could see, faintly, through the dark tinted front window, masts of sailboats rocking back and forth, appearing alternately on one side, then the other, of the red neon sign which hung from twine in the window's center and said simply, 'BEER'.

Captain Hanscomb's was a dump. It was dark. It smelled. There was no carpeting on the floor, only linoleum tile, dull and worn with pieces missing. In the center of the available floor space, Formica-topped tables had been placed hap-hazardly, each surrounded with chrome-framed dinette chairs of different colors and in various states of disrepair. There were booths along the wall, opposite the bar, with seating that could only be described as brown 'leatherette'. Each had been patched to varying degrees with duct tape. The walls were paneled with pine. At the front, near the only window, was a dart board. The wall around it had been badly damaged by errant shots which had accumulated over the years to form a dull textured background of a thousand holes. Everything else in the room had been provided by distillers and brewers as promotional items, most, judging from the worn appearance, had been there for some time.

Directly across from John, under the faded Carling Black Label poster, the phone continued to ring. The bartender, a slight man in his fifties, made no particular effort to answer it, preferring instead to continue a conversation with the couple, ten years his senior, at the far end of the bar. Finally, after what seemed forever, he shuffled back to John's end and picked it up. John managed to catch his eye and signaled him to bring another beer. The first had gone down easily.

The man poured while talking, looking around at each of the customers, including John, as he did.

Aside from the couple, there was only one other person in the bar; a small, muscular man with dark, longish hair, who was seated in one of the dilapidated booths facing the front door, away from Russel. He was the one, John had noticed, who had been feeding coins into the jukebox, causing the annoying stream of sound. He was there when John arrived almost fifteen minutes earlier, sitting alone, nursing a beer. He did get up once. John had seen his reflection in the filthy bar mirror as he passed behind him, made a brief call from the pay phone in the dark hallway between the men's and ladie's rooms, and returned to his seat. No one else had come in or left.

John watched as the bartender eased in his direction. "It's for you," he said, handing the receiver to Russel. John waited until the man had returned to his conversation at the far end of the room before he spoke. He pushed his finger into his right ear to hear over the music.

"Hello." John answered quietly.

The voice was the same as before, when he had called from the truck stop, "Go to the men's room. Go in the stall...and wait." The phone went dead.

"Hello? Hello?" He lowered the receiver, "Shit."

John left the phone on the bar, pounded the last of his beer, and got up. He was dizzy momentarily, but quickly came around. He reached down and grabbed his duffel bag from the rail near the floor and started for the restroom. He took a deep breath. This was it.

The stiff springed hinges slammed the door closed, almost hitting him as he entered. His nostrils immediately filled with the combined scent of stale urine and toilet disinfectant cakes. He looked around at the men's room. As he expected, it was as dirty as the rest of the place. The walls above the beige ceramic tile were painted seafoam green and covered as high as a man could reach with graffiti. The floor was rough plywood, as if it was being redone, though the stains indicated that it had been this way for some time. There was a trough urinal along the wall to his left, next to the door, offering a full view of one's privates to people in the hall. Directly across from it, a single stall, separated by a partial wall of deep stained wood. Next to it, the cracked porcelain sink under a high window, which was open outward from the bottom permitting an occasional whiff of fresh air to enter the tiny room.

The plywood creaked under him, as John entered the stall and closed the swinging door. He put his duffel on top of the toilet tank to keep it away from whatever may be living in the wood below and waited.

He could hear Merle Haggard singing again, loud, even from the other room. He unzipped the top of the bag and checked to make certain the baggie with the finger was there. Satisfied that it was, he closed the duffel.

He'd been in the bathroom less than a minute when the door swung open again. After it slammed, he heard a man's voice. It had a trace of accent, French, or possibly Spanish. "John Russel?"

"Yeah," he answered.

"Stay there. Pass the bag out under the door." The voice said. "C'mon. Hurry it up."

John did as he was asked. He heard the man rummaging through the luggage before he heard him zip it closed.

"Okay. Now stay in there, with your back to the door. Put your hands on the wall above the toilette. Hurry."

John leaned forward his arms outstretched, his hands flat against the filthy yellow tile. The door to the stall opened and almost immediately the stranger began to pat his hands against John's body, beginning first with the area around his chest and under his arms, to his back, and finally to his ankles, surveying every bit of him along the way for weapons and microphones.

Apparently, convinced that John was unarmed, the man went on. "Outside, at the end of the main dock, there is a white seaplane, my plane." John started to turn around to see who was talking. "Stay where you are. I am taking this bag with me. To the plane. You will wait here, at the bar for exactly five minutes. Then you will walk to the plane and we will leave. You don't show, I'm not waiting. Got it?"

John nodded.

A second later, the springs tightened, slamming the door, and the man was gone.

John felt the tension lesson with the man's departure, but he knew he couldn't afford to let down. He wasn't about to give the finger to a stranger and let him walk away with it. He would pause only long enough for the man to leave and then he would follow. The plane could be bullshit for all John knew. He couldn't let the man out of his sight.

John hurried out of the bathroom, coming out just in time to get his first good look at the man, the Merle Haggard freak with the long dark hair. John walked past the bar to the front window and watched as the man walked down the long dock with John's duffel. At the end of the breakwall, there was a float plane. John kept watching. The man continued along the dock. At the corner he turned right, toward the aircraft. He kept going to the end, where he jumped down onto the pontoon, opened the door to the cockpit, and tossed the duffel inside.

"'Nother beer?" The bartender called to John, fearing he would escape without paying.

"Oh. No, thanks." John reached into his tennis shoe and produced a damp wad of bills. He peeled off a Canadian twenty and threw it on the bar. The couple a few feet away paid no attention to him. The bartender nodded without smiling. John turned back to the window and looked both ways. The boardwalk was pretty much empty. A lone fisherman sat stoically at its edge, his line dangling motionless in the water. A woman passed quickly with a bag of groceries and turned onto the main dock, heading for her boat.

John brushed his hair from his forehead, took a deep breath, and pushed the heavy wooden door open. The harbor air was fresh and warm the sun felt good on his face, a pleasant relief from the cavern of the bar. The collection of stale smells gave way to pine, the jukebox to halyards, banging on the metal masts of sailboats. And another sound; the sound of the airplane's engine.

He turned left, running on the boardwalk, heading for the dock. He was squinting, waiting for his pupils to adjust to the onslaught of light. He hadn't gotten ten yards from Captain Hanscomb's front door when he realized that there was a silhouette of a man turning the corner at the end of the row of buildings.

"Hey, Russel," the silhouette said, "I want to talk to you."

The uniform. The hat. The deputy. Damn.

John spun around and ran back to the bar.

"Hey!" The deputy yelled, chasing after him. "Hey, c'mere!"

John bolted back into the depressing tavern to the astonishment of the bartender, who nearly fell over, tripping over the rubber mesh mats behind the bar as he retreated from the oncoming maniac. The older couple, to John's right, in the corner where the bar met the wall, were so comatose with whiskey that they didn't even notice his return.

The door shut behind him and he paused briefly, trying to figure out what to do next. Then the breeze again, and the light from outside. A figure behind him.

"Hey. Stop. Right there."

Not likely. The engine revved louder in the harbor. Russel grabbed the top of the nearest empty stool and hurled it to the floor between him and the man at the front door. He did the same with the next and the next, picking up speed as he did, heading for the bathroom, blasting through the stiff swinging door. He leapt onto the edge of the sink, reached up to the top of the open window and pulled with all of his strength. His fingers filled with pain as the rough metal frame dug into them, but he kept pulling, harder. He heard the door opening behind him and the cop yelling for him to get down as the long guide on the side gave way and the window collapsed outward under the weight of his body. He felt a hand on his ankle. He began to kick wildly, landing a lucky hit on the young officer's chin. The grip released his leg and he fell more than eight feet, tumbling with legs launched over his head in an awkward open somersault to the sidewalk below. First on his feet momentarily then, as the knees buckled, over on all fours, his hands slamming onto the concrete.

A woman, who had been walking with her husband and young son, screamed as John landed in front of her, grabbing her child and backing away into the circle of other, equally stunned, pedestrians.

The deputy appeared at the opening over the badly bent window, "Stop him!" he yelled, but nobody dared.

John ran past storefronts, dodging people as he went, rushing for the end of this long row of brick buildings. He came to the last one and made a wide turn toward the harbor. He was running at full speed when the deputy appeared in front of him, stationary with his gun drawn.

"Stop, dammit!" he ordered.

But John couldn't, even if had wanted to, which he didn't. While the timid crowd peered around the corner behind him, he slammed with the full force of his inertia into the deputy, sending the pistol flying thirty feet into the shallow water at the edge of the boardwalk and the man to his back. Down the dock, his hair, a dry heap of curls blowing backward as he ran. His navy sweatpants flapped in the passing wind and the city of Toronto, painted on the back of his tee shirt contorted as he pumped his arms for extra speed. Onlookers, curious of the repetitive pounding of John's tennis shoes on the boards, poked out of small souvenir shops along the heavy wooden pier to see what was causing the rumbling.

Even louder, the sound of an engine. The plane. He looked to his right as he neared the far corner of the first dock. He saw the sputter of blue smoke from the exhaust manifold on the side of the white seaplane. He turned, still at full speed, his breath thin and heart squeezing out its best energy. The plane was beginning to drift away from the pilings. Faster. He could hear the much younger deputy gaining from behind, screaming at him to stop. Sirens. Shit.

The huge propeller began to turn slowly. The plane was six feet from the end of the dock, still facing toward the shore, but beginning to turn around, to the channel, to the open bay.

John could almost feel the deputy breathing on him from behind. He was still twenty feet from the end of the dock and almost thirty now from the rear tip of the plane's right pontoon. With a final burst of everything he had, he kept going. Five feet, then four, then, like an Olympic long jumper over the edge.

For a moment all the sound stopped and motion slowed; the screaming and the engine, the sirens and the wind, silent. His arms flailing in wide silent circles at each side of his body, his legs running against nothing as he flew over the clear water. He could see fish, and rocks under him, distorted in the ripples. And he wondered as one can only do in the split second of crisis. If he would ever see Shelby again.

"Ahhhhh!" he screamed, loud at first, then garbled as every pore in his body was jolted by the freezing water. He sank completely under before pushing his way up to the surface.

John shook the moisture from his eyes. The plane was moving, pulling away. He started to swim, kicking as hard as he could with the heavy running shoes. The soaked clothing resisted, but he was making progress. He could hear the deputy on the dock over him still yelling for him to stop. The sirens stopped, the sound replaced by the airplane engine. The wind from the prop blew him back as he fought to gain position on the escaping pontoon. Then, with one final extension of his arm, he had it. He managed to get his other hand on the slippery metal and, with both, to pull himself up onto it. His right leg dangled into the water as he slid further toward the right hand door of the cockpit.

The pilot pushed the throttle forward and the wind blew harder at John's wet clothes as he pulled himself to his knees. He supported himself with a tight grip on the wing stantion with his right hand, moving his left to the handle of the door. The plane began to bounce as the waves and speed increased, nearly throwing him off. John yanked the handle and the latch released. The pilot pushed the throttle more as John forced the door open against the prop wash and fell into the plane, his chest resting on the seat.

"Jesus. You couldn't wait thirty seconds?" He said, gasping, pulling himself the rest of the way inside, just as the rough bouncing stopped and they were airborne. He turned, upright in the seat and put on the belt that hung at his side. Behind him, his Montreal Canadien's duffel bag, and, in it, the finger.

The dark-haired pilot steered the plane upward, and John had all he could do to suppress the temptation to strangle the bastard, despite the obvious consequences. But as John sat shivering in the waterlogged clothing, he could only glare at the man across the cockpit.

The plane ascended over the lake, heading north, following the shoreline, flying low, dipping occasionally, sometimes violently like a roller-coaster, when it hit sudden gusts of wind. After a few minutes, the pilot turned to John, smiling.

"Ya know, pal, for a minute there," he paused, "I didn't think you were gonna make it."

44

"Here he comes," Frank Doran announced from the porch.

Vincenzo Domati, who had been inside the main room of the lodge, shuffled out. He was dressed in a tailored double breasted suit. He could see Miguel's white float plane circling over Lake Naganosh, preparing to land. "That's good Franky. That's good." He turned around, slowly on the porch and Doran took his arm lightly to help him back over the transom. Inside, the old man waved to his son, Angelo, who immediately rushed across the room to relieve Doran, and to help his father into a large leather chair at the far side of the sparsely furnished hall. Domati sat, facing the front door. Frank returned to the screened porch.

A breeze had come up over the lake and chilled the air slightly, though it remained in the sixties. "Angel, would you please light the fire?" Domati asked.

"Yes, Mio," his son dutifully responded. Soon, the logs were ablaze. He grabbed another and tossed it on for good measure, before replacing the hinged steel screen. It began to crackle and sputter until the bark ignited in a bright flash of orange.

Domati signaled Angelo to come closer, coughing weakly at the same time. "Angel, come here." When he did, his father went over the details of the plan. "I want you to stay beside me, no matter what."

"Okay, Papa."

"When Russel is here, make him stand there in the middle of the room, so I can see all around him. And you watch his eyes, like I taught you. If he has a weapon, he will look at where it is. Watch his body. He is an amateur. If he is wired, and somehow we miss it, he will touch himself where it is. You watch. Call Franky."

Angelo did as instructed and Frank Doran soon arrived trailing a puff of smoke, standing directly in front of the don, chewing on his Cuban cigar.

"Franky, this is it. This is the last thing. Do this. Then you go to South America." Doran nodded. The old man coughed more violently, pulling his handkerchief out of the top pocket of his suit, to expel the phlegm. "You will be there, in the middle, where I can see everything. Between me and him. Now go and wait for him at the dock."

Doran chewed down hard on the butt, gnawing at it, his nerves growing prickly, he rocked almost imperceptibly from the ball of one foot to the ball of the other. He was about to leave when he heard the sound of voices, echoed from the hallway behind him, on the far side of the blazing fireplace. He heard rhythmic squeaking, the sound of bearings needing oil; the sound of Harris Loring's wheelchair as it was pushed closer by Nino Domati, who waddled behind.

"What about...him?" Doran was uncomfortable asking, and hoped Domati would not think that he was overly curious. But he was becoming increasingly fearful. "I don't like him being here, Vincenzo. Not with Russel coming. You know that."

The man was hauntingly silent for what, to Frank, seemed a long interval, before he started to shake slightly around the edges. It looked, at first, like a convulsion. Frank thought Domati might be having a stroke, until he realized the old man was beginning to laugh. "Oh, Franky," he said, half coughing, "What am I supposed to tell him? That he can't be here? I tried, Franky, I tried.

But this is what he wants. What can I say?" The laughter reduced to a deep cough and the handkerchief came out again. He gathered himself, replacing the wet hanky, then continued more seriously, "I know what you're saying, Franky. Nino will keep him hidden in the back, in the kitchen. It'll be okay."

Almost as his father said it, Nino appeared momentarily in the far corner, where the hallway opened into the main room. He was panting, the short walk from the mansion next door too much for the desperately out of shape, middle-aged man. He was pushing Harris Loring ahead of him in a wheelchair; using it to support himself as he walked. He turned an immediate right, saying nothing to the others, pushing Loring through one of two oversized swinging doors that led to the kitchen. Frank heard the squeaking wheelchair slow, and stop. He chewed down on the soggy tobacco. "I still don't like it. Not at all."

Ignoring Doran's comment, Domati went on, "Franky, go on. Wait outside for the plane to land. You'll bring him in. Miguel should stay with the plane. Go," he ordered, calling after him, "And stop worrying." His voice lowered as Frank disappeared, "You'll be out of this soon enough."

Frank was just as happy to get out of there, anyway. The fire was heating the room to an uncomfortable level. What the hell did the old man need with a fire in August? As the logs crackled behind him, Doran made his way to the porch, out, and down the half dozen steps to the grass. He reached into his shirt pocket, found the last of his De Christo Capo cigars, bit the end and lit it. The blue smoke lifted briefly in the air, then dissipated. He drew it in, inhaling a little, and watched the lake. He could hear the engine of Miguel's seaplane approaching. In a few minutes, it would be landing.

Inside, Don Domati continued his preparations, waiting for Doran to leave, before speaking. "Angelo, get me the gun." While he waited, he slipped a thin leather dress glove over his right hand.

Angelo left the room, returning moments later with a package, a small brown paper bag. He reached inside and produced a standard issue, thirty-eight caliber, FBI service revolver, agent Morse's weapon, wrapped in cellophane. Carefully, he handed it to his father.

The eighty-six year old, stern and resolute, removed the wrapper and checked the weapon thoroughly, before he slipped it, as he had done hundreds of times before, into the right front pocket of his suit pants. From this location, seated as he was, he could keep his gloved hand in his pocket and, with the gun's handle resting on the seat of the chair, he could fire easily, while barely moving. "Make sure that your brother stays in the kitchen. Make sure they are quiet. I don't want Russel to know they're in there. Tell Nino to stay out of the food, if he can, and pay attention to what's going on."

"I understand Papa Mio."

"Good."

The fire had reduced to a steady burn with sections of the first small logs now glowing as hot embers. Domati sat and waited, his son by his side, standing as he had been ordered, leaning on the tan leather chair. It was one of only two in the room, the only other seating, two excessively long sofas, each positioned in front of a fireplace at either end of the great hall. Directly in the middle of the back wall was the bar, dark oak, dented and dull. Several stools surrounded it. Twenty feet away, was the antique billiard table, floating, isolated in the center of the room. Above, connecting the stone walls, massive beams reached the entire distance from front to rear, forming a row of triangles, six feet apart, and extending from the chimney on one end to the chimney on the other. The floor was hard and polished wood, interrupted only rarely by hand-made wool rugs of varying sizes and colors. The room was more than a hundred feet long and nearly forty wide dwarfing the two men as they waited for John Russel to arrive.

The engine outside whined louder, coming close over the trees. Frank Doran watched the white plane as it first skimmed the tops of the waves before settling into the water itself and landing against the onshore wind. He walked over the deep lawn, toward the dock, which jutted straight out into the lake. The pavilion that was built on top of it years before and once used as a dance hall, had been modified; the floor removed, to create a monstrous hangar for seaplanes and boats, so they could not be detected from the air. Doran arrived at the edge of the pier as Miguel turned his plane around in the middle of Lake Naganosh and headed for the pavilion.

He was still going fairly fast and the bumpy water bounced John Russel around in his seat as the plane drew closer to the shore. When they were about a hundred yards from the side of the long brown building, the side lifted up mechanically, like a garage door. There was a man standing inside, operating the controls, but John was too far away and was being jostled too violently to make out who it was.

When they were only twenty feet from the dark opening, Miguel cut the engine, and the plane drifted the remainder of the way into the cavernous darkness. It was then that John recognized Frank Doran, standing at the door, puffing, as always, on his illegal cigar. Doran pushed a large button on the wall and the door began to close behind the plane. It was dark inside, the only light coming from a row of small windows that encircled the building near the top. Others, larger ones, had been boarded up, many years before. Miguel opened the airplane's door and jumped down onto the pontoon on the left side of the plane. He stretched to reach a line that was tied permanently to a piling on the main dock that circled the interior. It had been draped over a low floating dock that protruded from the left side of the building. Miguel yanked it hard and secured it to a cleat near the rear of the float. The rope tightened causing the plane to swing around to the left, and stop four feet short of the side wall, bobbing slightly and rocking from side to side in the water. There was another low dock, John noticed, on the right side, his side, of the plane. He was tempted to get out, but decided instead, to wait. His heart rate was rising, but he dared not make a move. The flight had been thankfully uneventful and he was so relieved to have made it onboard, that his entire body let down and, exhausted, he had actually drifted to sleep briefly en route. But now, he was wide awake and almost as excited as he was afraid; hopeful that Shelby would be here; that she was still alive as Domati had promised.

Soon he felt a rush of fresh, cool air as his door was opened from the outside and there, glaring in at him was Frank Doran. A puff of blue preceded his comment. "Well, Mr. Russel. Here we are," he said quietly, then ordered John to get out of the plane. John reached behind the seat to grab the duffel bag, but Doran stopped him.

"I'll get that. You just get out and wait over there." Doran pointed to the corner of the small dock, where steps led upward to the perimeter dock on a higher level. He reached into the area behind the seat in the cockpit and pulled the bag out. "C'mon. Let's go." Doran indicated with a nod of his head that John should head up the stairs. "C'mon." He followed behind, giving instructions to Miguel. "You wait in here. Make sure you're ready to go. All right?"

"I'll be ready," the pilot answered, his accent still heavy with Spanish.

Russel reached the top of the stairs and walked, with Doran close behind him, to a door at the shore side of the building. He opened it and emerged from the darkness into the bright sun and the northern air. Aside from the random squish, his footsteps made no sound, muffled as they were by the soggy tennis shoes. He could hear Frank's loafers behind him though, banging on the planks. When he stepped onto the grass at the end of the dock, Doran stopped him.

"Hold it. Right there."

John did as he was told. He turned around to see what the murderer was up to. Doran bent down and unzipped the duffel, patting around inside with his hand. He glanced up at John as he pulled out the baggie containing the rotten remains of Bobby Merrimac Wilson's severed fingertip. He held it up, close to his face, to take a better look. John could see, even from a distance, that the ice had melted again and that it had now turned an ominous dark green. Doran turned away, disgusted. "What else do you have in here, Russel?"

Without waiting for an answer he knelt again, tossed the baggie on the lawn, and resumed his search, turning the duffel upside down and shaking it.

John watched as his wet clothing fell to the ground at Doran's feet. He threw the bag to the side, bit down on the tobacco and motioned to a nearby tree. "Now get your ass up against that tree. Lean forward, hands against it. Spread your legs."

Doran patted him from the top of his body down to his legs, searching for a weapon or listening device. Satisfied there was none, Doran spun John around, facing him. He reached into the pocket of his slacks and produced a small, flat tin about three by five inches in dimension. He opened it, revealing a soft milky colored substance. "Give me your hand." John was puzzled, but obeyed. He watched as Doran pushed the tip of each of John's fingers into the paraffin, making a clear impression of his prints, a process the FBI man had used many times to create various identities. One day, perhaps soon, he might need to be John Russel.

He closed the container and put it away. "C'mon. They're waiting inside." John walked slowly through the soft grass toward the screened porch and the front door of the lodge. Doran picked up the baggie and followed close behind. John breathed in deeply, trying to be calm, but he was shaking. He had no gun, no way to defend himself. If Domati wanted to kill him, he certainly would, especially after getting what he wanted. But he had plenty of opportunities and hadn't. And why bring him here? Domati already had the duffel bag on the plane. He sensed that Vincenzo Domati did nothing without a reason, but he had no idea what it could be.

John was becoming physically ill at the thought of dying; a feeling enhanced when he imagined that Shelby would also be killed. A man of his word, Domati had said. But Jesus, these people are killers. What could their word be worth?

John felt heaving deep in his gut, increasing in intensity until he could not keep it from surfacing. He stopped and bent over thinking he was going to vomit. He hung his head low, with his hands on his knees but nothing came out. Doran looked on, saying nothing, waiting. It was the same feeling, John imagined, that the condemned must experience as they take the long final walk. Doran had seen it before.

After a few seconds, John stood up, breathing in the freshness and, at least momentarily, felt somewhat better. He could see to his left several of the lodge's many cabins, each situated to afford maximum privacy in the shade of tall pine trees. Maybe that was where they were keeping his wife. On the shore to his right, he could just make out the far corner of the mansion, the rest hidden from view by dense forest. The area in front of the main lodge was park-like and pristine. On any other day, in would be beautiful.

He turned to look out over the water, the sun glistening in each small blue wave, like it would be now at Duck Lake, his own lake. He breathed again, his nostrils filling with the scent of the foliage, and closed his eyes, for the tiniest moment, but long enough to see every bit of his life, before turning back to the old wooden lodge and offering his surrender to the inevitable.

Solemnly, he ascended the four wide wooden steps to the screen door, opened it and went inside. When he saw the Domatis, Angelo and Don Vincenzo, in the room ahead, he stopped, unable to move again until Doran pushed him. "Let's go."

The huge hall was silent, except for the slushy suction sound of John's shoes echoing around the hard room, mixing with Doran's more substantial steps bouncing in between; two rhythms blending into one, then stopping all together with John facing the old man in the chair, just ten feet away.

Neither Angelo nor Doran spoke, deferring to the don, who cleared his throat, sputtered, coughing slightly, then began in a low almost inaudible tone. "Mr. Russel, thank you for coming. I know it wasn't easy to get here. Did you bring it?"

John nodded. Speech was impossible. He surveyed the room, instinctively looking for exits, for places to run.

"Let me see it."

Frank Doran interrupted, "I have it here, Vincenzo." He left John and handed the baggie to the old man, waiting by the chair for his response.

Domati held it up, even with his chin, looking at the contents. "So, this is what we will all risk our lives for..." he shook his head, "It's amazing to me..." He squeezed the bottom of the clear plastic bag, forcing the finger to turn and move up toward the top. He could see the flesh, now a collection of shades of yellow and green, and the murky liquid that surrounded it, some water from the ice and some from the finger itself. "Here, Franky. Check it out." He handed the thing back to Doran who walked to the back of the room, to the bar, where he reached into his pocket and took something out; something small, wrapped in plastic. The don spoke to John.

"I must first tell you that your wife is okay, Mr. Russel and that, if that really is what it's supposed to be, we will all be done with this soon."

"Where is she?" John asked, looking around the room again.

"She is not here, Mr. Russel. She is safe." He sat up, turning to look over his shoulder at Frank Doran who was busy at the bar. "Franky, what do you think?"

John could see that Doran had unwrapped the object, and laid it on the surface of the bar. It was what was left, half approximately, of a small bone. He had opened the baggie, too, and its contents poured out on the dull dark wood. A horrible, putrid scent rose from the area, so strong that even John could detect it from where he stood across the room. Doran seemed unfazed and continued with his work, comparing the saw marks where the finger had been amputated with the marks on the half bone, the bone he had stolen from the table at the hospital in Northport, while Dr. Hoffman was busy reassembling the rest of Bobby Merrimac Wilson's skeleton. Frank had saved it for this day, so he could be absolutely certain that the finger was legitimate; that it matched.

It seemed a long time had passed before Doran responded. "Yeah. That's it."

"Give it to Angel," Domati ordered before beginning his lecture to John. "You see, all of the death...everything...could have been avoided if your father would have just done what he was supposed to do. Do you see that? Why would he do this? The result is the same. What could he have hoped to prove?"

Domati didn't expect John to answer. So he stood silent, watching Doran hand over the disgusting finger to Domati's son, and return to the middle of the room, next to John. He could see a pistol tucked into Doran's pants and wondered if maybe he could grab it, but he decided it was too risky.

Angelo looked at the rotting body part, and, holding it at arm's length, left his father's side, and walked across the worn wool rug to the fireplace. The old man watched him move the screen aside and, without hesitation, drop the only remaining evidence of the conspiracy into the glowing coals.

The finger sputtered and crackled. It smoked as the remaining skin burned away, and steamed as the liquids inside boiled, bubbling out of it. John watched too, stunned and horrified. Doran smiled, still puffing on his cigar, happy to be finally rid of the proof. "Well, Russel...I guess that's it..." He was anxious to get on with his own departure.

John felt Doran's hand close around his bicep. Jesus. He had his orders, too. Jesus. But Domati interrupted.

"Franky," Domati said seriously, "Wait."

Doran released John's arm. He had a puzzled look on his face. Angelo was back at his father's side, staring at Doran. "What's going on, Vincenzo?" The old man sat silently. "Angel?" But he too said nothing.

"Franky, I hope you understand. This is why you are here. Why Russel is here. You are a smart man. You have to see. You are the only link. Without you there is no connection..."

"But, Vincenzo, I..." Frank Doran began to back away from Domati. John edged backwards even more.

"You are the last one who was there. I'm sorry Franky."

The explosion of the pistol ripped through Domati's gabardine slacks. The first bullet hit Doran's right arm, spinning him toward John with his back to Domati. He yelled with pain, but the sound was cut short as Domati fired again and once more after that. The second bullet entered Doran's right shoulder just under the blade and exited in a burst of blood from his chest. John, in shock could not move except to shield his eyes from the liquid. He noticed as he did that Frank Doran was staring directly at him, his eyes shiny and wide. Doran's last cigar had fallen halfway out of his mouth, but was stuck, glued by saliva, to his lower lip. Blood was beginning to fill his mouth and spill down the brown leaf as he fell onto John. Try for his gun. Grab it. But it was impossible to wrench it from the trained man's instinctive grip. The third shot tore into the back of Doran's skull and shattered the top of his forehead into small fragments that scattered everywhere, some landing on John, some vaulting across the expanse to the front door as Doran collapsed, sliding down John's leg to the floor.

John, even as terrified as he was, but clear in the moment, recognized this was it; the sliver of time when all decisions must be made. He jumped back, pulling his feet from under Doran's mutilated skull. There was no hope of getting the gun. He had fallen face down, crushing it under him. John lifted his eyes from the dead man and before he even knew what his own body was doing, leapt forward, toward the Domatis. Angelo, so stunned by this action, froze in place.

John flew through the air, arms outstretched, reaching. He dived for the chair and Domati, landing with his chest on the man's knees. He managed to wrap his hands around the gun and tear it loose from the Mafiosi, knocking him and the leather chair to the floor at the same time.

With the gun in hand, John scurried around behind Domati. He grabbed the old man around the neck with his left hand and held the pistol to his head with the other. Domati lay still, his feet propped up by the seat of the chair. Angelo started to lunge at John who was on the floor, on his knees looking up at the large Italian.

"Hold it. Stop right there!" John shouted, "Don't come any closer."

Abruptly, Angelo obliged, hovering over the two men.

Nino, who had heard the commotion, charged out of the kitchen, "What the hell is happening out here?" He was holding a sizable chunk of white bread in his hand which he dropped after seeing the situation with John and his father, and started to reach for his own weapon. But he wasn't fast enough. John turned around, facing him, pointing his own gun momentarily at him. "Stop!" John again pointed Karen Morse's thirty-eight at Vincenzo's head. Nino swallowed the last bite, and he too froze in place, leaving only the residual rolls of fat moving from his inertia. "Okay. Okay." He held his hands up in front of him.

"Take your left hand and get your gun. Drop it on the floor and kick it over here," John commanded, but Nino did nothing. "Now." Realizing he had no choice, he did as John asked.

John collected the firearm and stuffed it into the elastic waistband of his sweat pants. "Okay...now..." He was forcing himself to calm down, to reason. His hand was shaking. "Okay, Mr. Domati. Let's get up. C'mon. Let's get up off the floor."

John helped the old man to his feet as carefully as he could. It was not his intention to hurt anyone, but he still kept his arm firmly around the man's neck. "Now...where is she?" He asked. "Where is my wife?"

Domati said nothing. There was a noise from the kitchen. A squeak. "What's that? Who's in there?" Russel asked, still panting from fear and shock, his frustration growing, "Have you got her here?"

Finally, Domati spoke. "Now Mr. Russel, this is not going to get you anywhere," he said softly and slowly, "There is no reason to do anything stupid now. And, if you let me explain it to you, you'll see that there's nothing you can do at all. So please, let's just calm down."

John was adamant, "Not 'til I see what's in there. C'mon." John hauled Vincenzo Domati by the neck, dragging him across the floor, around Nino, closer to the kitchen door, while his sons watched, unable to help. When he was close enough, he kicked the door and it swung open. "Come out of there," he yelled at the opening. "Come out or I'll kill him. I swear to God." John couldn't believe those words had come from him. He had already shot a man once in his life, the guard at Michigan Scrap Metal, he knew he could do it again.

He heard the squeaking again, coming closer, and the voice. "Just take it easy, Russel, settle down." The tone was harsh. It was tough and American. East Coast. New York, maybe. He knew John by name.

While he was distracted, with his back turned, Nino tried to surprise John from behind, but his weight bent the flooring. John heard him and backed away in an arc, dragging Domati with him, until his back was against the wall next to the open door. "I told you to stay put. Now stop right there." John ordered, waving the pistol at him.

Nino lied, "Take it easy. I'm not doing anything."

The squeaking approached from the kitchen, growing louder.

"No." Domati tried to stop Loring from coming out.

"Oh Vinny, what the hell do I care now?" The gruff voice shot back and Harris Loring emerged in his wheel chair. John saw him at first, only from behind. His hair, what remained of it, was bright white and long, too long, John thought for a man his age. He caught his first glimpse of Doran's body, bleeding on the floor in front of him. "Oh, jeez, what a fuckin' mess, God." His legs were weak, but with the considerable strength that remained in his upper body, he spun his chair around to face John. "So you're the doctor's kid..." he said. There was a slight whistle as air flowed over loose dental work. The men stared at each other, each sizing the other up.

Who the hell was it? What did he have to do with this? How did he know John's father? One thing was sure. He was not afraid of John Russel.

"You don't know who the hell I am, do you?" The old man smiled, revealing the source of the strange noises, the false teeth, old and ill-fitting. He had strong eyes, but they were lost in the sagging flesh around them. "Hey, Vinny," he started to laugh, "He has no idea who the fuck he's talking to." The laughing stopped. "Look, Russel, put the gun down."

"I want my wife."

"What are you gonna do, kill us all? How do you think that's gonna get your wife back?" He wheeled his way over to the fireplace. "You got nothin'. Nothin'." He turned back to John. "You don't know these guys, Russel. Hurtin' Vincenzo Domati is gonna get her killed, that's what it's gonna do...and you right behind her."

"He's right, Russel." Angelo jumped in. He took a step closer to John.

Domati started to cough. The choking grip around him was too much.

The man in the wheelchair continued fearlessly, "Let him go. Keep the gun. Just let him sit down. Angelo, pick up that chair for your dad." Domati's eldest moved slowly, afraid to spook John. He righted the leather chair, positioning it next to the wheelchair. "Let him go, Mr. Russel."

John looked intently into the man's hard eyes. He was right. He couldn't win. They still had Shelby. He loosened his grip on Domati and the old man slipped slightly downward. Instantly, Nino raced to help him. John flinched but didn't fire. He watched, with his back to the wall, as Nino helped his father into the chair. Domati struggled for air, coughing, then sat back in the soft cushion, rubbing his neck. If anyone had tried such a thing forty years ago he would have broken their balls, but now he hadn't the strength.

"I have told you Mr. Russel, that I am a man of my word," Domati began. "You will have your wife back."

The man in the wheelchair was angry. He rolled up close to John and stopped less than three feet in front of him. He wrinkled his square forehead, scarred from a difficult early life, and raised his finger, pointing at John like a weapon, "You want your wife...you want your wife. You know something? I don't give a damn what you want. How's that?" The air whistled through his dentures. Even though the man was unarmed, his manner was threatening. John held the pistol to his side and listened as the ominous verbal attack continued. "If it weren't for your father...well, it's his fault...he was stupid..."

Domati tried to stop him, but it was too late, "No, Jim..." He caught himself.

"Fuck Vinny, what do we care? We lived, right?" The man shot back, still staring at Russel, "Go ahead, take a good look..."

John felt the uncontrollable waves come over him, rising from his feet. The wall supported him.

"Yeah. You're gettin' it. Your wife, humph. I lost everything...wife, family, my son...and you expect me to give a shit what happens to you? Well I don't. Your father was dumb and he got what he deserved. You're lucky this isn't up to me or you and your wife'd both be floating face down in the fucking Lake St. Clair..." The grisly old man spun again in his chair, this time rolling away until John stopped him.

He raised the gun, his hand devoid of fear, steady with rage. "Hold it...right there. Turn around." John waited.

The man stopped, then slowly turned, pulling at one of the wheels, until he and John were again facing each other. He was smiling. "Hey, Vinny," he whistled, "I think he knows who I am." Domati said nothing.

John walked away from the wall, closer to the man, pointing the gun at his face. Everything else in the room disappeared in his anger. He could only see the man in the chair. He moved even closer, inspecting every line of the man's face. He circled his chair, and John could see other deeper scars through the strands of white on the man's balding head. He came back in front of him and knelt down, the gun still aimed at the old man's head, and John Russel stopped, with the barrel touching the rough flesh between his eyebrows.

"It's you, isn't it?" John whispered, "I know who you are." He continued quietly, perfectly still, studying this foul mouthed ghoul. And he did know. He was staring into the eyes of Jimmy Hoffa.

It was he who had caused all of this. His idea that sucked his father into the darkness of their sick world, that got Uncle Henry killed, and Keenan, and his neighbor, John Holloway...and the list went on. John stood up straight, still pointing his pistol at Hoffa. He was strangely calm now, still and resolute. Whatever hatred he had for guns had passed. He could kill again. He thought of the others, his parents, and Shelby; all woven into this selfish man's plan. Maybe she was dead.

John trained the gun sight directly at Hoffa's nose. His finger closed on to the trigger. His lip pursed out, he breathed in deeply. The Domatis knew John was serious. They knew when a man would kill, when the fear was gone. And they watched, motionless, like statues.

Hoffa broke through the tension of this last moment, "Go ahead," he said, "What difference does it make?"

Domati, used the opening to speak, wheezing at John, "Wait, Russel. Think about it." This was the distraction that saved Hoffa's life.

It interrupted his concentration and John briefly looked over at the Mafiosi, listening.

"You will kill Jimmy Hoffa...and then we will kill you and your wife, no one will win. But it doesn't have to be that way. Look. Look at him lying there." He pointed to Doran's body, now surrounded in blood. "You killed him. That's why I brought you here; why I brought both of you here."

"What?" John didn't understand.

"You've got the gun. Look at it. Look at it closely. Do you recognize it?"

John didn't. He wouldn't know one from another.

"You don't, do you? It's the one you had. That you left in my car. And even if you weren't holding it now, your prints are the only ones on it. I would have left it here anyway." The old man began to chuckle, coughing as he did, "And you know what's funny, what makes me wanna laugh?...I'll tell you..." He started to break up completely, "Now, there are no more bullets in it..."

Hearing this, Angelo rushed toward John. John turned and without thinking, pointed it at his attacker. As Angelo froze in place, by reflex, he pulled the trigger. Nothing. Domati's son started at him again.

"Hold on, Angel," Domati instructed. "Like I keep telling you Russel, I am a man of my word, that is my strength. Now listen to me. You killed him. That's fine. Self defense. Nothing will happen to you. The finger is gone. You have no more proof of what we did twenty years ago. It's your word against...well it's just your word, Russel. And you can go ahead and tell the whole fucking world that you saw Jimmy Hoffa....alive, but no one is going to listen. They think you're some kinda nut, they'll crucify you. And you can't prove anything."

John was listening to Domati, the gun at his side, no longer aimed at Hoffa.

"We will go. Then you will have Shelby." It was the first time he had used her name and the sound of it shocked John.

"Angelo, bring the phone," Domati commanded. "Listen."

John took it and held it to his ear, "Hello."

There was nothing at first. Then, her voice, "Junior," she said, "I'm okay. I'm okay." The line went dead. John dropped the phone on the floor and it bounced noisily over the wood, coming to rest against the wall.

Domati went on, "You see, Mr Russel? She is fine," Domati reassured him before continuing. "It will look like Frank Doran did it all, everything; I will make sure *that* is the story that is told, that it is believed. We have people, powerful people, who will tell that story, you will see. If you are smart, you will never hear from us again. And we will never hear from you. I never wanted things to go this far. I have no wish to harm you or your lovely wife." Domati's tone became almost conciliatory, "I am sorry that you have been through this, but this is the end now. Good bye, Mr. Russel."

John stood, dumbfounded, the gun dangling at his side. Angelo Domati helped his father to his feet, and helped the don as he shuffled toward the front door. Nino waited until his brother and father were outside. When they were, he wheeled Hoffa out after them and lowered him, one step at a time to the grass. That done, he returned to the lodge.

John Russel was in shock. He collapsed into the overstuffed leather chair, still clutching the pistol. He watched as Nino pulled on black gloves and disappeared into the kitchen. When he came out, he had a piece of salami in one hand and a dish towel in the other. While he gnawed at the lunch meat, he wiped furiously, destroying any fingerprints they may have left in the room. He picked up the empty baggie and wiped the bar, the pool cues, the area around the doors and finally the chair where John was sitting, stupefied. Nino picked up the cell phone from the floor and tucked it under his substantial arm. He was careful, as he completed his rounds, not to step in the significant pool of blood that Frank Doran had created in the middle of the room. He went to the fireplace, threw the plastic bag and phone into the flames, and watched as they melted into distorted blobs eventually disintegrating, leaving behind only a stream of black smoke. After wiping the mantel, the fireplace screen, and the card table on the porch, he wiped his way outside and was gone.

Shelby was alive. The thought ricocheted through John's mind. When would he see her? Jesus. He looked at the dead man on the floor in front of him. Prick. The Mafia was amazing. They made things turn out the way they wanted. Domati was right. He was clean. He made sure of that, letting Doran do all the dirty work. They couldn't prove that he so much as whispered the name, let alone connect him to Jimmy Hoffa. There was a body; a body that had been positively identified, that the FBI dug up in John's lawn. How perfect was that? There were plenty of people to blame; his father, Swain, Doran, Baglia; everyone, except those who were really responsible, Domati and Hoffa himself. And, of course, there was John Russel.

He heard the sound of the sea plane, its engine surging to life. He heard it rev up faster, then grow faint as it lifted from the surface of the lake into the dusk. Then there was no sound left, but the soft crackle of burning logs and his own breathing.

The plane was less than two miles from the lodge and crossing through fifteen hundred feet, when Miguel pointed down at something below. Domati stretched to see out of his small window, behind the pilot. There on the shore, in full camouflage, the RCMP swat team was moving along the shore, toward the lodge, hugging the forest, diving for cover when they heard the float plane overhead. Hoffa was on the other side of the plane and couldn't see them.

Ten minutes later, Angelo looked out of the right window and saw two Royal Canadian Mounted Police helicopters traveling fast in the opposite direction, about a mile away and a thousand feet lower than the plane.

"Can they see us?" Nino asked from the seat farthest back, where Miguel had placed him for proper balance.

"No." Miguel assured him, but taking no chances, he pulled back on the stick to increase the angle of ascent. "Even if they did, they can't catch us. We'll be outta here before they can get a plane."

Soon they rose higher, each of the Domatis, heading home; Angelo to Miami, Nino and Don Vincenzo to Detroit; and Jimmy Hoffa, disappearing again, as would Harris Loring, forever.

John had no concept of time. He had no idea how long he had been sitting in the chair. He hadn't realized that his grip on the pistol had loosened and it had fallen into the crack of the smooth upholstery beside him, and now rested against the arm, where the powder from Domati's shot had blackened the hide, burning it from the discharge.

He had just been sitting, staring defocused into the space, eventually erasing the sight of Doran's body from his mind. The bastard got what he deserved, betrayed and murdered by people he trusted. Just as people who had placed trust in him had been ruthlessly eliminated.

Until now John's view of such violence, had been objective. He had seen death only on the news. He was isolated from it by the television, by the media. The things he had experienced happened only to others. They were to be topics of country club discussion, not shared experiences. And certainly never to be actually witnessed in person.

He felt his whole being dissolve into the comfortable chair. He was oddly relaxed. He believed that Domati would release Shelby, as he had promised. John had to smile at the concept; that he had more confidence in the integrity of a notorious mobster, than he did in Stanley Messing; someone who was sworn to protect him, but who, without a second thought, would have deliberately risked his life and Shelby's for his own gain. Maybe the Mafia should run the damn government. They'd certainly be a lot more effective. And we wouldn't need as many prisons, he thought, looking again at Doran bleeding on the floor.

Suddenly the silence was shattered by the deafening crash of glass as a uniformed man burst through the front window of the lodge, rolling several times across the room until he was even with John and leveling an automatic rifle at him. Then a second slam as the kitchen door swung around ripping away from its top hinge as it hit the sandstone wall. Another dull green camouflaged man appeared and trained a rifle on Russel. Six more raced through the screened porch and knelt into position, pointing weapons at John, waiting to fire. But amazingly, John, stunned, was unable to react or even move at all. Then, the thunderous roar, the helicopters landing out front.

A minute later, there was a voice at the door, and John turned as Garnetti, Karen Morse, and the Mountie, Sam Baylor entered, each with pistol drawn, sweeping the room aiming them everywhere, as they had been trained.

"Hold your fire, men. Hold fire." Baylor commanded, and the swat team eased their fingers from the triggers.

"John." The familiar female voice, Christine Ferrand rushed in behind the men, "John. You're all right. Thank God." She hurried across the floor ignoring Doran and threw her arms tight around John, bending to press her cheek to his, whispering, "Thank God."

John embraced her, smiling, "Hi, Chris."

"Ahh," she pulled back, half joking, "We've got to get you a shave." She was right, he was a mess. She walked over closer and looked at the body, "Doran."

John nodded. They would assume that he killed Frank Doran. Just as Domati said. Once again, the old man was right. What the actual truth was, didn't really matter. It never had. John had every justification.

By this time the FBI agents were hovering over him, Garnetti used a pen to pick up the pistol from beside John's leg, lifting it dangling upside down from the trigger guard, "Bag this, Forester, please."

The agent produced an evidence bag and held it open, and Garnetti dropped it in. "Well John, it's good that you're safe," he said.

"At ease, men," Baylor commanded and the sharpshooters broke from their positions, dropping the weapons to their sides. "Sergeant," he ordered one of them, "Search the grounds."

John could see Karen Morse leaning to take a closer look at the fire. She was poking at the logs with an iron tool, but, finding nothing, she returned it to its rack and turned around, looking at John.

"I'm sorry, Agent Morse, I didn't mean to…"

"It's all right, Mr. Russel. Don't worry about it."

"C'mon, John." Chris helped him to his feet. She wiped several small fragments of bone and tissue from his forehead with her thumb. "Let's get you home."

She walked with him to the door, and when they were on the porch beyond earshot of the others, she asked, "What really happened here, John?"

He wanted to tell her everything, but he couldn't bring himself to do it. He sloshed down the front steps, stopping on the lawn, and looked back at her, waiting on the porch for an answer. There he was, in the glow of the final sun of the August day, in his navy sweatpants and black shirt with the picture of Toronto on the back, one of only four people in the world, who knew exactly what happened to Jimmy Hoffa.

And all he could say was, "Nothing."

45

The FBI wanted to take him to Harper Hospital, at the Medical Center at Wayne State University, but there was no way John was going there. He'd been through enough already to last more than one lifetime. He didn't really want to go to any hospital, but Christine had talked him into it, insisting that his injuries be examined. He acquiesced and agreed to go to Cottage Hospital, near his home in Grosse Pointe. It was more like an exclusive hotel than a healthcare institution, and his private room allowed John to relax under the care of his own doctor. While he was there, though, there had been a parade of visitors, mostly close friends, and John was happy to be reminded of his much more normal life. The shrapnel wound in his calf had just about healed, and his array of cuts and contusions had been inspected and treated. All in all, the doctor said, he was in pretty good condition, considering. He had been given a pain killer, though, to help him relax.

The last person he saw, before passing out cold, was Christine Ferrand.

"John," he remembered her saying through the fog, "Messing wants to see you tomorrow, to debrief."

"Tell him to kiss my ass." John laughed. The drug was beginning to take effect.

"We'll talk later, John. You just rest."

"What about Shel? Have you heard anything?"

If she answered, he was asleep before he heard it. It was a wild visual ride, filled with images of Shelby and guns and planes; of tossing and spinning, and finally being shaken back into consciousness.

"John, John..."

It was a woman's soft voice. Christine. He worked his eyes open and saw her in the hazy light. Morning. He had been sleeping for hours.

"Chris?"

"John, wake up, they found her...Shelby, she's here."

He assumed that his dreams were continuing, "What?"

"Really, John. Wake up!"

There was a second figure, agent Morse, in his doorway and with her, another. He was awake now and beginning to focus. The soft, pink light of dawn cut in through his window, throwing shafts across the room. He could just make out the tone of the beautiful brown hair, highlighted against the wall. And her eyes. Hazel eyes.

She saw he was awake and she ran, nearly pushing Chris to the floor as she landed on his bed and grabbed John around the neck, squeezing hard and crying, "Junior. Junior," before collapsing on his chest, sobbing.

"It's okay, Shel. It's okay...Jesus, I love you...Thank God you're all right." John whispered, holding her as if he could squeeze her soul through his skin into his own. His heart pounded with hers, one against the other as she slid up to his face, her lips to his, and kissed him.

"I thought you were dead, Junior, I thought I'd never see you again..."

Christine backed away, into the hall, closing the door behind her. "How did you find her?" She asked Morse.

"We didn't. She just walked in off the street...to our office."

"What'd she say? Where was she?"

"She won't say anything. She won't discuss it."

Shelby lay next to John, on the bed, "What the hell happened? What happened to Doran? That pig...I'll rip his throat out..."

"Too late, Domati shot him."

"Domati?"

"Shhh, they think I did it."

"What?"

"I'll tell you about it later."

They were interrupted when Christine knocked and peeked in, "May I come in?"

Shelby Russel, always proper, instinctively sat up on the side of the bed, "Sure, Chris."

"I went by your house this morning and I got both of you some jeans and stuff. I hope you don't mind." She handed Shelby a small suitcase. "I thought you might want to change before we go."

John didn't like the sound of that. "...Go? Where?"

"We've got an appointment, at the MacNamera Building, with Messing."

John hesitated for a moment. He looked at his wife, worn and frazzled, but as beautiful as he could ever remember. And he couldn't convince himself, to expose her to any more of this insanity. He got up from the bed, and felt every injury again. He opened the suitcase, his hospital gown blowing open behind him, located a pair of pants and a golf shirt, and, without a word, vanished into the small bathroom in the corner of his room; a few minutes later he reemerged, dressed.

"Chris, can I borrow your car?"

Neither she nor Shelby knew what he was up to, but she agreed, "What's left of it." She held out the keys.

John was smiling broadly as he snagged them with one hand, while holding Shelby's tight with the other. "I promise, I'll be more careful this time. Where is it?"

"Right out front, John, but…"

"Thanks."

He had prayed for this moment and nobody would stop him now. He breezed past Chris, hauling Shelby shrugging behind him. He left the room, marching happily down the long corridor, swinging his arms, holding hands with his wife, like a school child, almost skipping with delight. Other patients and staff leaned out of doorways to see what the commotion was, but ducked quickly back in to avoid the crazy man. He reached the nurse's station at the corner, and turned right, toward the elevator.

The nurse at the desk called after him, "Mr. Russel, you can't just leave. Mr. Russel, the doctor hasn't released you yet. Mr. Russel?"

Down to the first floor. Out past the guard's desk, through the marble lobby, Shelby still in tow, through the electric doors. Outside.

"Junior, what are you doing?" she asked, but he didn't respond, instead whistling an innocuous disjointed melody.

"There it is."

Christine's black Mercedes convertible, badly dented on one side, was parked across the main circular drive, on the far side of the blacktop, hugging the lawn.

He released her hand just long enough to run around to the passenger side and open the door, taking it again to guide her in.

Once behind the wheel, he started the engine, and then, to Shelby's surprise, pushed the button and the tan top lifted up and disappeared into a compartment behind them, allowing the bright morning inside. John leaned to her and they kissed.

There was a small group of reporters camped across the street, spread out in the parking lot of a nearby business, waiting for word of his exit. John gunned the motor, jammed the car into gear, and raced out to the end of the driveway, aimed directly at the group. He honked and Shelby began to laugh uncontrollably. The first of the press, astonished, stood and pointed, "It's him!" the man yelled.

John raised his hand, waving. "Good-bye," he shouted back, before turning out, tires squealing, flying down the street. The next four hours were heaven.

The sun beamed into the car. The day was warm, nearing hot, and blowing through their hair while they drove north. It was time spent rehashing events, comparing what each had been thorough, piecing together the horrible story. John knew why Shelby hadn't offered any information to the FBI. He knew she had been told not to. He also knew it wouldn't serve any purpose. There was no reason for either of them to expose themselves to any of it. As long as they were together again, and alive, they agreed, that they didn't really care if anyone knew the truth, ever. The hardest part to John was deciding whether to tell Shelby about Hoffa.

She was hounding him, "Okay, at the camp, or lodge, or whatever, who, besides Doran, was there?"

"His sons...one from Miami, scary looking guy, and the other one, Nino, huge...you've seen him on TV, gotta weigh three hundred..." He tried to digress.

"Who else?"

John decided it was best to keep the secret, even from her, fearing that the information might put her in danger again someday. "Nobody." He was a terrible liar and he could tell that she didn't believe him. He could see she was pouting, but he would not waiver.

"Oh," she said, then nothing for the rest of the trip.

When they pulled into Duck Lake Road, the first thing John noticed was the 'For Sale' sign at 'Holly's Retreat' as they drove by. At their own cottage, John grimaced as he was confronted again by the gaping rectangular hole in his lawn. It was still surrounded by the yellow police tape. The grass around it was badly overgrown. The house itself seemed fine. The window on the left wall, still covered by the plywood board, would need to be replaced, and the floor in the living room refinished to remove the blood stains, left from Benny Tenino's murder. The bullet holes would have to be patched, and the place could use a good cleaning. But it remained, as always, the cottage; John's favorite place in the world.

Shelby started immediately, putting the place in order, and John went back outside. He stood on the porch, breathing in his own air, listening to the geese squawking as they flew overhead. He walked back down the two-track drive, past the car to the far corner of the hole. He tugged at the tape until it came free from the far tree, where it had been tied. The FBI had driven a thin metal support into the ground at the corner nearest the driveway to hold the tape. John yanked it out and stepped on it, pulling the tape until it broke. He took the long piece he had freed and walked down the driveway toward Holloway's house. When he found a suitably narrow section, he tied the yellow plastic across it to form a barrier, the first line of defense against inquisitive intruders.

On the way back to the cabin, he checked the shed. Inside, he discovered that it was completely empty and only dusty outlines were left where there had been tools and fishing gear. He walked around to the lake side, where he kept the small boat and his canoe. Both were missing. So were his oars, his outboard motors and gas cans, his lawn mower, all of his gardening equipment, and a hose. Purloined, he assumed by Joey Greydog. John chuckled as he returned to the house. The Indian was right, there were too many visitors.

In the short time he'd been gone, Shelby had managed to transform the place into amazingly livable condition. She had dragged the rug from the second bedroom to cover the stains on the wooden floor and rolled the one that had been there, and was also badly stained, into the corner. She was working in the kitchen, spritzing and polishing. The furniture, which had been tossed everywhere in John's escape, had been returned upright. She had opened all of the windows and the breeze from the forest replaced the staleness of the empty residence.

John surveyed the bookcases and the shelves that had once contained his father's journals. There were many photographs of his family and one of dad with Uncle Henry, taken on one of the dozens of visits to the lake. John picked it up. He couldn't really blame them for what they had done, it must have made sense to them at the time.

John put the picture back in place, next to the others. There was a television on the shelf below, and resting on top of it, the remote control. He pushed the button and the set came to life. John recognized the scene immediately as the front steps of the federal building. There was a female reporter standing in the foreground with a microphone. "...and now we take you back live to our anchor desk for more on this developing story..." John was barely paying attention. He went to the refrigerator and found one of three cans of beer that remained and opened it. Shelby was still cleaning, now in the back of the house, in their bedroom.

John sat down at the counter between the kitchen and the living room and watched as a hastily conceived graphic treatment spun into position on the television screen. It said, simply, 'HOFFA: SOLVED' in thick red stylized type against a background of question marks. The anchorman started talking "...one of the most intriguing cases of this century has come to a close. The mystery surrounding the disappearance of former Teamster's president

James Riddle Hoffa, may have finally come to a stunning and dramatic conclusion late yesterday with the discovery of the body of fugitive FBI agent, Frank Doran..."

John took a sip of beer. This ought to be good, he thought.

"...it is unclear what actually happened, but this much, we do know. Sometime late yesterday during a raid at the Lake Naganosh Lodge in northern Ontario, FBI agents discovered..."

Shelby appeared at his side, curious.

"...killed in self defense by a man once suspected himself of some involvement in the case..." The newsman was obviously interrupted off camera. "I'm told now that we will go live to the MacNamera Building where Assistant Attorney General Stanley Messing is about to make a statement..."

"That's right, Bob," the young woman began, "As you can see behind me, there is a lot of activity here. There are several members of the FBI and Justice Department and also of the Attorney General's staff. He is stepping to the podium now."

They cut to a closeup of Messing arriving through the large brass revolving door in the center of the building and stepping to the microphone at the podium. The same podium he had set up everyday for a week, just in case. Following closely behind, was Messing's assistant, Jack, who joined Garnetti and Morse in a row behind him.

"Thank you for coming ladies and gentlemen," he began, "I have a lot of information today, so please, if you would, refrain from questions until I am finished with my statement. Thank you." Messing looked down at a stack of three by five cards, his notes, piled on the podium in front of him, but hidden from the cameras. "The Justice Department has concluded its ongoing investigation into the disappearance and now confirmed death of Jimmy Hoffa. The investigation, which began over twenty years ago, has resulted in the recovery of irrefutable and conclusive evidence culminating in the positive identification of the body discovered on July twenty-eighth of this year as that of James Riddle Hoffa. The body was located as a result of information provided to the bureau by one Dominic Baglia, now deceased. Mr. Baglia claimed to have been responsible for disposing of the body on August 5th, 1975 as part of a conspiracy involving the Tenino crime family, Antonio, Michael, and Benito, and Frank Doran, former agent in charge of the Detroit office of the FBI, all deceased. The murder of Mr. Hoffa seems to be financially motivated, with the perpetrators seeking to prevent Mr. Hoffa from regaining control of the Teamsters Union. It was apparently their belief that such control might lessen their influence and interfere with their access to the union and various union funds. I will add, however that this is largely conjecture since those involved are no longer able to testify in this case."

"No shit." John took another sip of the cold liquid.

Messing continued, "Mr. Hoffa's remains will be returned to the family tomorrow for internment. We consider the case closed and expect to bring no further charges." He put the last card down and looked up smiling, proud of his delivery. "I would like to acknowledge some of the fine agents that were personally responsible for bringing this matter to a successful conclusion; Agent Karen Morse..."

John watched as the camera panned to Karen, and then to Bob Garnetti.

"...and to Bob Garnetti, whom I am pleased to announce has accepted the position of Special Agent in Charge of the Detroit office of the FBI. We will now accept questions..."

"That's not what happened..." Shelby couldn't believe it.

John pushed the 'off' button on the remote control. "C'mon, Shel." He hugged her gently, "Let's go for a walk."

The sun was not far from the horizon, the day almost over, when they emerged from the path that led from the cottage to Lake Michigan. The air was warm and still, the sky devoid of clouds. Miles out, they could see the islands, North and South Manitou, and, except for a seagull walking ahead on the smooth sand, there was nothing. They found a log, most of a tree, and sat watching the sun as it touched the straight horizon, throwing its orange light into the water.

They sat close, hand in hand, saying nothing. They kissed in the last light of the sun and in the dark that quickly followed. John felt the incredible passion rise uncontrollably within him as Shelby's love surrounded him, both of them screaming with the pleasure of each other in this wonderful moment of freedom, before rolling over softly on their backs, fingers still entwined, and lying still, catching their breath under the moon that had sneaked above them and reflected from the dark water.

John thought of his father and mother and how many times they had been together on this same beach and wondered if they had ever made love in the cold sand as he and Shelby had tonight.

He wondered about Bobby Merimac Wilson, who never had this joy, whose life had no value, who just was, but wasn't anything. He thought of Henry Swain and Benny Tenino, his neighbor, Bill Holloway and Charley Keenan.

John Russel wondered about it all, as he lay there with Shelby, two worn and polished stones; tossed from the water by a storm, and in the calm afterwards, unable to ever roll back.

"Jesus."

The End

Printed in the United States
1940